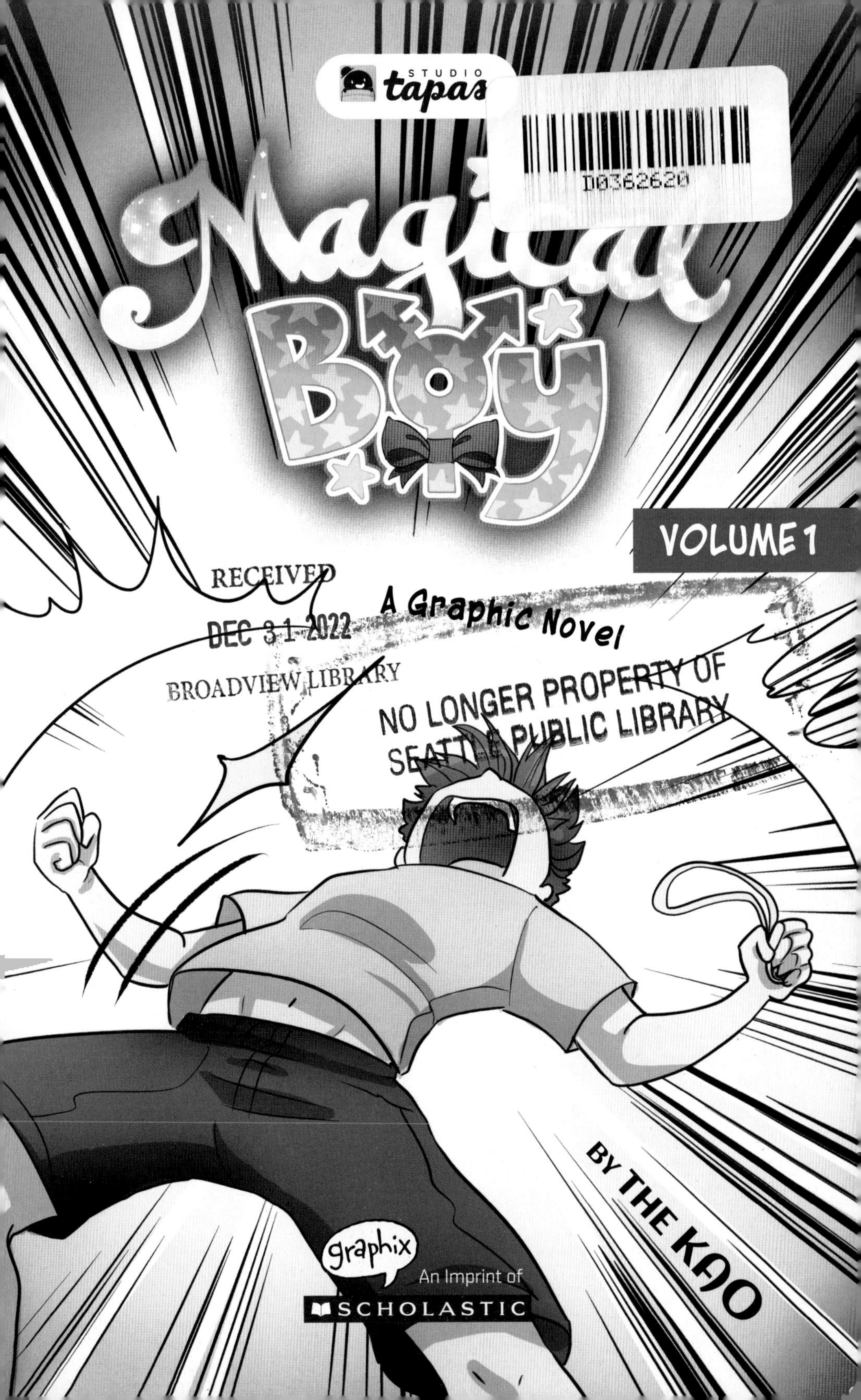
STUDIO tapas
Magical Boy
VOLUME 1
A Graphic Novel
BY THE KAO
graphix
An Imprint of
SCHOLASTIC

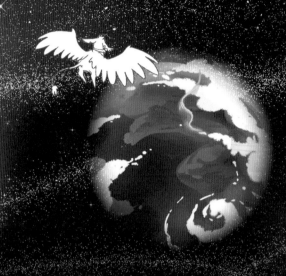

CONTENT ADVISORY:
THIS GRAPHIC NOVEL CONTAINS INSTANCES OF DEAD NAMING, HOMOPHOBIA, TRANSPHOBIA, MISGENDERING, AND FORCED GENDER EXPRESSION THAT MAY BE DISTRESSING TO SOME.

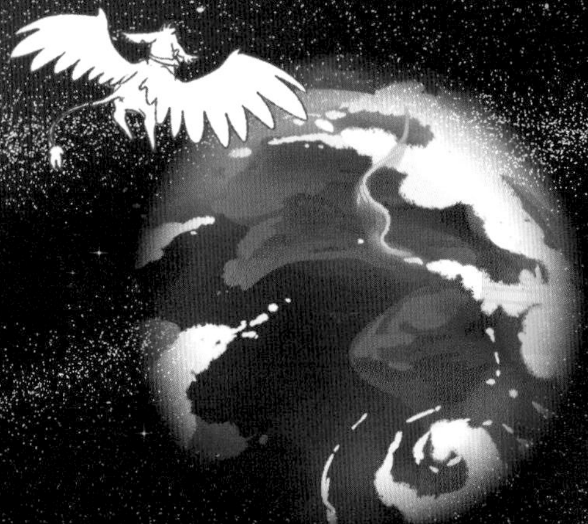

First published online in 2018 by Tapas. All rights reserved. Published by Graphix, an imprint of Scholastic Inc., *Publishers since 1920*. SCHOLASTIC, GRAPHIX, and associated logos are trademarks and/or registered trademarks of Scholastic Inc.

ISBN 978-1-338-77552-5 (PB)

ISBN 978-1-338-72553-2 (HC)

10 9 8 7 6 5 4 3   22 23 24 25

Printed in China   62

First edition, November 2021

Edited by Michael Petranek and Lori Wieczorek

Book design by Jeff Shake, Salena Mahina, and Cheung Tai

Lettering by Dezi Sienty

For Tapas:

Edited by Brooke Huang

Colored by Dojo Gubser

Art assistance by Sera Swati

Additional assistance by Selena Ahmed

Editor in Chief Michael Son

Dear Reader,

Magical Boy is a story I've been wanting to tell for a long time. I wanted to create a story about a hero who embarks on a messy, funny, difficult, outrageous, and ultimately rewarding journey, and I wanted that hero to be someone who all readers—but especially transmen—can cheer on and relate to.

Like any good story, there will be conflict. There will be times when Max faces hardships and obstacles to his transition, and some of those will be from Max's own internal struggles as well. He's a teen who's still going through the messy process of figuring out who he is as a person in many aspects. There are people in his life who won't understand him, and there will be times when he doubts himself.

I know that *Magical Boy* will be tough for some to read at times. I wanted to create a story that is authentic and true to experiences that many transmen have faced, but please don't doubt that I have the best intentions for Max. I know that *Magical Boy* can't be representative of every transman's experience, but I hope that you'll find his journey of self-discovery and overcoming the fictional obstacle of his Magical Girl lineage to be fun, compelling, and genuine.

Max is a character that I hold close to my heart, and I hope that you'll hold him close to yours, too.

—The Kao

Episode 1:
IT'S MAX

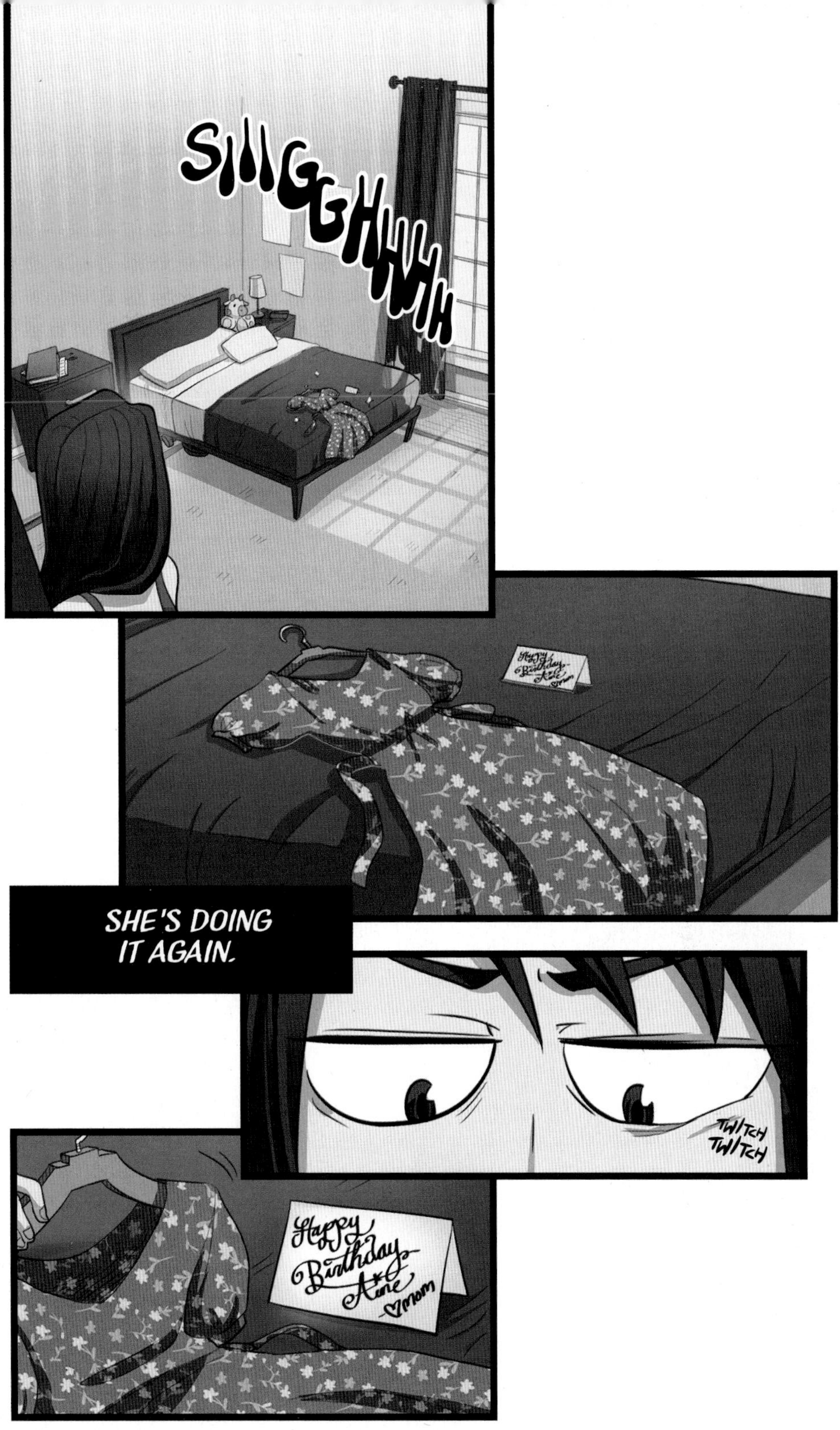
SIIIGGHHHH
SHE'S DOING IT AGAIN.
TWITCH TWITCH
Happy Birthday Anne
-♡Mom

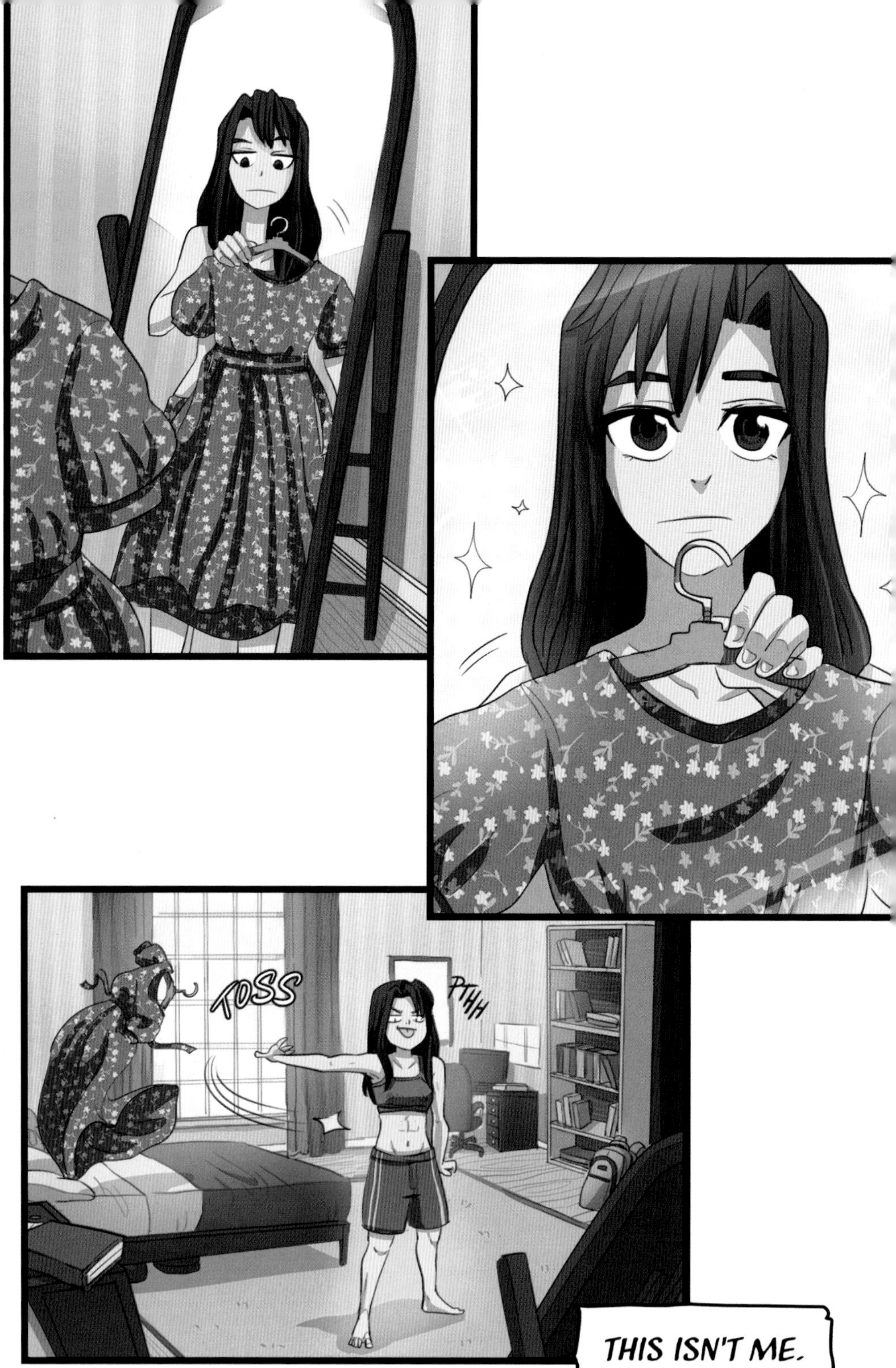
TOSS
PTHH
THIS ISN'T ME.

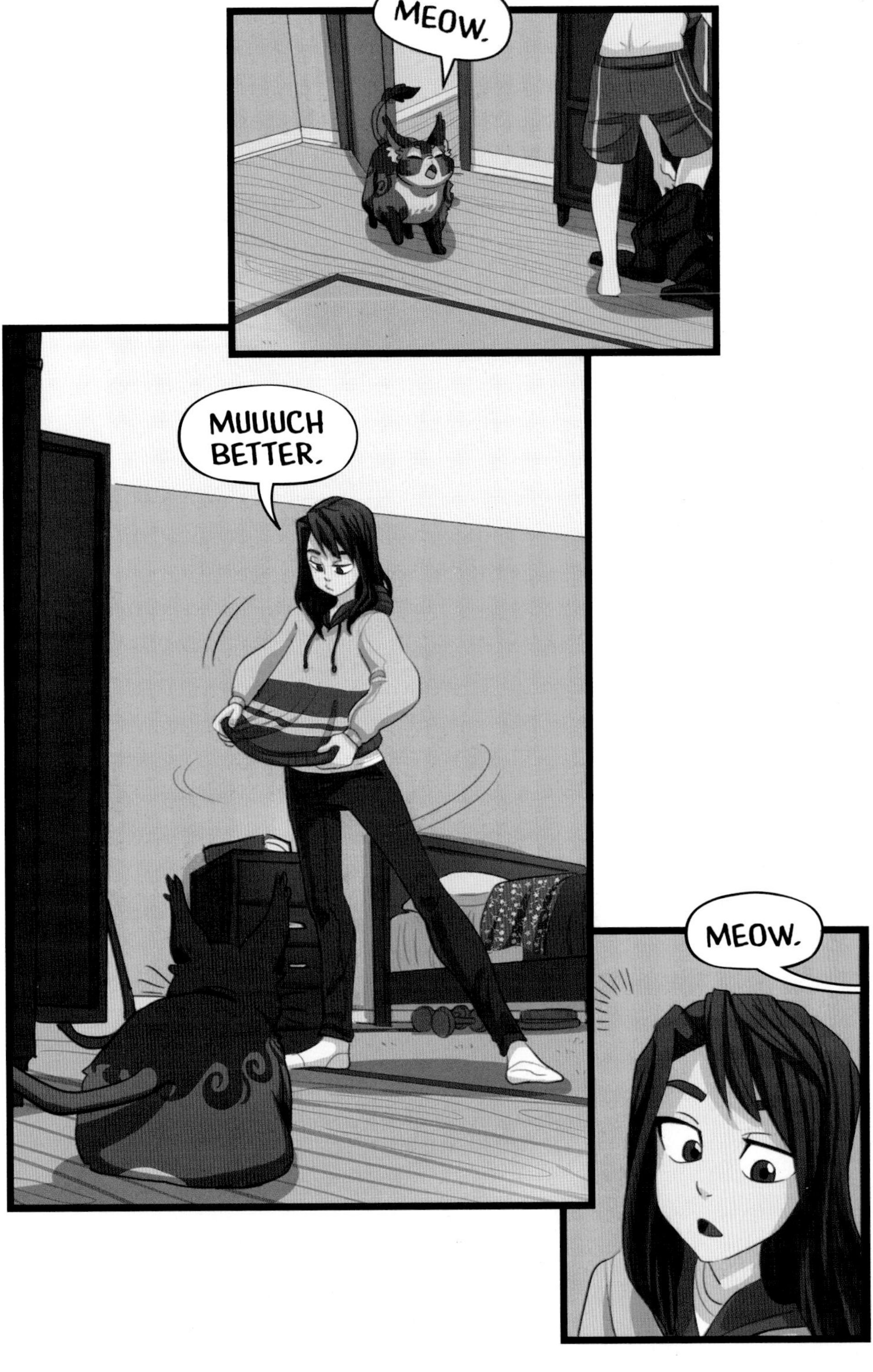
MEOW.
MUUUCH BETTER.
MEOW.

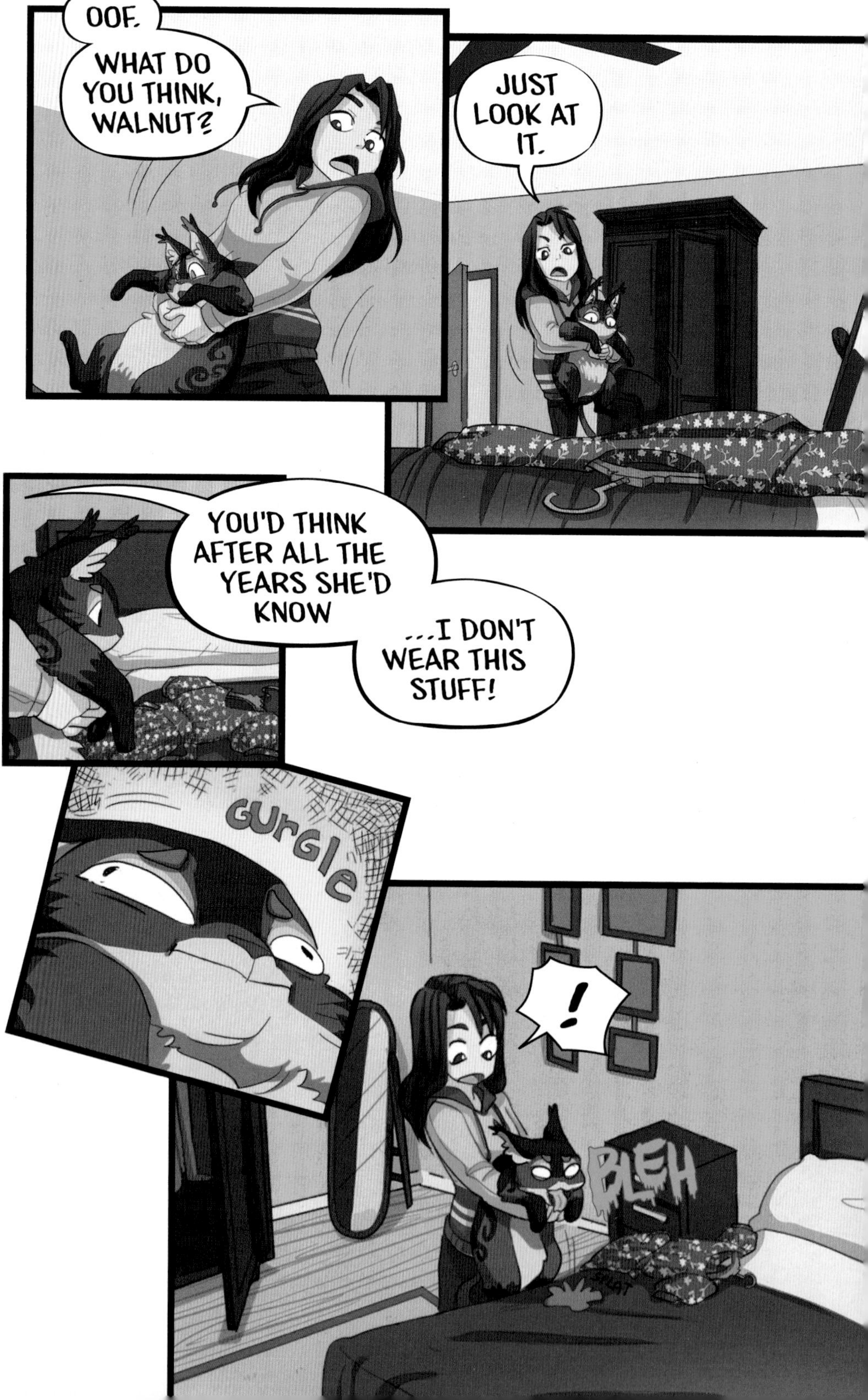
OOF.
WHAT DO YOU THINK, WALNUT?
JUST LOOK AT IT.
YOU'D THINK AFTER ALL THE YEARS SHE'D KNOW
...I DON'T WEAR THIS STUFF!
GURGLE
!
BLEH

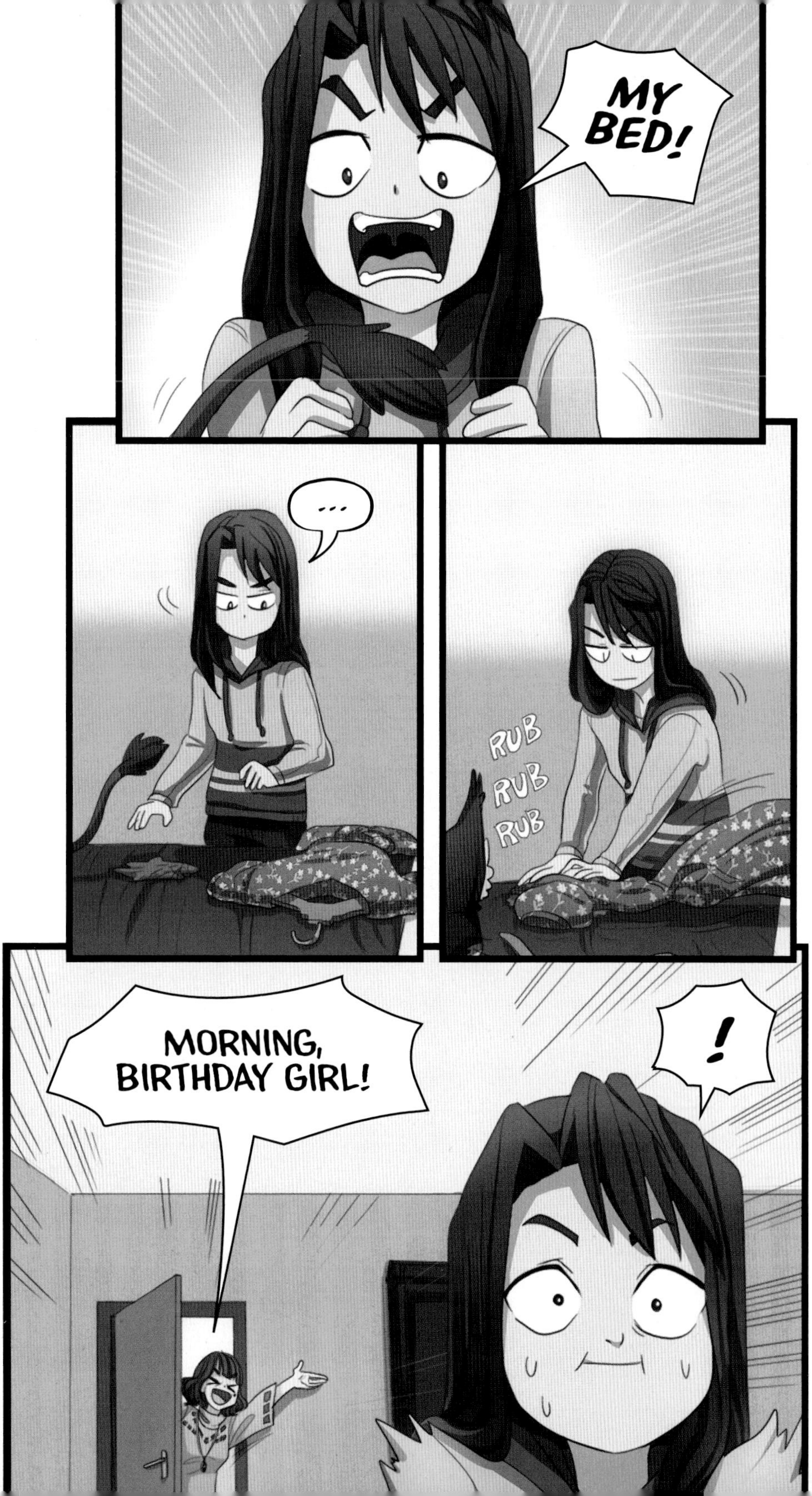
MY BED!
...
RUB
RUB
RUB
MORNING, BIRTHDAY GIRL!
!

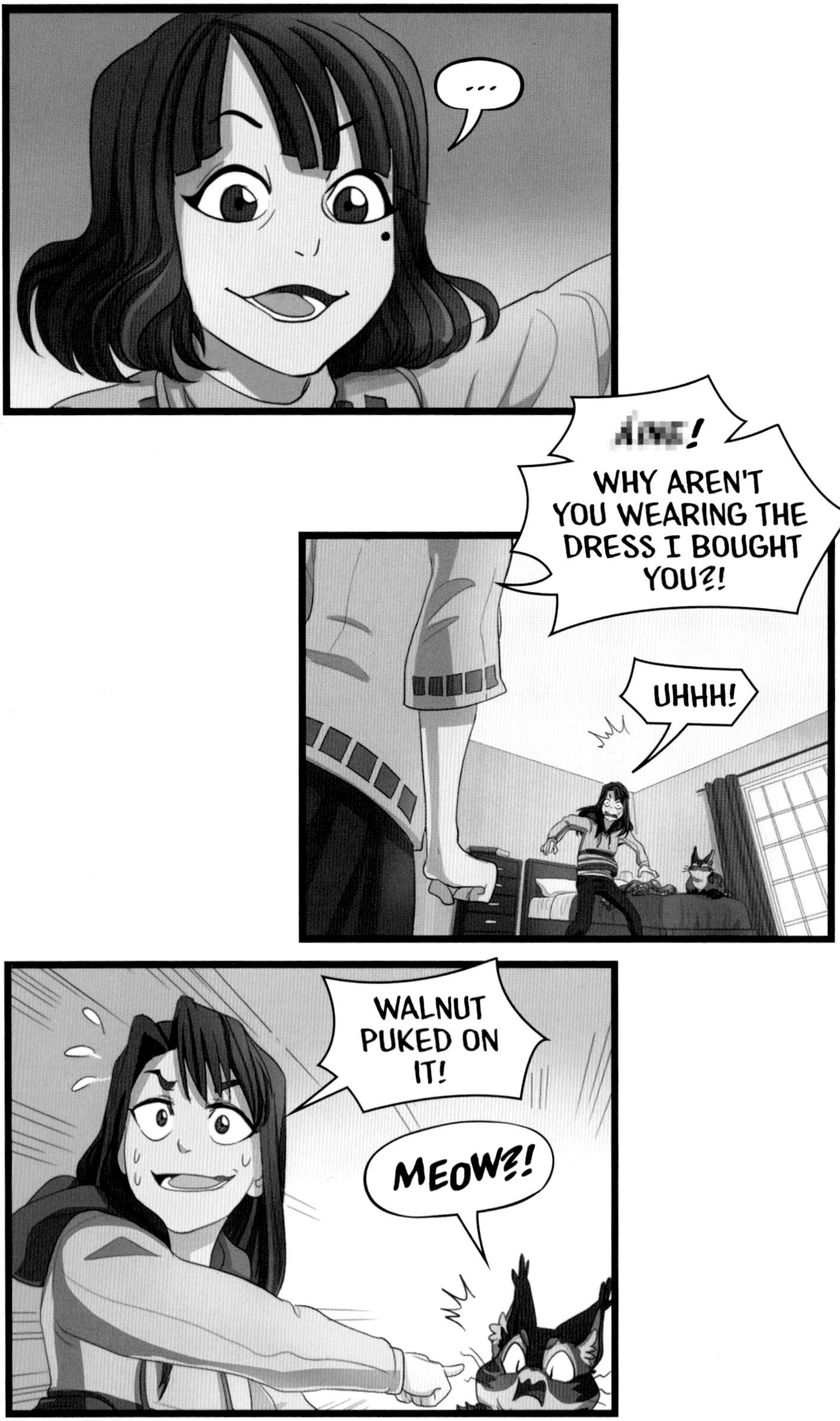
...
!
WHY AREN'T YOU WEARING THE DRESS I BOUGHT YOU?!
UHHH!
WALNUT PUKED ON IT!
MEOW?!

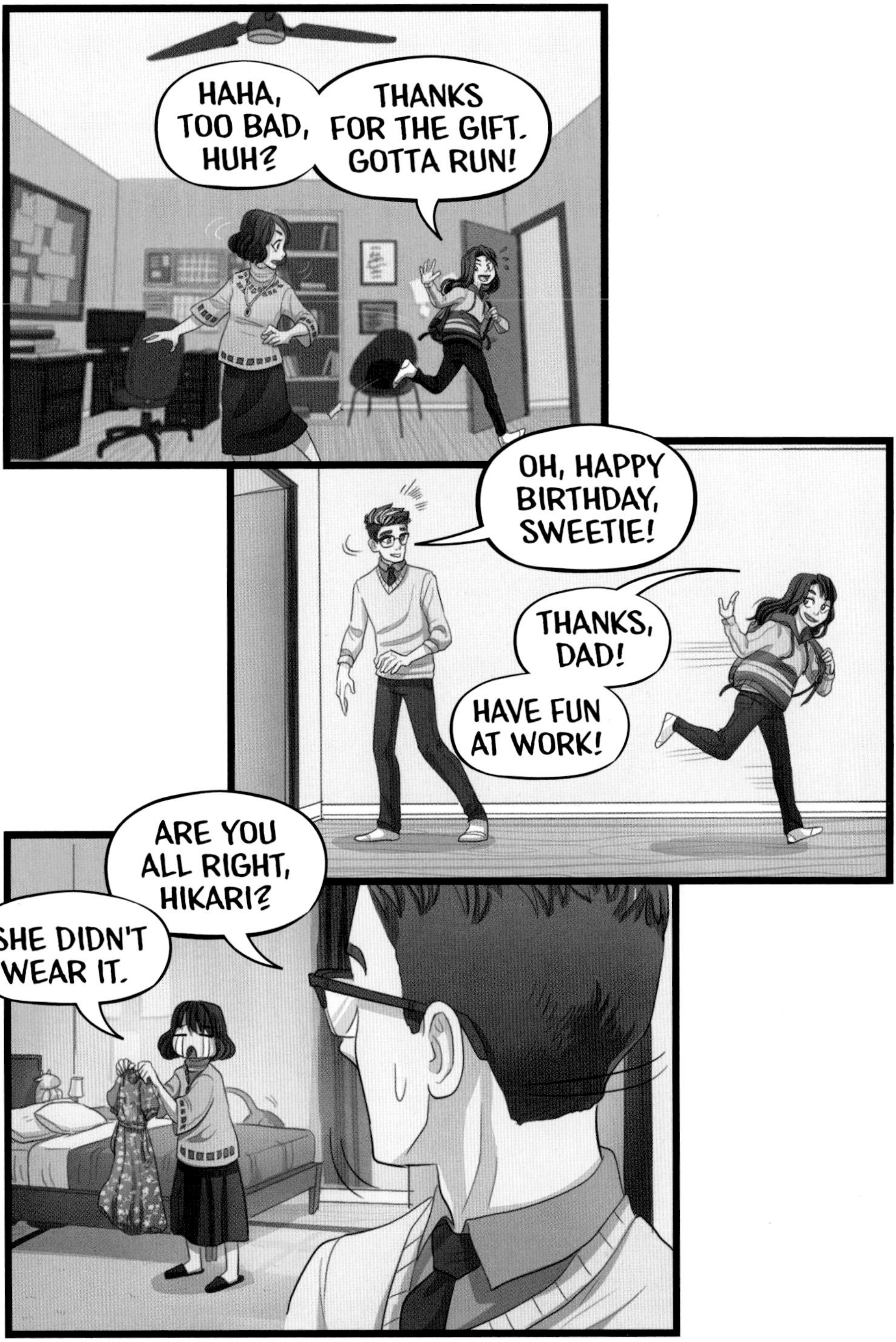
HAHA, TOO BAD, HUH?
THANKS FOR THE GIFT. GOTTA RUN!
OH, HAPPY BIRTHDAY, SWEETIE!
THANKS, DAD!
HAVE FUN AT WORK!
ARE YOU ALL RIGHT, HIKARI?
SHE DIDN'T WEAR IT.

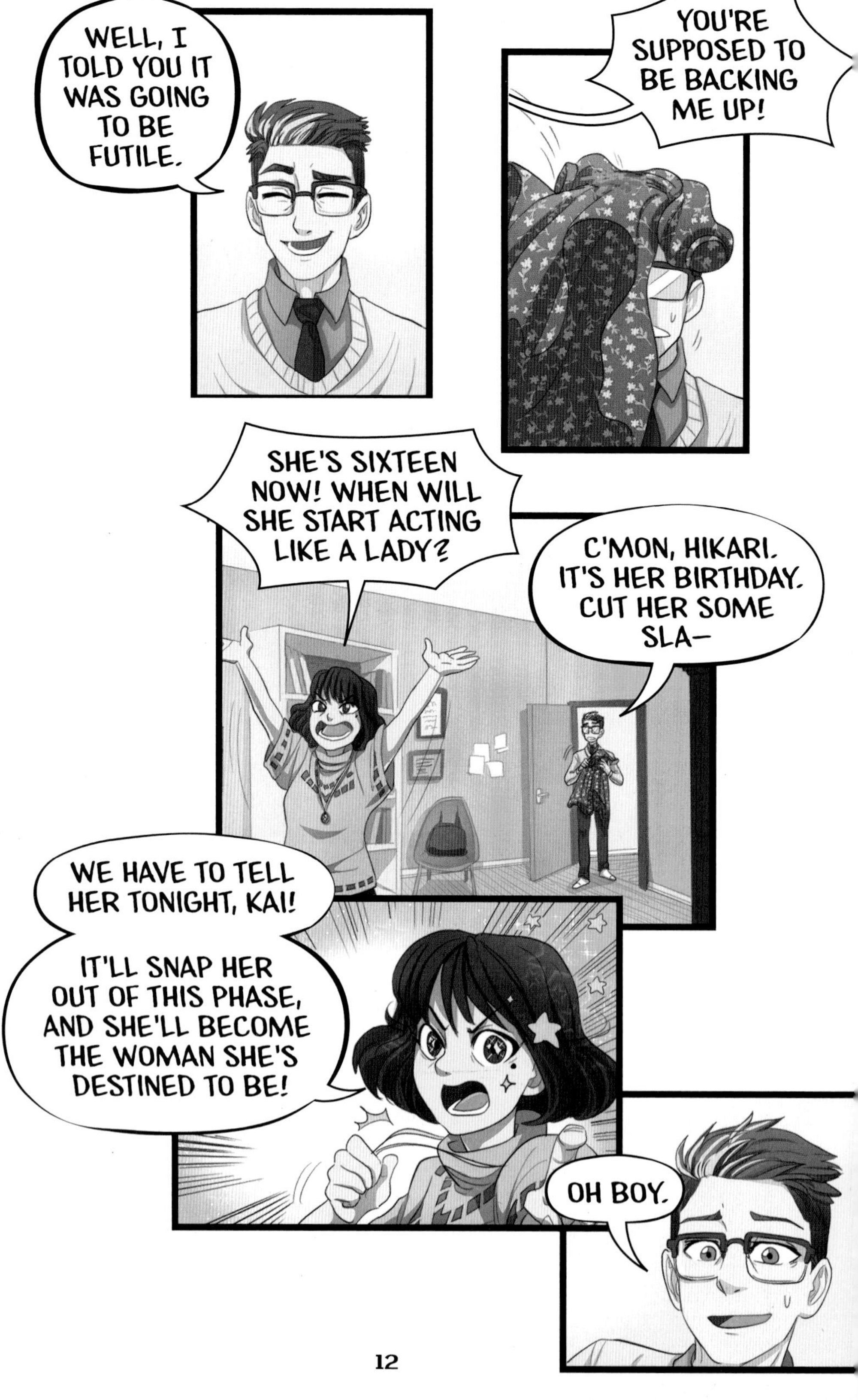
WELL, I TOLD YOU IT WAS GOING TO BE FUTILE.
YOU'RE SUPPOSED TO BE BACKING ME UP!
SHE'S SIXTEEN NOW! WHEN WILL SHE START ACTING LIKE A LADY?
C'MON, HIKARI. IT'S HER BIRTHDAY. CUT HER SOME SLA—
WE HAVE TO TELL HER TONIGHT, KAI!
IT'LL SNAP HER OUT OF THIS PHASE, AND SHE'LL BECOME THE WOMAN SHE'S DESTINED TO BE!
OH BOY.

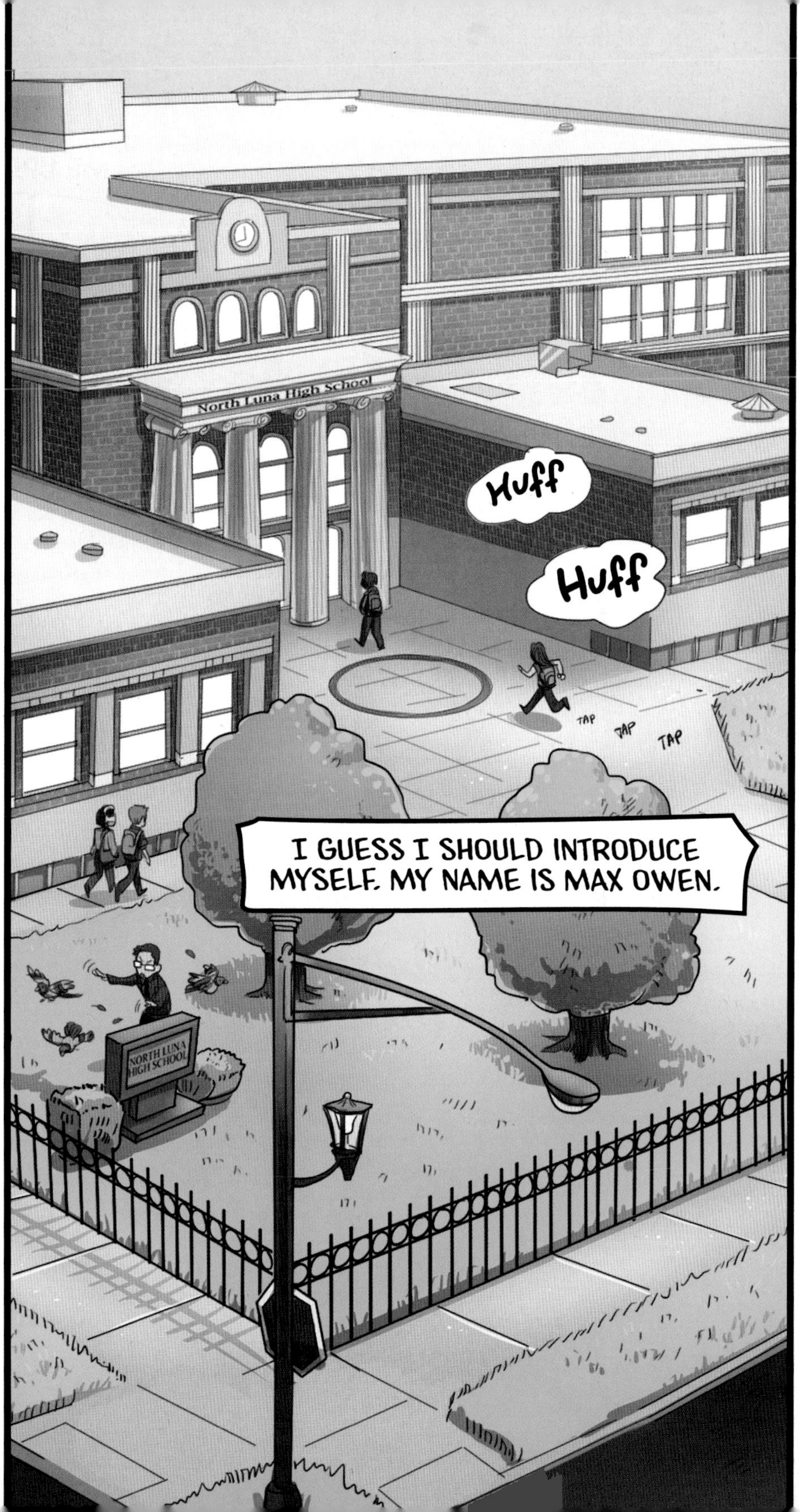
North Luna High School
Huff
Huff
TAP
TAP
TAP
I GUESS I SHOULD INTRODUCE MYSELF. MY NAME IS MAX OWEN.
NORTH LUNA HIGH SCHOOL

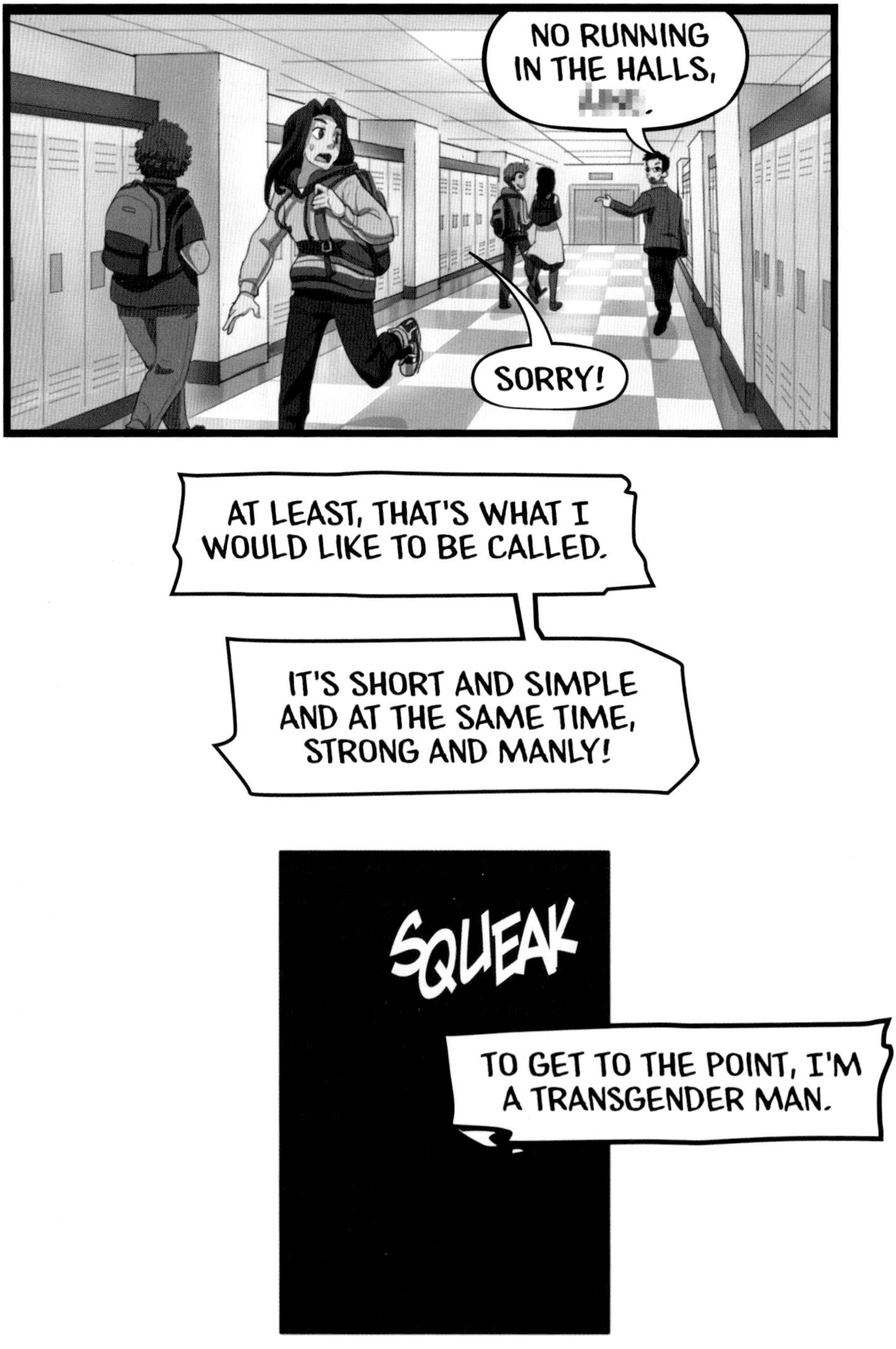
NO RUNNING IN THE HALLS,
SORRY!
AT LEAST, THAT'S WHAT I WOULD LIKE TO BE CALLED.
IT'S SHORT AND SIMPLE AND AT THE SAME TIME, STRONG AND MANLY!
SQUEAK
TO GET TO THE POINT, I'M A TRANSGENDER MAN.

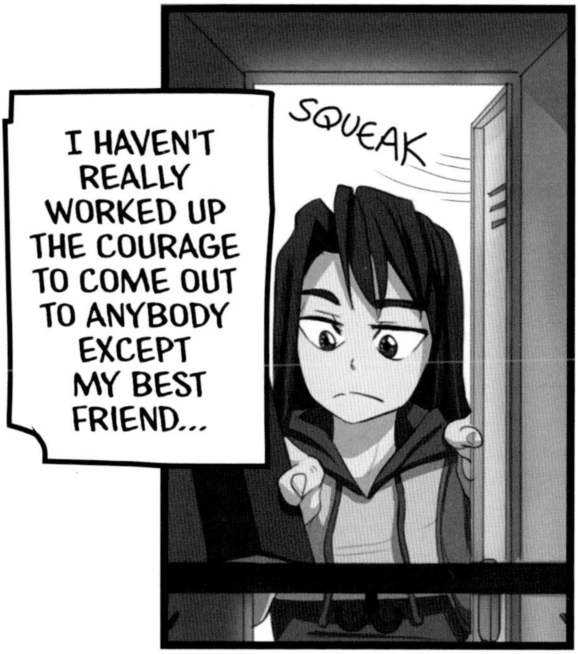
I HAVEN'T REALLY WORKED UP THE COURAGE TO COME OUT TO ANYBODY EXCEPT MY BEST FRIEND...
SQUEAK

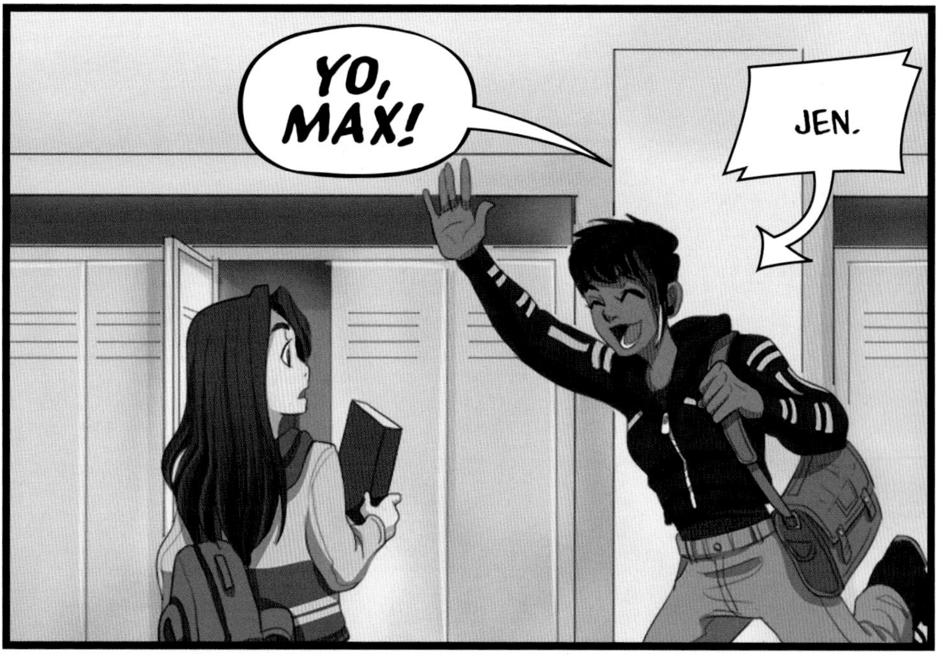
YO, MAX!
JEN.

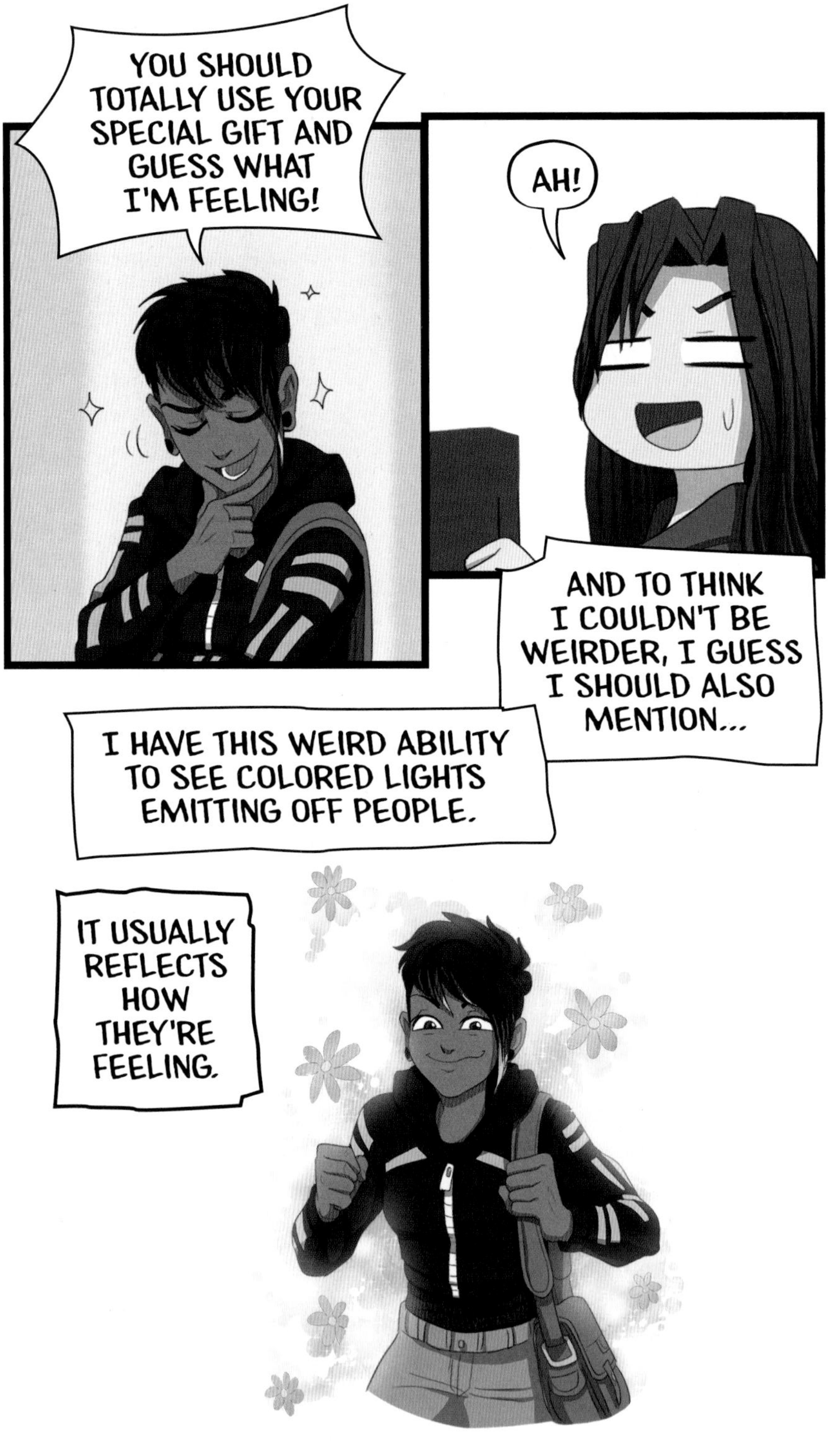
YOU SHOULD TOTALLY USE YOUR SPECIAL GIFT AND GUESS WHAT I'M FEELING!
AH!
AND TO THINK I COULDN'T BE WEIRDER, I GUESS I SHOULD ALSO MENTION...
I HAVE THIS WEIRD ABILITY TO SEE COLORED LIGHTS EMITTING OFF PEOPLE.
IT USUALLY REFLECTS HOW THEY'RE FEELING.

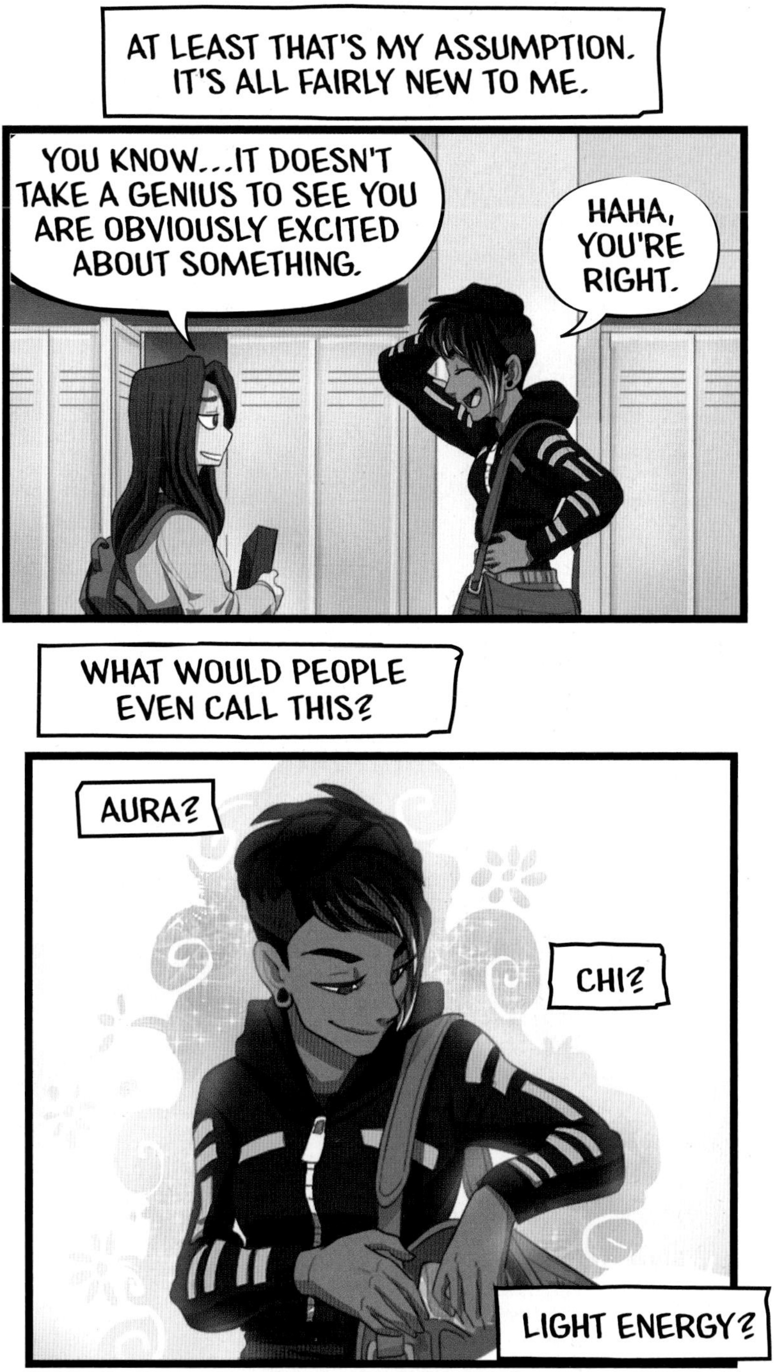
AT LEAST THAT'S MY ASSUMPTION. IT'S ALL FAIRLY NEW TO ME.
YOU KNOW...IT DOESN'T TAKE A GENIUS TO SEE YOU ARE OBVIOUSLY EXCITED ABOUT SOMETHING.
HAHA, YOU'RE RIGHT.
WHAT WOULD PEOPLE EVEN CALL THIS?
AURA?
CHI?
LIGHT ENERGY?

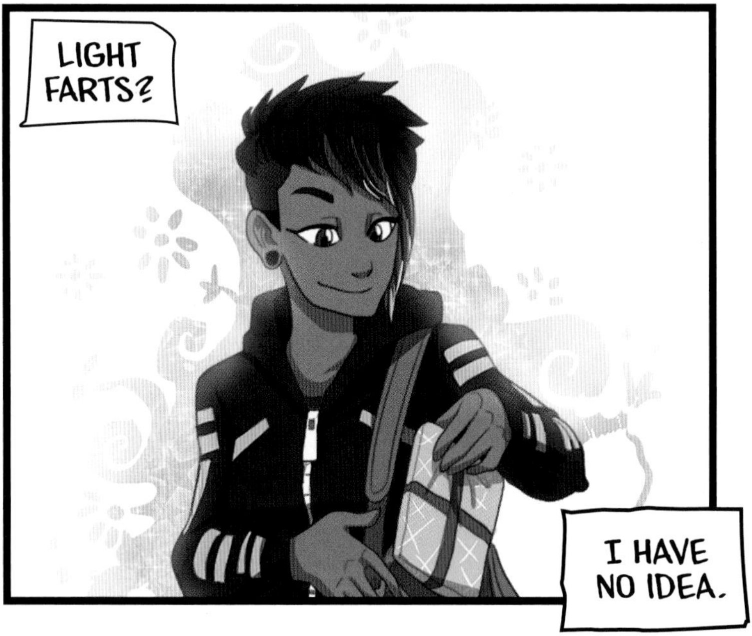
LIGHT FARTS?
I HAVE NO IDEA.

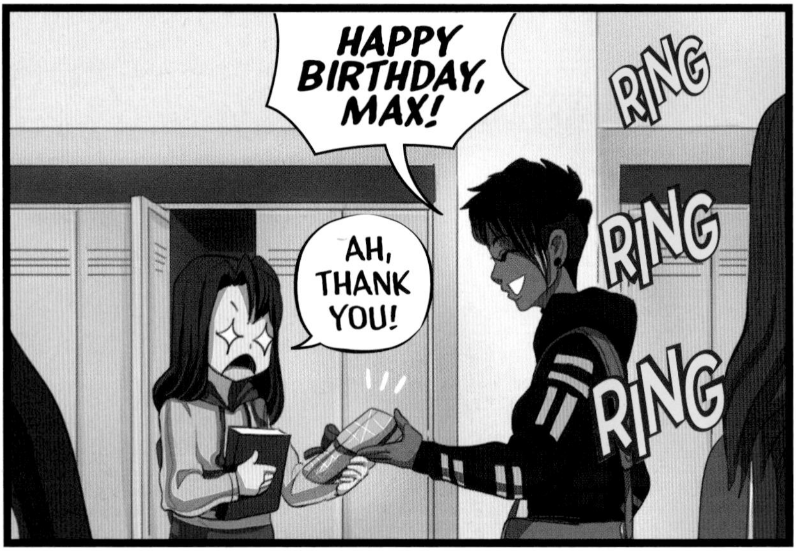
HAPPY BIRTHDAY, MAX!
RING
RING
AH, THANK YOU!
RING

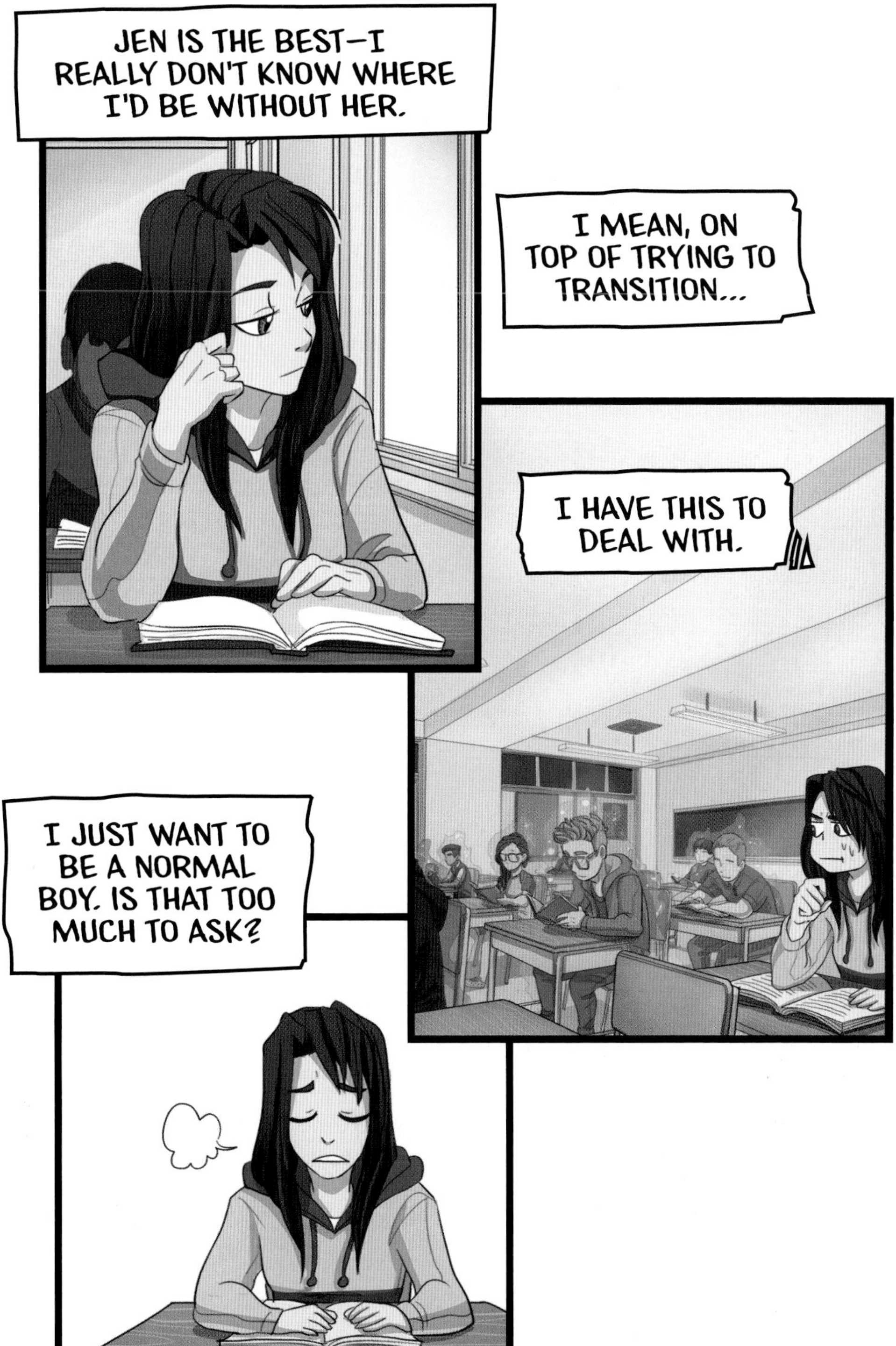
JEN IS THE BEST—I REALLY DON'T KNOW WHERE I'D BE WITHOUT HER.
I MEAN, ON TOP OF TRYING TO TRANSITION...
I HAVE THIS TO DEAL WITH.
I JUST WANT TO BE A NORMAL BOY. IS THAT TOO MUCH TO ASK?

SLAM

MAX, DID YOU OPEN THE GIFT YET?

AH, NOT YET.

DUDE, WHAT ARE YOU WAITING FOR? OPEN IT NOW!

OKAY, OKAY.

CRINKLE

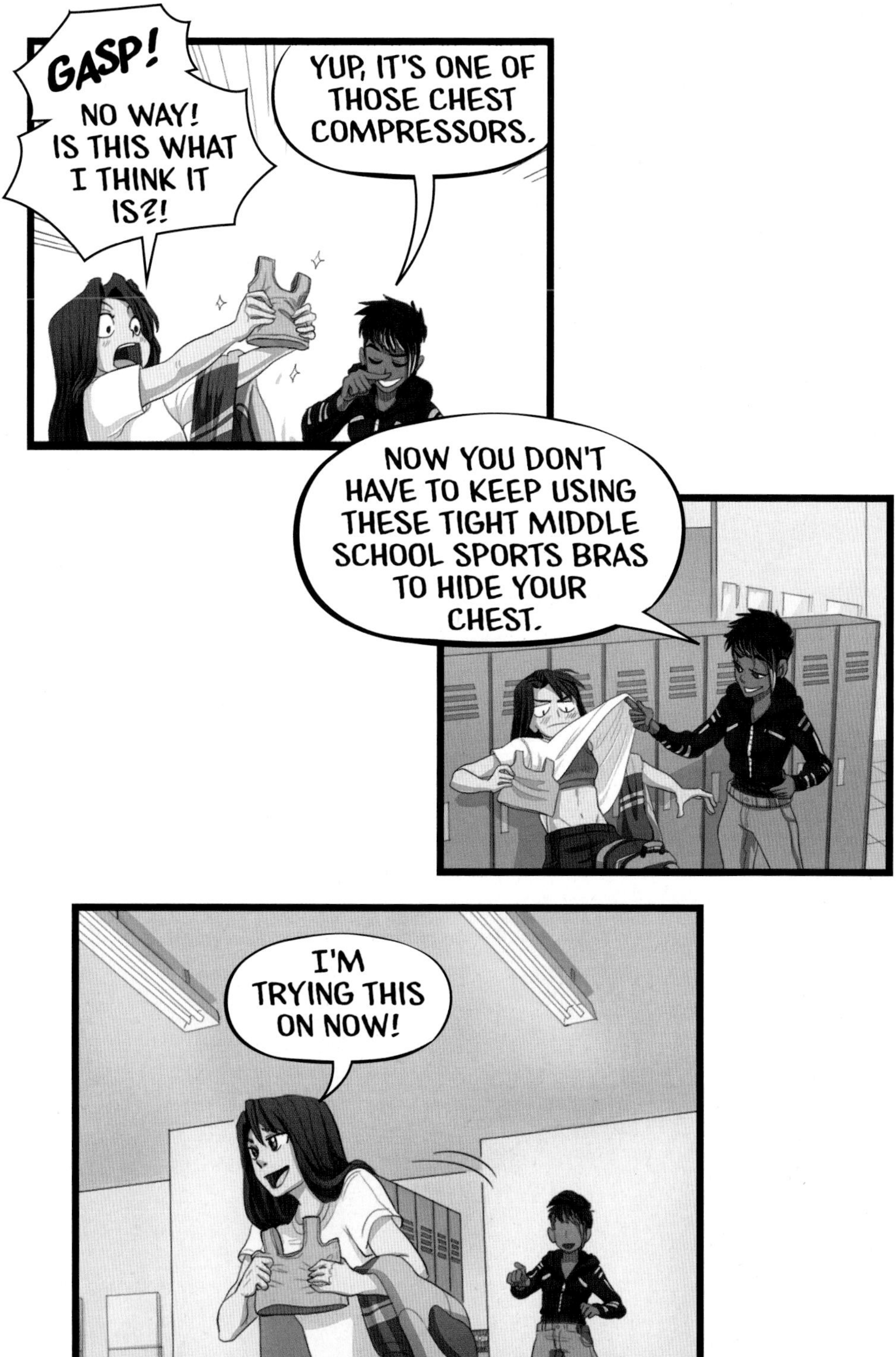
GASP!
NO WAY! IS THIS WHAT I THINK IT IS?!
YUP, IT'S ONE OF THOSE CHEST COMPRESSORS.
NOW YOU DON'T HAVE TO KEEP USING THESE TIGHT MIDDLE SCHOOL SPORTS BRAS TO HIDE YOUR CHEST.
I'M TRYING THIS ON NOW!

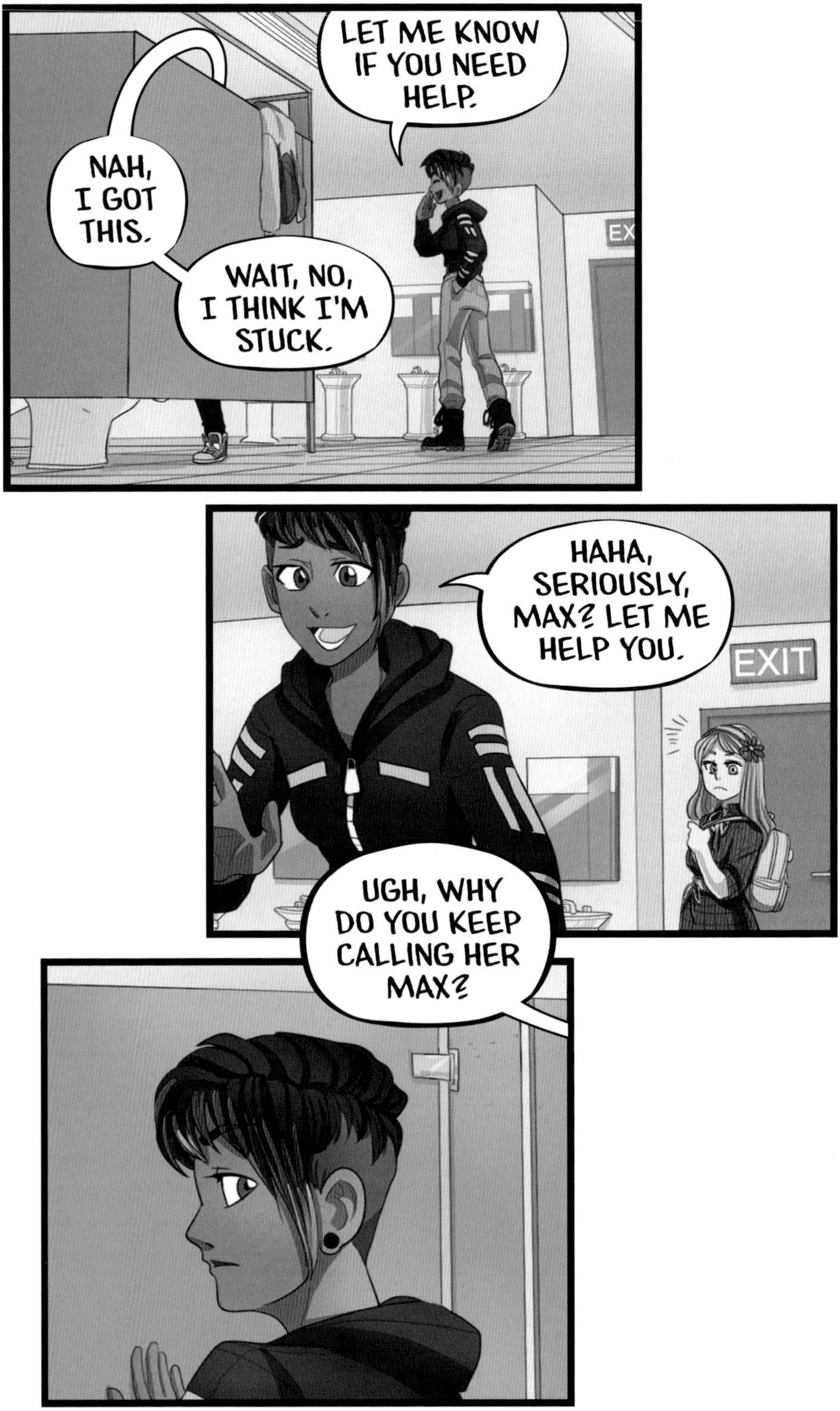
LET ME KNOW IF YOU NEED HELP.
NAH, I GOT THIS.
WAIT, NO, I THINK I'M STUCK.
HAHA, SERIOUSLY, MAX? LET ME HELP YOU.
EXIT
UGH, WHY DO YOU KEEP CALLING HER MAX?

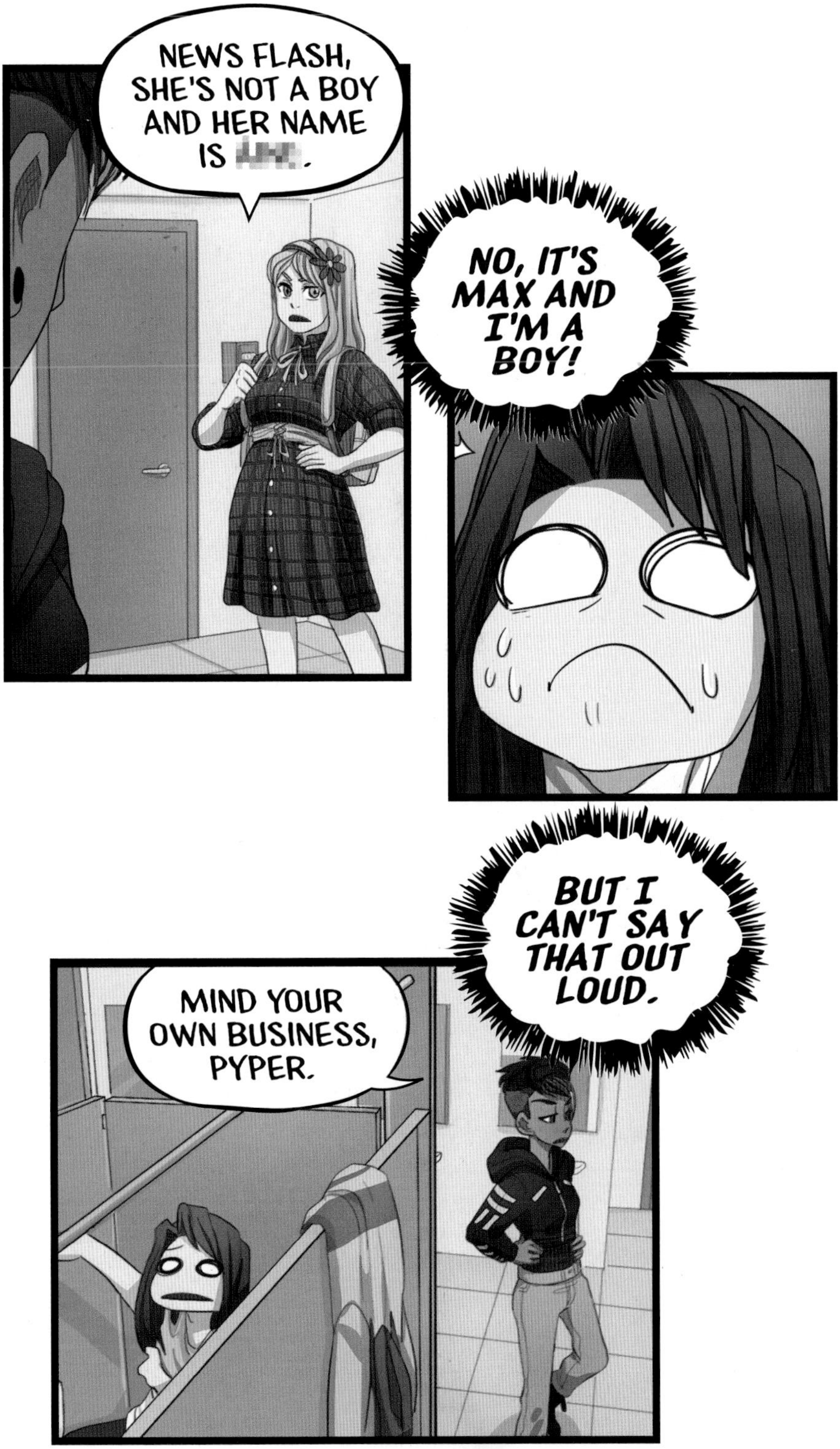
NEWS FLASH, SHE'S NOT A BOY AND HER NAME IS [redacted].
NO, IT'S MAX AND I'M A BOY!
BUT I CAN'T SAY THAT OUT LOUD.
MIND YOUR OWN BUSINESS, PYPER.

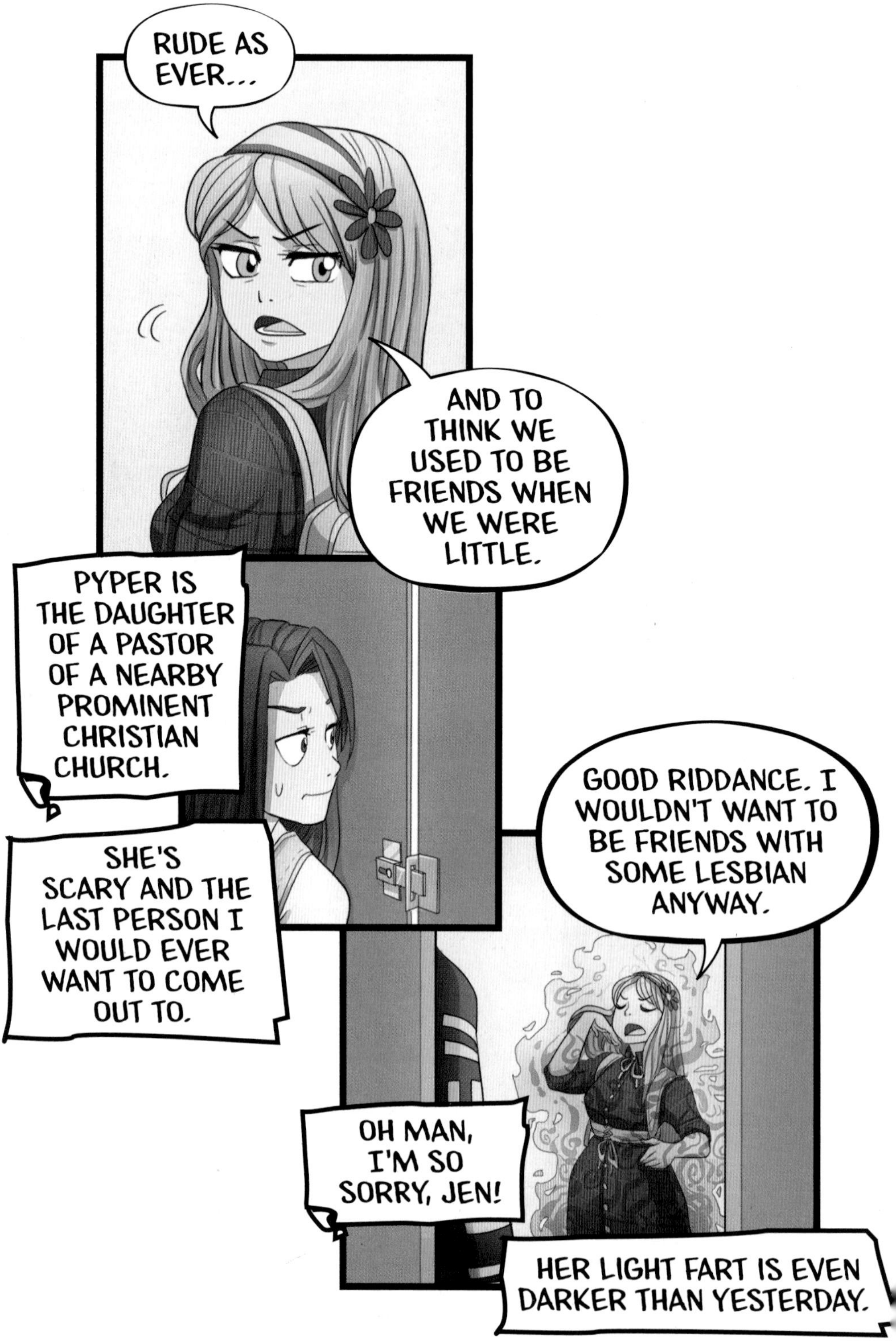
RUDE AS EVER...
AND TO THINK WE USED TO BE FRIENDS WHEN WE WERE LITTLE.
PYPER IS THE DAUGHTER OF A PASTOR OF A NEARBY PROMINENT CHRISTIAN CHURCH.
SHE'S SCARY AND THE LAST PERSON I WOULD EVER WANT TO COME OUT TO.
GOOD RIDDANCE. I WOULDN'T WANT TO BE FRIENDS WITH SOME LESBIAN ANYWAY.
OH MAN, I'M SO SORRY, JEN!
HER LIGHT FART IS EVEN DARKER THAN YESTERDAY.

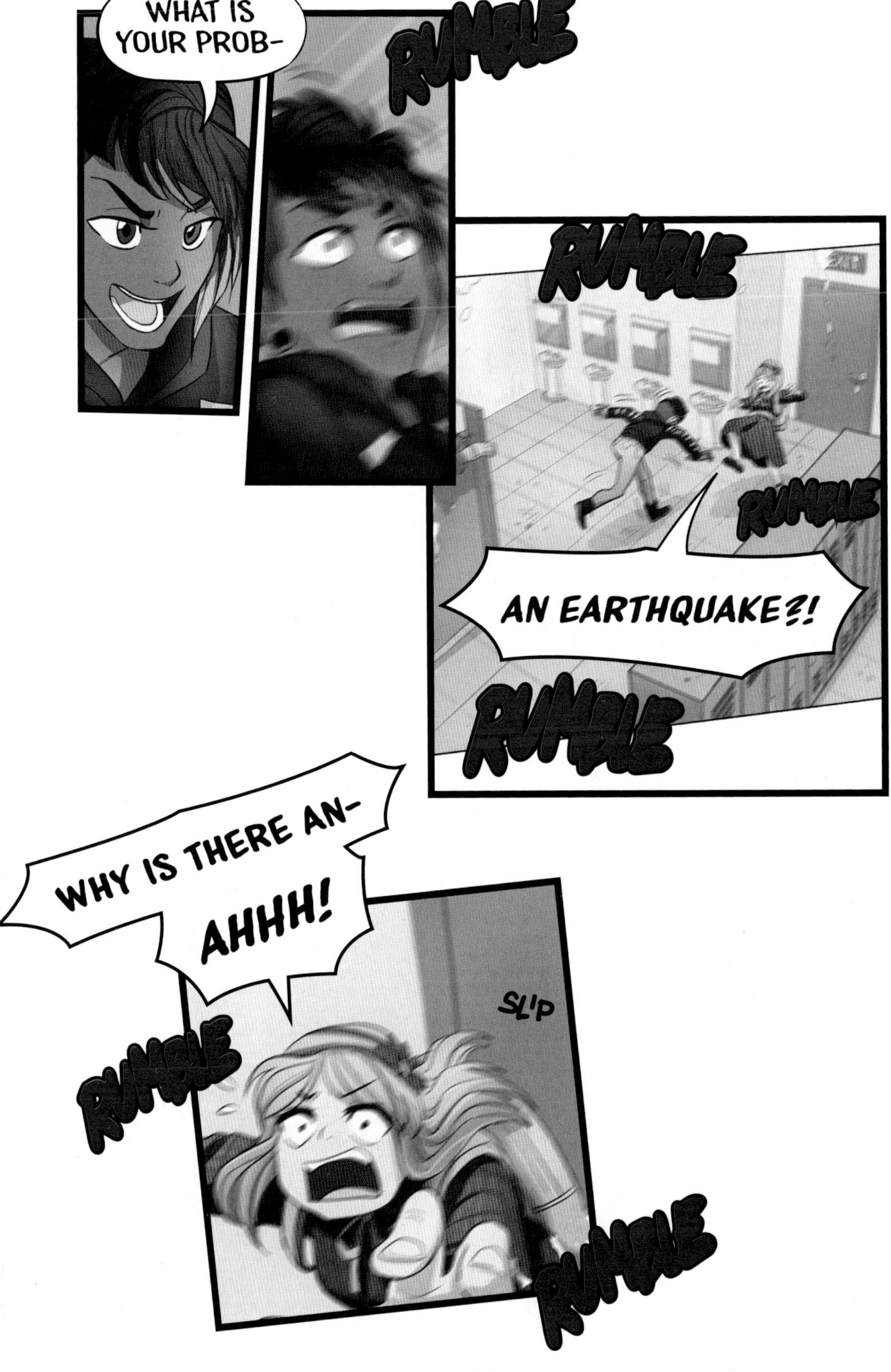
WHAT IS YOUR PROB-
RUMBLE
RUMBLE
RUMBLE
AN EARTHQUAKE?!
RUMBLE
WHY IS THERE AN-
AHHH!
SLIP
RUMBLE
RUMBLE

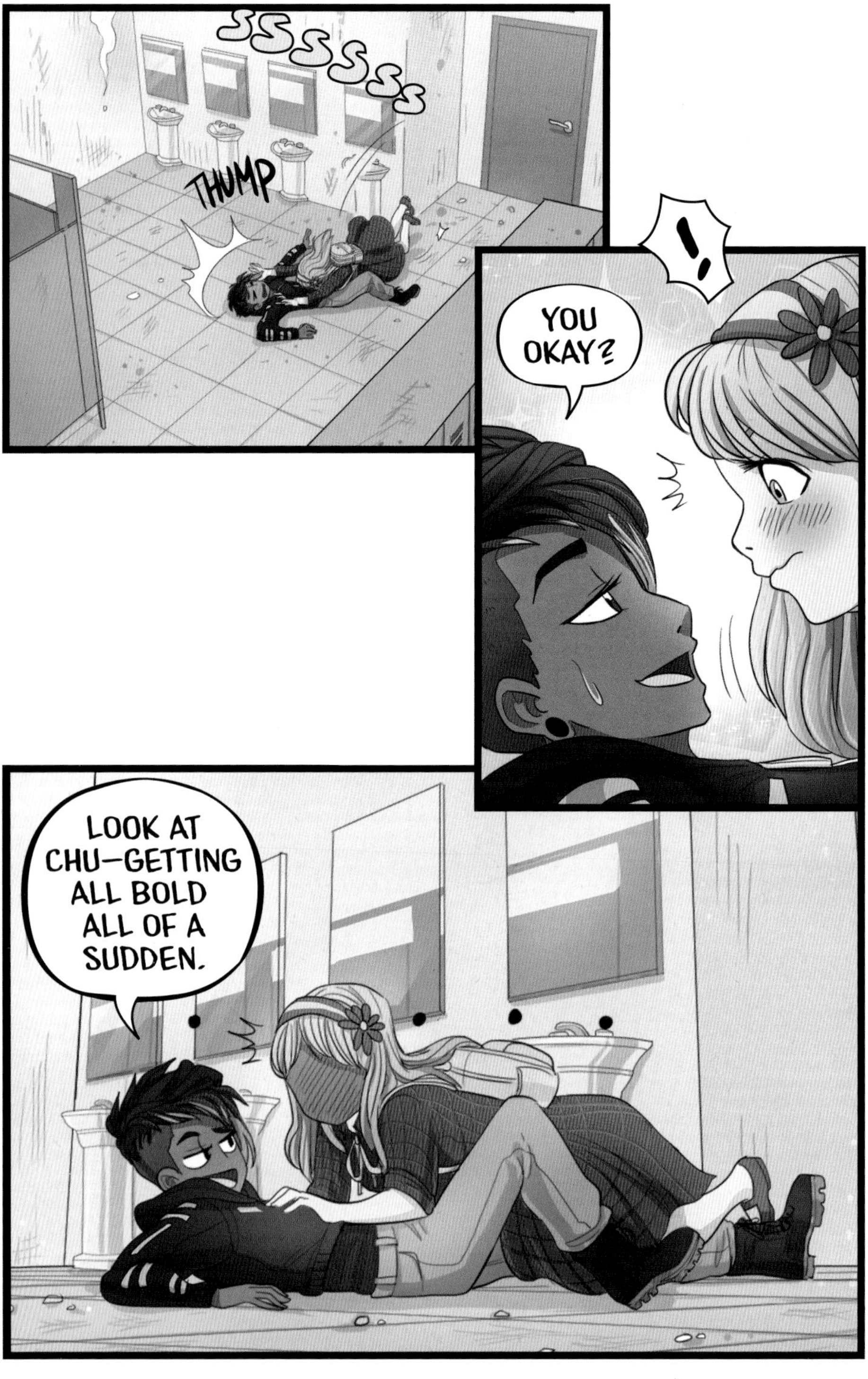
SSSSSS
THUMP
!
YOU OKAY?
LOOK AT CHU—GETTING ALL BOLD ALL OF A SUDDEN.
. . . .

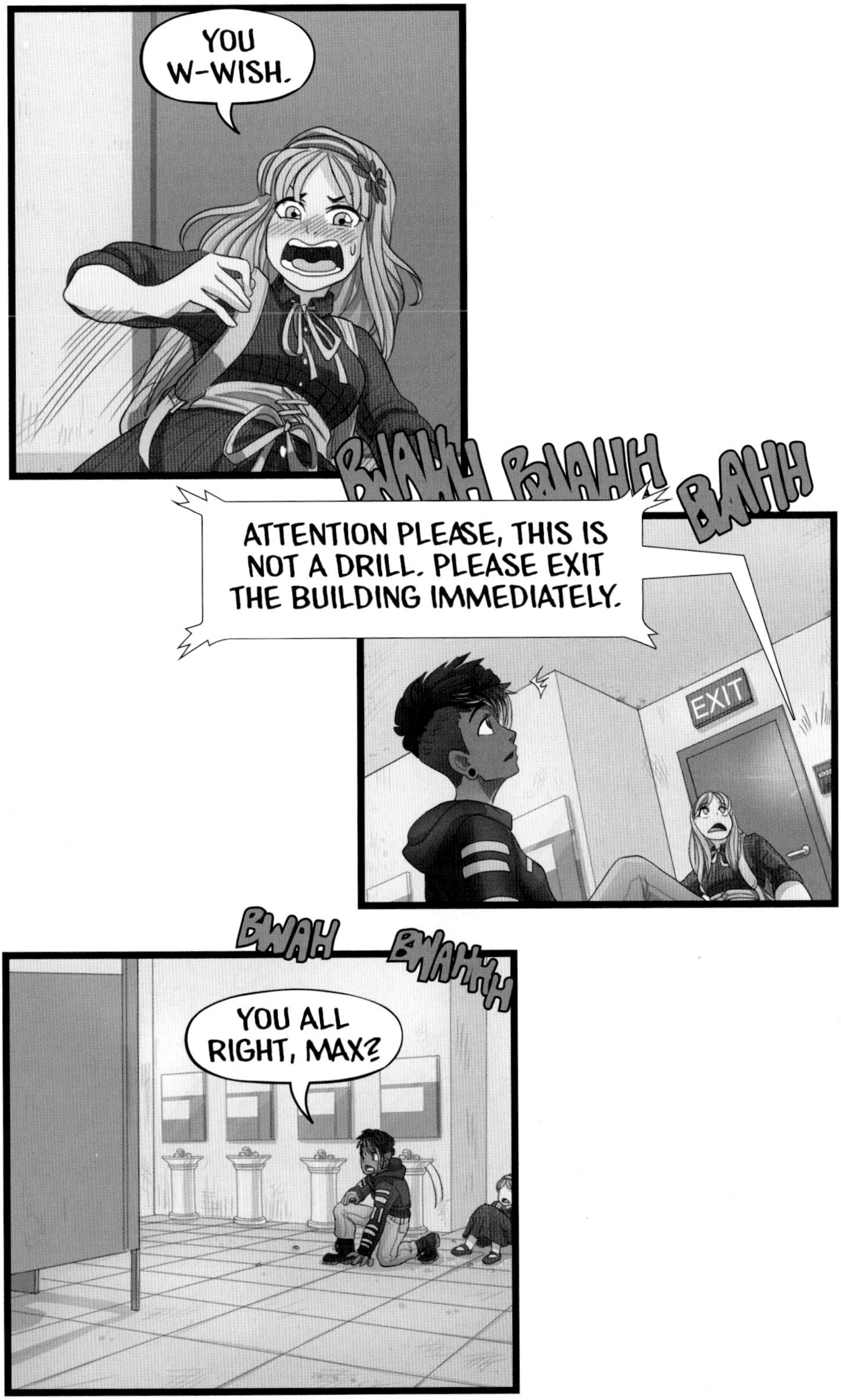
YOU W-WISH.
BWAHH BWAHH BAHH
ATTENTION PLEASE, THIS IS NOT A DRILL. PLEASE EXIT THE BUILDING IMMEDIATELY.
EXIT
BWAH BWAHHHH
YOU ALL RIGHT, MAX?

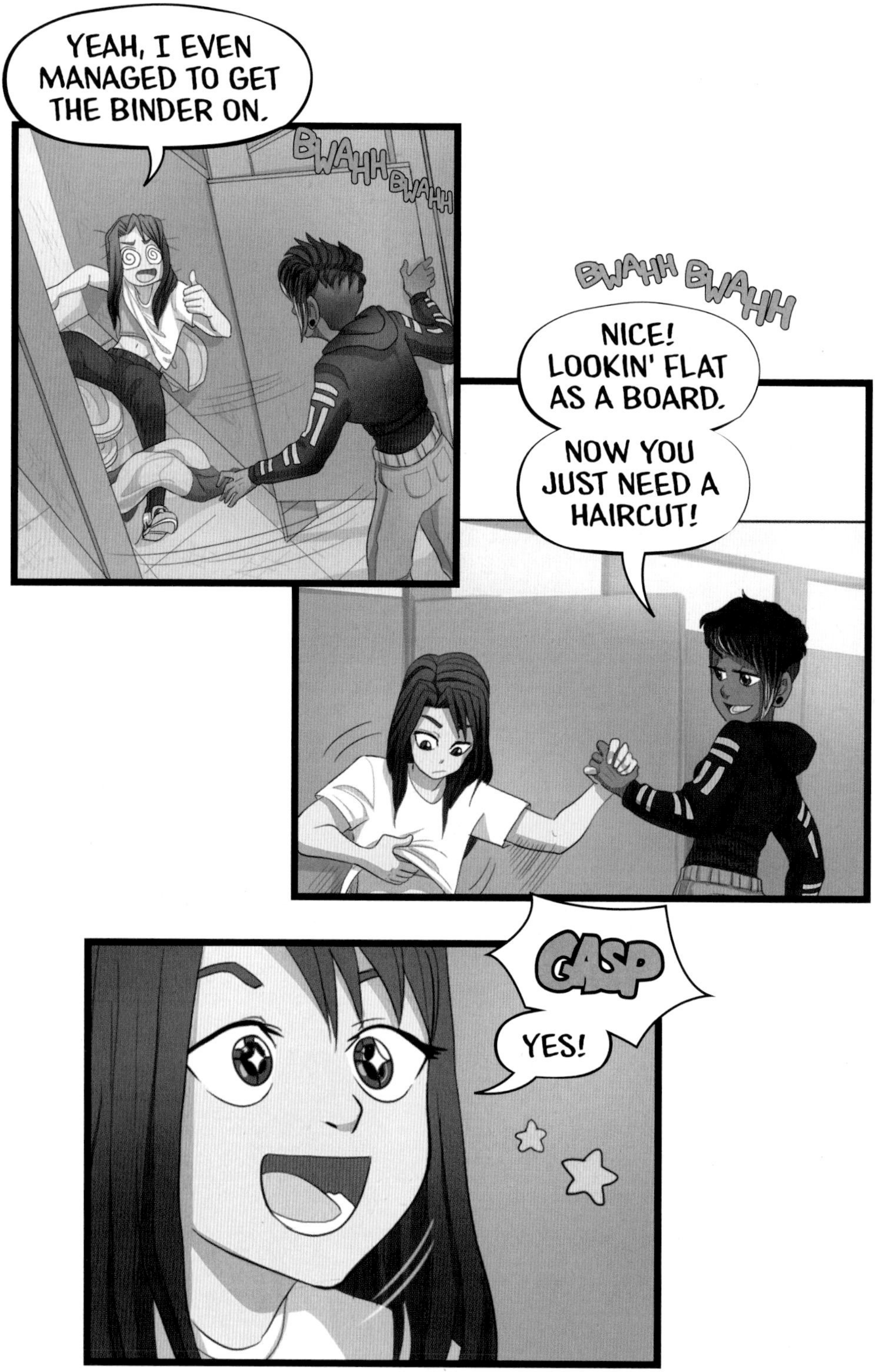
YEAH, I EVEN MANAGED TO GET THE BINDER ON.
BWAHH BWAHH
BWAHH BWAHH
NICE! LOOKIN' FLAT AS A BOARD.
NOW YOU JUST NEED A HAIRCUT!
GASP
YES!

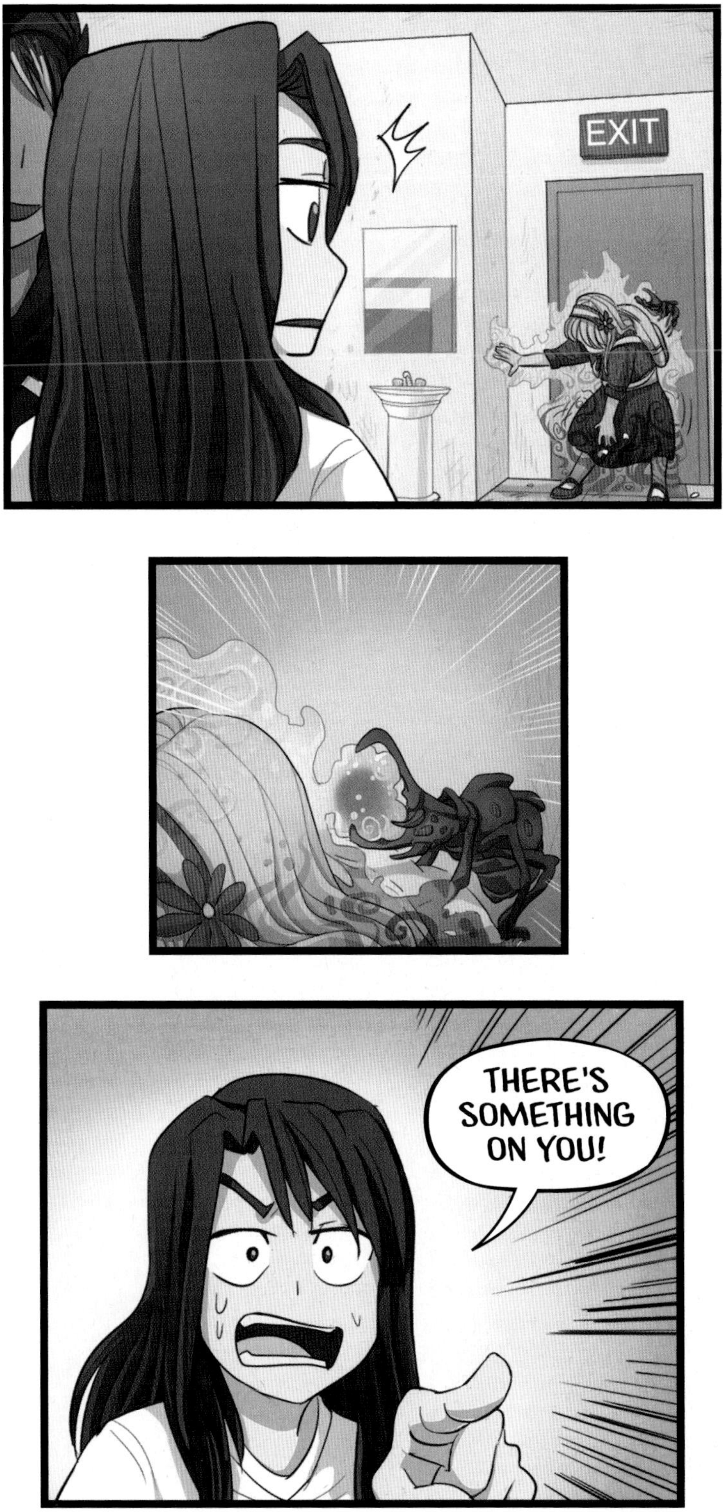
EXIT
THERE'S SOMETHING ON YOU!

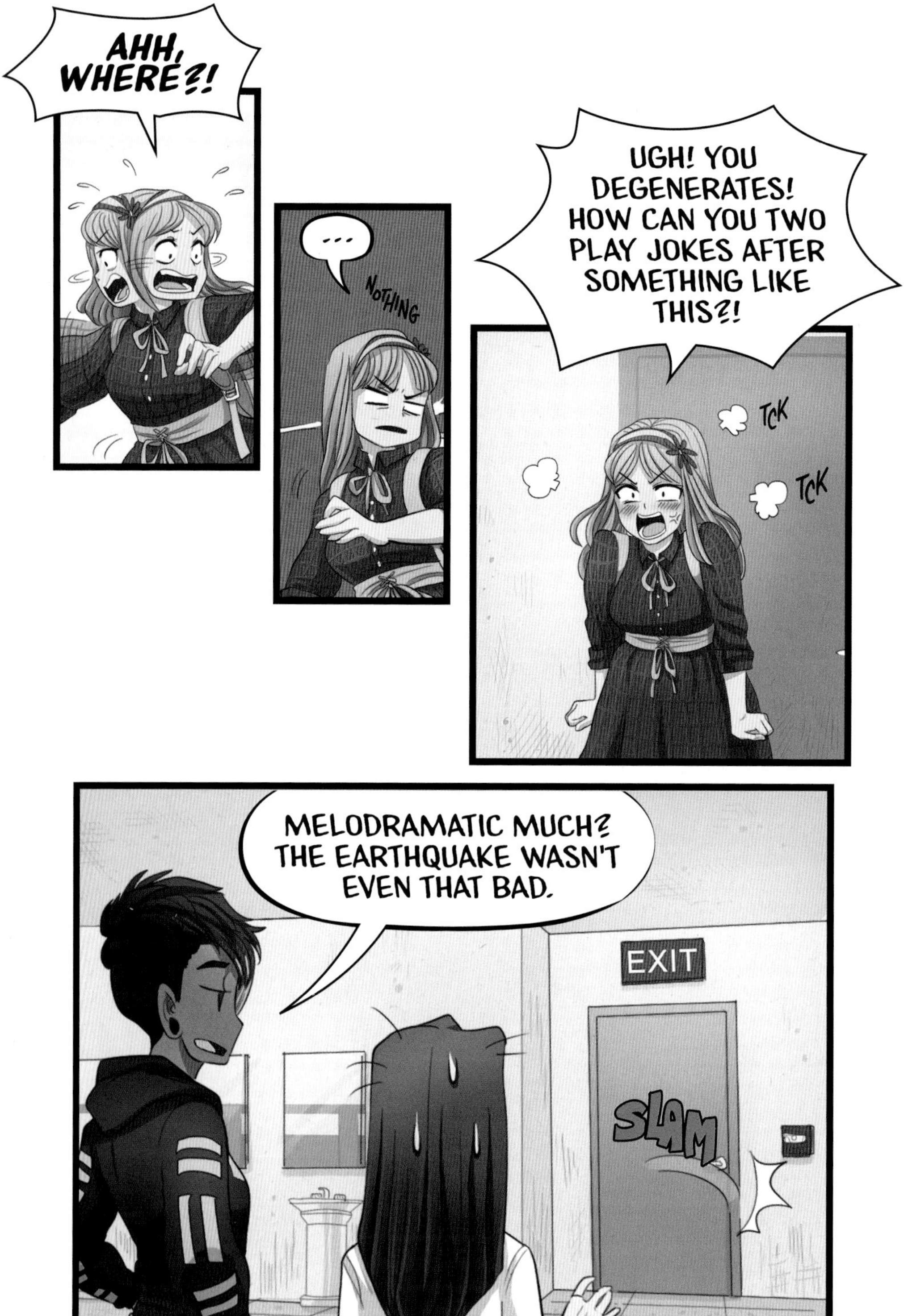
AHH, WHERE?!
...
NOTHING
UGH! YOU DEGENERATES! HOW CAN YOU TWO PLAY JOKES AFTER SOMETHING LIKE THIS?!
TCK
TCK
MELODRAMATIC MUCH? THE EARTHQUAKE WASN'T EVEN THAT BAD.
EXIT
SLAM

ANYWAYS, GOOD ONE, MAX.

I REALLY THOUGHT I SAW SOMETHING. I GUESS NOT...

C'MON, LET'S GET OUT OF HERE AND SEE WHAT'S GOING ON.

HM.

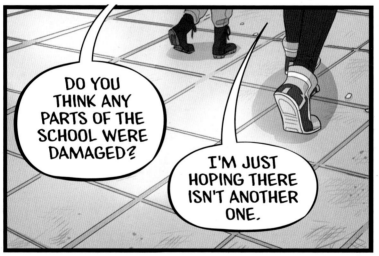

DO YOU THINK ANY PARTS OF THE SCHOOL WERE DAMAGED?

I'M JUST HOPING THERE ISN'T ANOTHER ONE.

TCK

TCK

WIGGLE WIGGLE

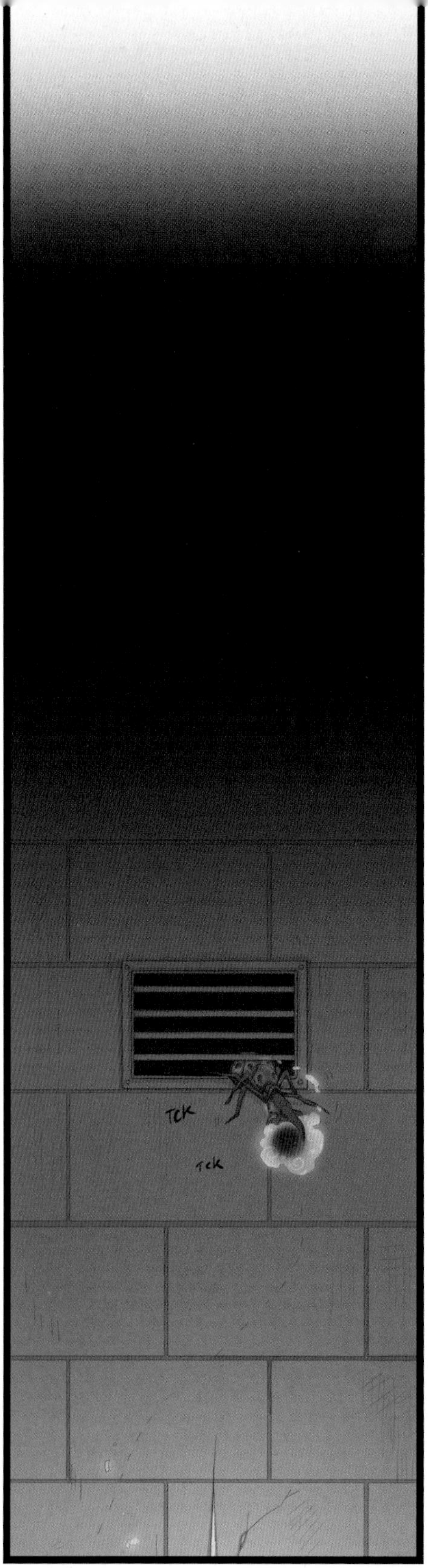
TCK
TCK

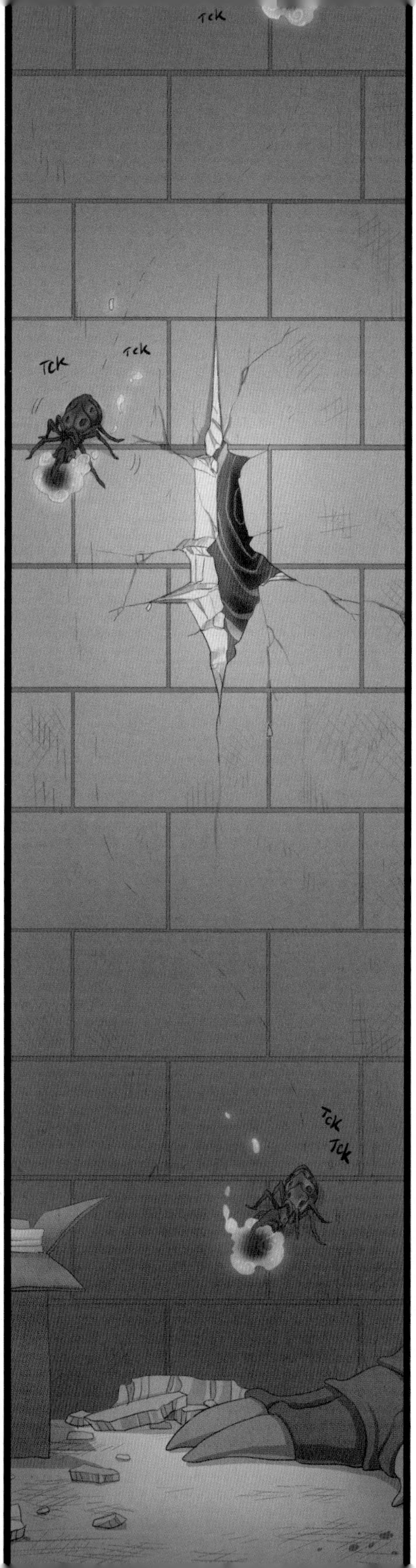
TCK
TCK
TCK
TCK
TCK

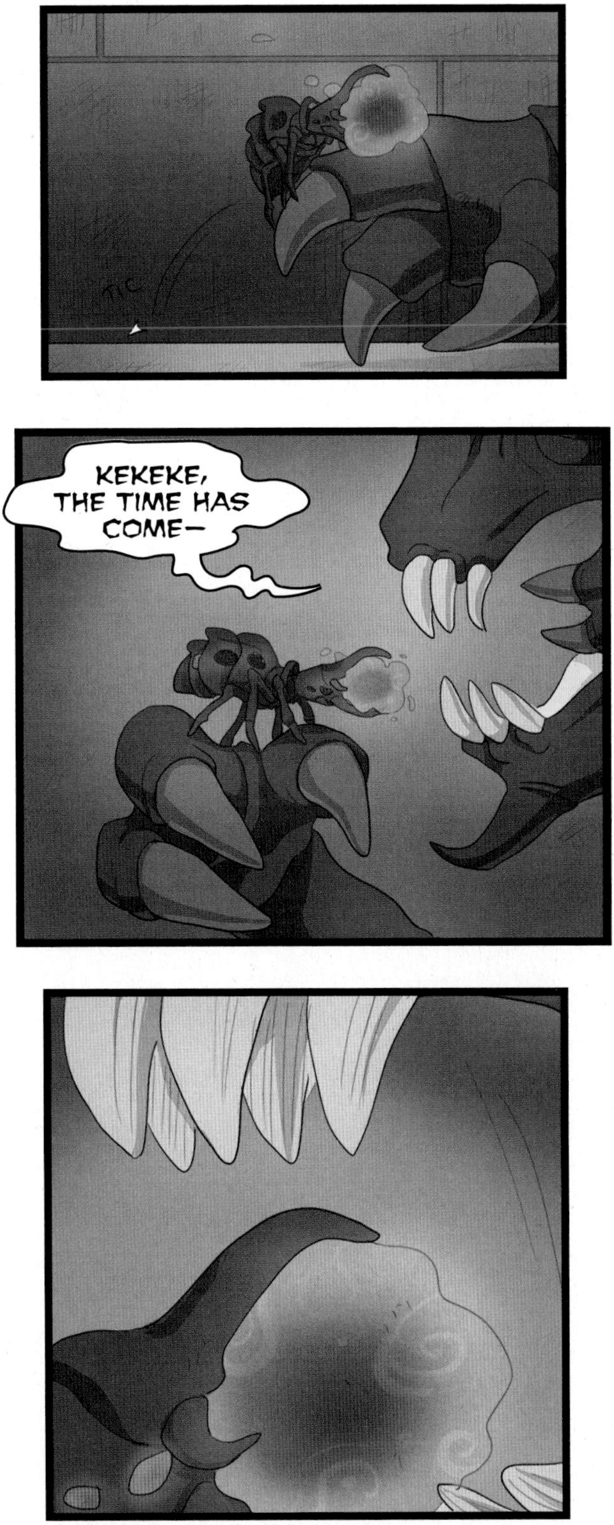
TIC
KEKEKE, THE TIME HAS COME–

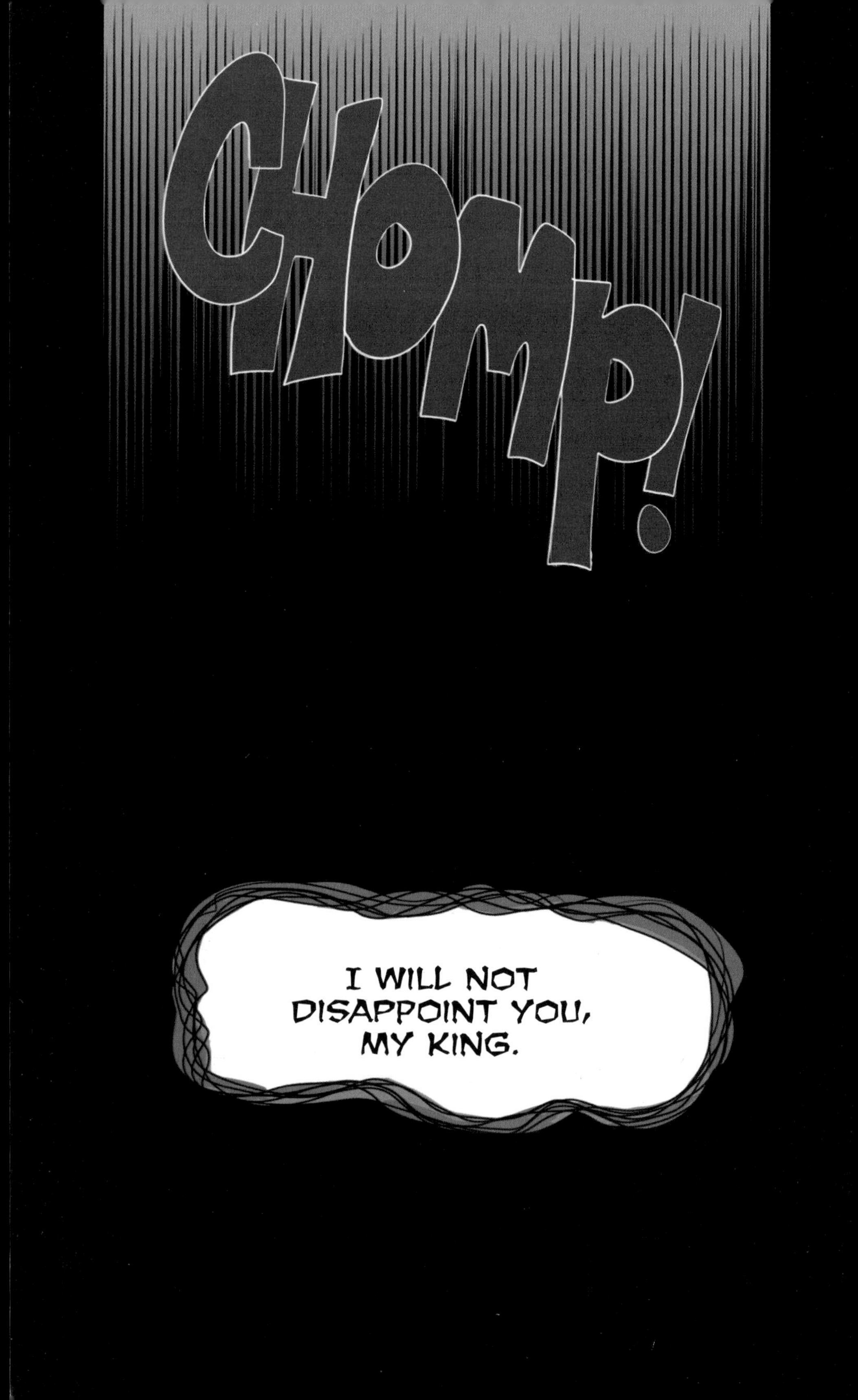
CHOMP!
I WILL NOT DISAPPOINT YOU, MY KING.

Episode 2:
COMING OUT

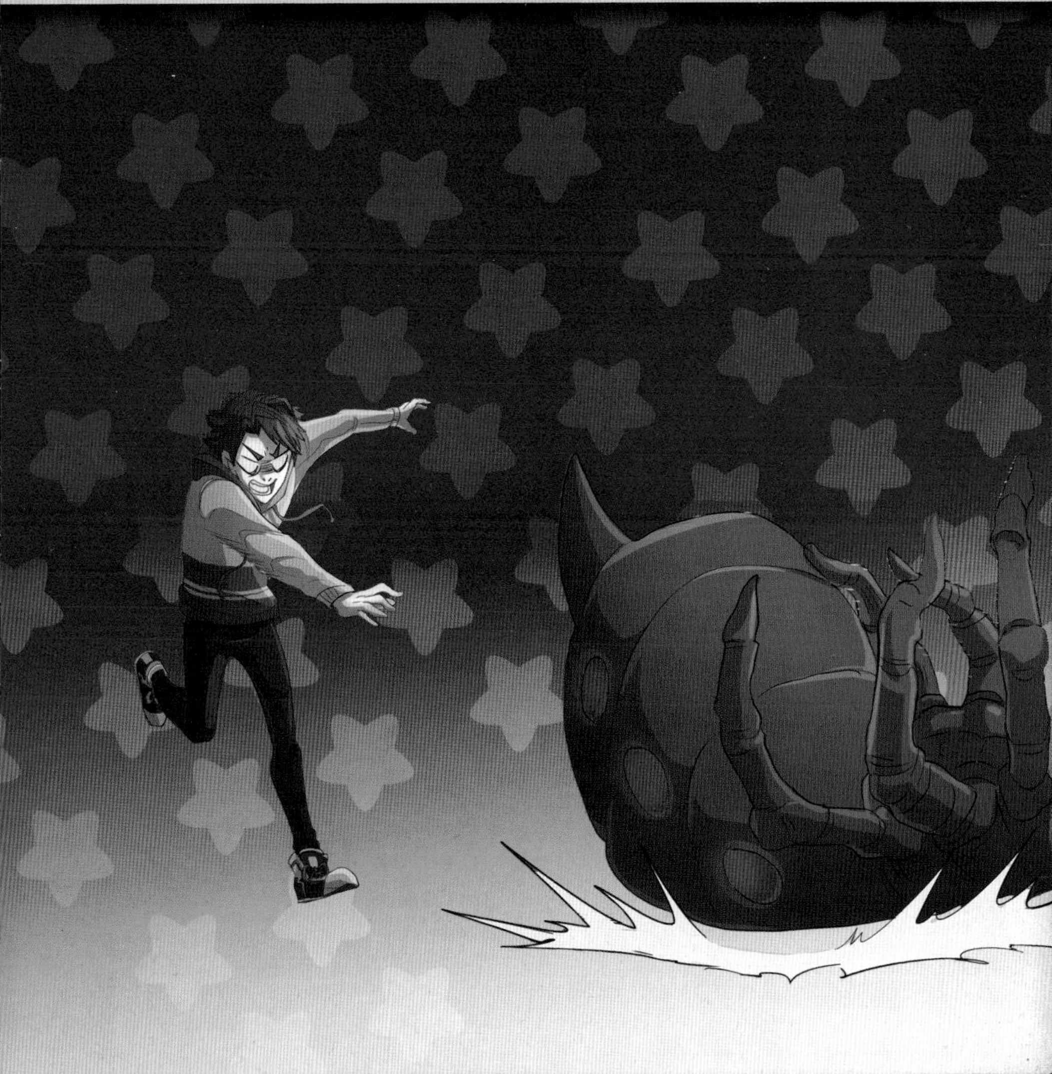

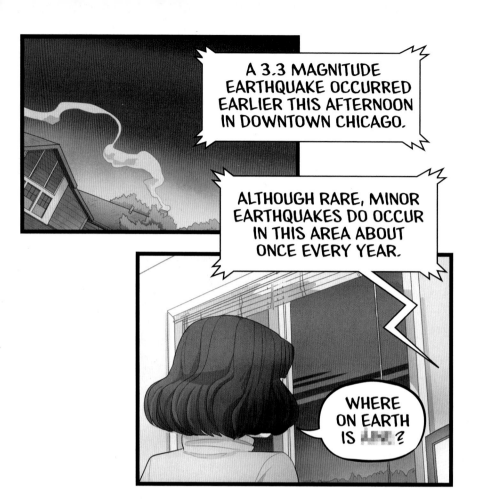

A 3.3 MAGNITUDE EARTHQUAKE OCCURRED EARLIER THIS AFTERNOON IN DOWNTOWN CHICAGO.

ALTHOUGH RARE, MINOR EARTHQUAKES DO OCCUR IN THIS AREA ABOUT ONCE EVERY YEAR.

WHERE ON EARTH IS ███?

IT'S BEEN HOURS SINCE SCHOOL'S BEEN OUT. YOU'D THINK SHE WOULD CALL AFTER AN EARTHQUAKE.

NO SERIOUS DAMAGES OR INJURIES WERE REPORTED IN THE CHICAGO AREA.

SHE'S PROBABLY HANGING OUT WITH HER FRIENDS.

IT **IS** HER BIRTHDAY. AND LIKE THE NEWS SAID, THE EARTHQUAKE WASN'T BAD.

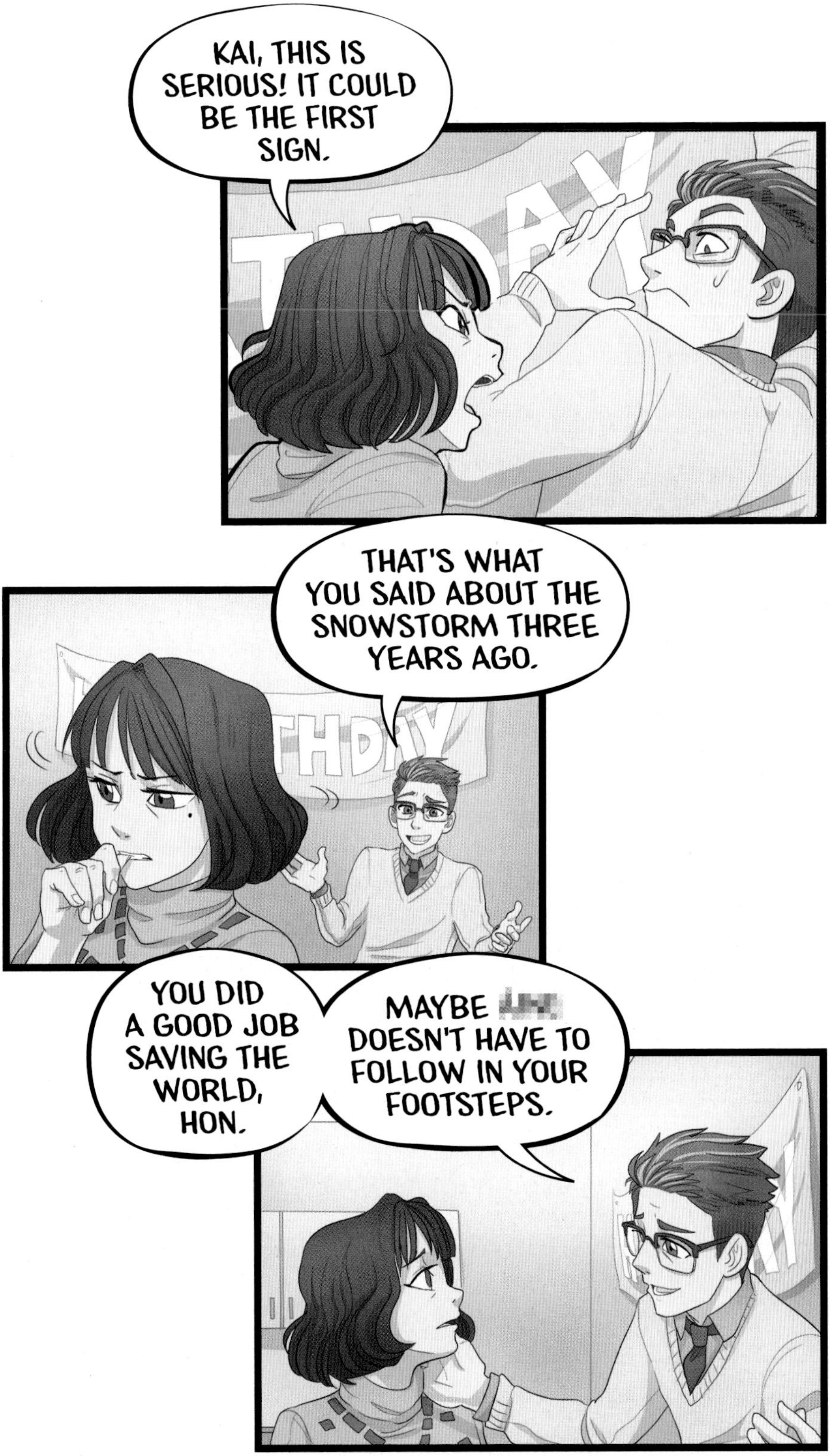
KAI, THIS IS SERIOUS! IT COULD BE THE FIRST SIGN.
THAT'S WHAT YOU SAID ABOUT THE SNOWSTORM THREE YEARS AGO.
YOU DID A GOOD JOB SAVING THE WORLD, HON.
MAYBE DOESN'T HAVE TO FOLLOW IN YOUR FOOTSTEPS.

MAYBE...
JINGLE
CREAK
SLAM
step
step

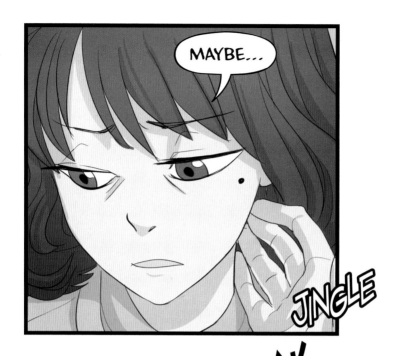

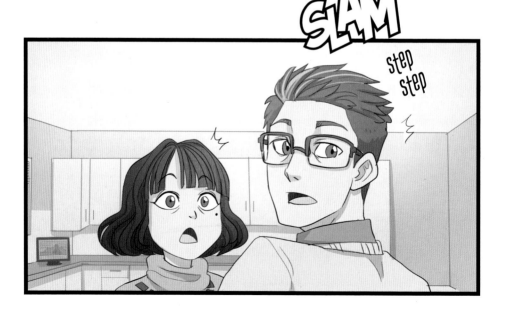

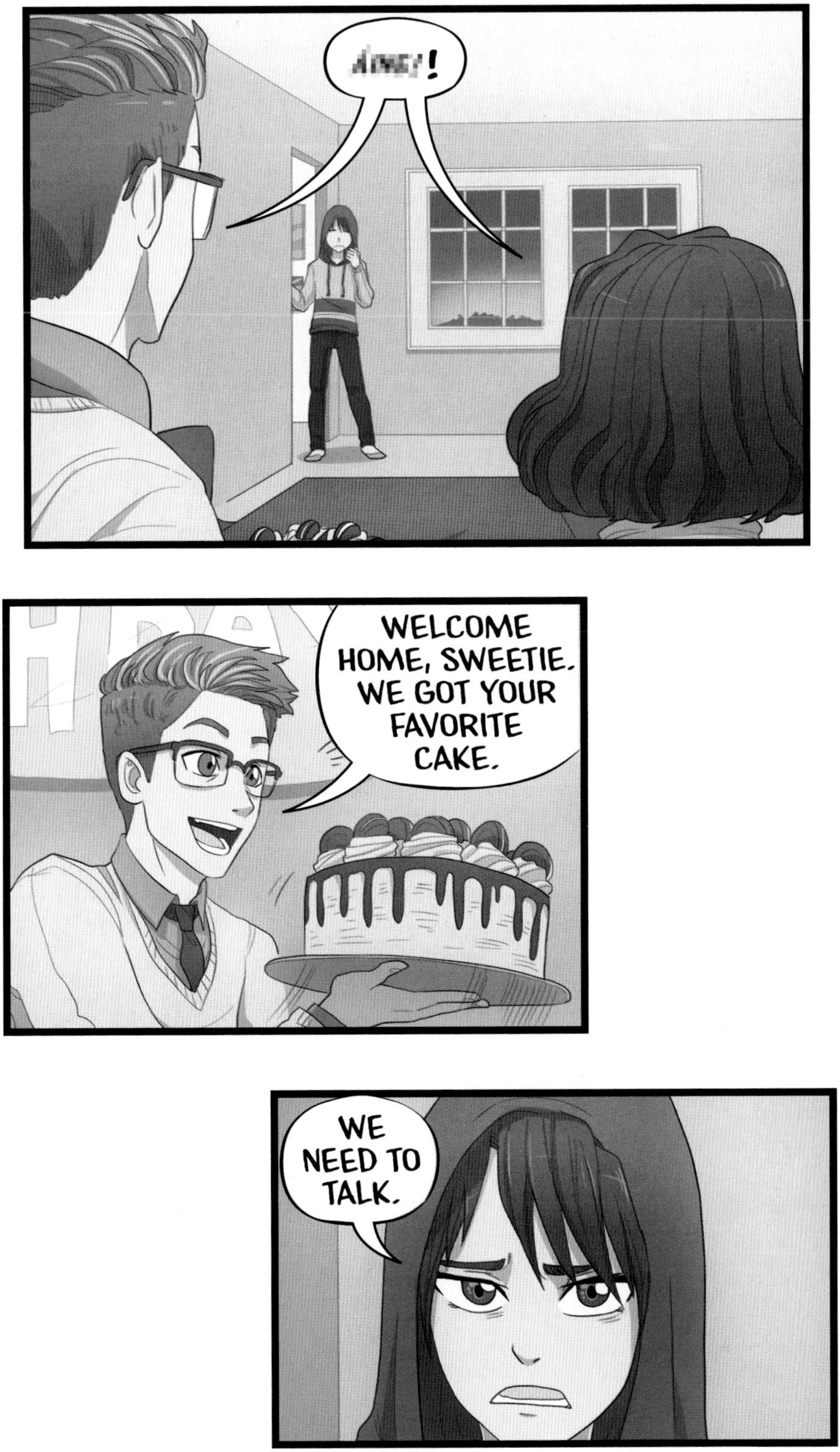
[redacted]!
WELCOME HOME, SWEETIE. WE GOT YOUR FAVORITE CAKE.
WE NEED TO TALK.

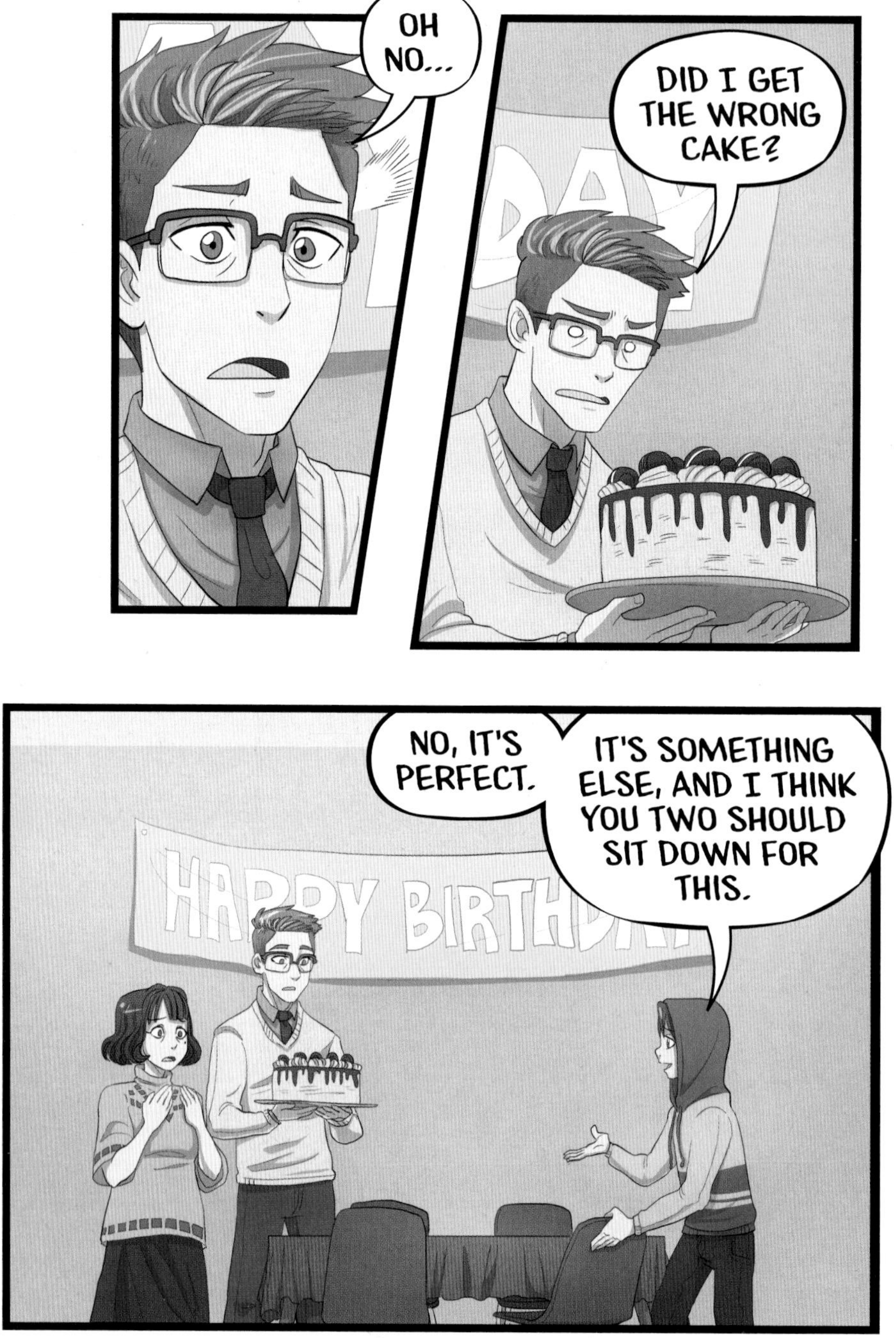
OH NO...
DID I GET THE WRONG CAKE?
NO, IT'S PERFECT.
IT'S SOMETHING ELSE, AND I THINK YOU TWO SHOULD SIT DOWN FOR THIS.
HAPPY BIRTHDAY

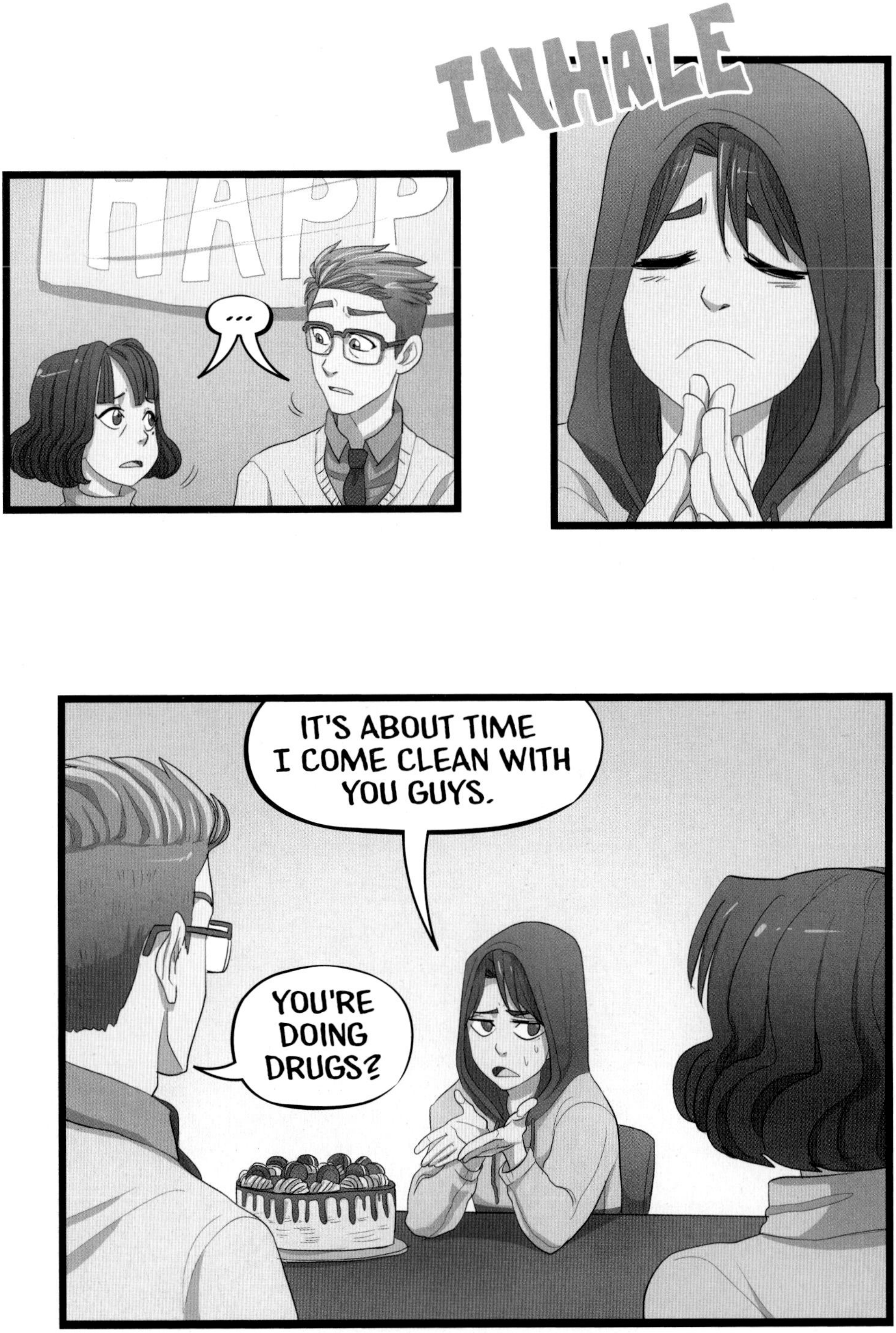
HAPP
...
INHALE
IT'S ABOUT TIME I COME CLEAN WITH YOU GUYS.
YOU'RE DOING DRUGS?

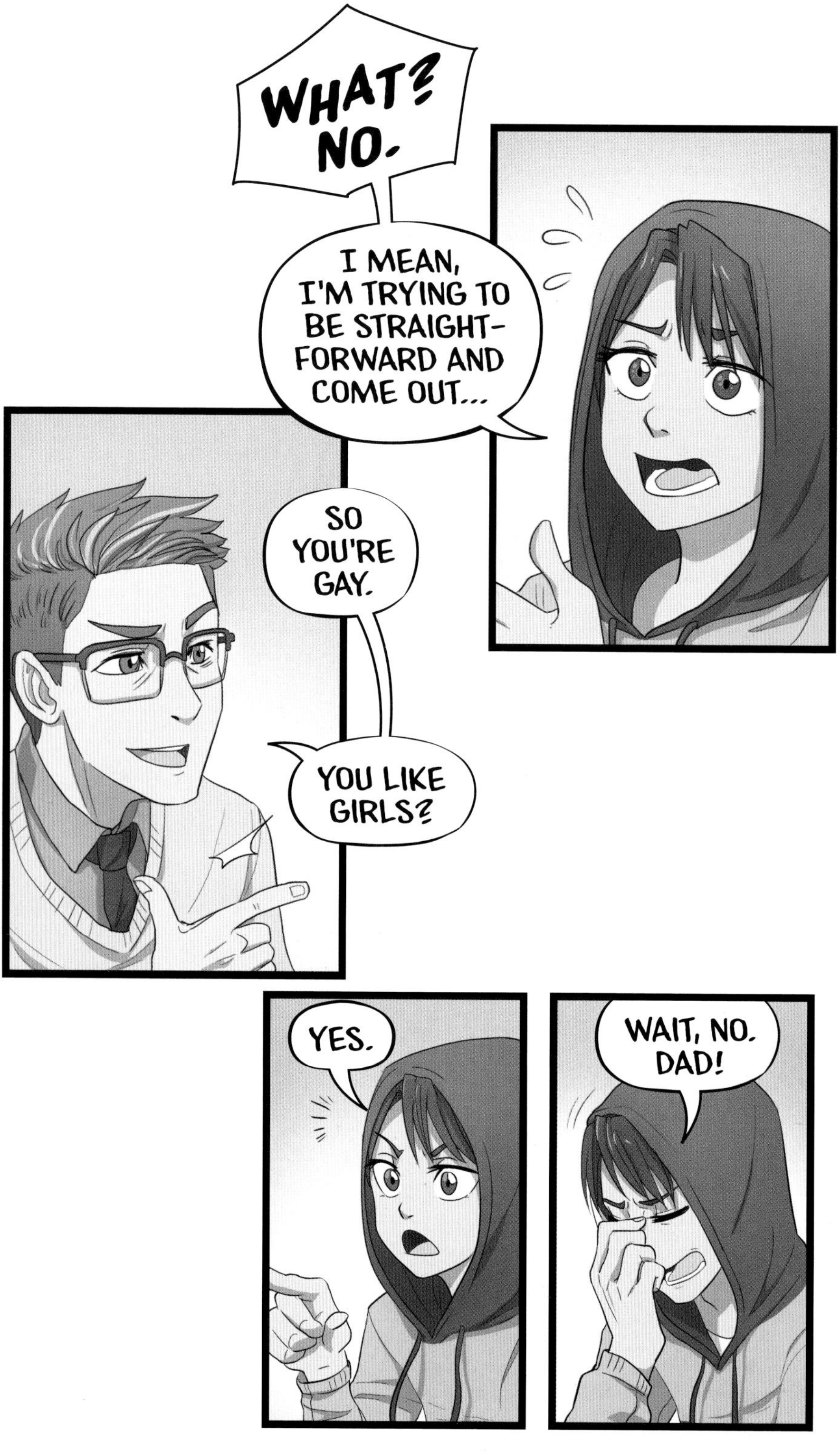
WHAT?
NO.
I MEAN, I'M TRYING TO BE STRAIGHT-FORWARD AND COME OUT...
SO YOU'RE GAY.
YOU LIKE GIRLS?
YES.
WAIT, NO. DAD!

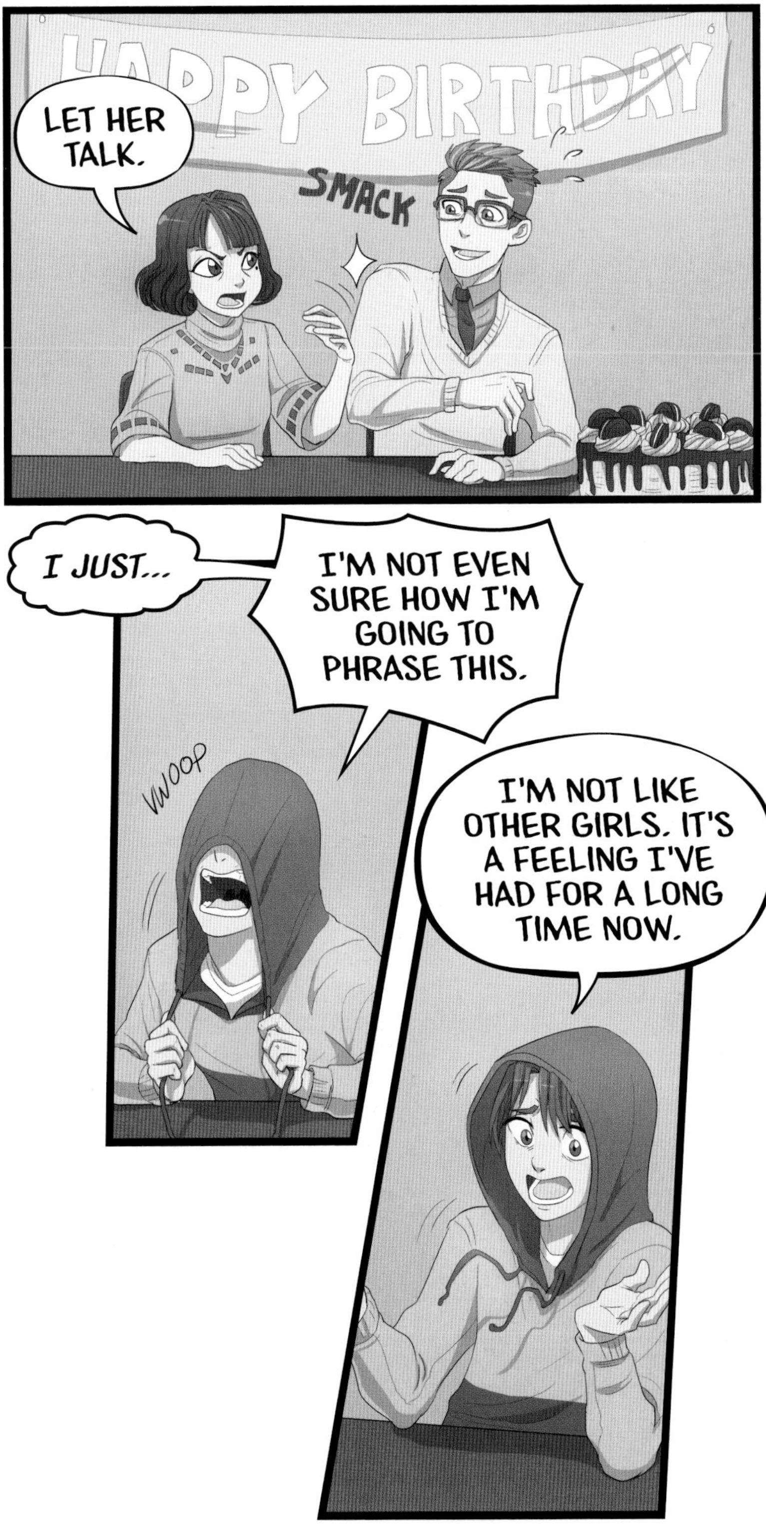
LET HER TALK.
SMACK
I JUST...
I'M NOT EVEN SURE HOW I'M GOING TO PHRASE THIS.
VWOOP
I'M NOT LIKE OTHER GIRLS. IT'S A FEELING I'VE HAD FOR A LONG TIME NOW.

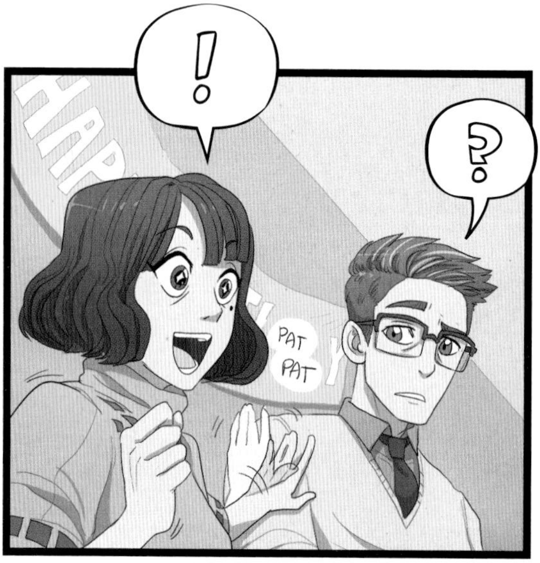
!
?
PAT
PAT

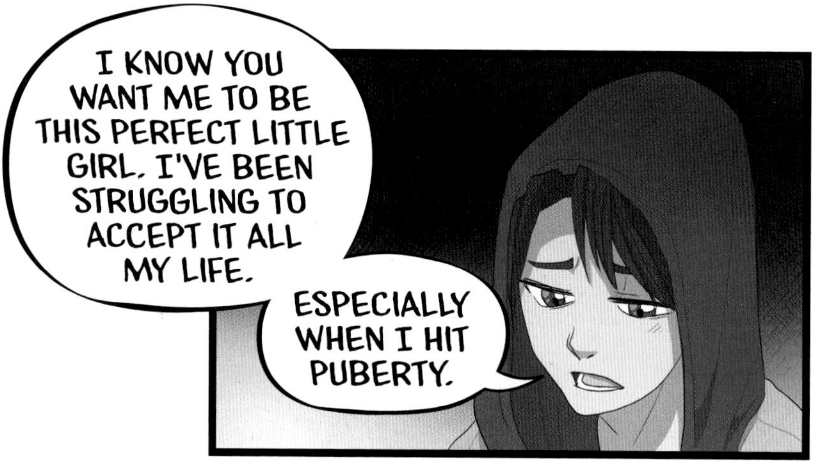
I KNOW YOU WANT ME TO BE THIS PERFECT LITTLE GIRL. I'VE BEEN STRUGGLING TO ACCEPT IT ALL MY LIFE.
ESPECIALLY WHEN I HIT PUBERTY.

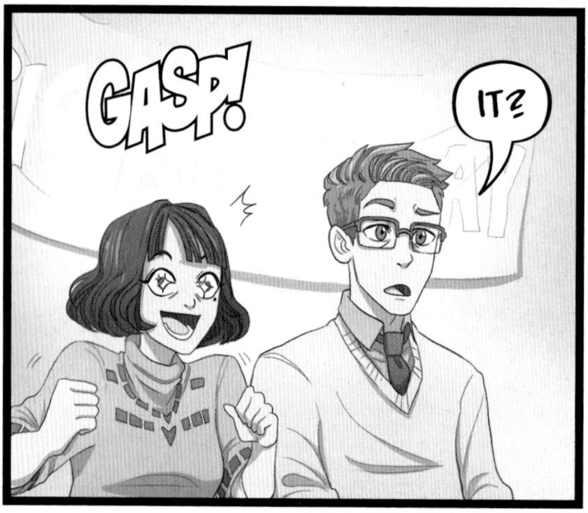
GASP!
IT?

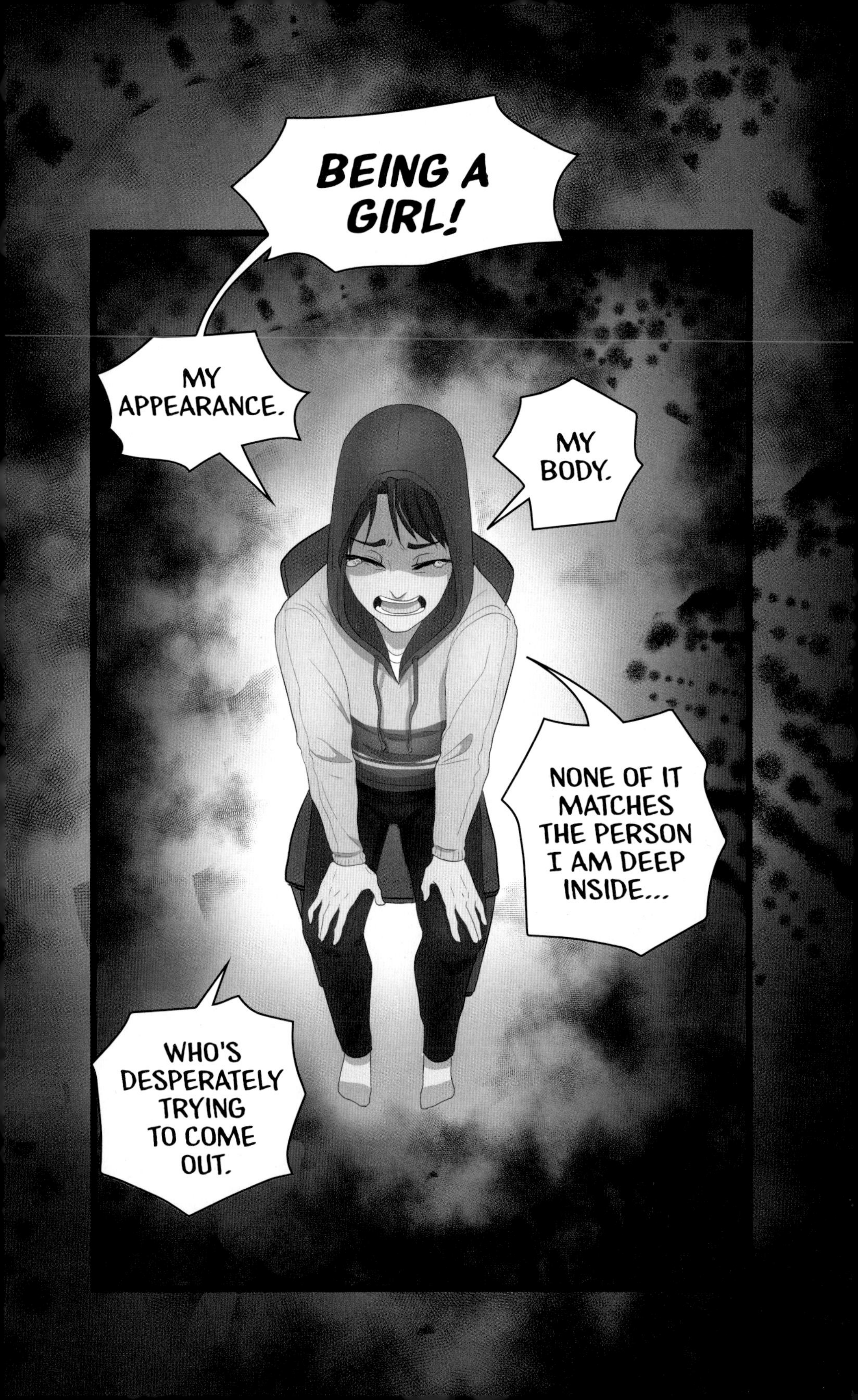
BEING A GIRL!
MY APPEARANCE.
MY BODY.
NONE OF IT MATCHES THE PERSON I AM DEEP INSIDE...
WHO'S DESPERATELY TRYING TO COME OUT.

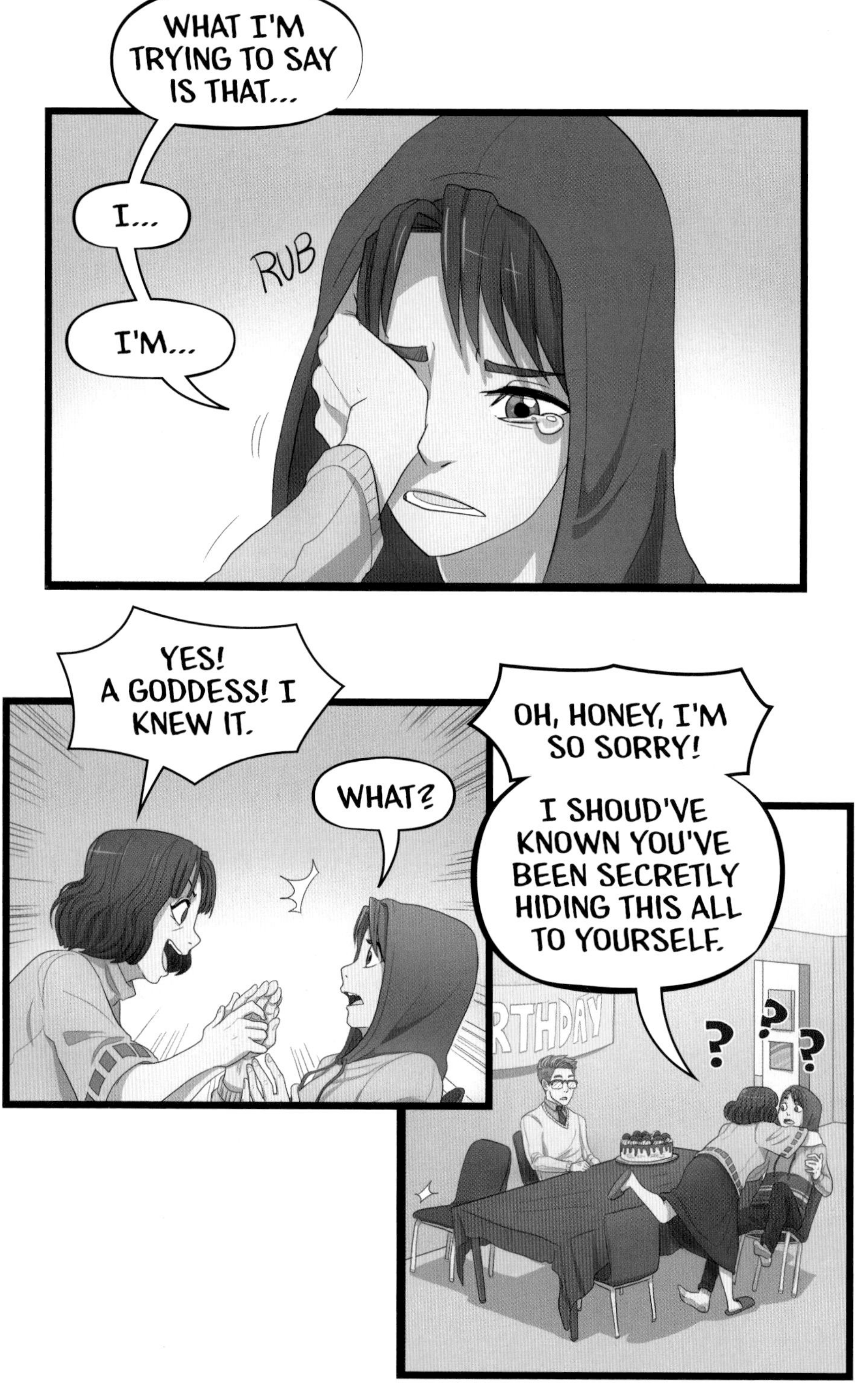
WHAT I'M TRYING TO SAY IS THAT...
I...
RUB
I'M...
YES! A GODDESS! I KNEW IT.
WHAT?
OH, HONEY, I'M SO SORRY!
I SHOUD'VE KNOWN YOU'VE BEEN SECRETLY HIDING THIS ALL TO YOURSELF.
RTHDAY
? ? ?

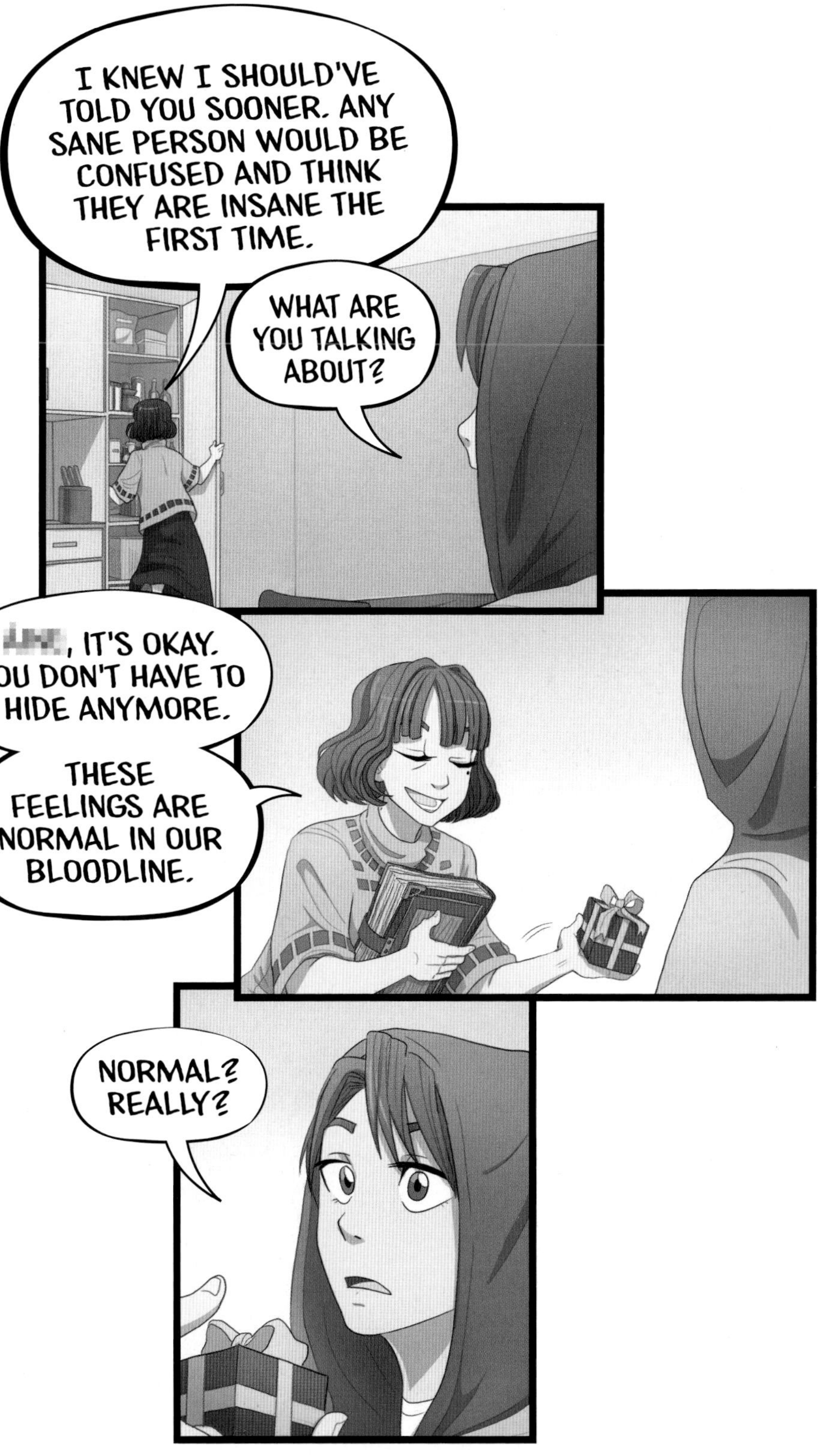
I KNEW I SHOULD'VE TOLD YOU SOONER. ANY SANE PERSON WOULD BE CONFUSED AND THINK THEY ARE INSANE THE FIRST TIME.
WHAT ARE YOU TALKING ABOUT?
, IT'S OKAY. YOU DON'T HAVE TO HIDE ANYMORE.
THESE FEELINGS ARE NORMAL IN OUR BLOODLINE.
NORMAL? REALLY?

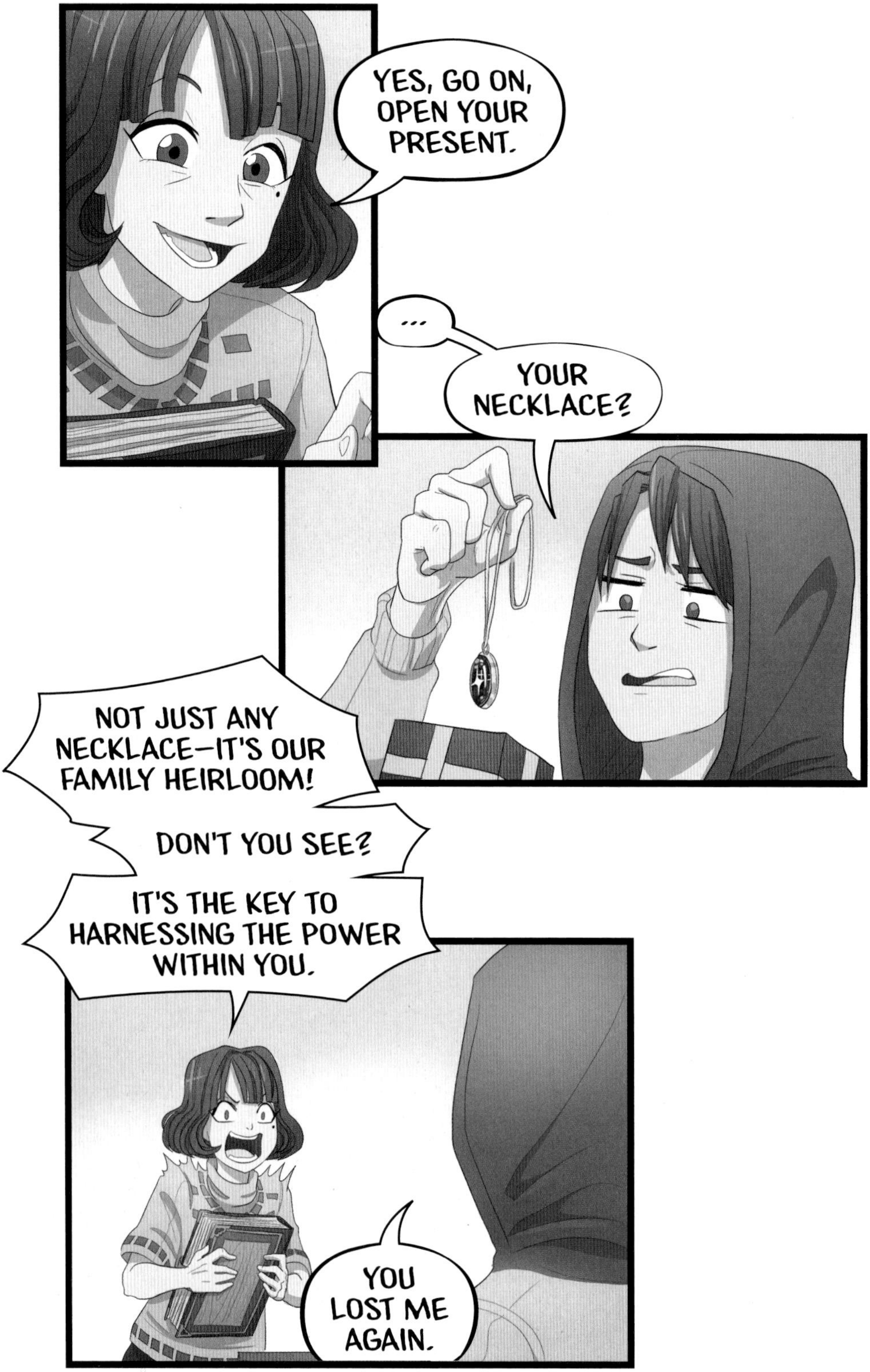

YES, GO ON, OPEN YOUR PRESENT.
...
YOUR NECKLACE?
NOT JUST ANY NECKLACE—IT'S OUR FAMILY HEIRLOOM!
DON'T YOU SEE?
IT'S THE KEY TO HARNESSING THE POWER WITHIN YOU.
YOU LOST ME AGAIN.

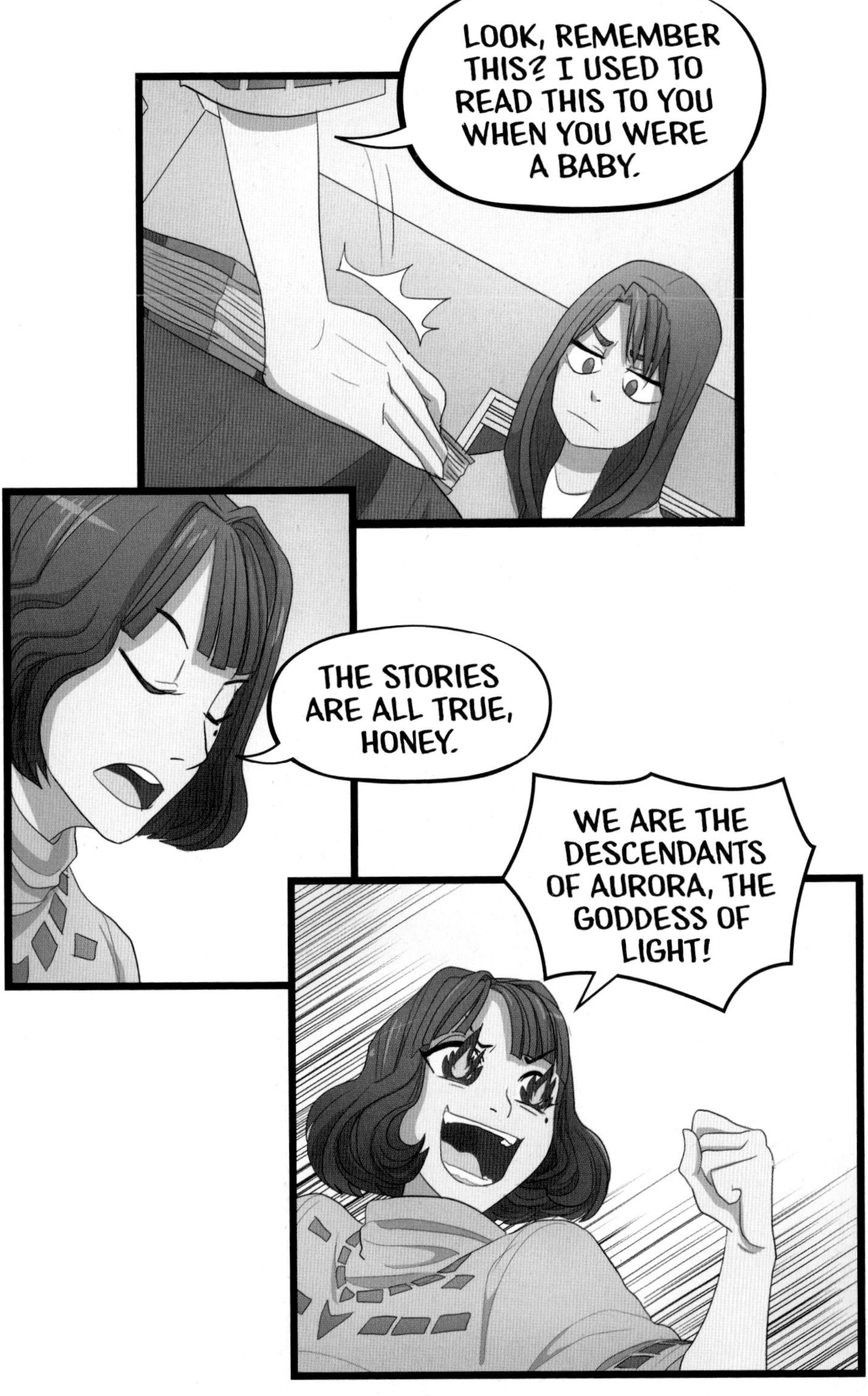
LOOK, REMEMBER THIS? I USED TO READ THIS TO YOU WHEN YOU WERE A BABY.
THE STORIES ARE ALL TRUE, HONEY.
WE ARE THE DESCENDANTS OF AURORA, THE GODDESS OF LIGHT!

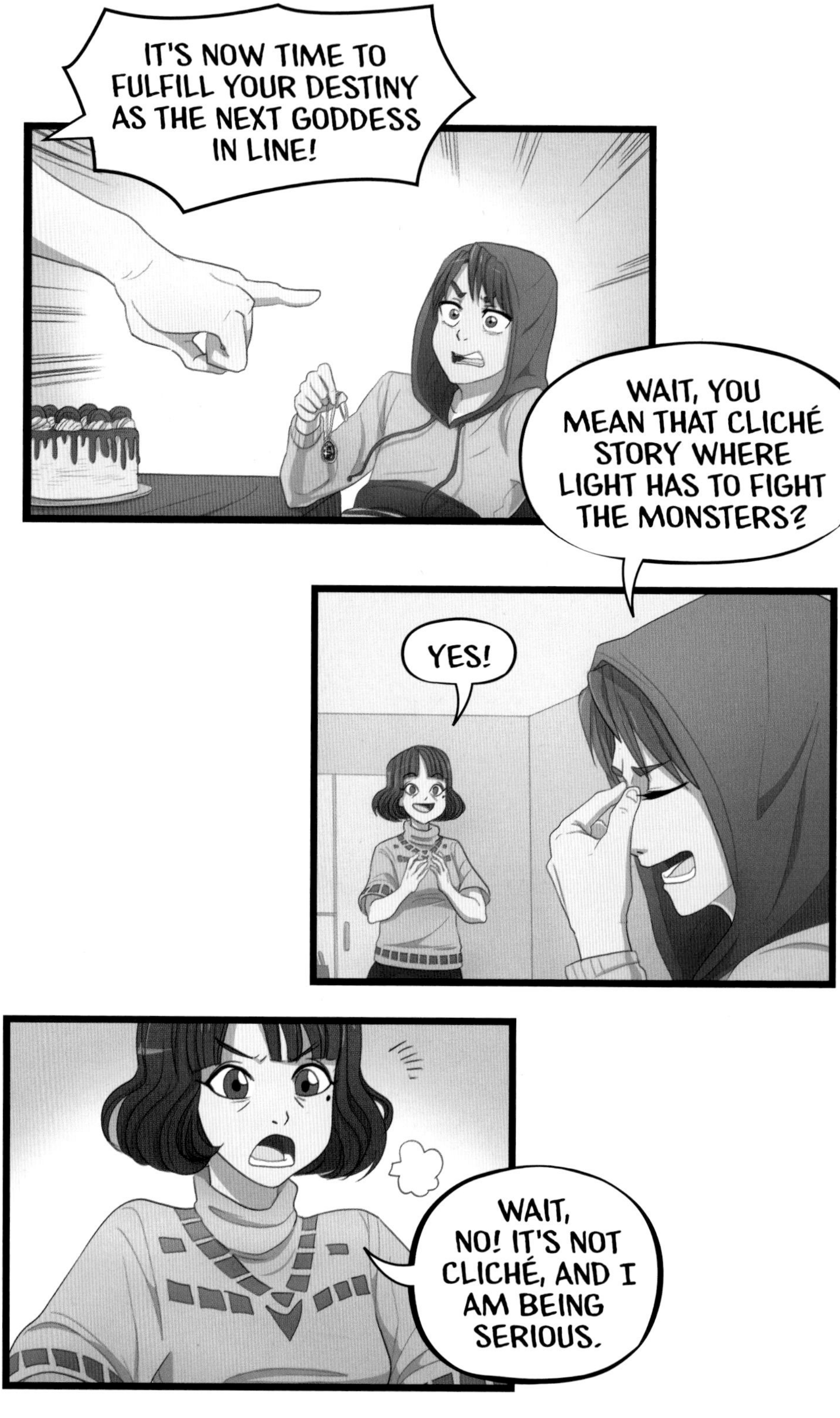
IT'S NOW TIME TO FULFILL YOUR DESTINY AS THE NEXT GODDESS IN LINE!
WAIT, YOU MEAN THAT CLICHÉ STORY WHERE LIGHT HAS TO FIGHT THE MONSTERS?
YES!
WAIT, NO! IT'S NOT CLICHÉ, AND I AM BEING SERIOUS.

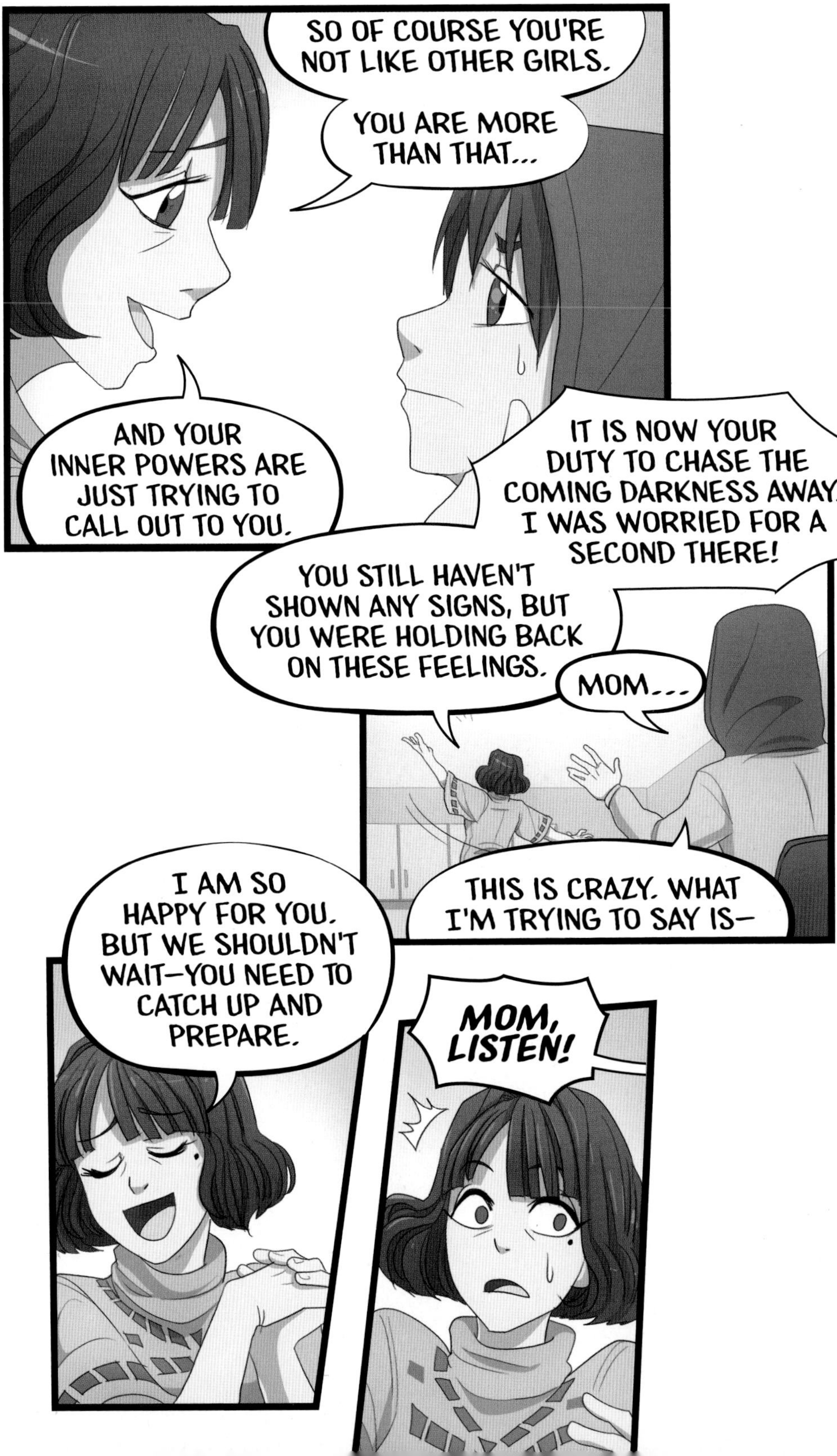
SO OF COURSE YOU'RE NOT LIKE OTHER GIRLS.
YOU ARE MORE THAN THAT...
AND YOUR INNER POWERS ARE JUST TRYING TO CALL OUT TO YOU.
IT IS NOW YOUR DUTY TO CHASE THE COMING DARKNESS AWAY. I WAS WORRIED FOR A SECOND THERE!
YOU STILL HAVEN'T SHOWN ANY SIGNS, BUT YOU WERE HOLDING BACK ON THESE FEELINGS.
MOM...
THIS IS CRAZY. WHAT I'M TRYING TO SAY IS—
I AM SO HAPPY FOR YOU. BUT WE SHOULDN'T WAIT—YOU NEED TO CATCH UP AND PREPARE.
MOM, LISTEN!

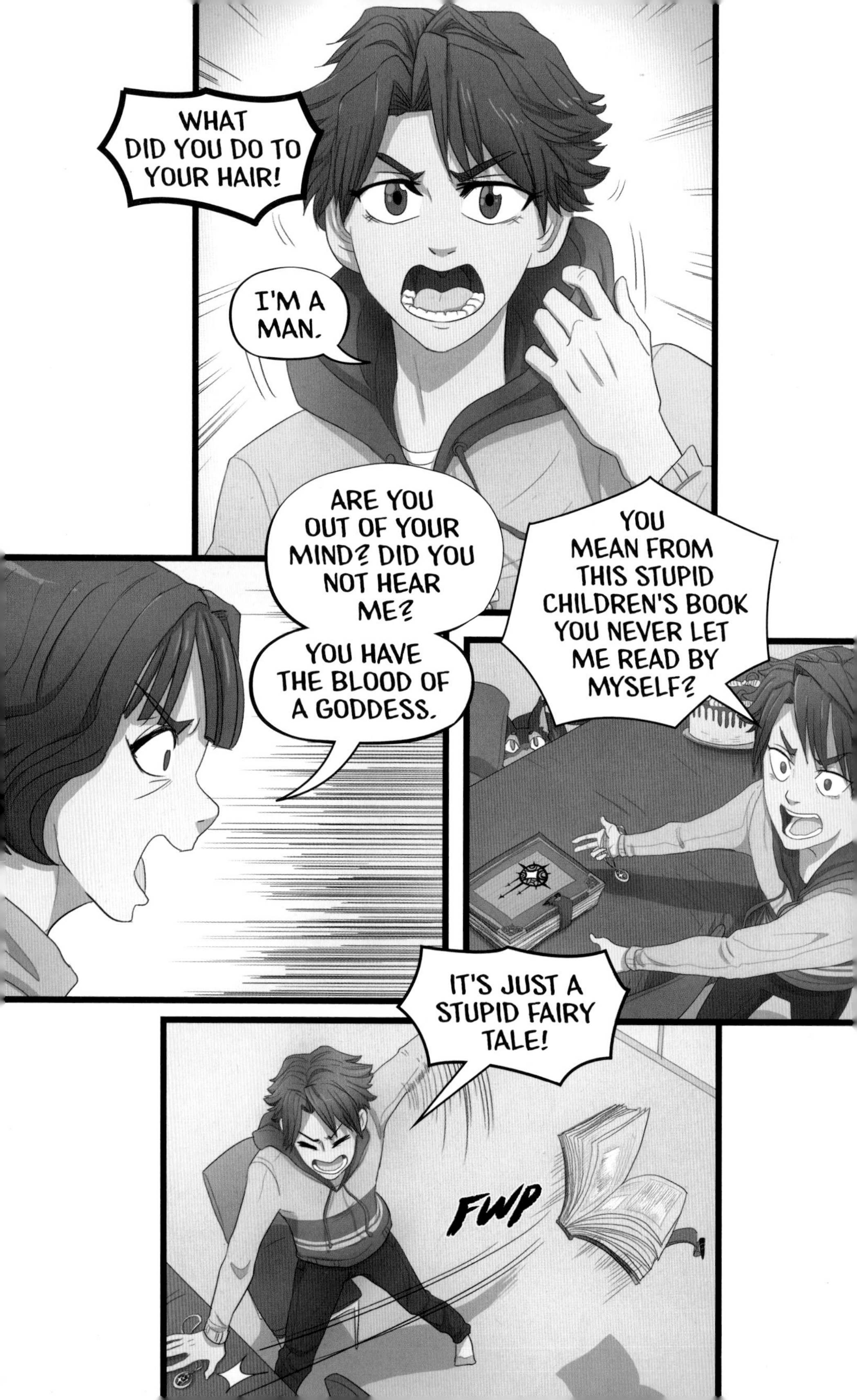
WHAT DID YOU DO TO YOUR HAIR!
I'M A MAN.
ARE YOU OUT OF YOUR MIND? DID YOU NOT HEAR ME?
YOU HAVE THE BLOOD OF A GODDESS.
YOU MEAN FROM THIS STUPID CHILDREN'S BOOK YOU NEVER LET ME READ BY MYSELF?
IT'S JUST A STUPID FAIRY TALE!
FWP

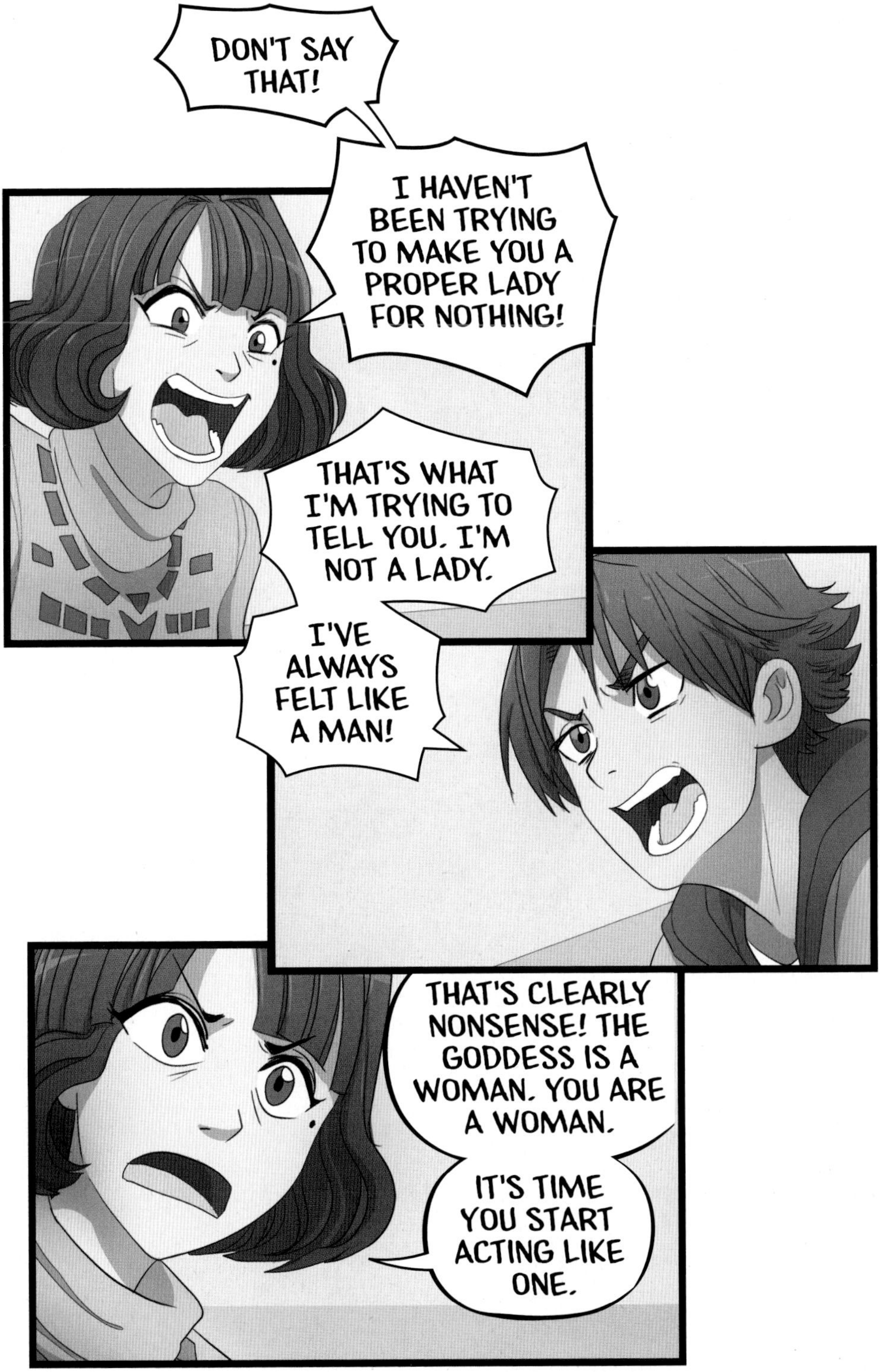
DON'T SAY THAT!
I HAVEN'T BEEN TRYING TO MAKE YOU A PROPER LADY FOR NOTHING!
THAT'S WHAT I'M TRYING TO TELL YOU. I'M NOT A LADY.
I'VE ALWAYS FELT LIKE A MAN!
THAT'S CLEARLY NONSENSE! THE GODDESS IS A WOMAN. YOU ARE A WOMAN.
IT'S TIME YOU START ACTING LIKE ONE.

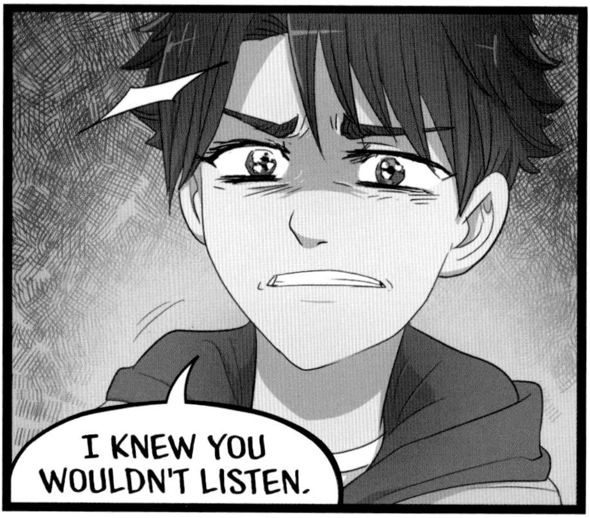
I KNEW YOU WOULDN'T LISTEN.

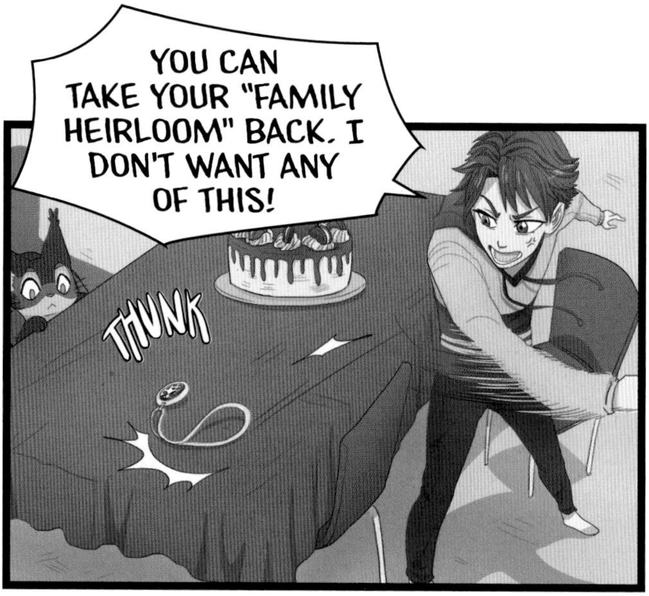
YOU CAN TAKE YOUR "FAMILY HEIRLOOM" BACK. I DON'T WANT ANY OF THIS!
THUNK

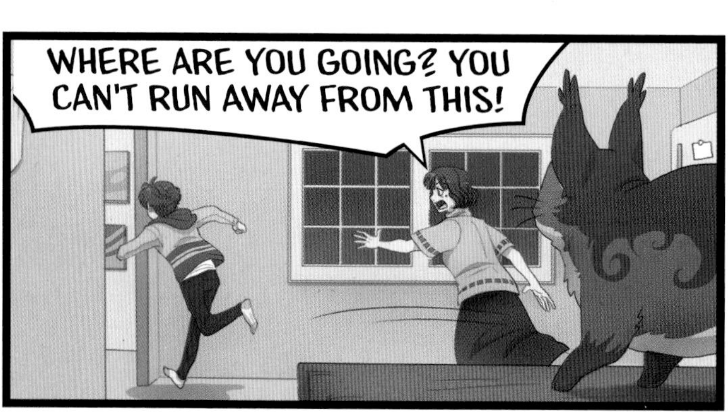
WHERE ARE YOU GOING? YOU CAN'T RUN AWAY FROM THIS!

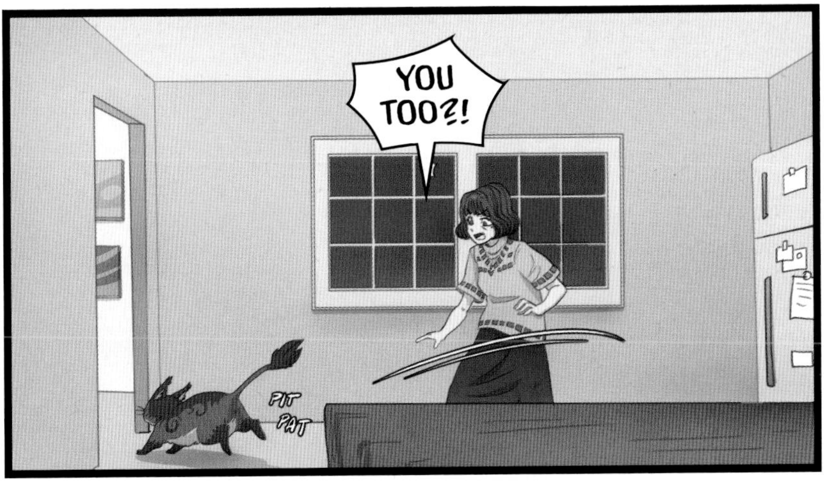
YOU TOO?!
PIT PAT

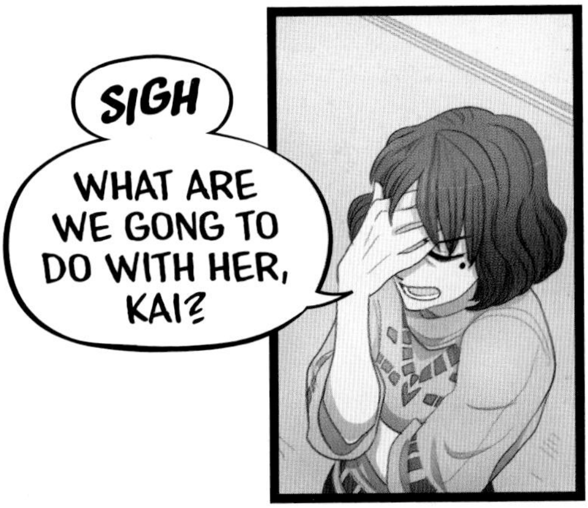
SIGH
WHAT ARE WE GONG TO DO WITH HER, KAI?

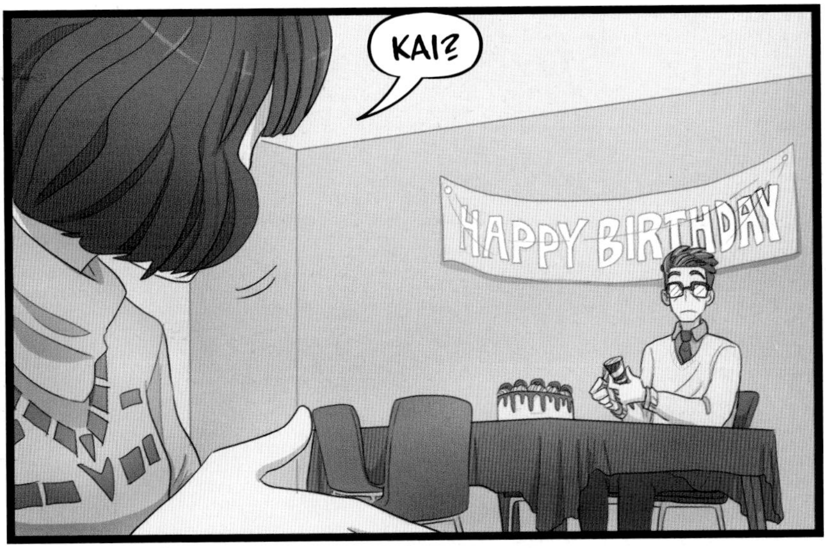
KAI?
HAPPY BIRTHDAY

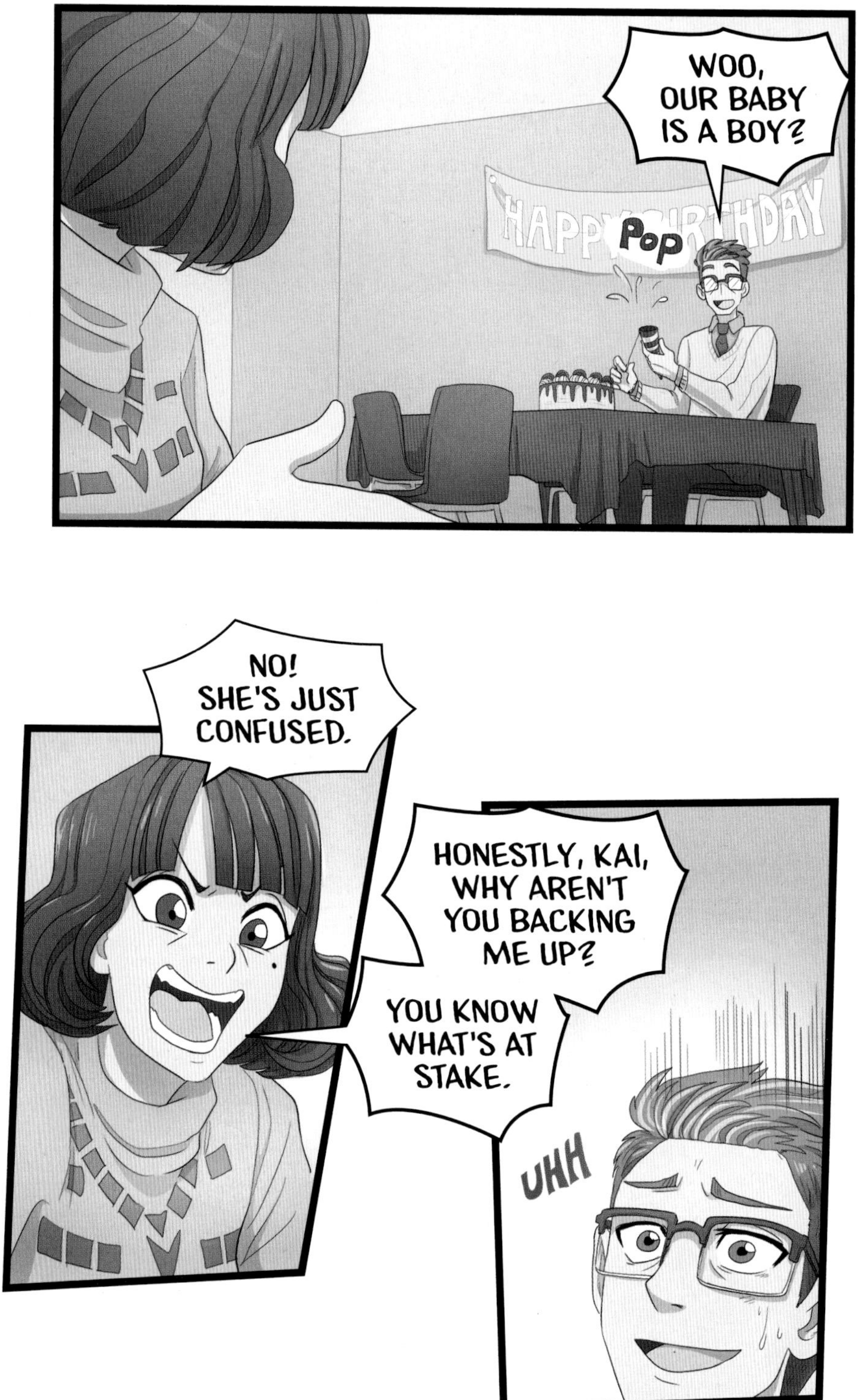
WOO, OUR BABY IS A BOY?
Pop
NO! SHE'S JUST CONFUSED.
HONESTLY, KAI, WHY AREN'T YOU BACKING ME UP?
YOU KNOW WHAT'S AT STAKE.
UHH

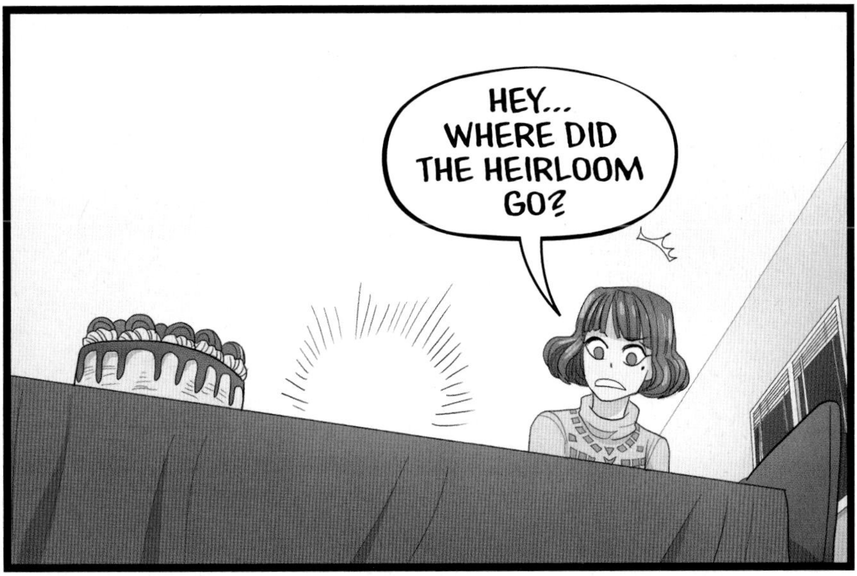
HEY... WHERE DID THE HEIRLOOM GO?

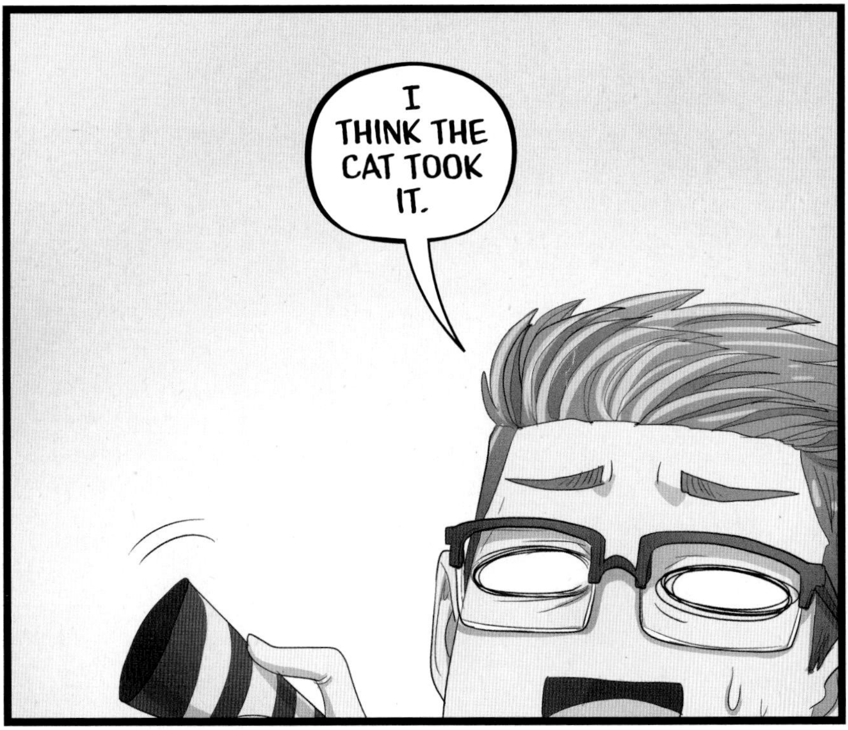
I THINK THE CAT TOOK IT.

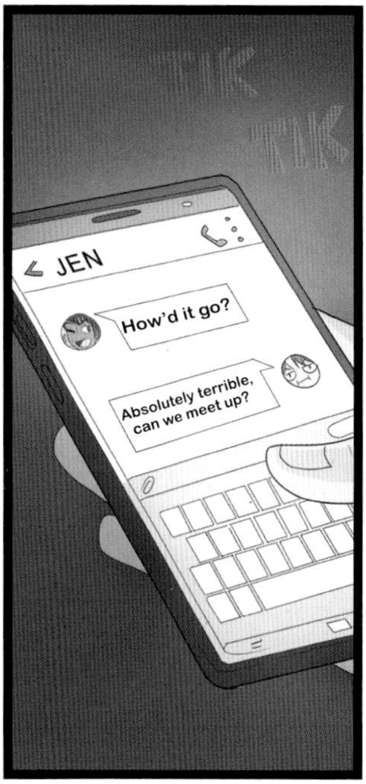
TK
TK
JEN
How'd it go?
Absolutely terrible, can we meet up?

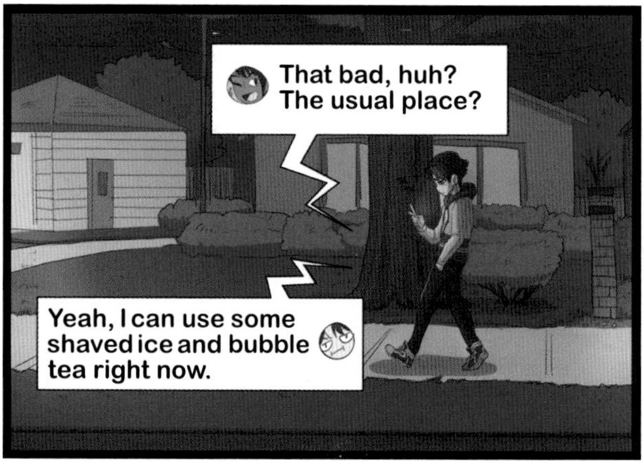
That bad, huh? The usual place?
Yeah, I can use some shaved ice and bubble tea right now.

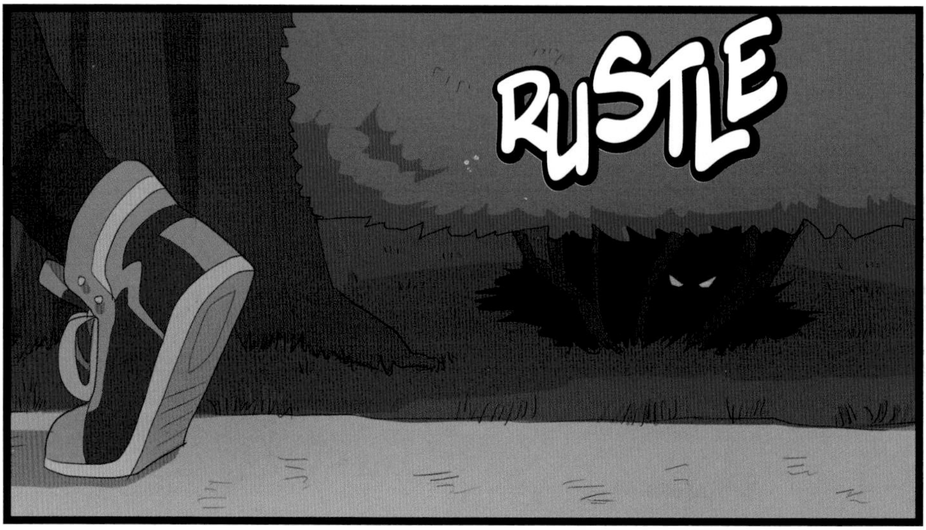
RUSTLE

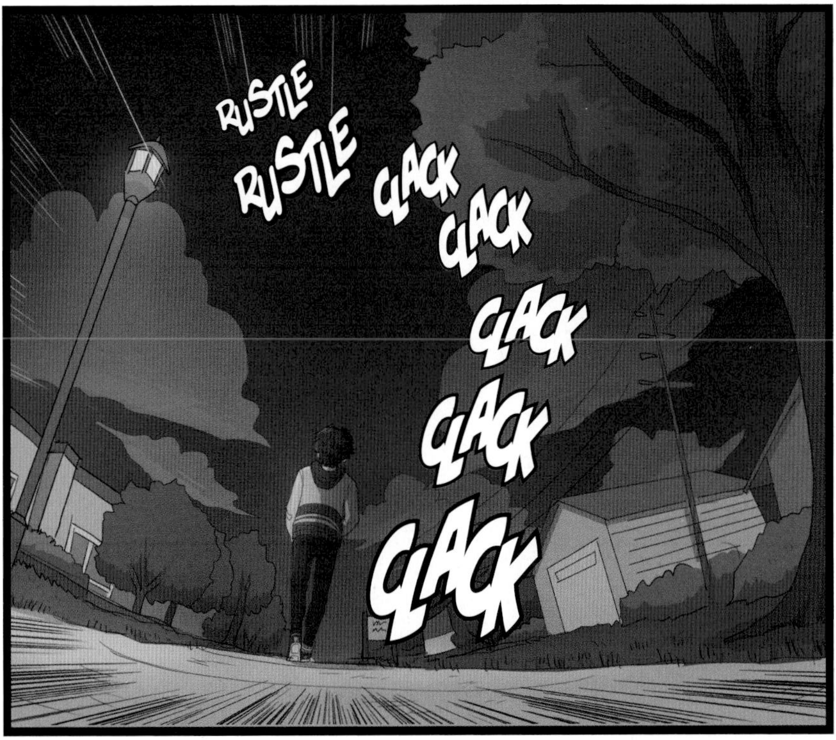
RUSTLE
RUSTLE
CLACK
CLACK
CLACK
CLACK
CLACK

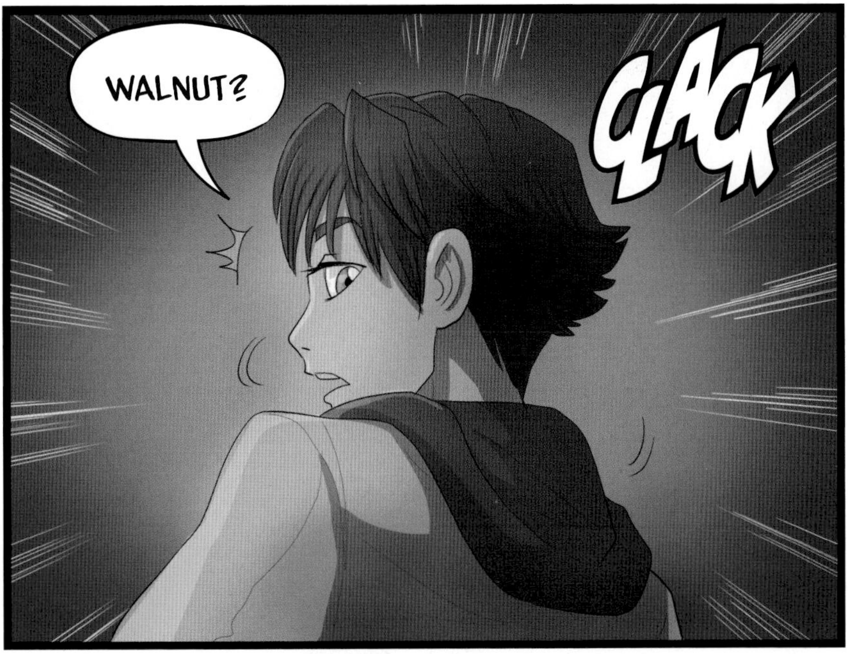
WALNUT?
CLACK

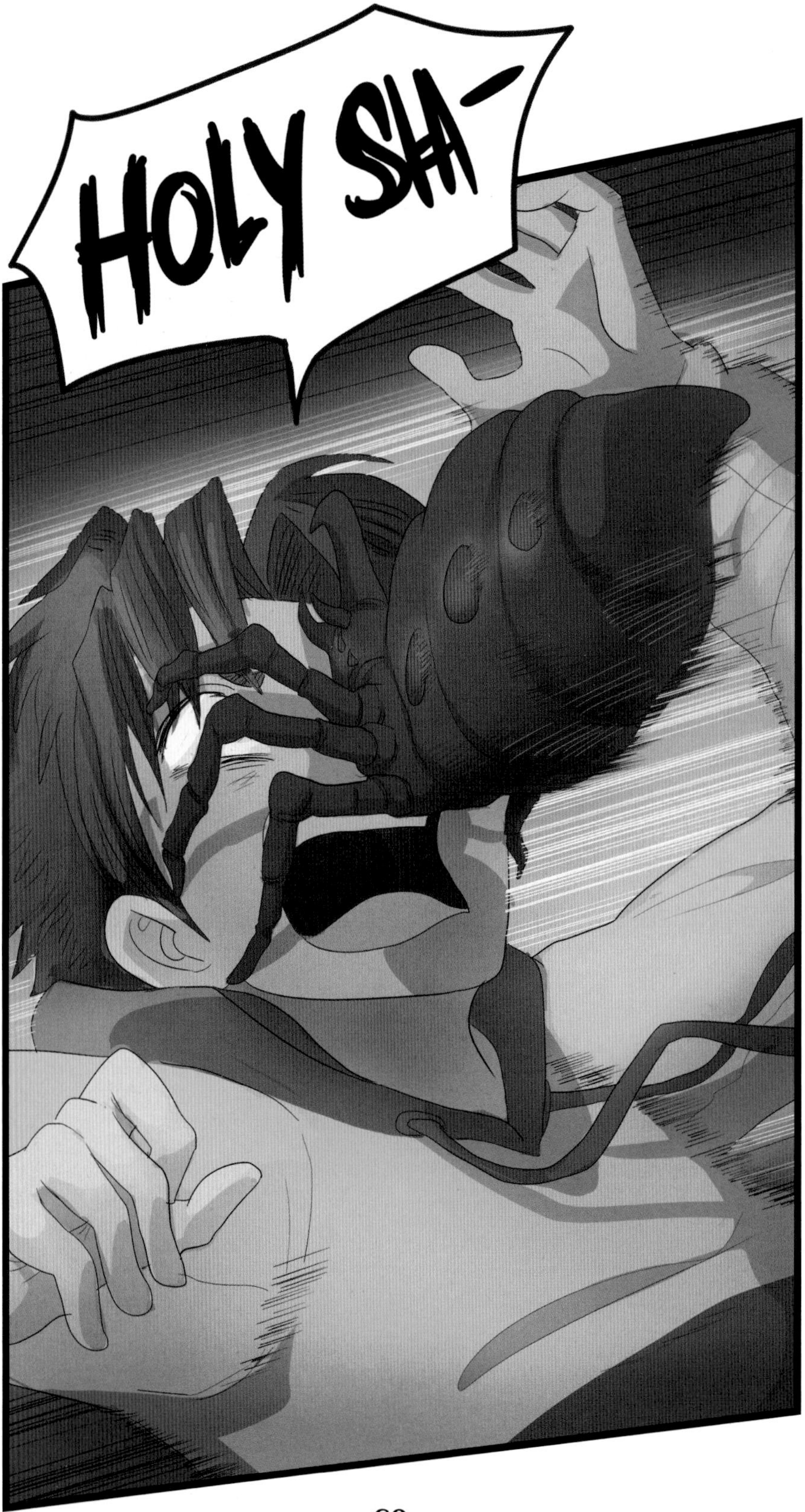
HOLY SH-

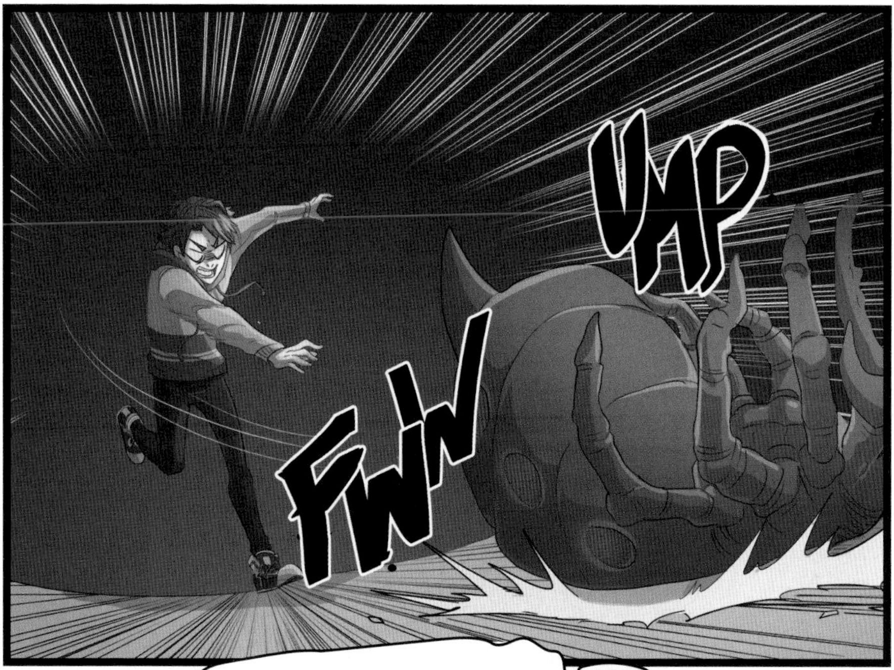
FWIN
UMP

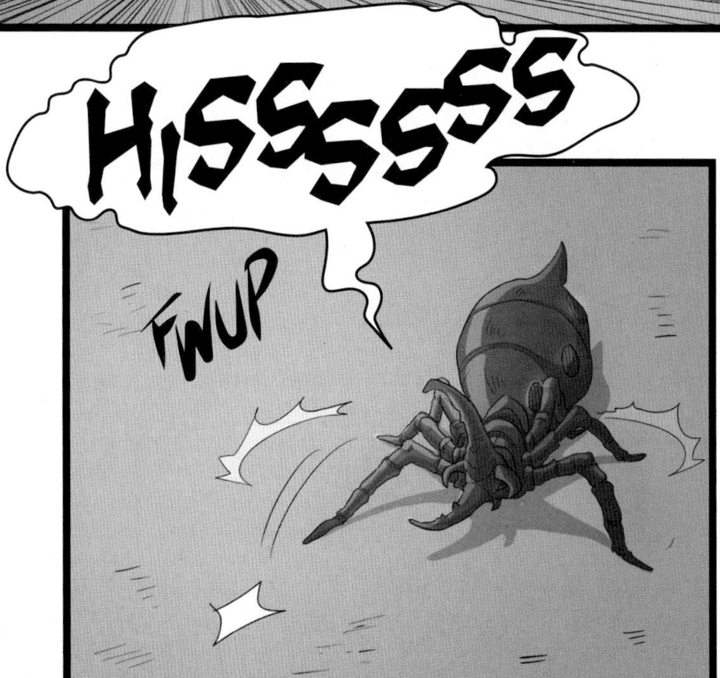
HISSSSSSS
FWUP

DON'T TELL ME THIS IS PART OF MOM'S...

...CRAZY STORY ABOUT MONSTERS.

!

HEY, WAIT! YOU GET BACK HERE!

SKIT

SKIT SKIT

SKIT SKIT

SKIT SKIT

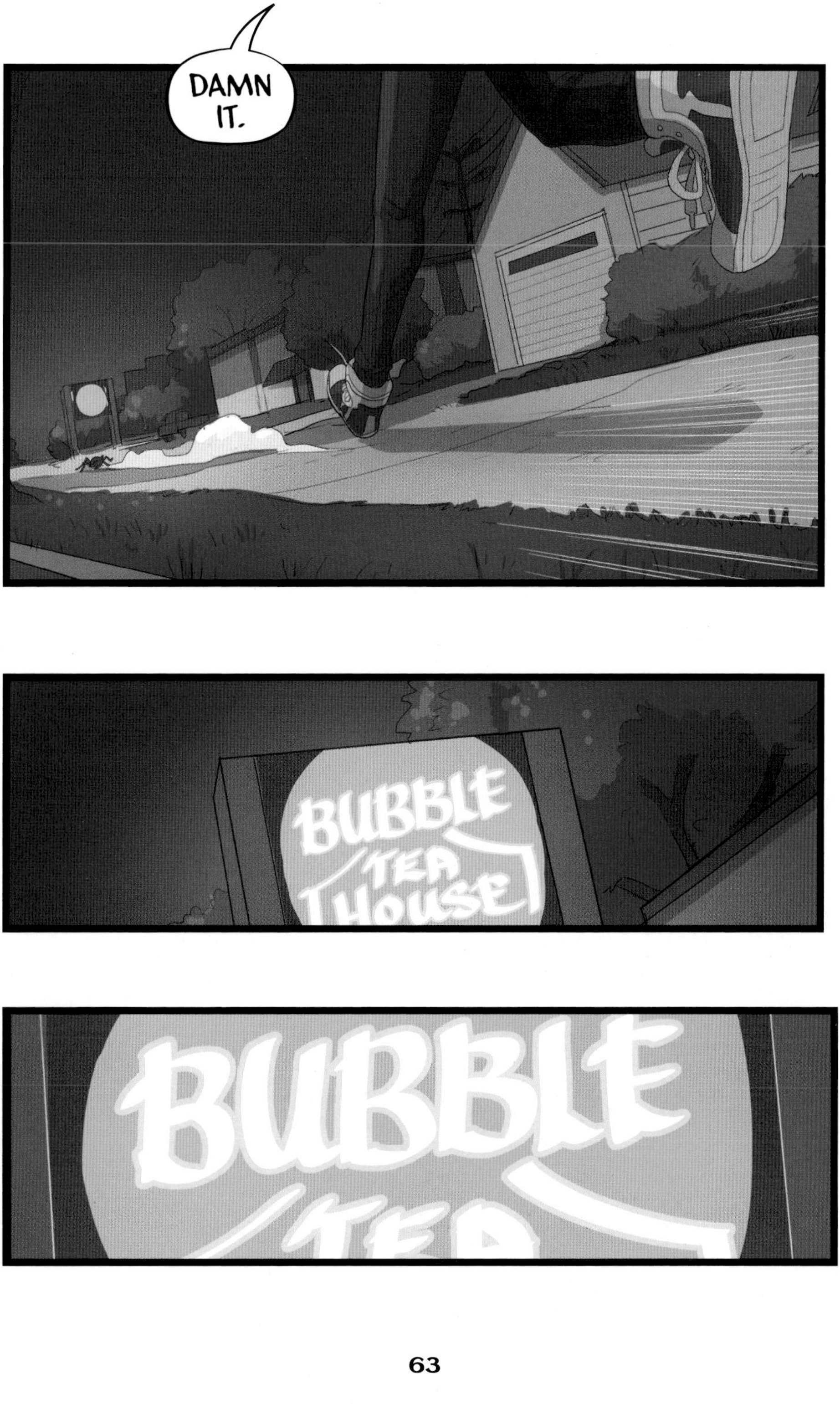
DAMN IT.
BUBBLE TEA HOUSE
BUBBLE

Episode 3:
IMPOSSIBLE

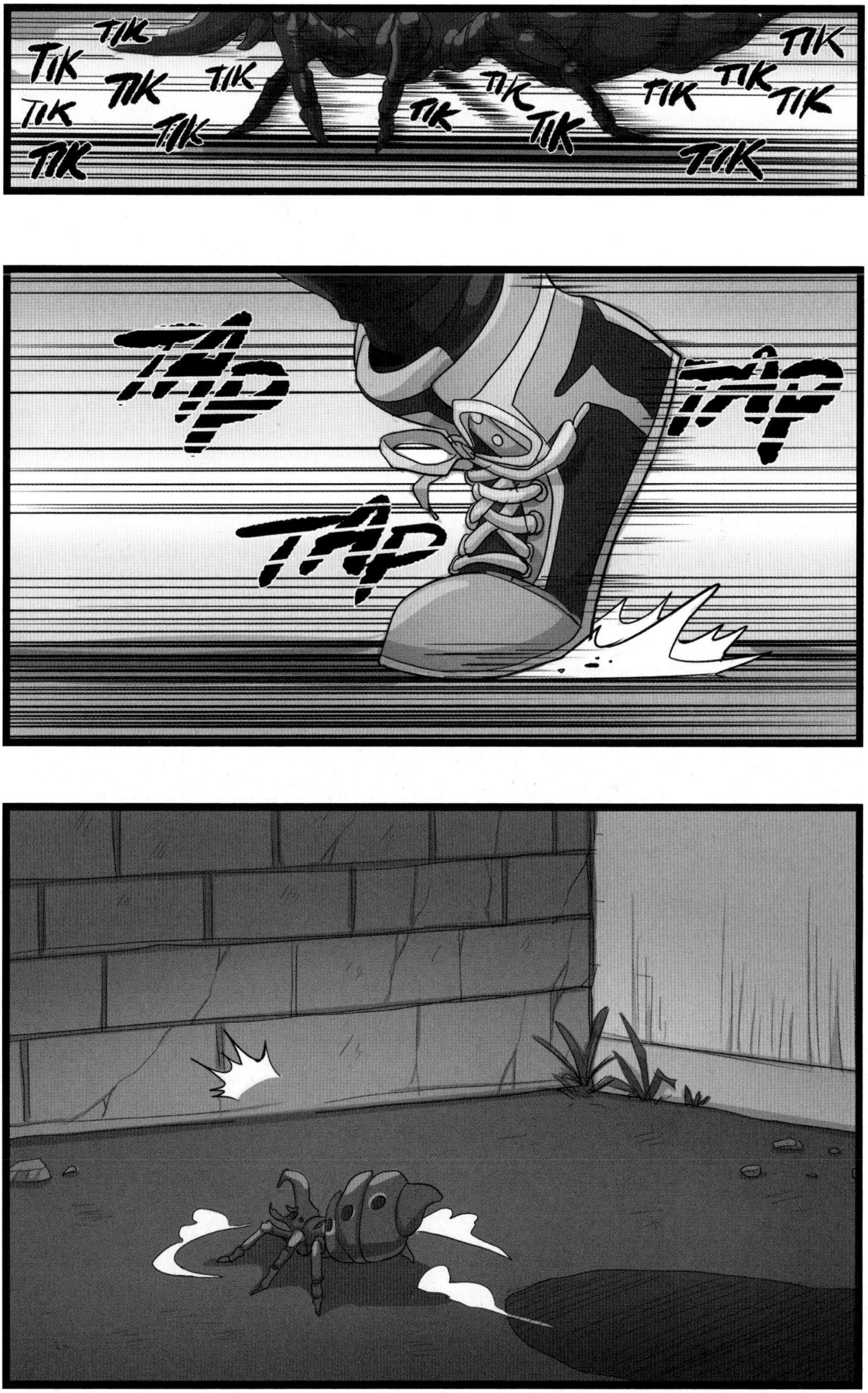
TIK
TIK
TIK
TIK
TIK
TIK
TIK
TIK
TIK
TIK
TIK
TIK
TIK
TIK
TIK
TAP
TAP
TAP

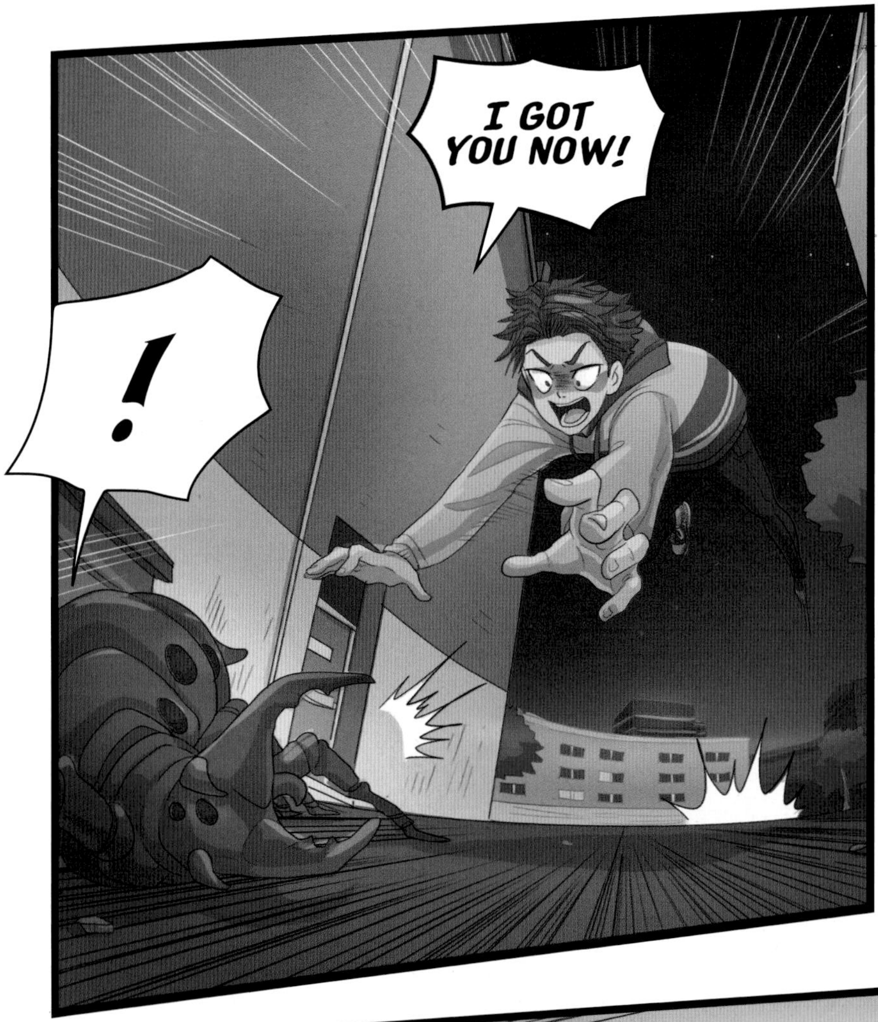
I GOT YOU NOW!
!

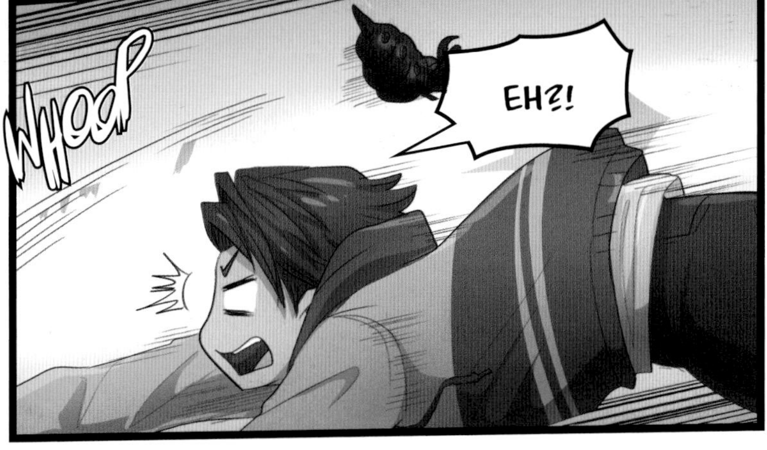
WHOOP
EH?!

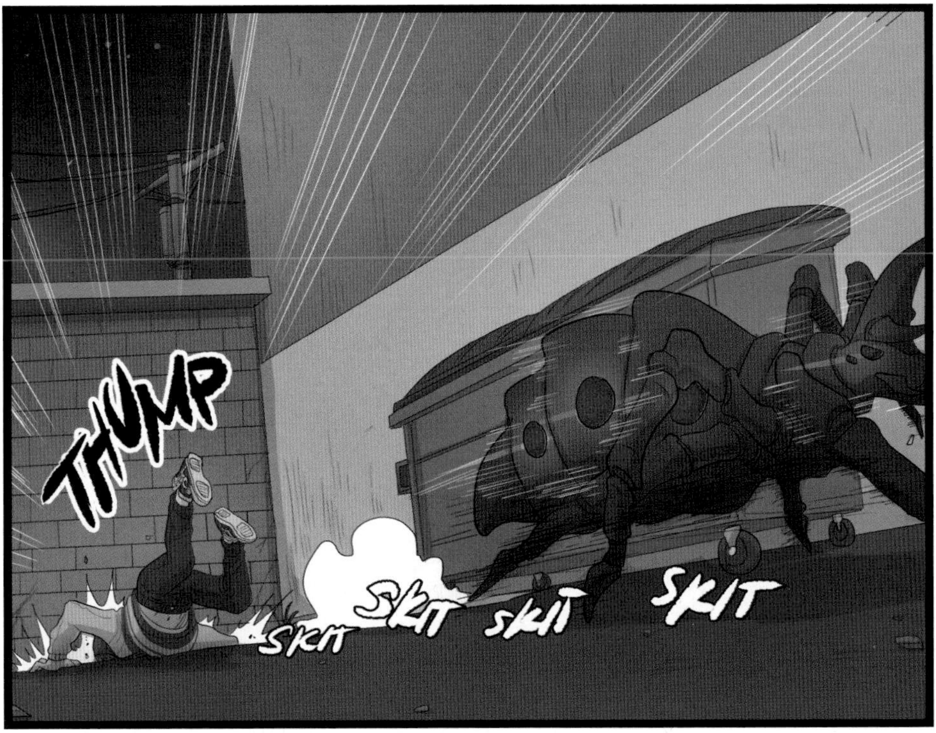
THUMP
SKIT
SKIT
SKIT
SKIT

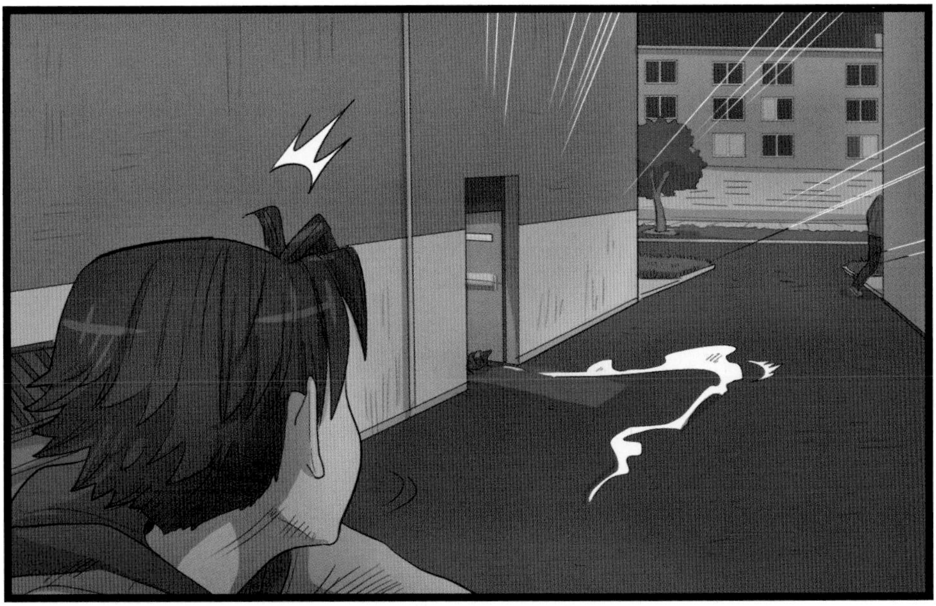

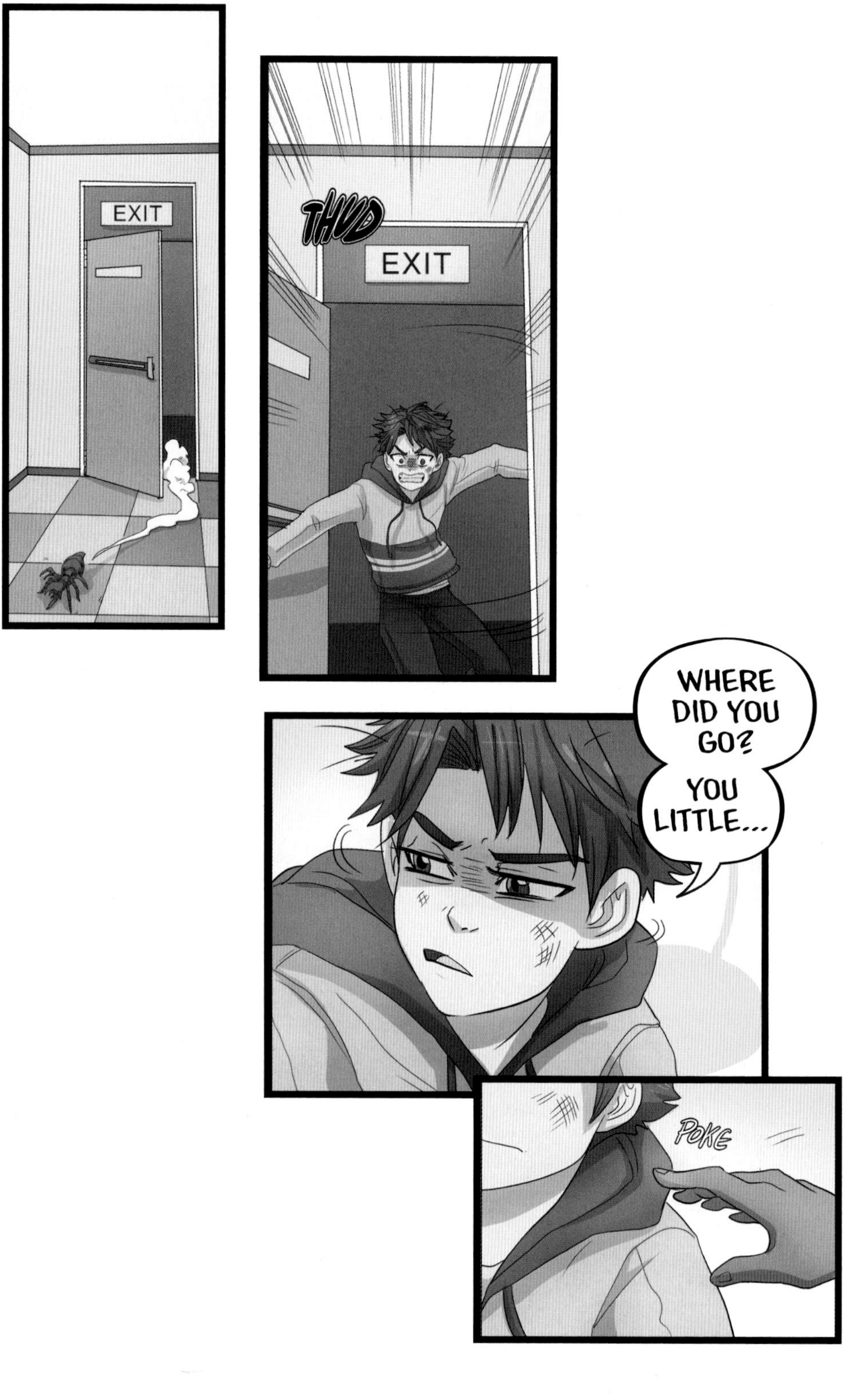
EXIT
THUD
EXIT
WHERE DID YOU GO?
YOU LITTLE...
POKE

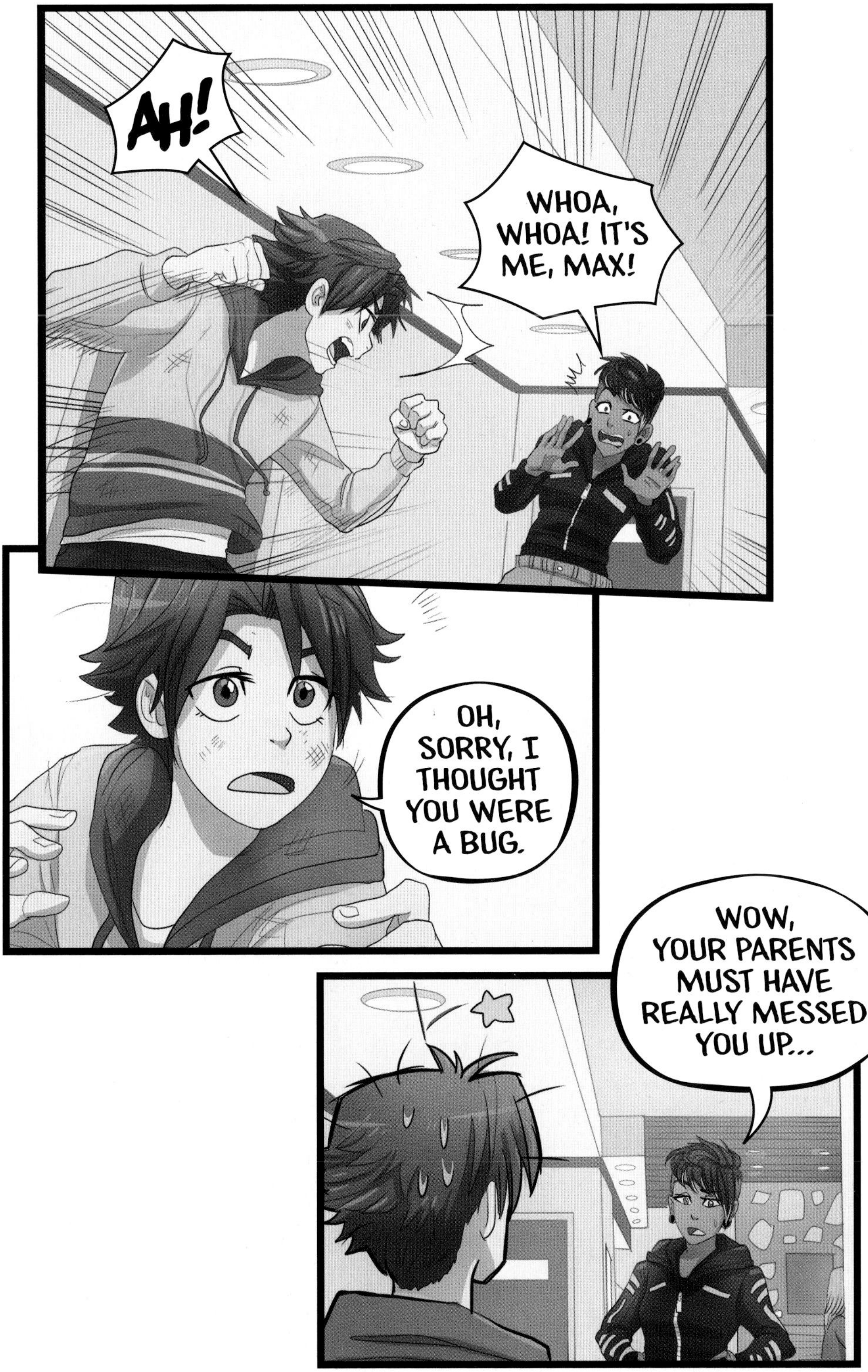
AH!
WHOA, WHOA! IT'S ME, MAX!
OH, SORRY, I THOUGHT YOU WERE A BUG.
WOW, YOUR PARENTS MUST HAVE REALLY MESSED YOU UP...

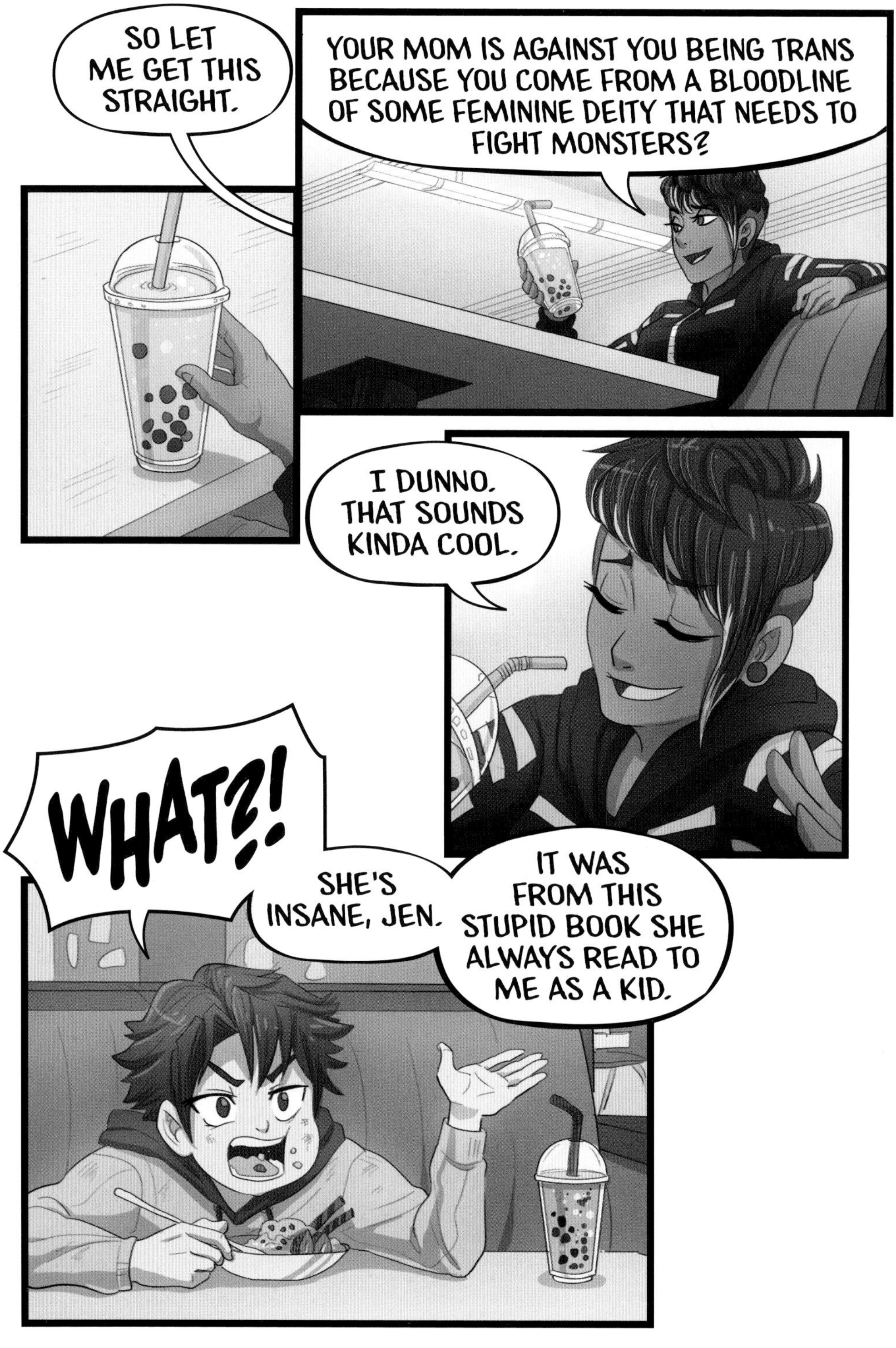
SO LET ME GET THIS STRAIGHT.
YOUR MOM IS AGAINST YOU BEING TRANS BECAUSE YOU COME FROM A BLOODLINE OF SOME FEMININE DEITY THAT NEEDS TO FIGHT MONSTERS?
I DUNNO. THAT SOUNDS KINDA COOL.
WHAT?!
SHE'S INSANE, JEN.
IT WAS FROM THIS STUPID BOOK SHE ALWAYS READ TO ME AS A KID.

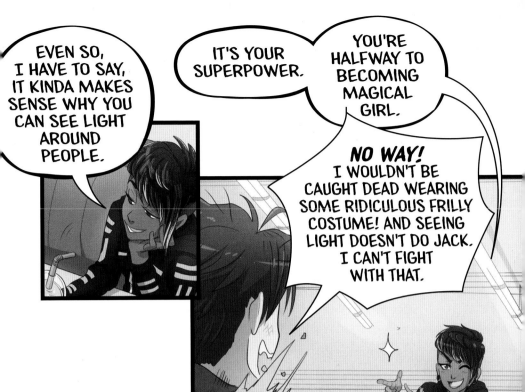

EVEN SO, I HAVE TO SAY, IT KINDA MAKES SENSE WHY YOU CAN SEE LIGHT AROUND PEOPLE.

IT'S YOUR SUPERPOWER.

YOU'RE HALFWAY TO BECOMING MAGICAL GIRL.

NO WAY! I WOULDN'T BE CAUGHT DEAD WEARING SOME RIDICULOUS FRILLY COSTUME! AND SEEING LIGHT DOESN'T DO JACK. I CAN'T FIGHT WITH THAT.

EVEN IF THIS IS SOME KIND OF DESTINY CRAP, IT SHOULDN'T MATTER WHAT GENDER I AM. I CAN STILL FIGHT EITHER WAY.

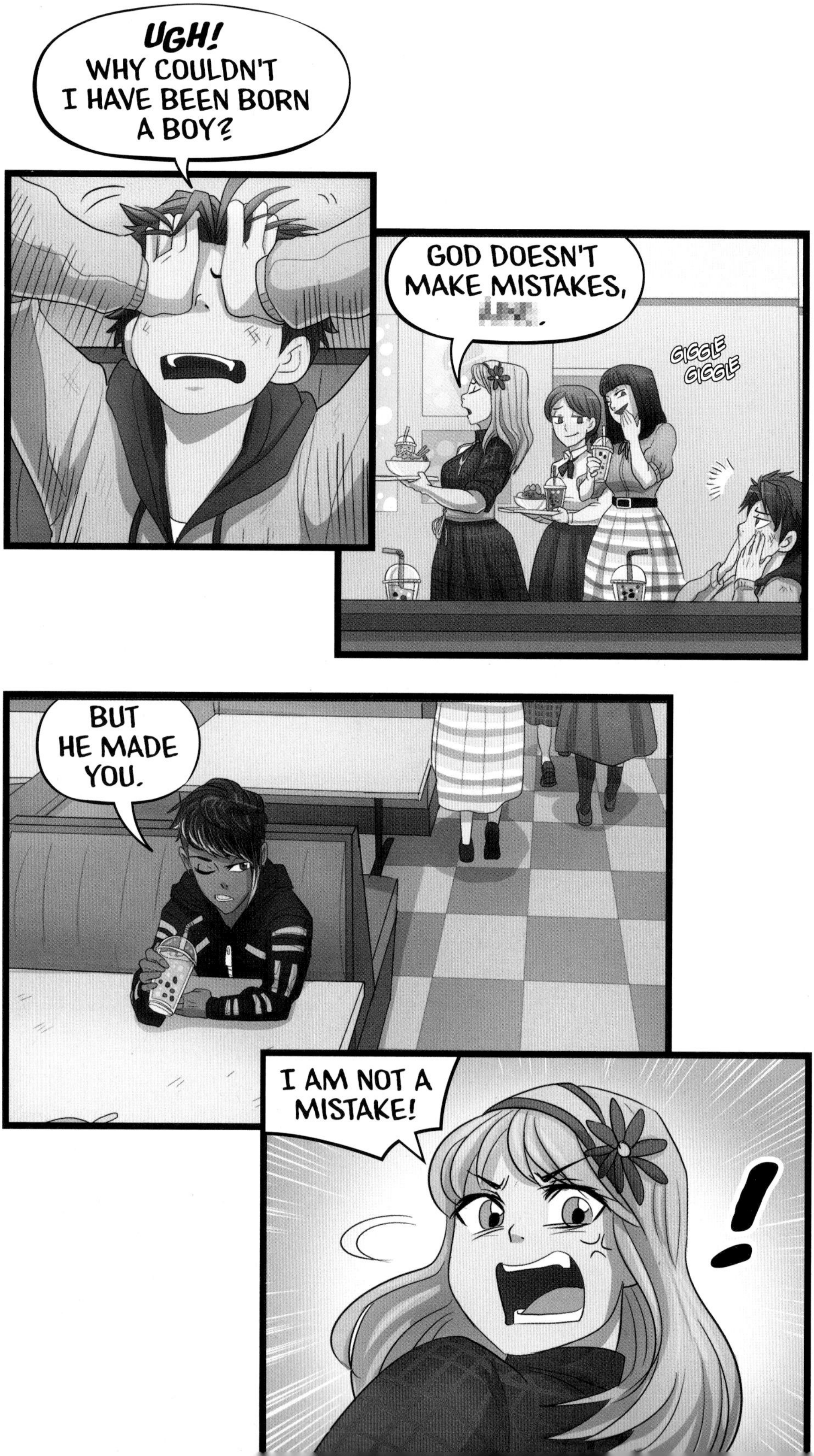
UGH! WHY COULDN'T I HAVE BEEN BORN A BOY?
GOD DOESN'T MAKE MISTAKES,
GIGGLE GIGGLE
BUT HE MADE YOU.
I AM NOT A MISTAKE!
!

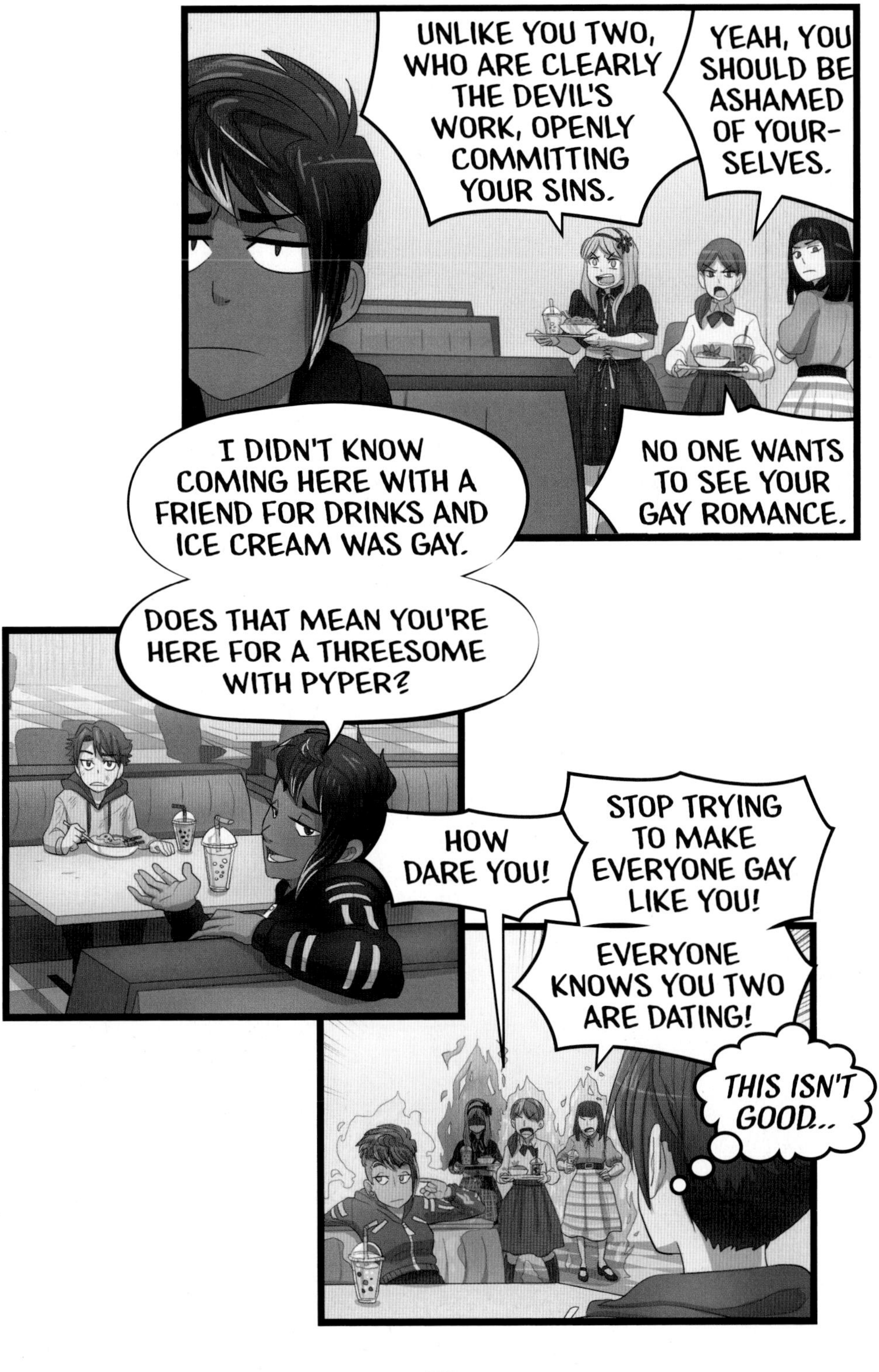
UNLIKE YOU TWO, WHO ARE CLEARLY THE DEVIL'S WORK, OPENLY COMMITTING YOUR SINS.
YEAH, YOU SHOULD BE ASHAMED OF YOUR-SELVES.
NO ONE WANTS TO SEE YOUR GAY ROMANCE.
I DIDN'T KNOW COMING HERE WITH A FRIEND FOR DRINKS AND ICE CREAM WAS GAY.
DOES THAT MEAN YOU'RE HERE FOR A THREESOME WITH PYPER?
HOW DARE YOU!
STOP TRYING TO MAKE EVERYONE GAY LIKE YOU!
EVERYONE KNOWS YOU TWO ARE DATING!
THIS ISN'T GOOD...

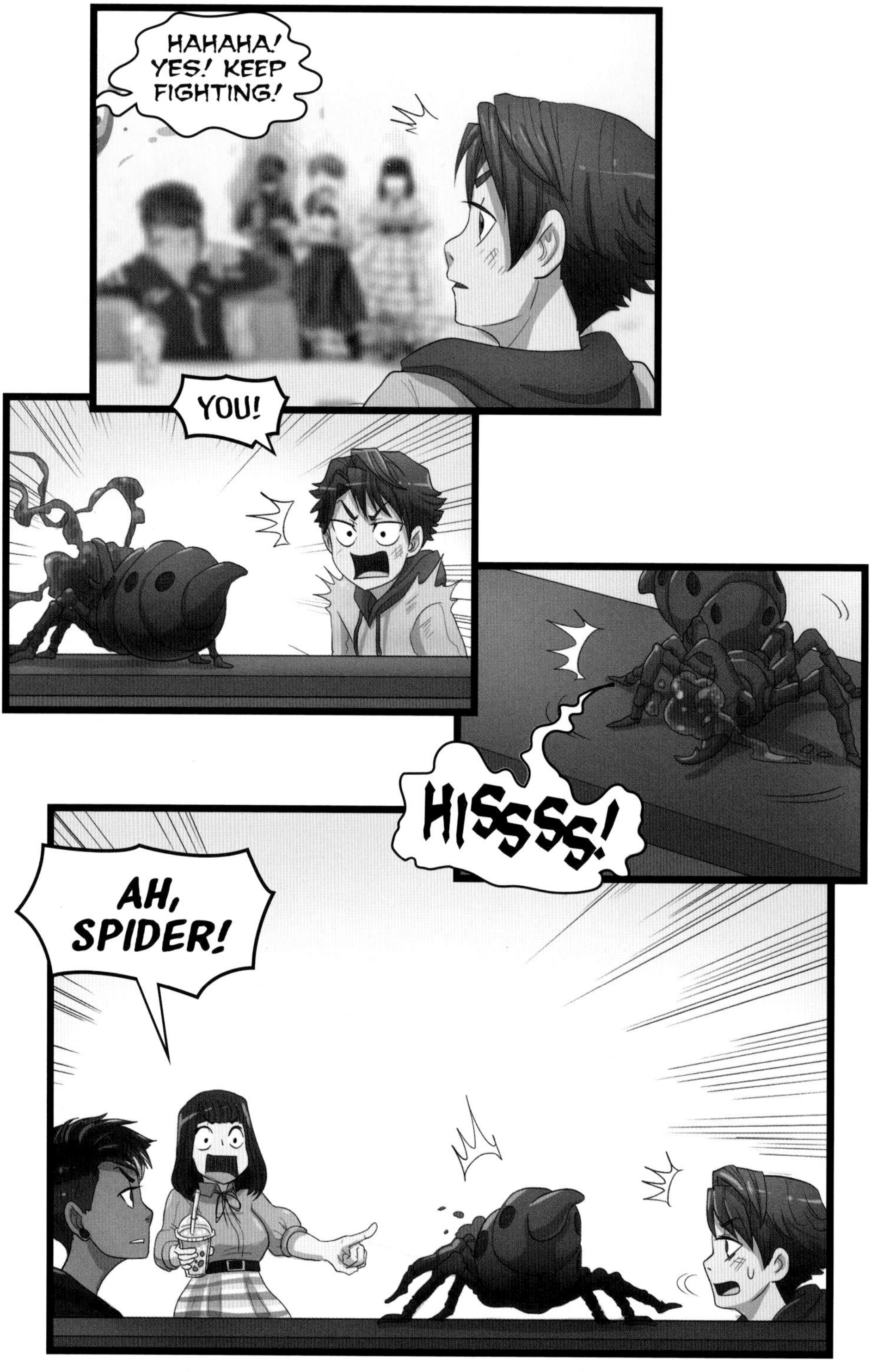
HAHAHA! YES! KEEP FIGHTING!
YOU!
HISSSS!
AH, SPIDER!

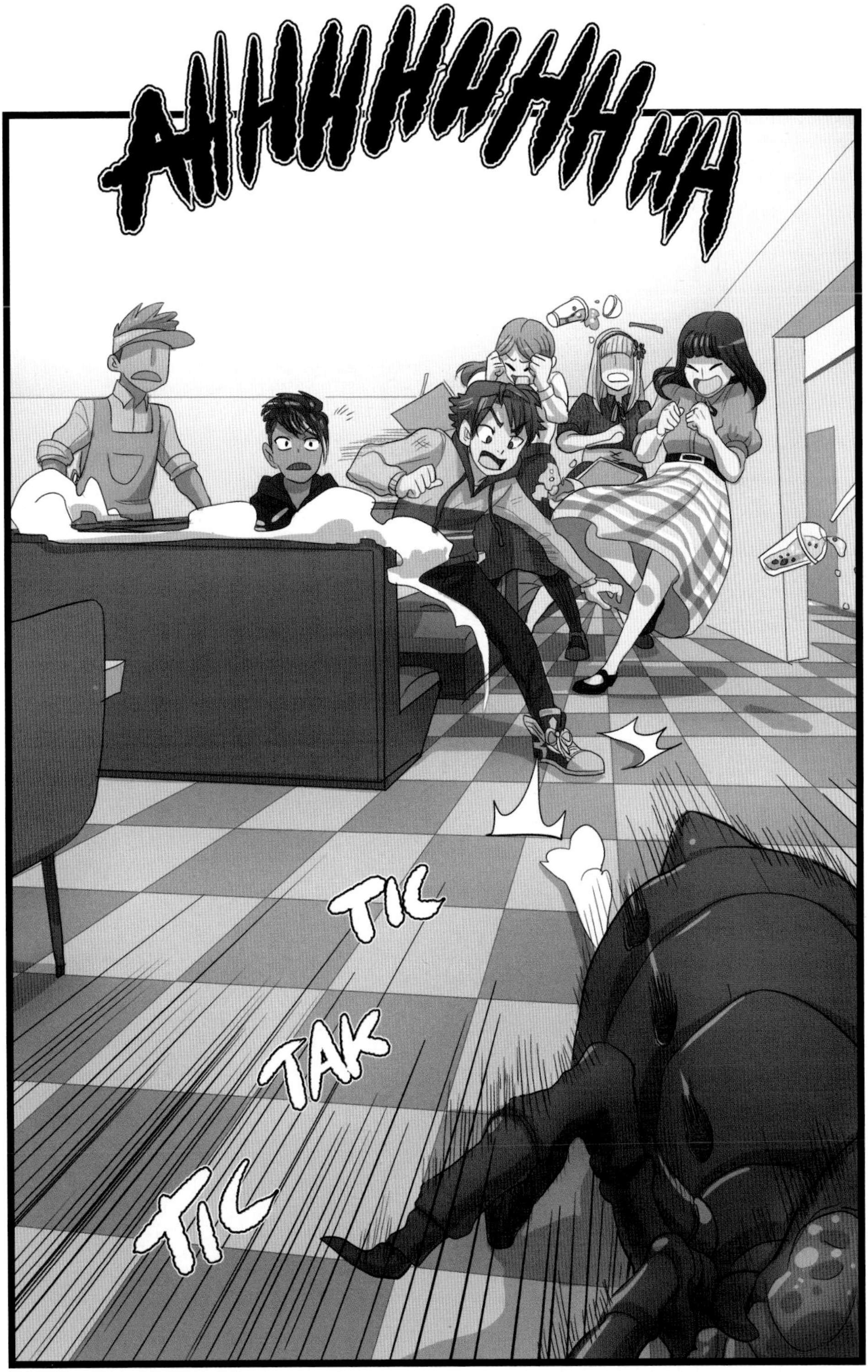
AHHHHHHHHHH
TIC
TAK
TIC

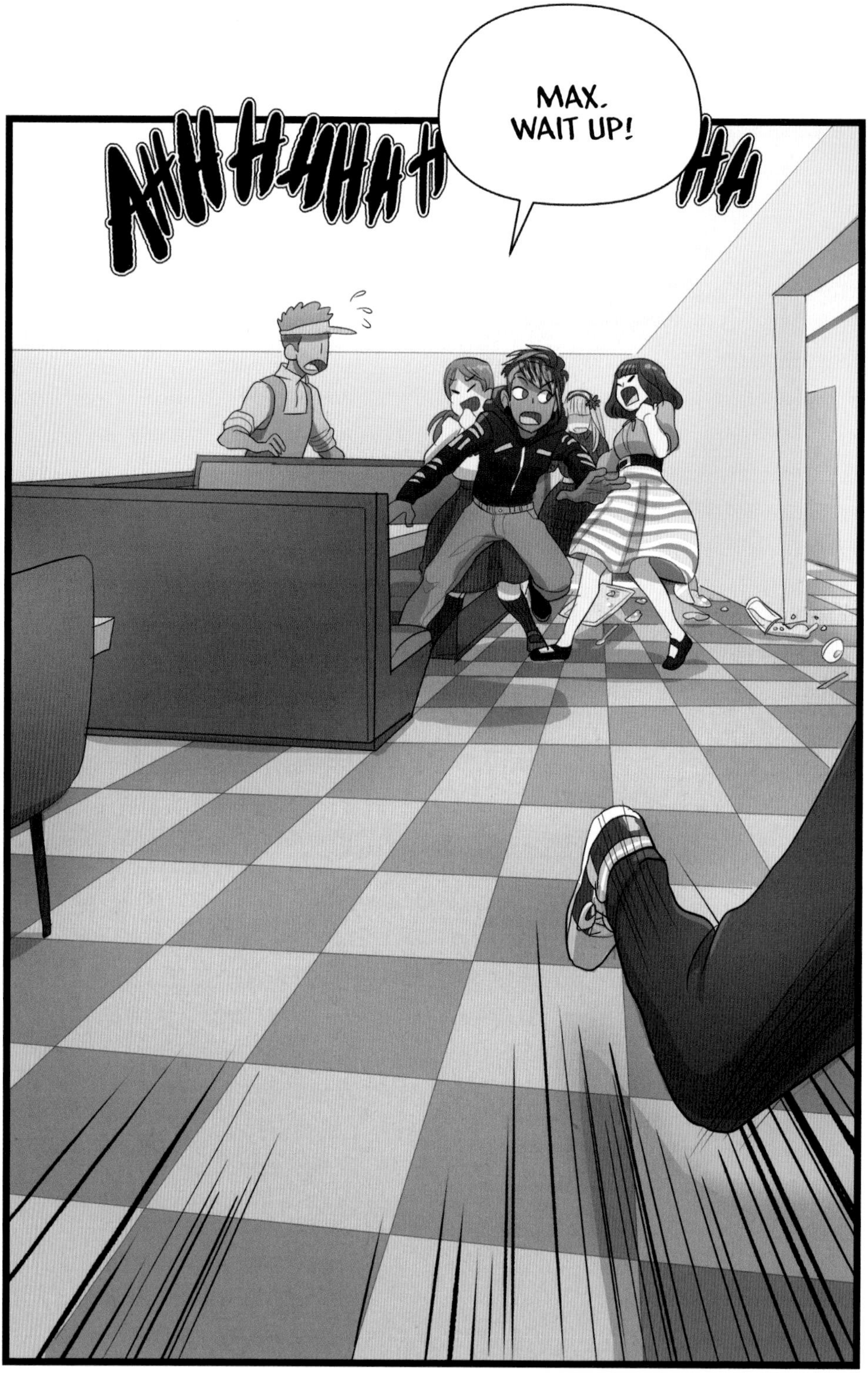
AHHHHHHHH
MAX. WAIT UP!
HH

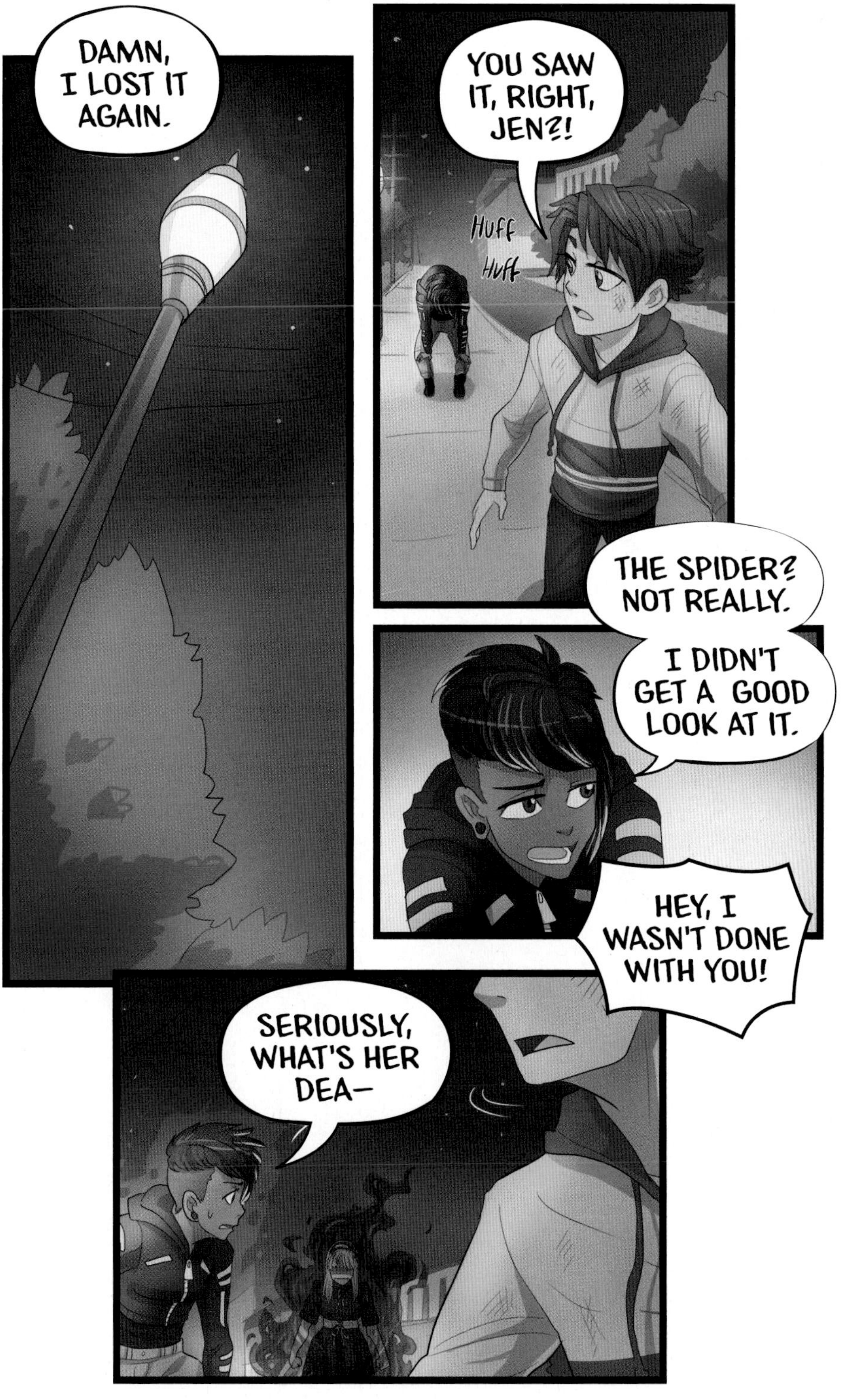
DAMN, I LOST IT AGAIN.
YOU SAW IT, RIGHT, JEN?!
HUFF
HUFF
THE SPIDER? NOT REALLY.
I DIDN'T GET A GOOD LOOK AT IT.
HEY, I WASN'T DONE WITH YOU!
SERIOUSLY, WHAT'S HER DEA–

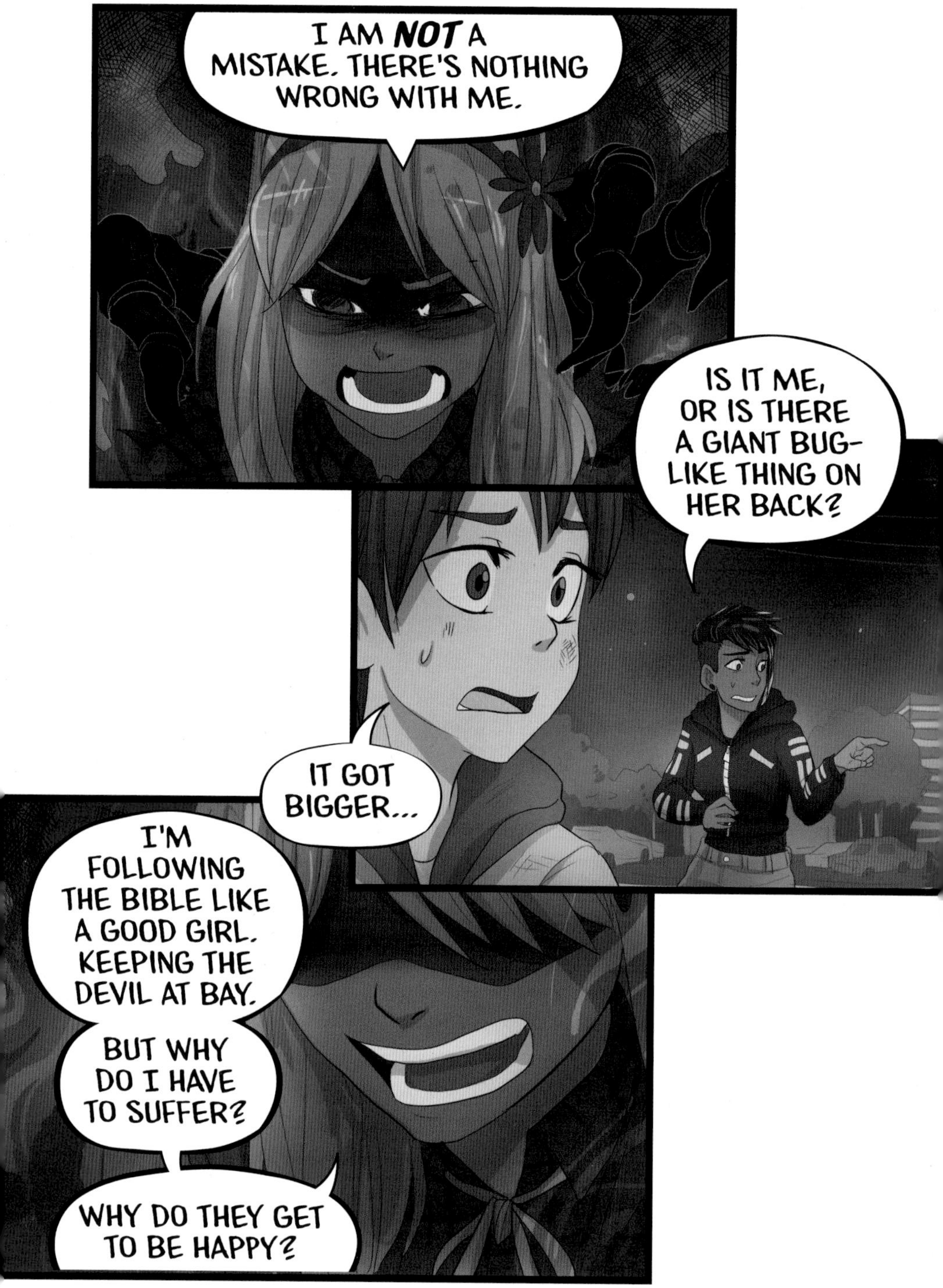
I AM NOT A MISTAKE. THERE'S NOTHING WRONG WITH ME.
IS IT ME, OR IS THERE A GIANT BUG-LIKE THING ON HER BACK?
IT GOT BIGGER...
I'M FOLLOWING THE BIBLE LIKE A GOOD GIRL. KEEPING THE DEVIL AT BAY.
BUT WHY DO I HAVE TO SUFFER?
WHY DO THEY GET TO BE HAPPY?

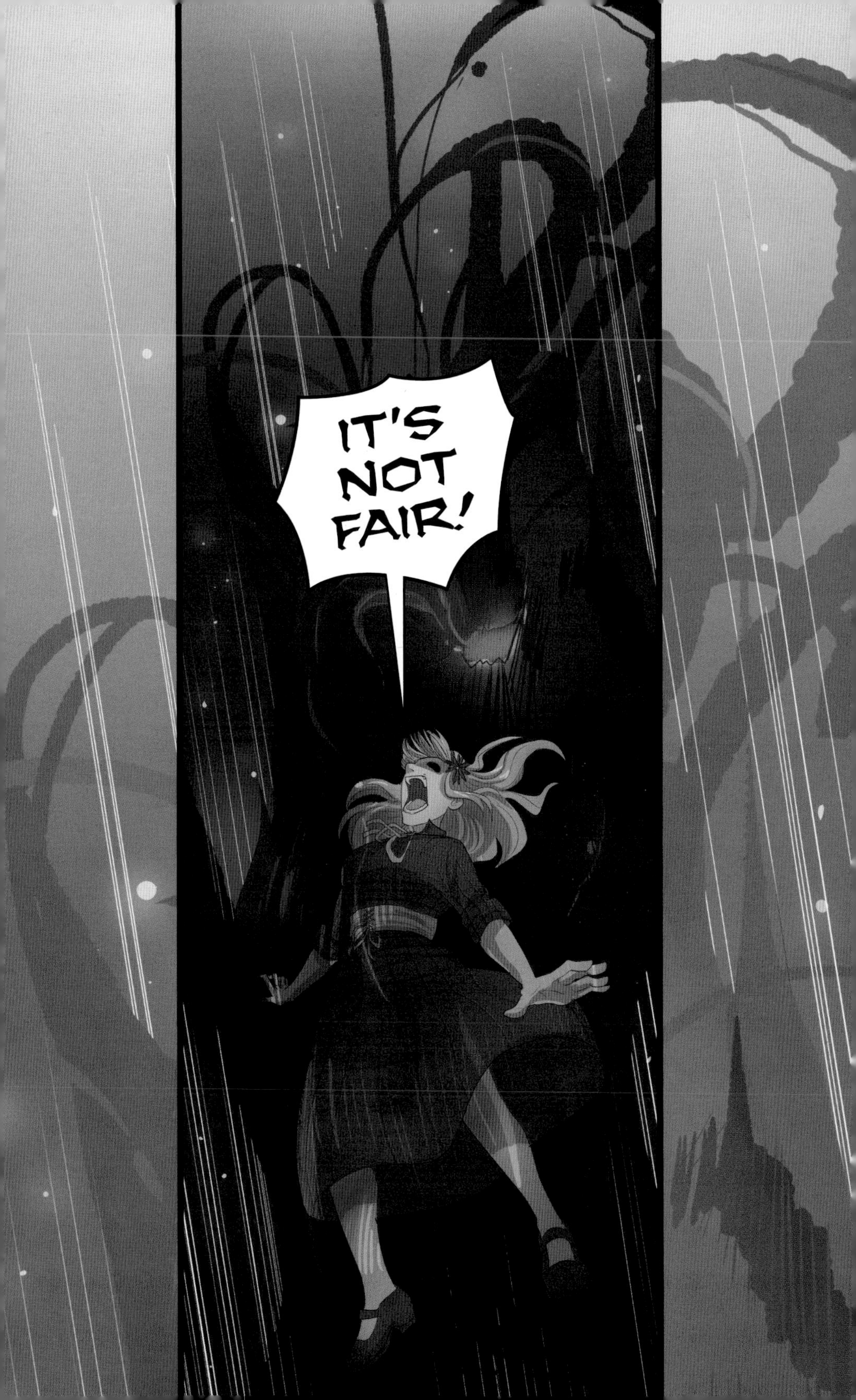
IT'S NOT FAIR!

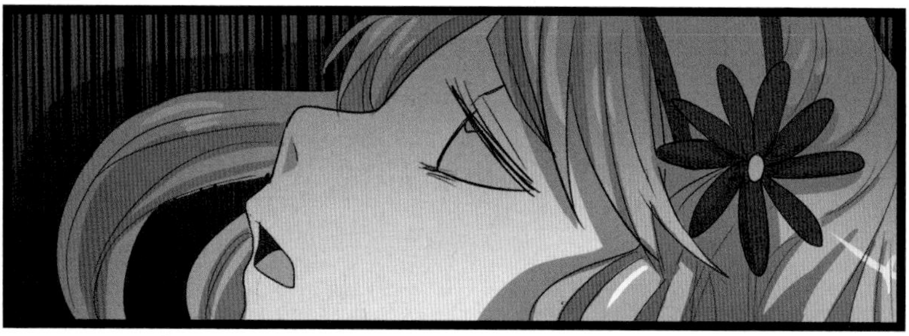

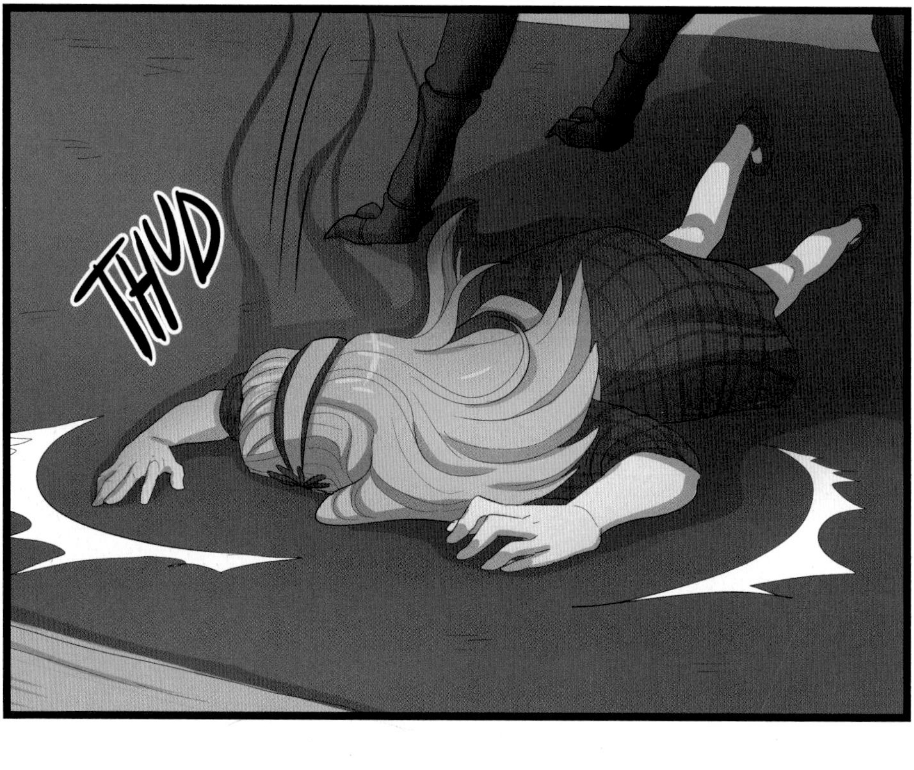
THUD

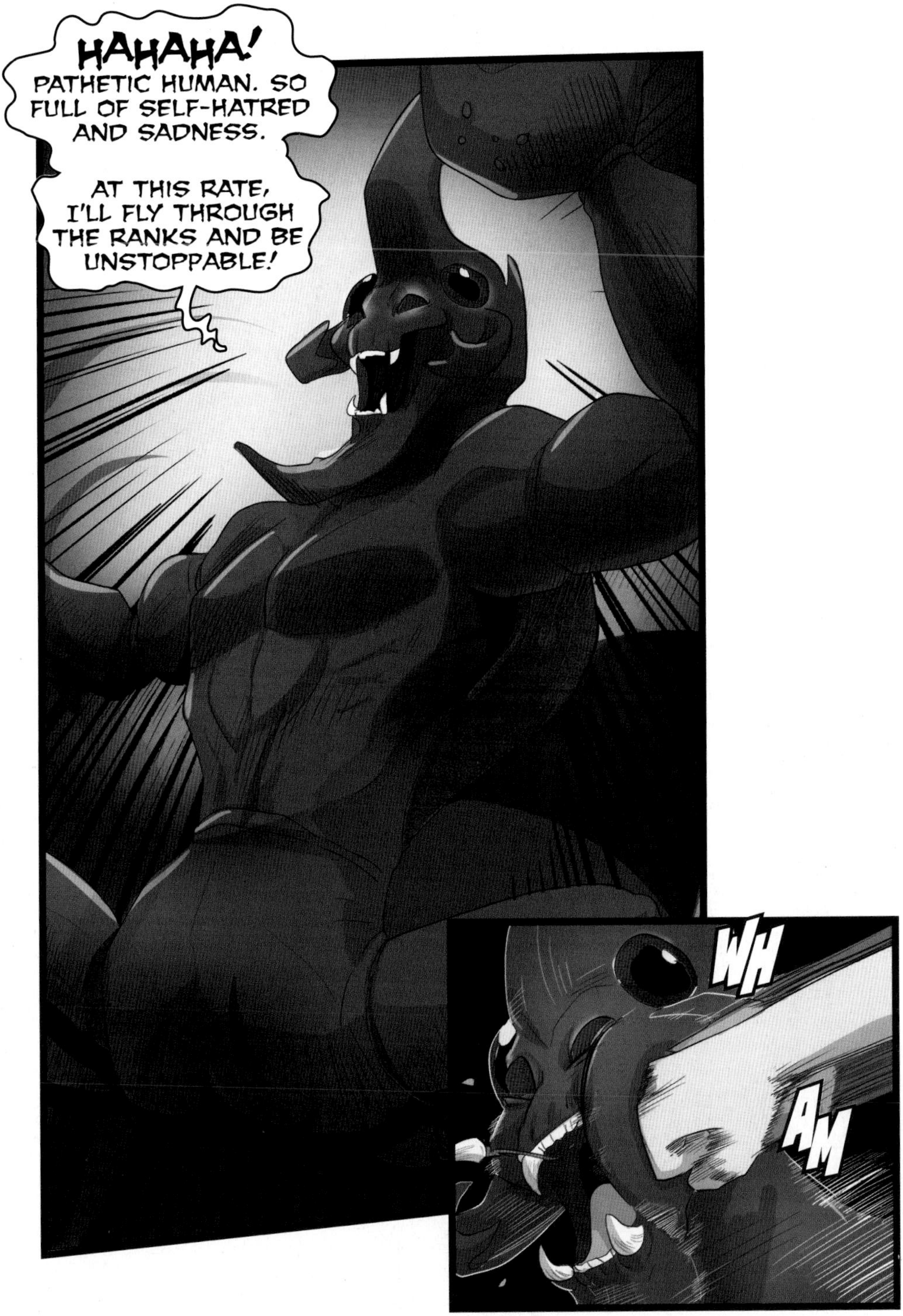
HAHAHA!
PATHETIC HUMAN. SO FULL OF SELF-HATRED AND SADNESS.
AT THIS RATE, I'LL FLY THROUGH THE RANKS AND BE UNSTOPPABLE!
WHAM

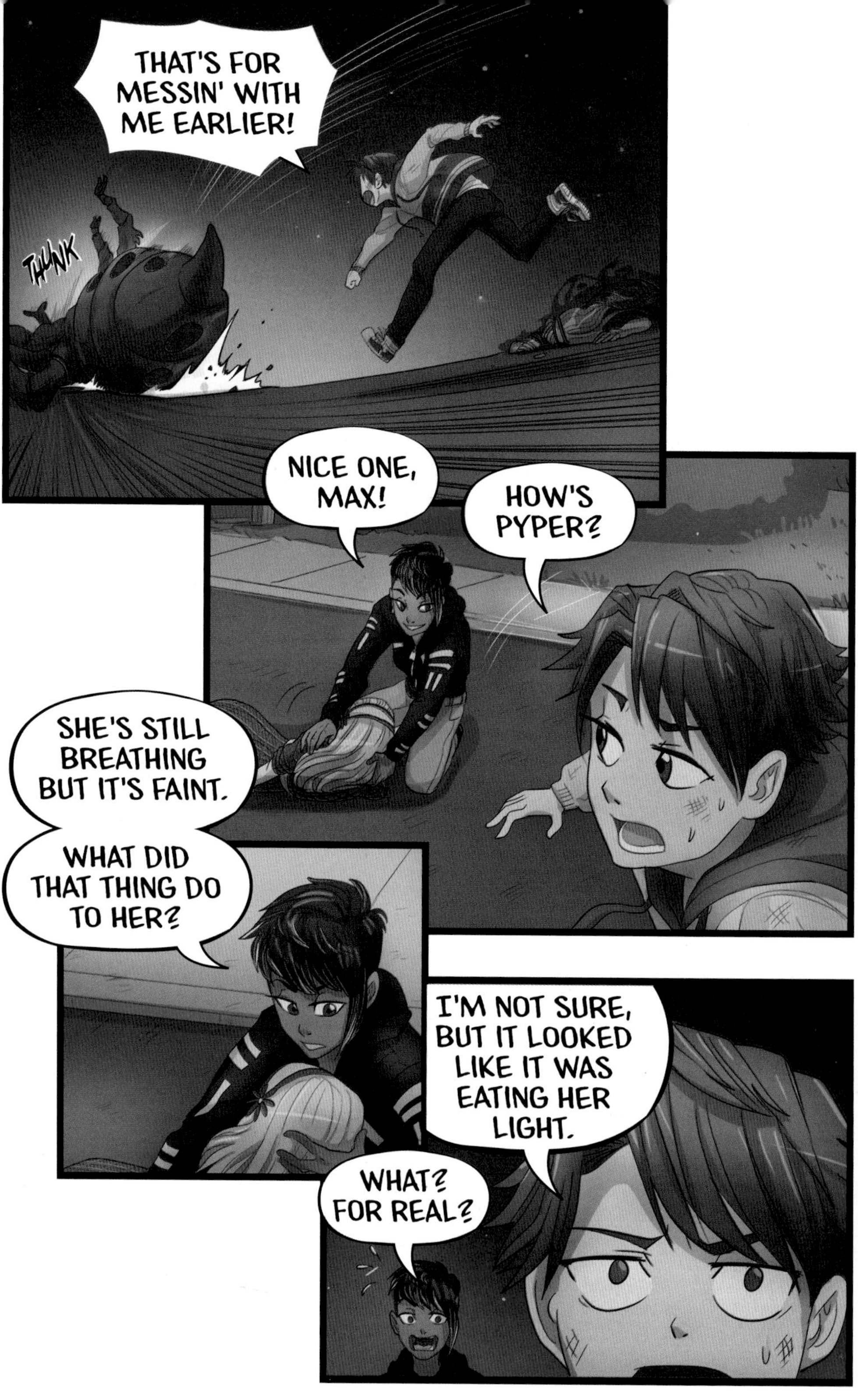
THAT'S FOR MESSIN' WITH ME EARLIER!
THUNK
NICE ONE, MAX!
HOW'S PYPER?
SHE'S STILL BREATHING BUT IT'S FAINT.
WHAT DID THAT THING DO TO HER?
I'M NOT SURE, BUT IT LOOKED LIKE IT WAS EATING HER LIGHT.
WHAT? FOR REAL?

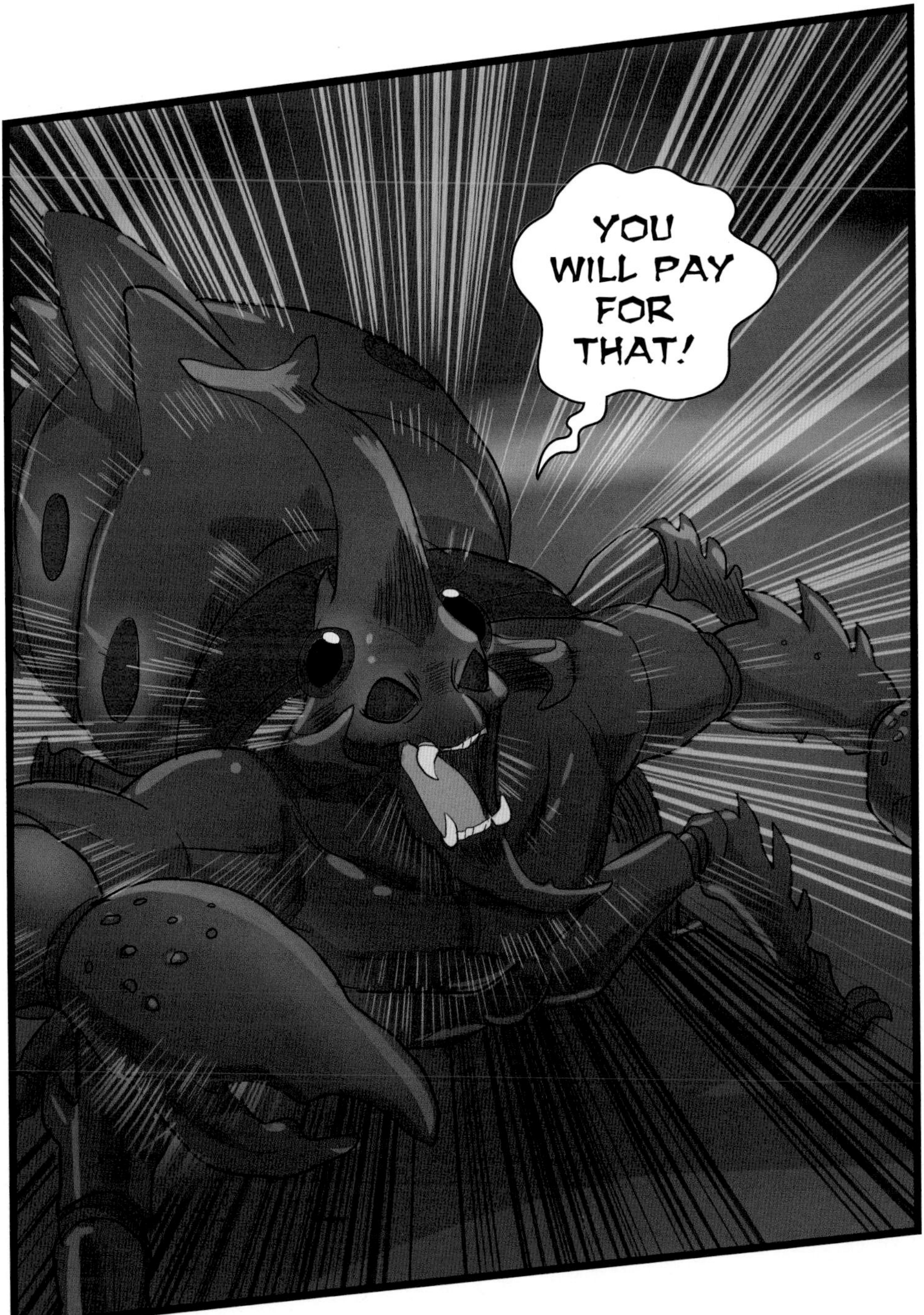
YOU WILL PAY FOR THAT!

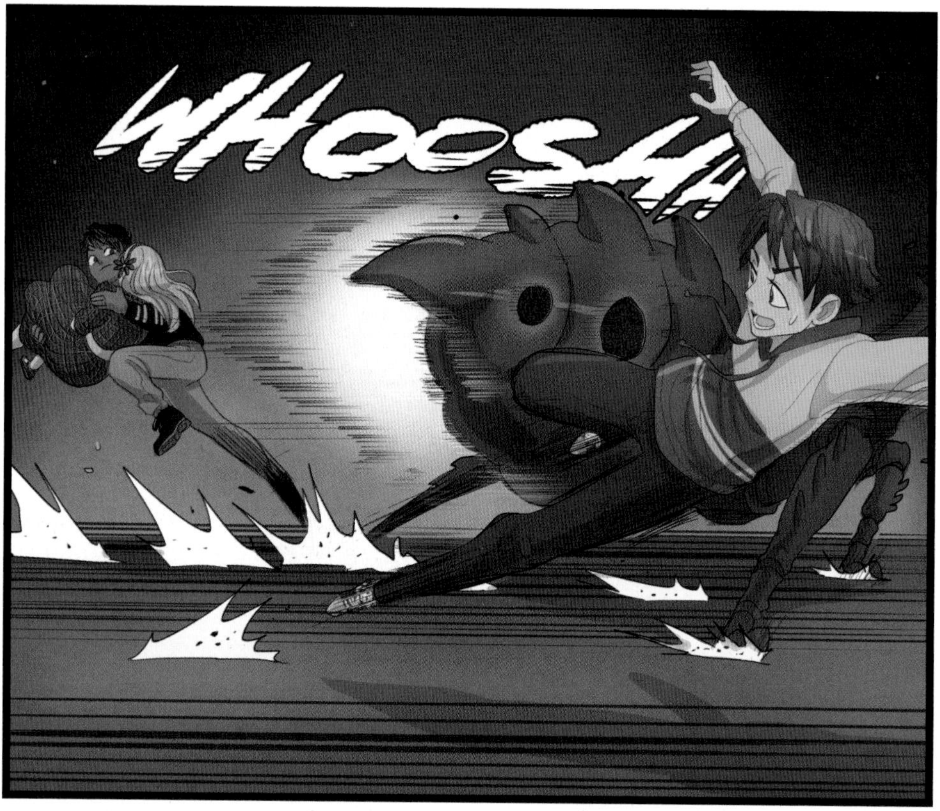
WHOOSH

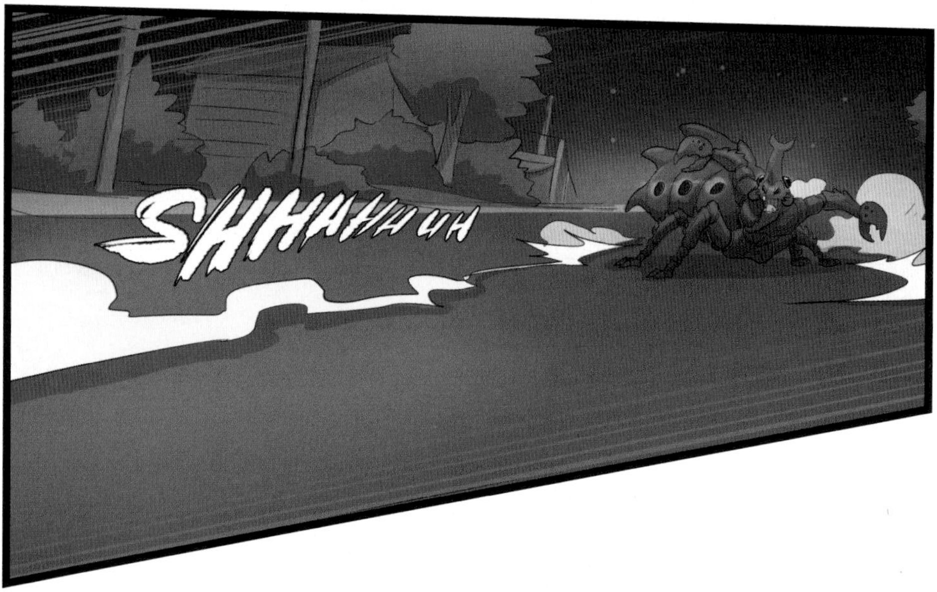
SHHHHHHH

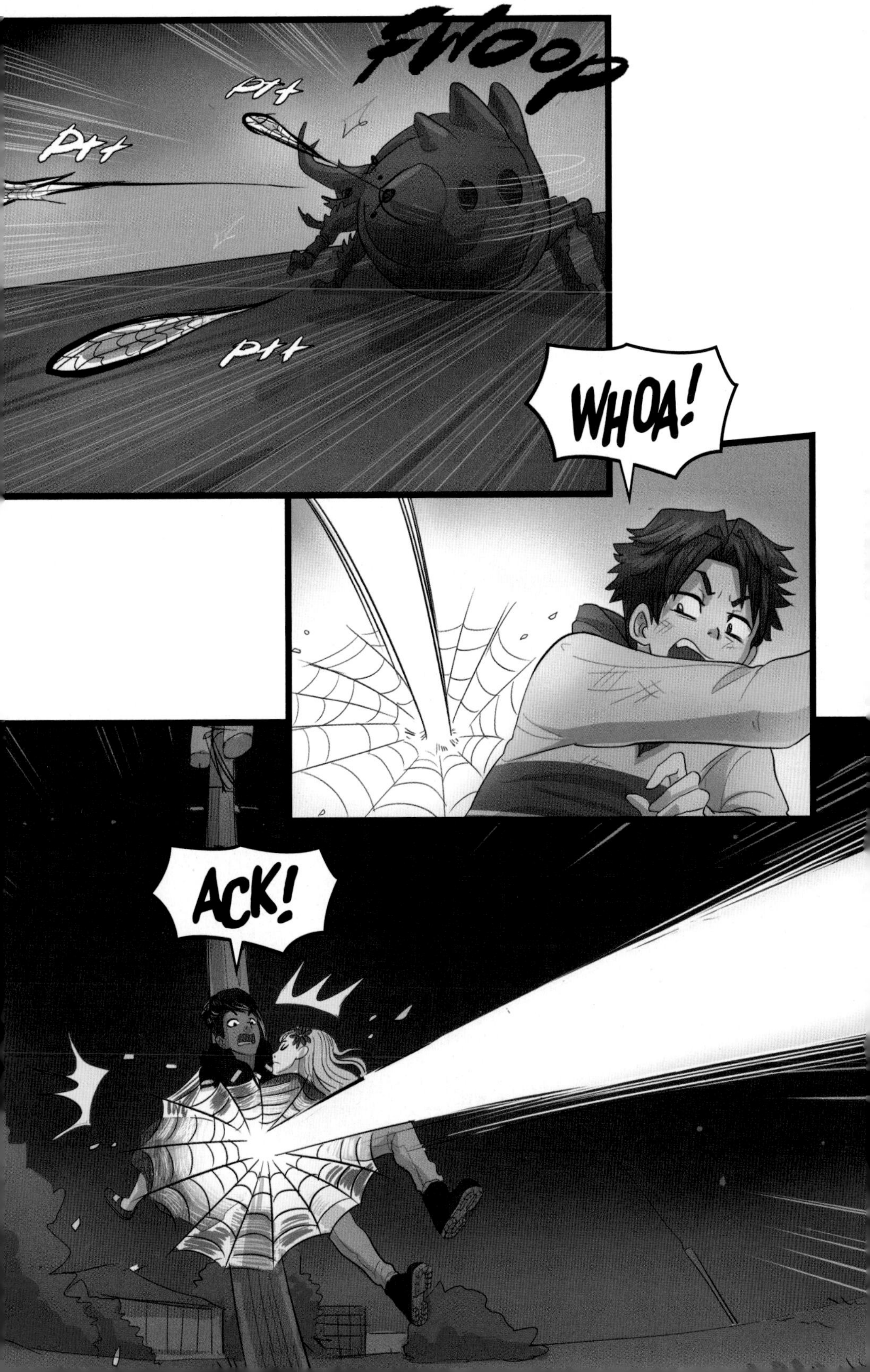
FWOOP
PTT
PTT
PTT
WHOA!
ACK!

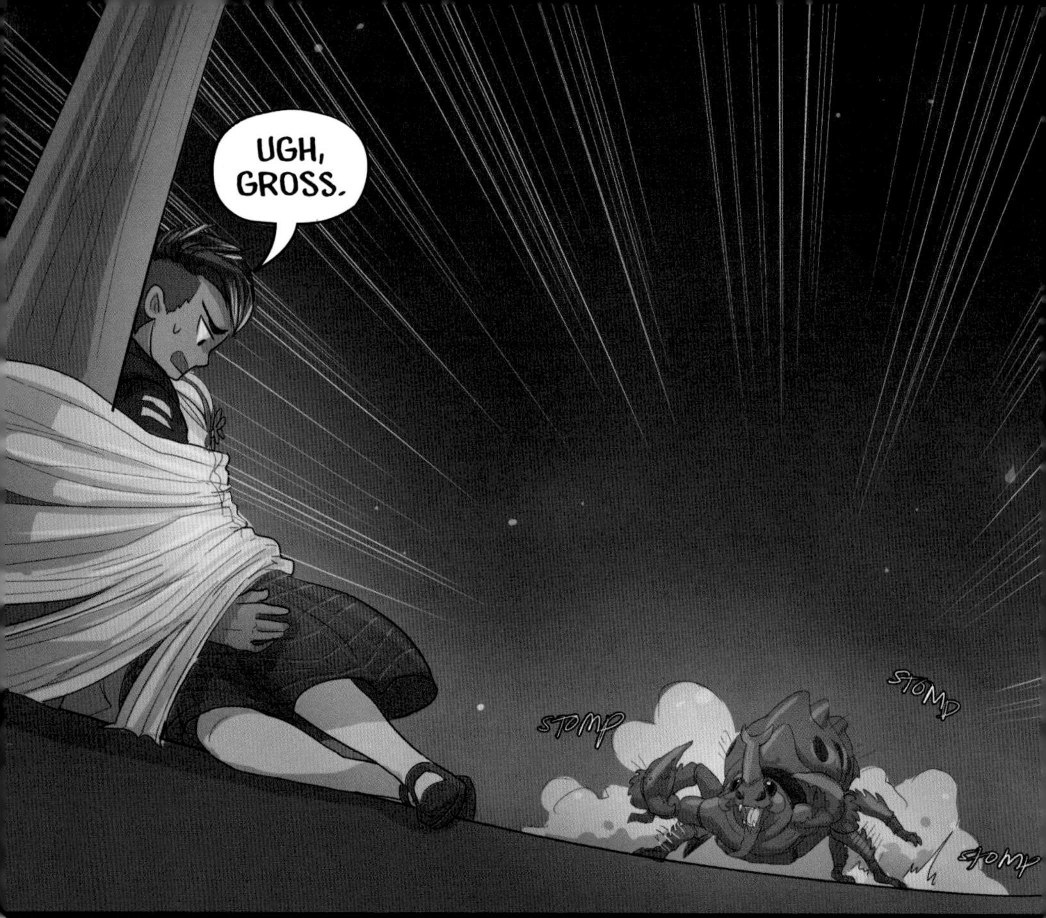
UGH, GROSS.
STOMP
STOMP
STOMP

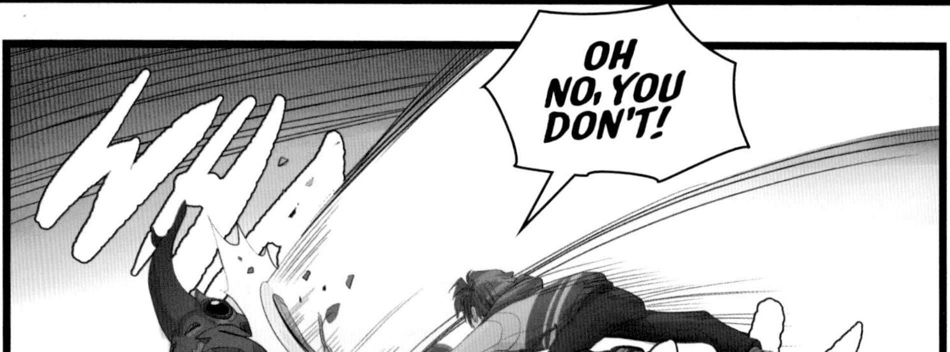
OH NO, YOU DON'T!

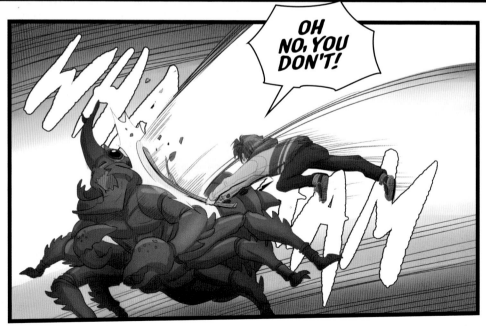

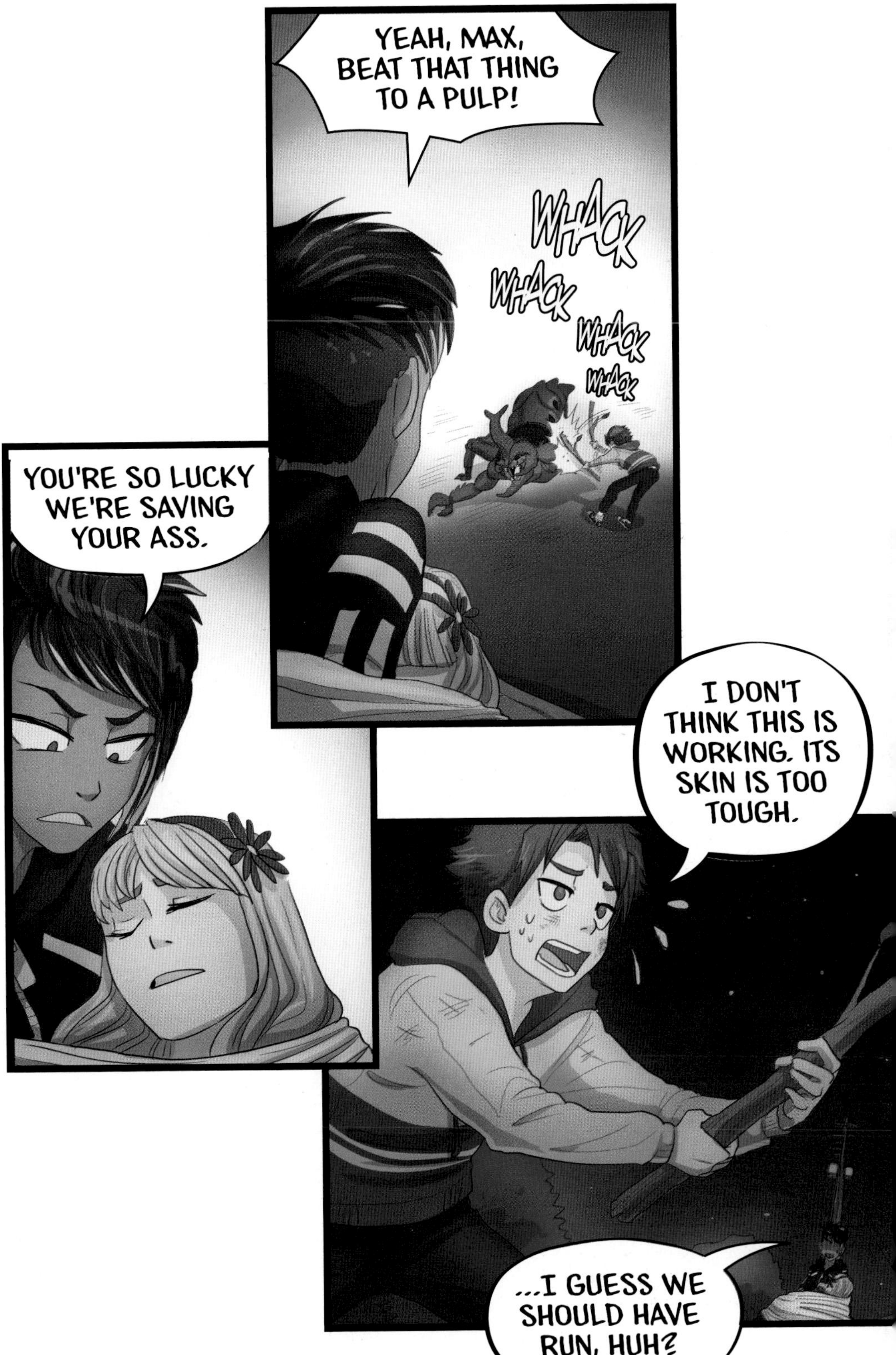
YEAH, MAX, BEAT THAT THING TO A PULP!
WHACK
WHACK
WHACK
WHACK
YOU'RE SO LUCKY WE'RE SAVING YOUR ASS.
I DON'T THINK THIS IS WORKING. ITS SKIN IS TOO TOUGH.
...I GUESS WE SHOULD HAVE RUN, HUH?

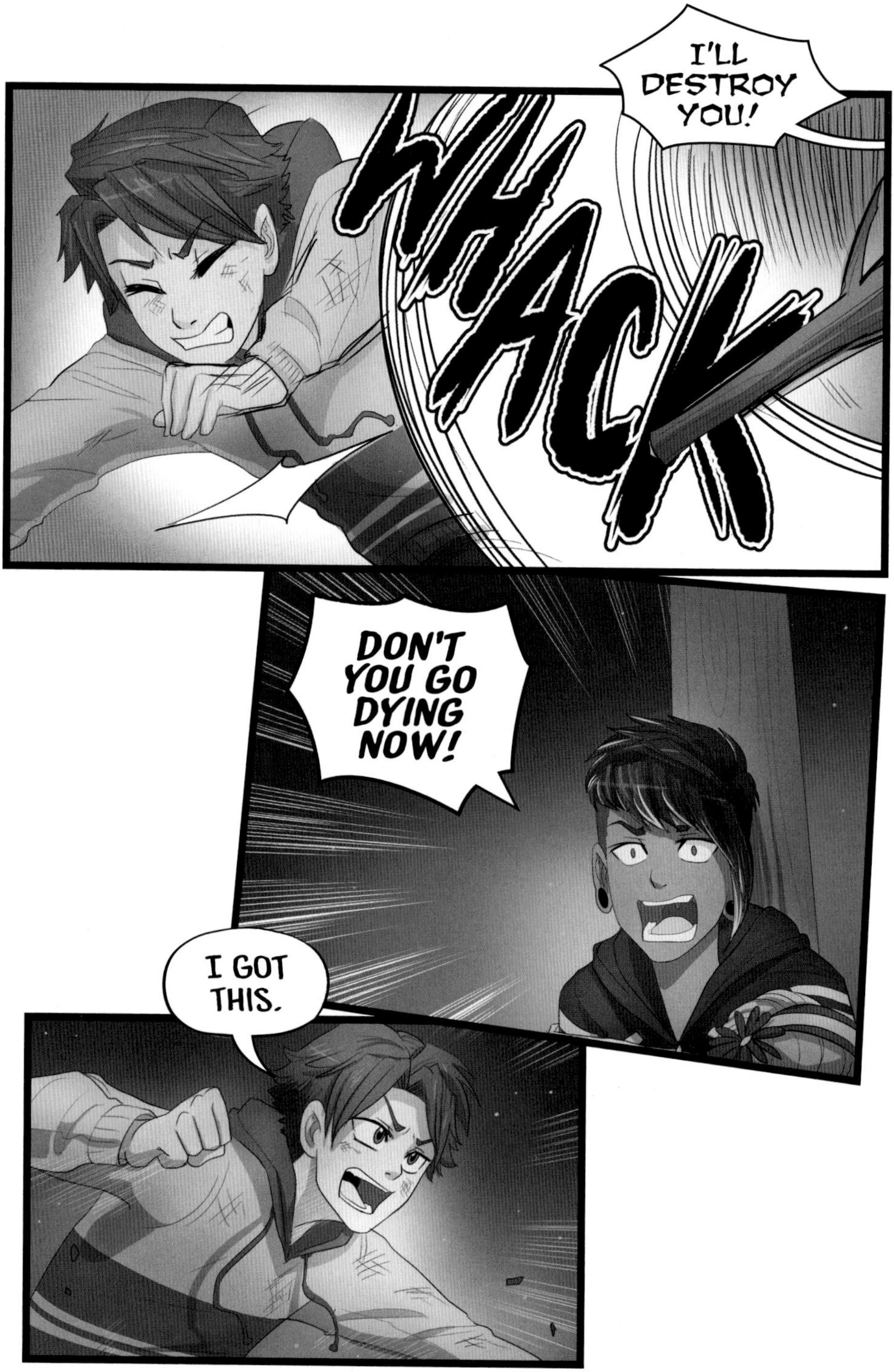
I'LL DESTROY YOU!
WHACK
DON'T YOU GO DYING NOW!
I GOT THIS.

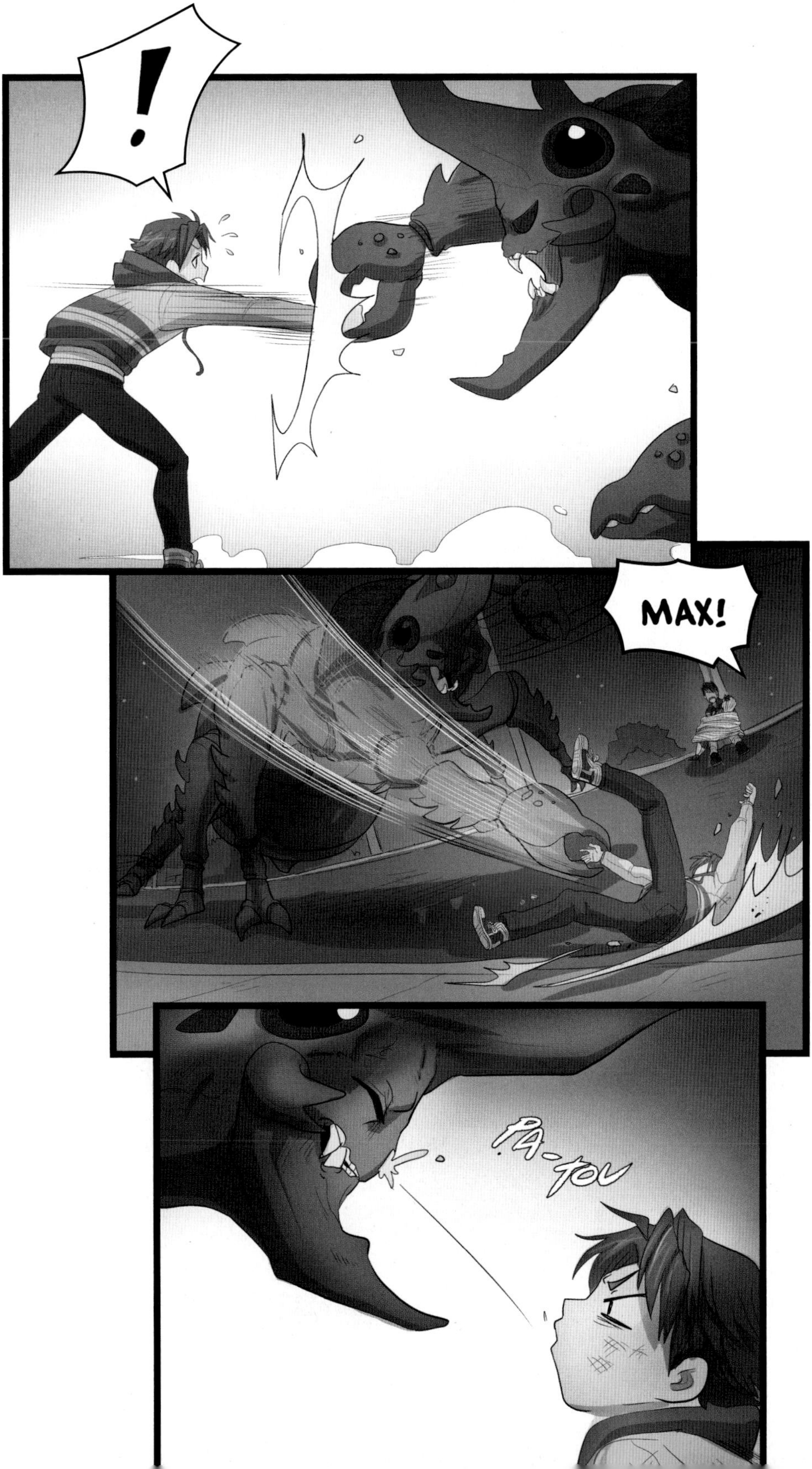
!
MAX!
PA-TOU

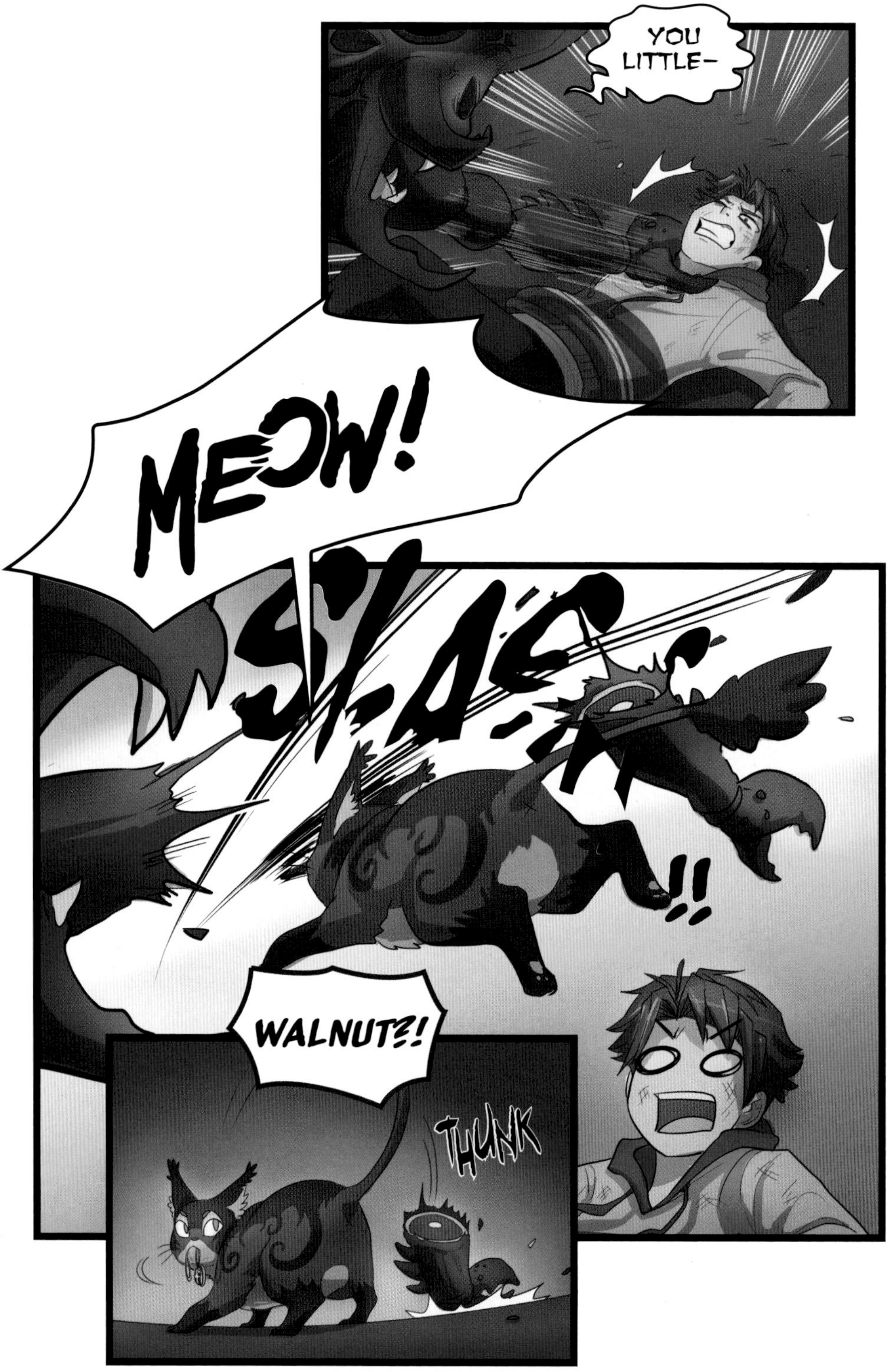
YOU LITTLE-
MEOW!
SLASH
!!
WALNUT?!
THUNK

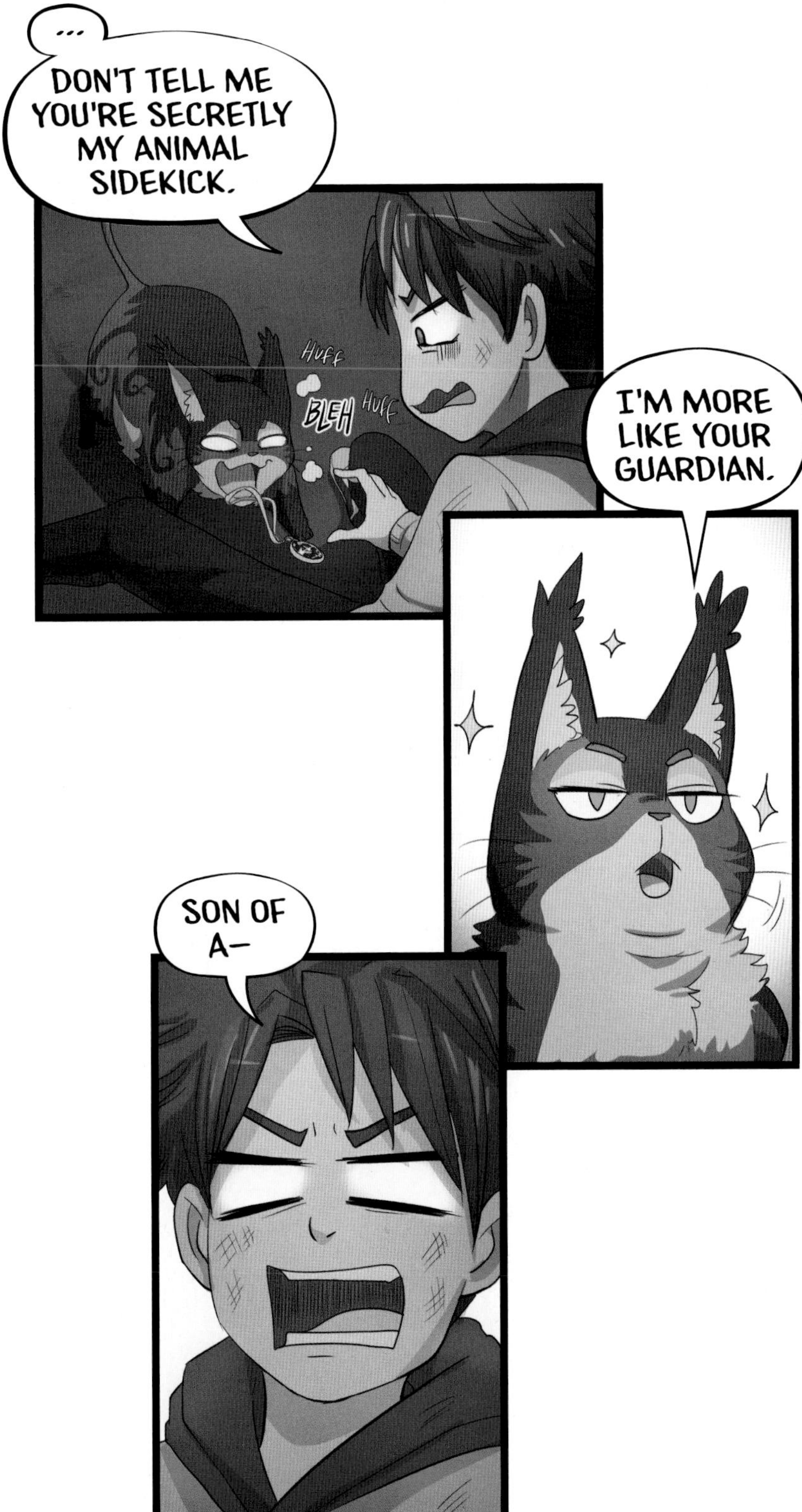
...
DON'T TELL ME YOU'RE SECRETLY MY ANIMAL SIDEKICK.
HUFF
BLEH
HUFF
I'M MORE LIKE YOUR GUARDIAN.
SON OF A—

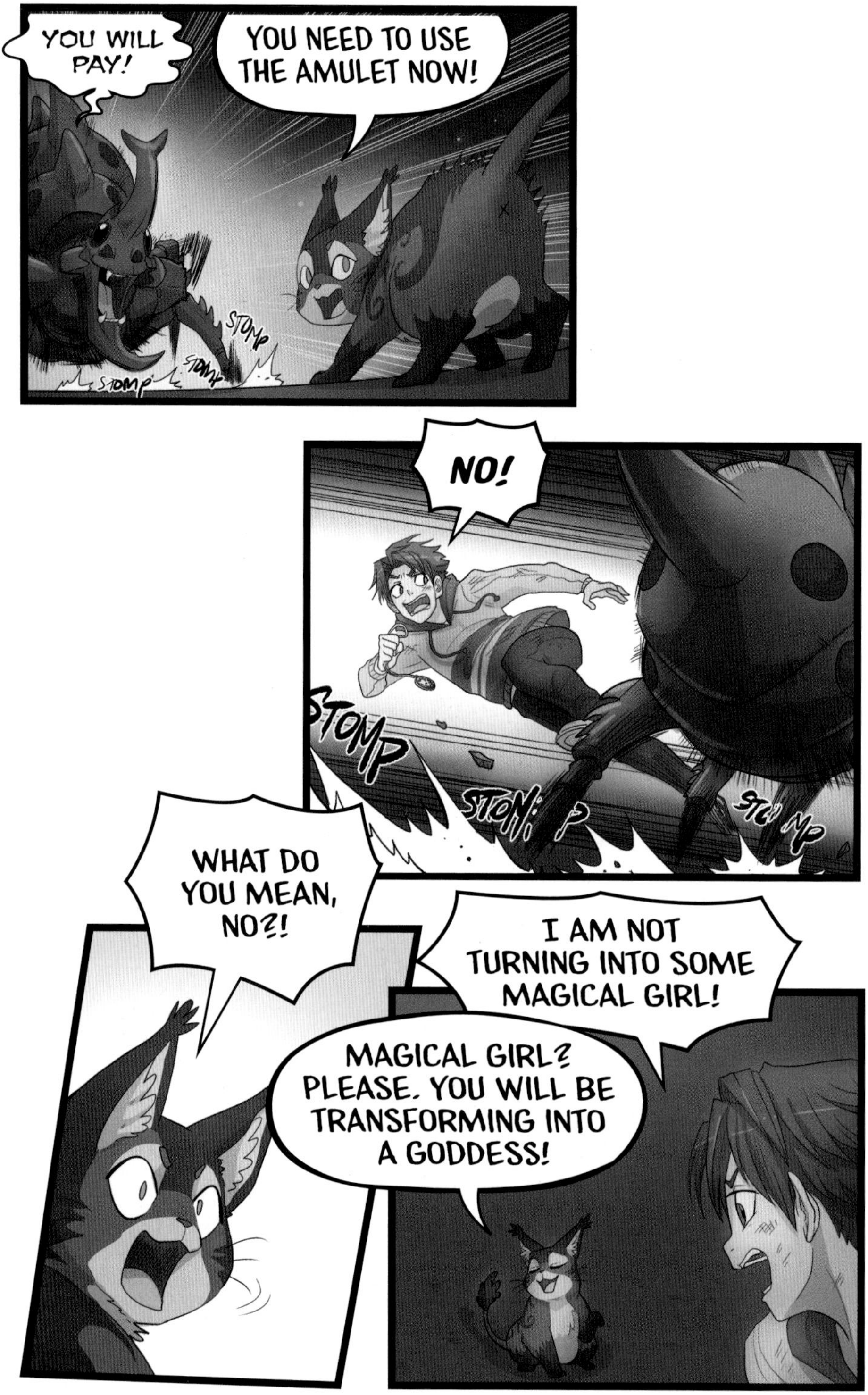
YOU WILL PAY!
YOU NEED TO USE THE AMULET NOW!
STOMP
STOMP
STOMP
NO!
STOMP
WHAT DO YOU MEAN, NO?!
I AM NOT TURNING INTO SOME MAGICAL GIRL!
MAGICAL GIRL? PLEASE. YOU WILL BE TRANSFORMING INTO A GODDESS!

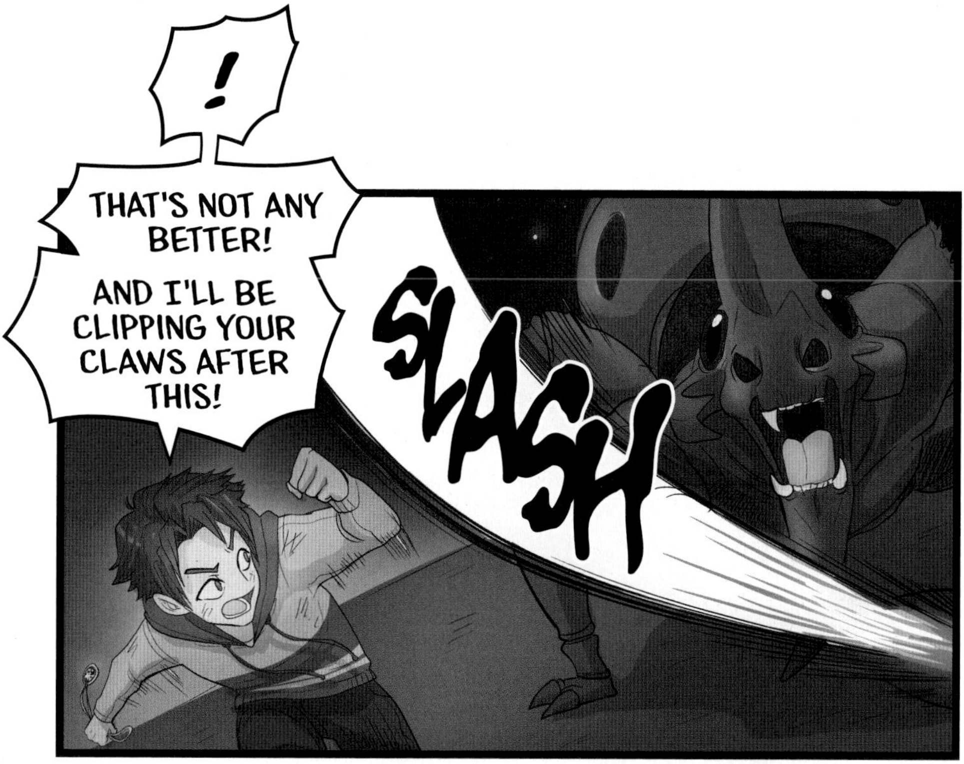
!
THAT'S NOT ANY BETTER!
AND I'LL BE CLIPPING YOUR CLAWS AFTER THIS!
SLASH

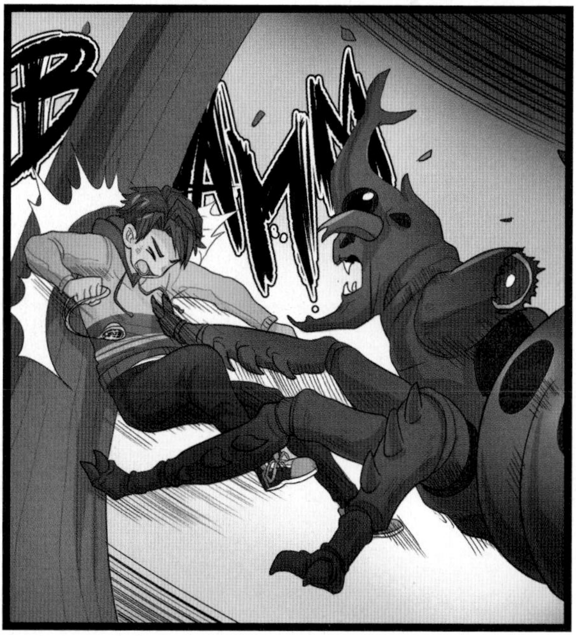
BAMM

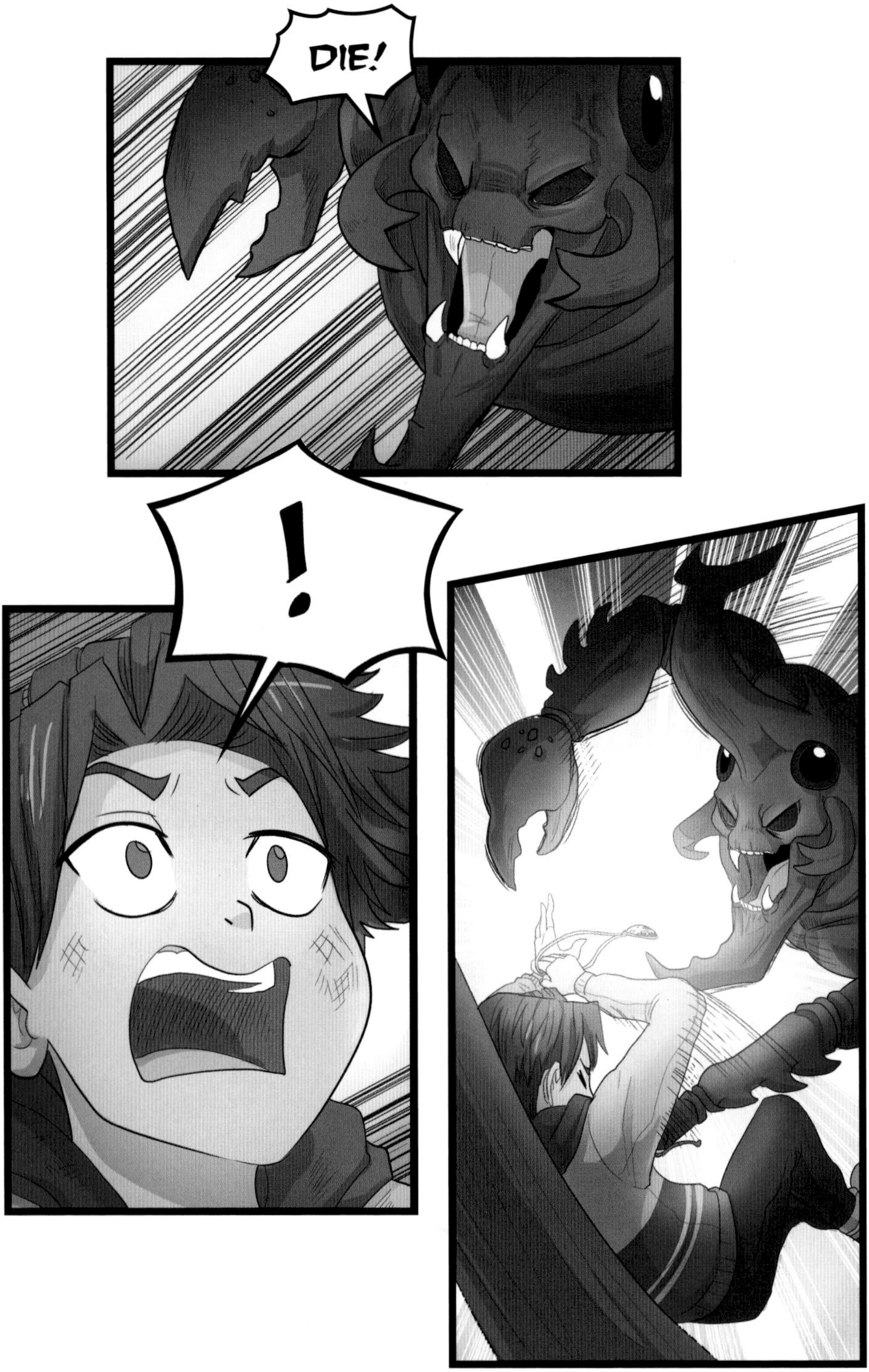
DIE!
!

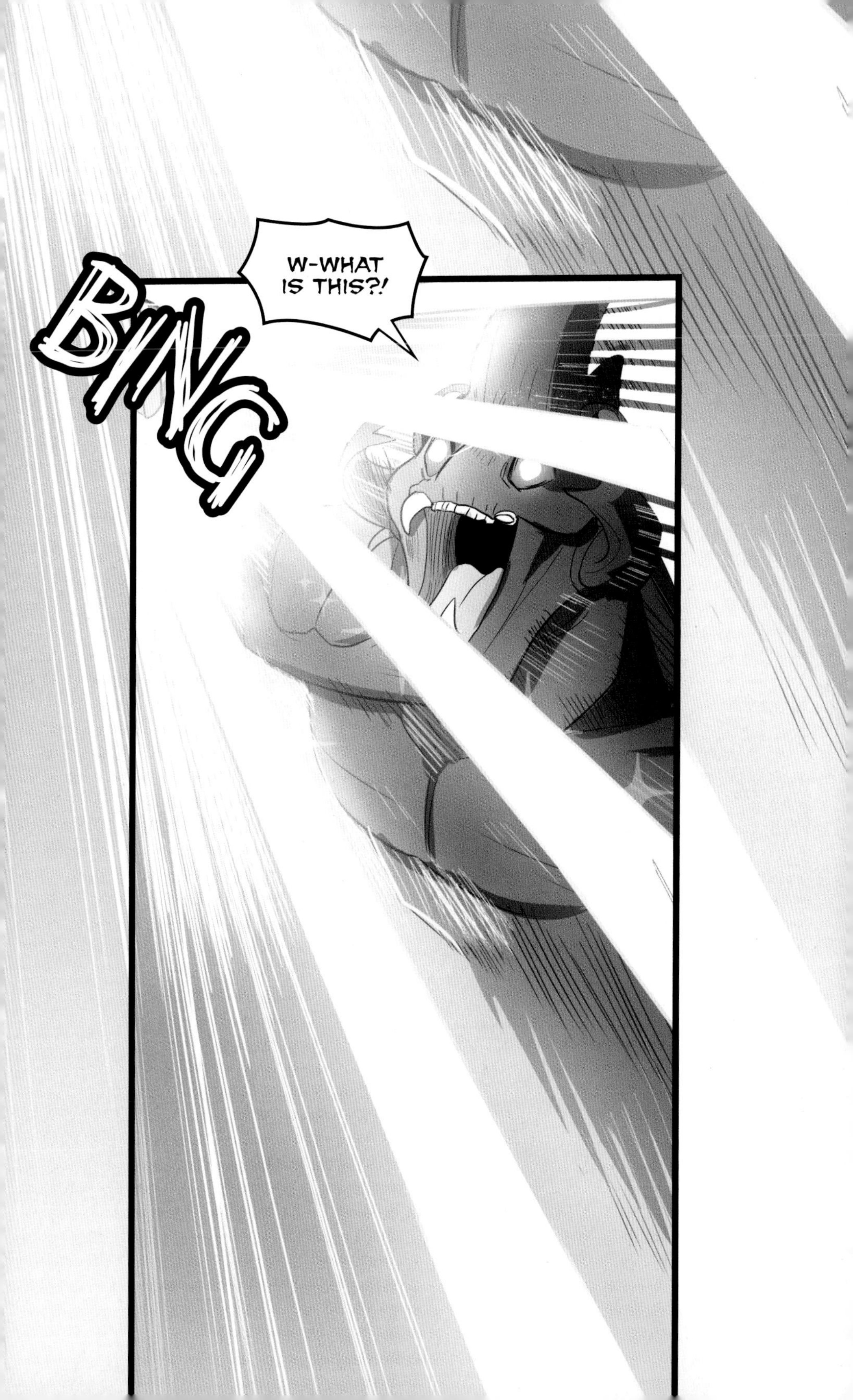
BING
W-WHAT IS THIS?!

IN THE BEGINNING

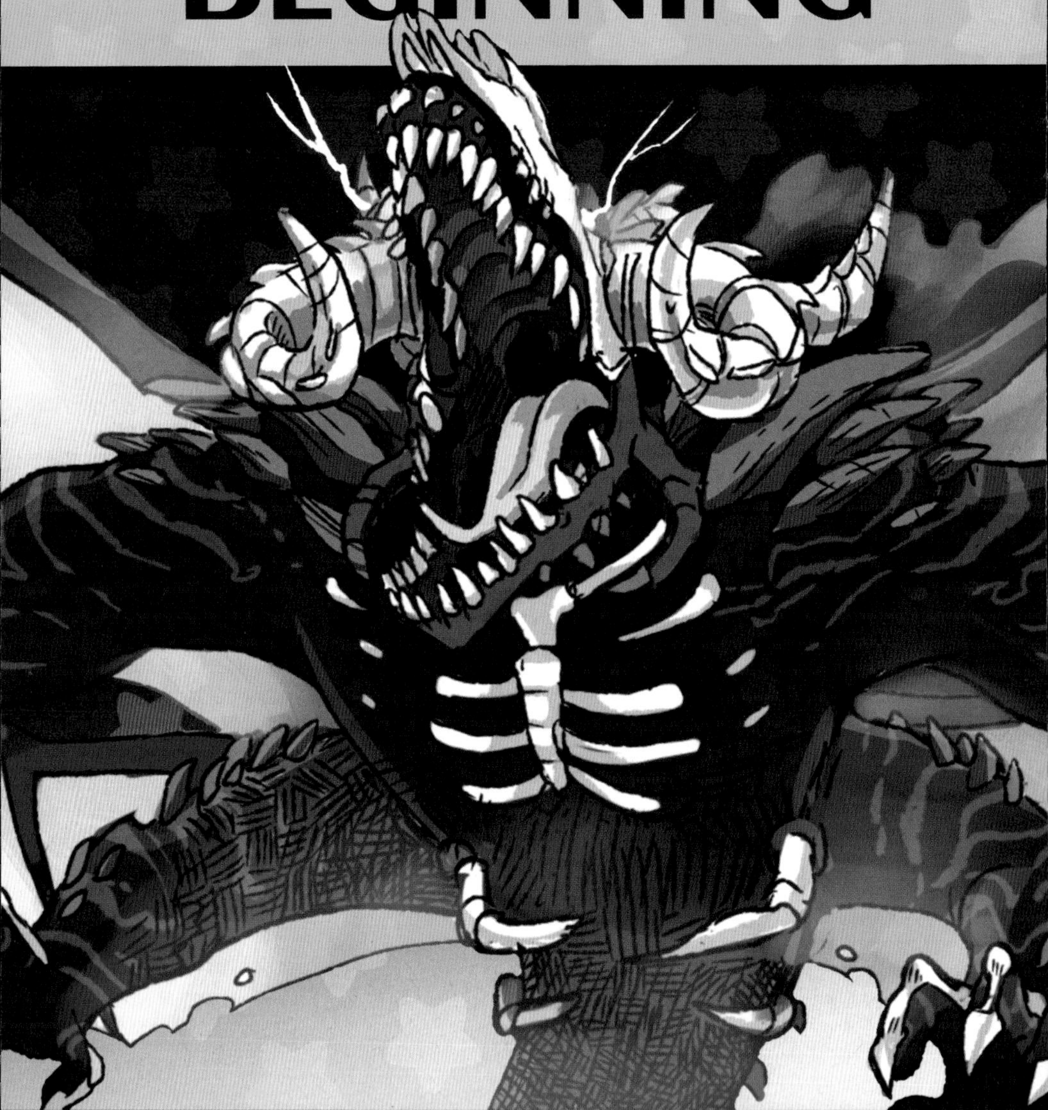

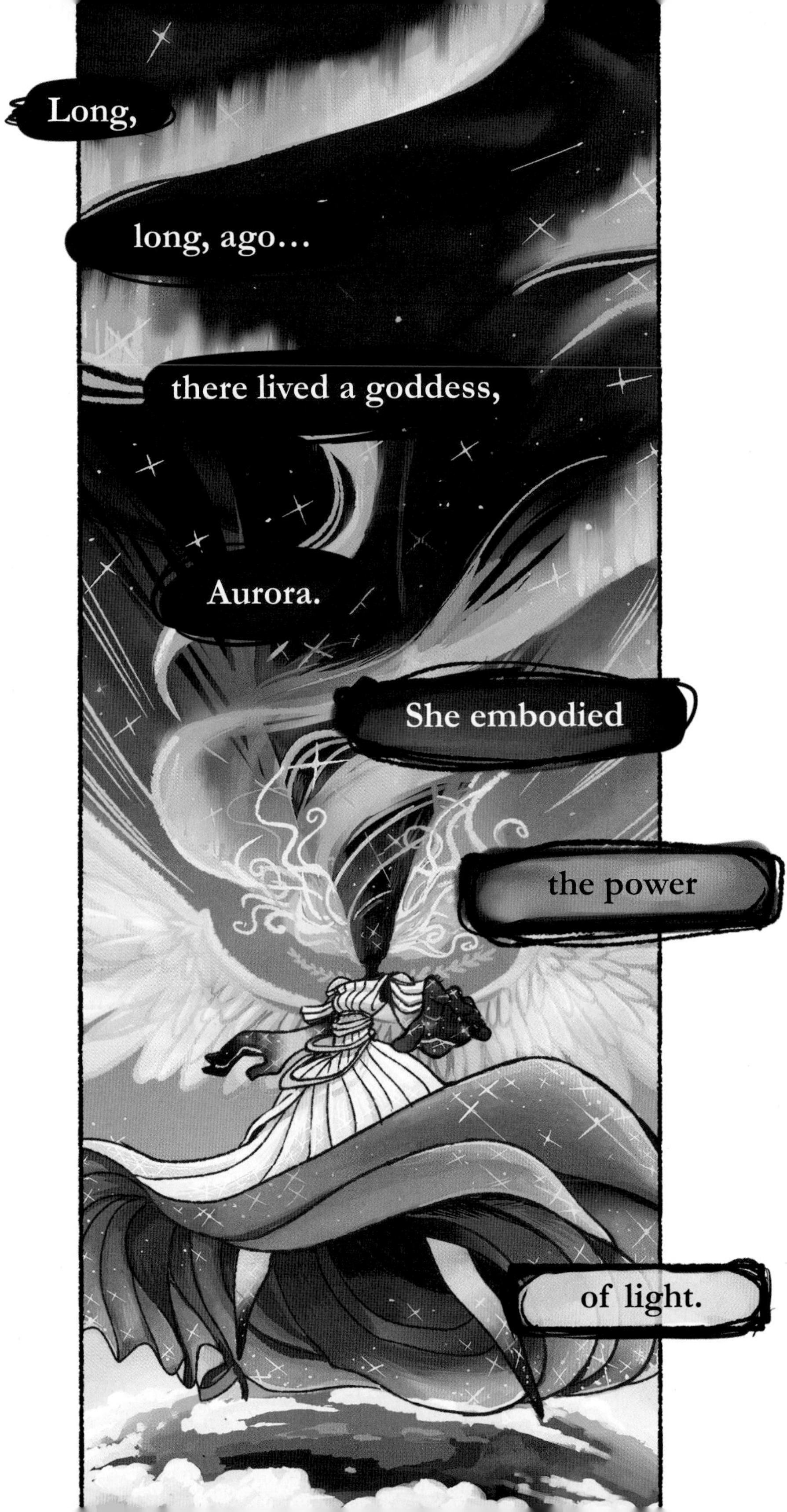

Long,
long, ago…
there lived a goddess,
Aurora.
She embodied
the power
of light.

It was she who
shined light on
the planet

against the dark deity.

DEVOID.

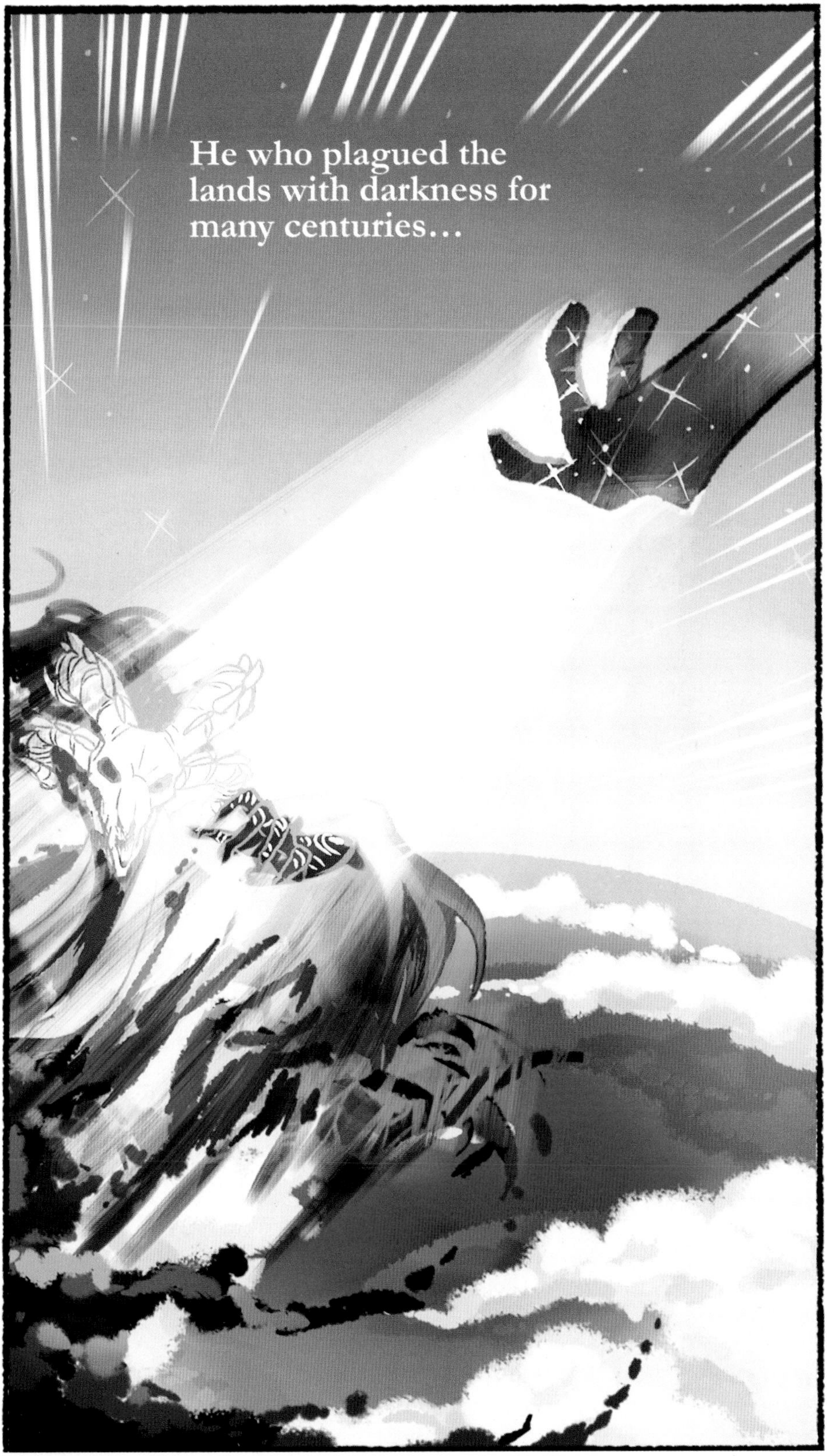
He who plagued the lands with darkness for many centuries…

with Aurora's light

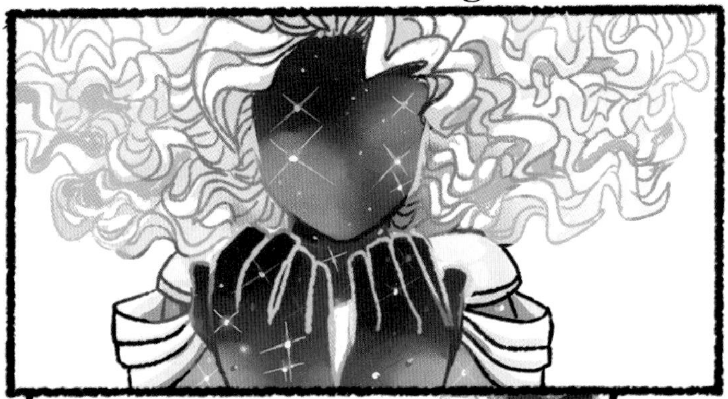

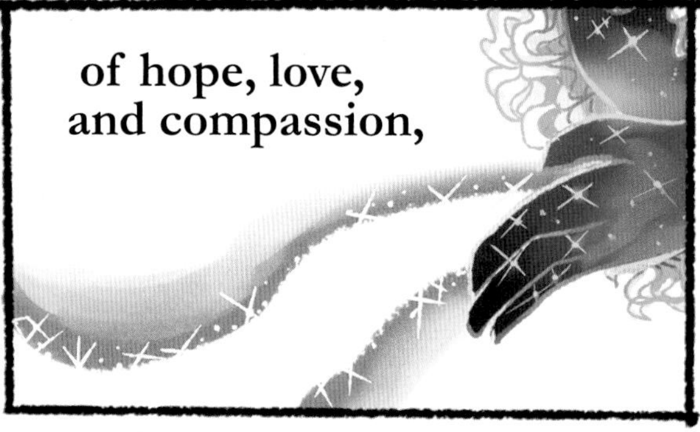
of hope, love,
and compassion,

all living creatures

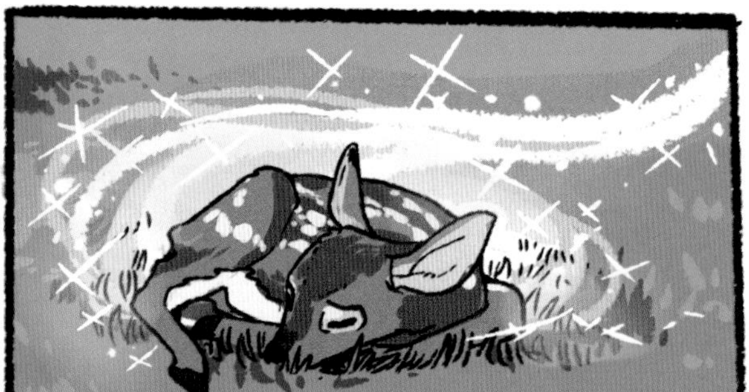

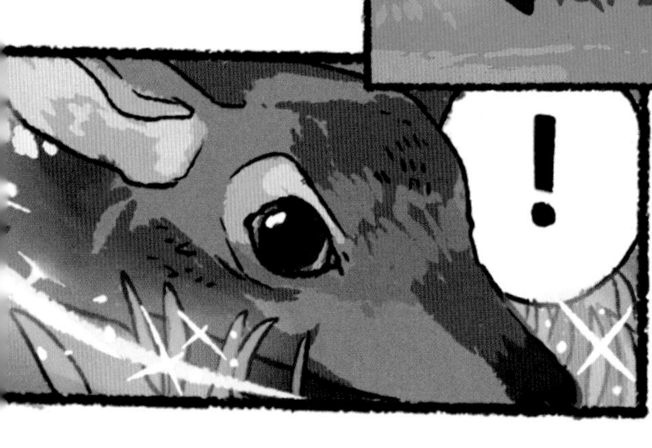
!

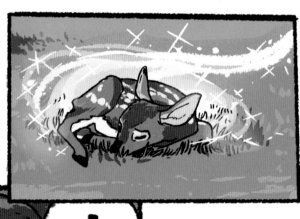

were able to flourish with overwhelming life force.

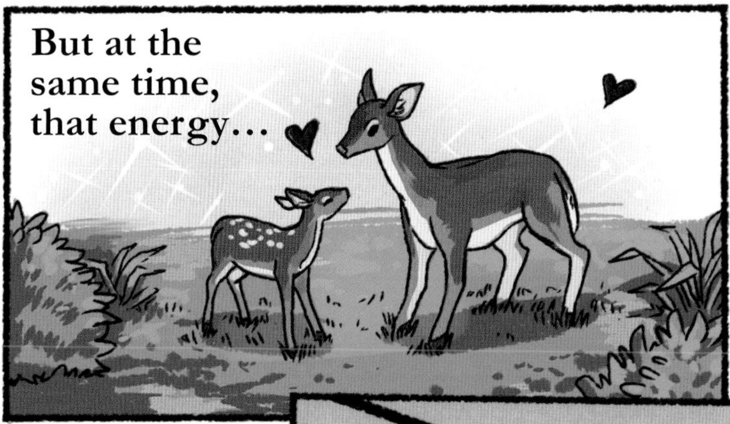
But at the same time, that energy...

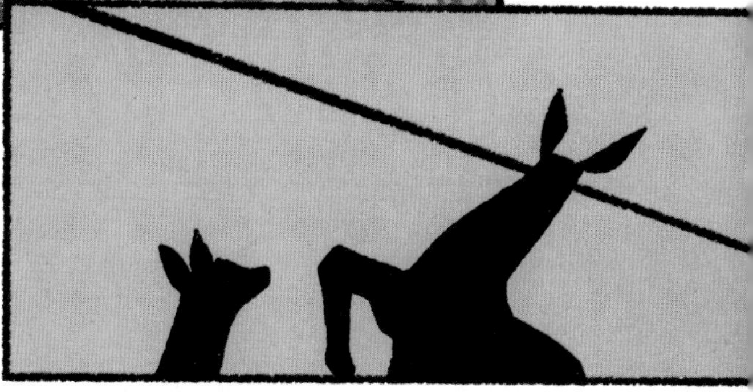

when tainted, became a darkened life force...

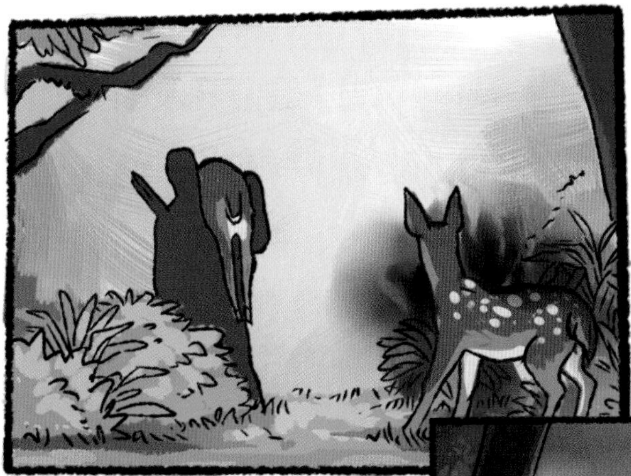

that gave Devoid strength.

Tired of living in the shadows,

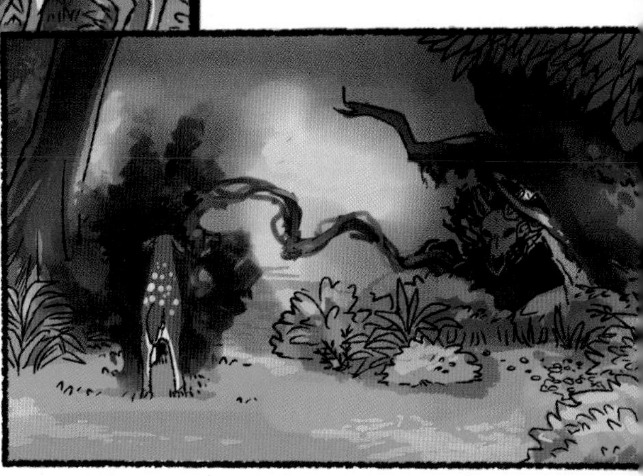

he began a reign of terror
among the people with his
monstrous creatures…

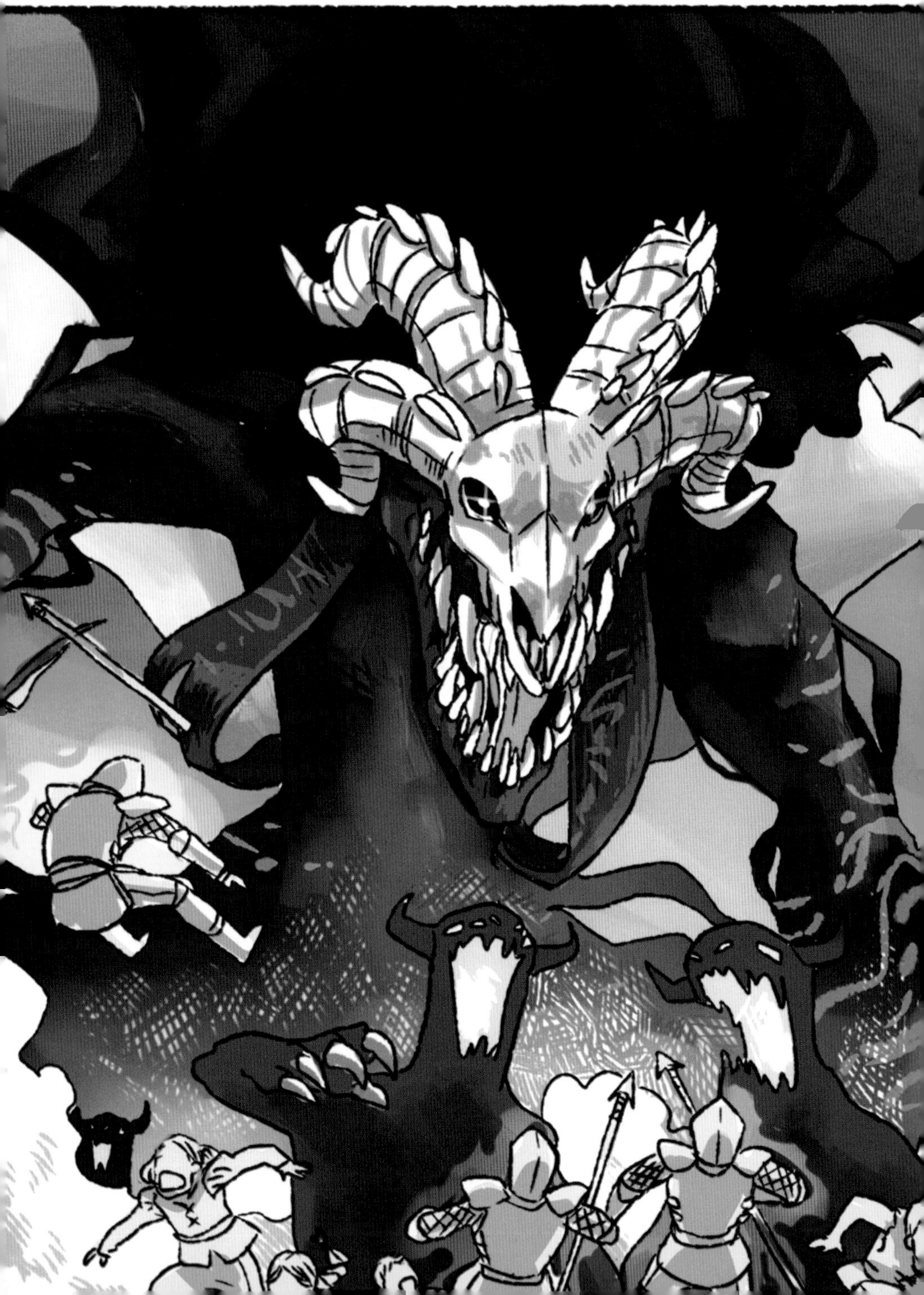

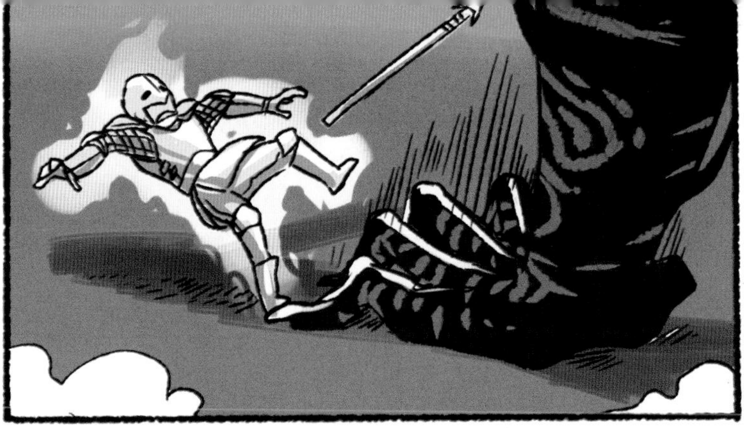

creating increasing amounts of fear, anger, and greed among them.

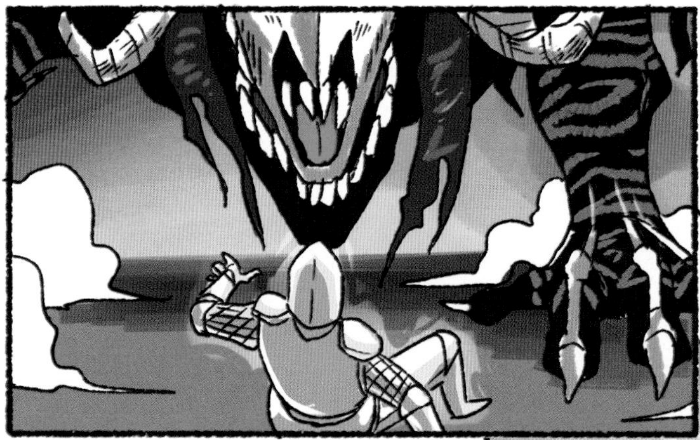

The light within these beings quickly faded...

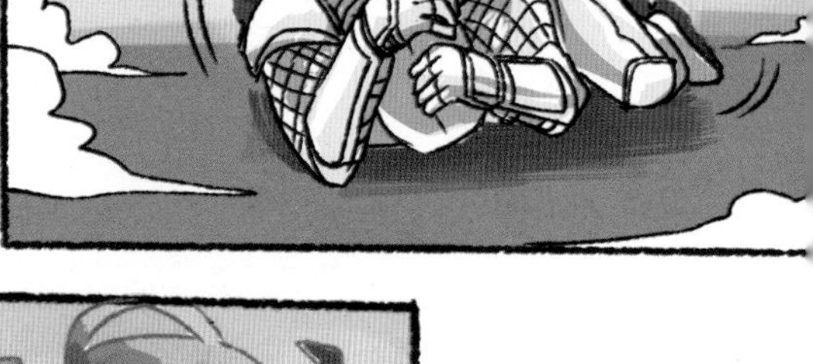

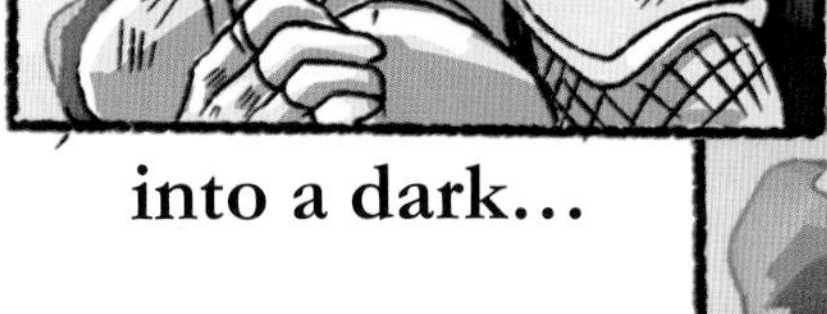

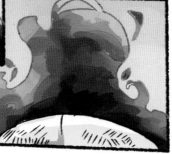

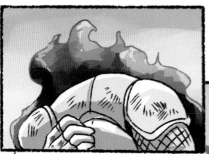

into a dark...

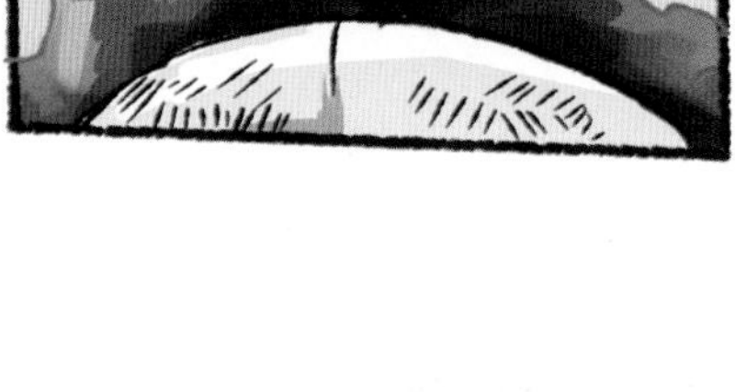

dense...

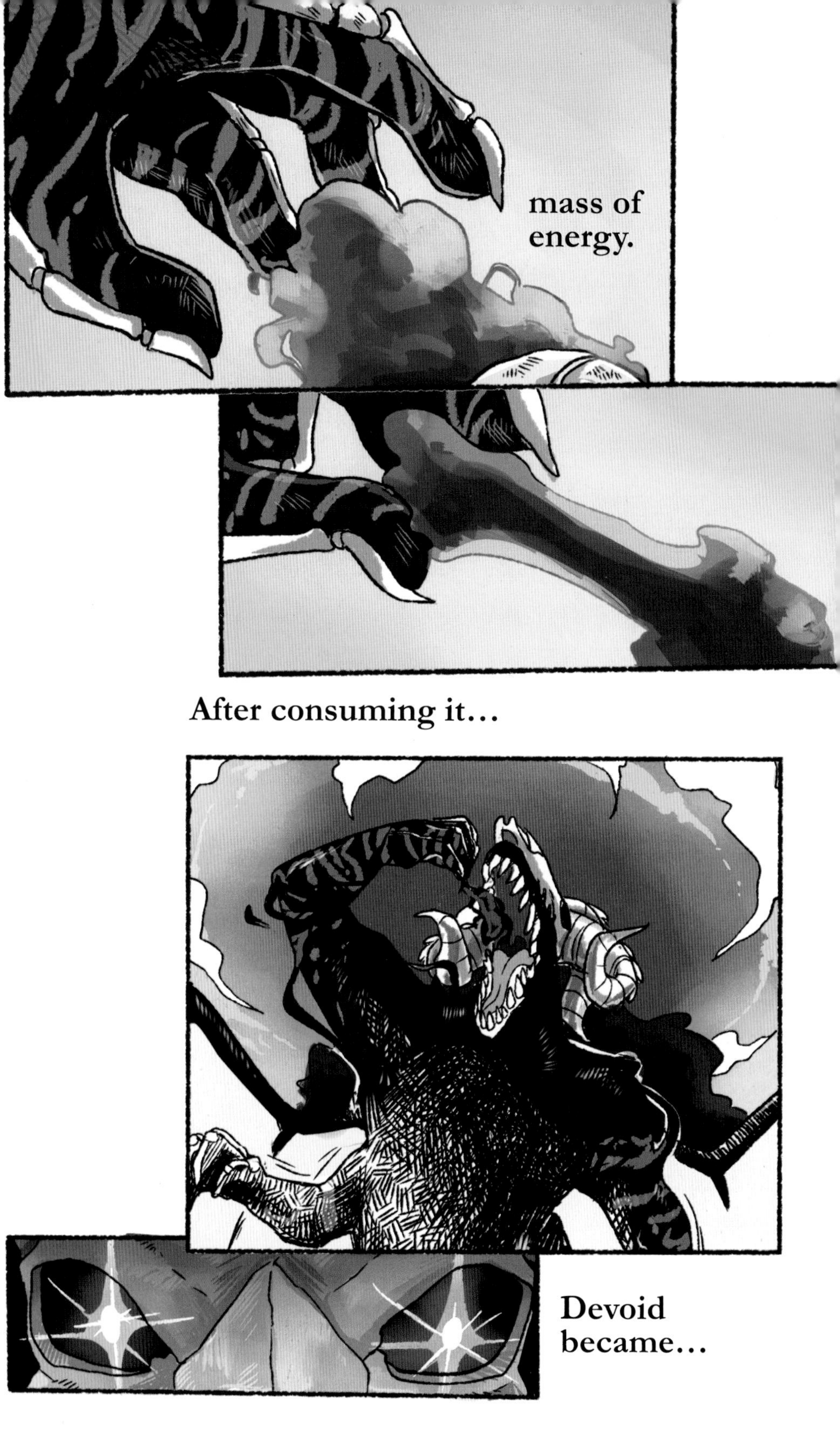
mass of energy.
After consuming it…
Devoid became…

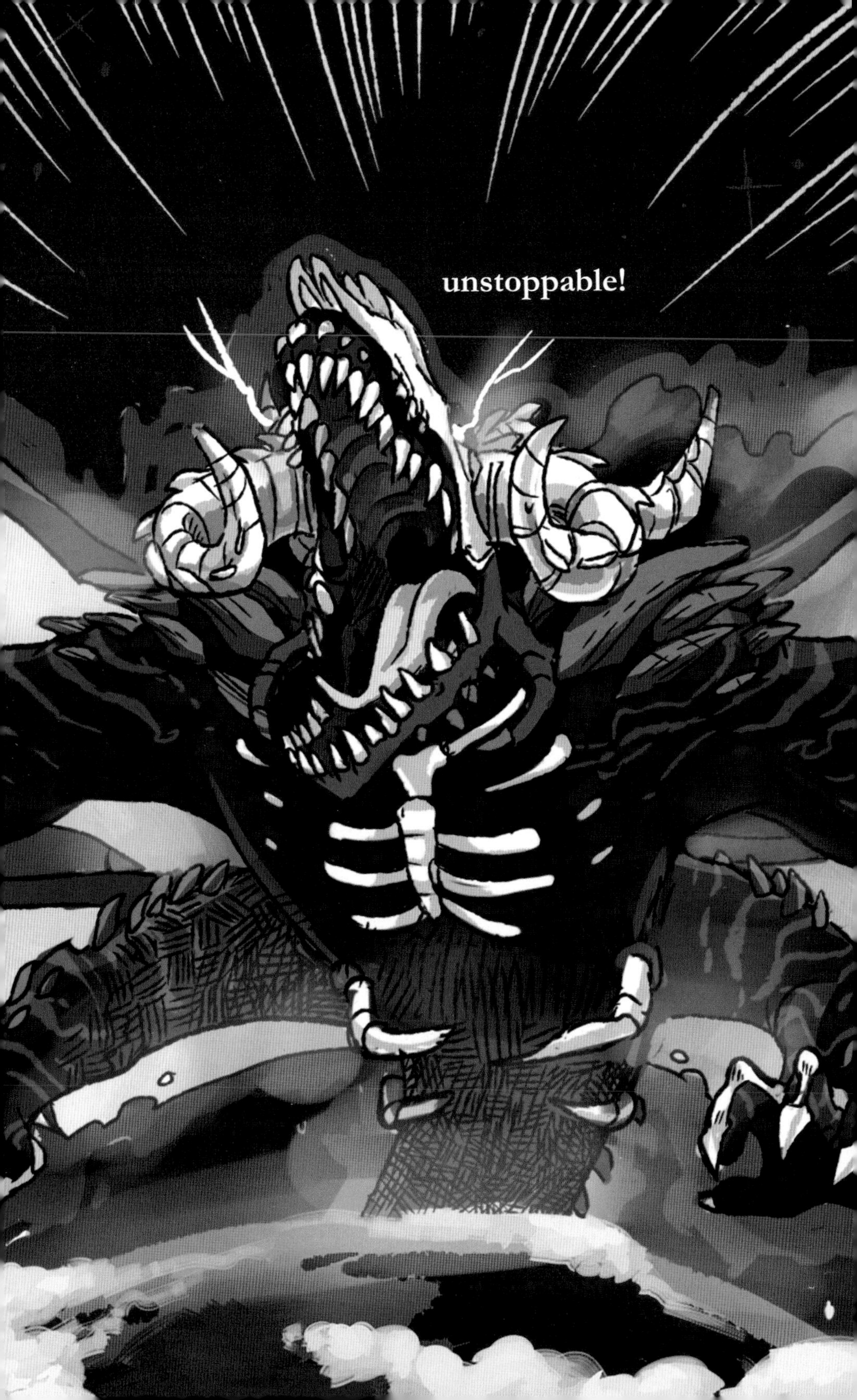
unstoppable!

Aurora knew she had to do something

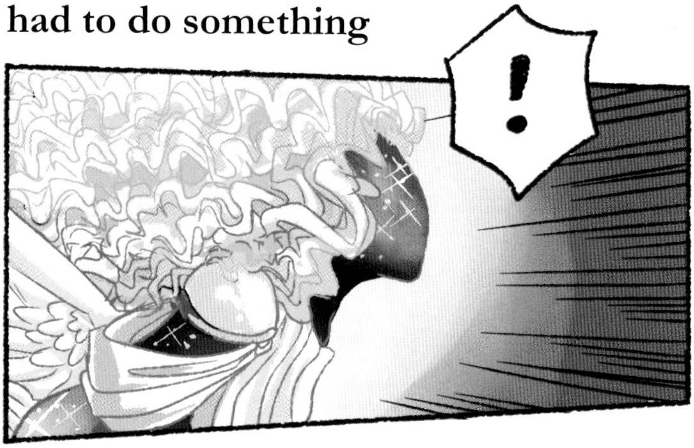
!

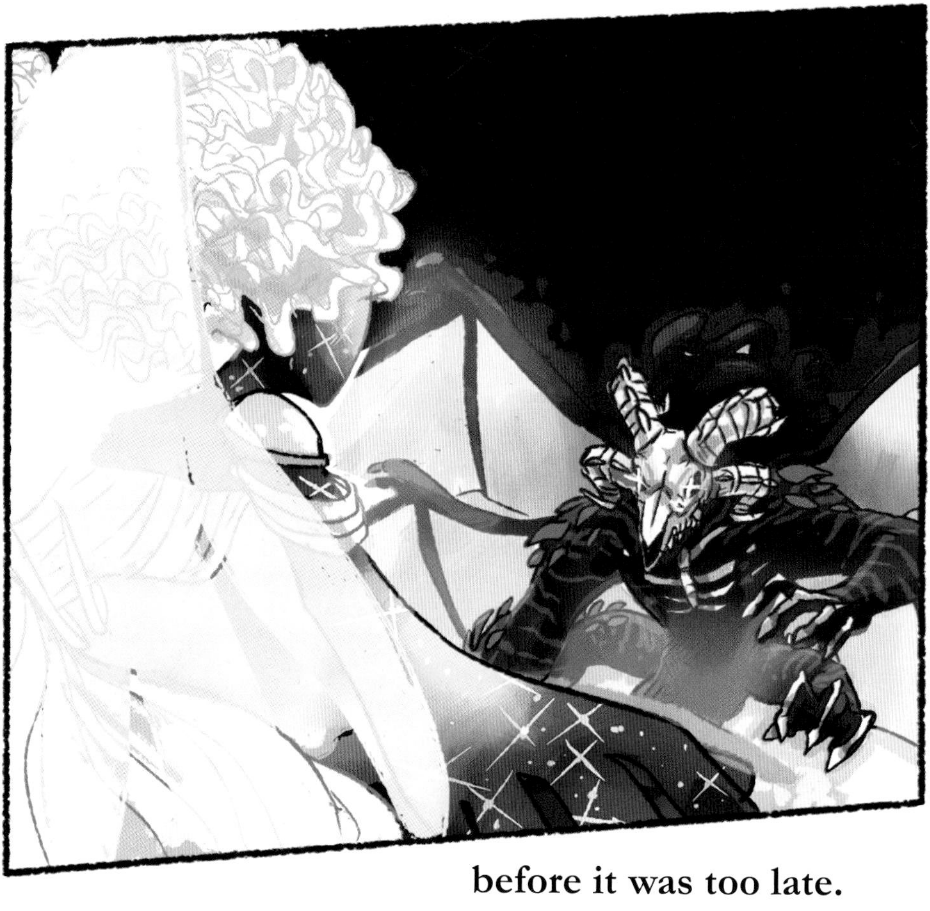

before it was too late.

With the help of her
trusty guardian,

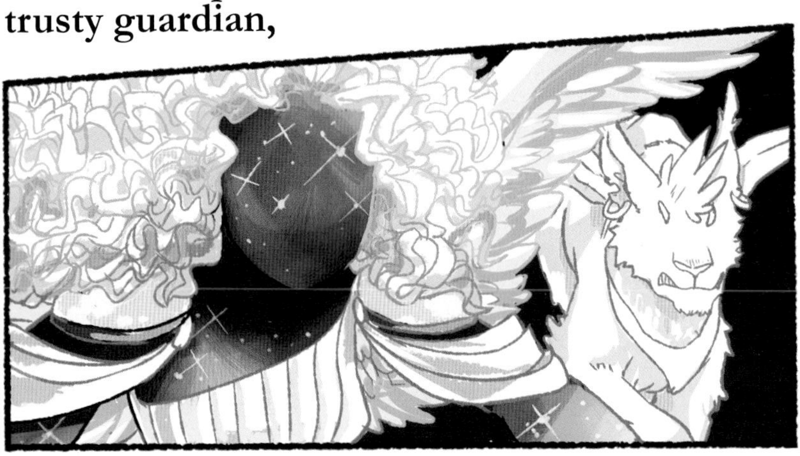

they dove into battle

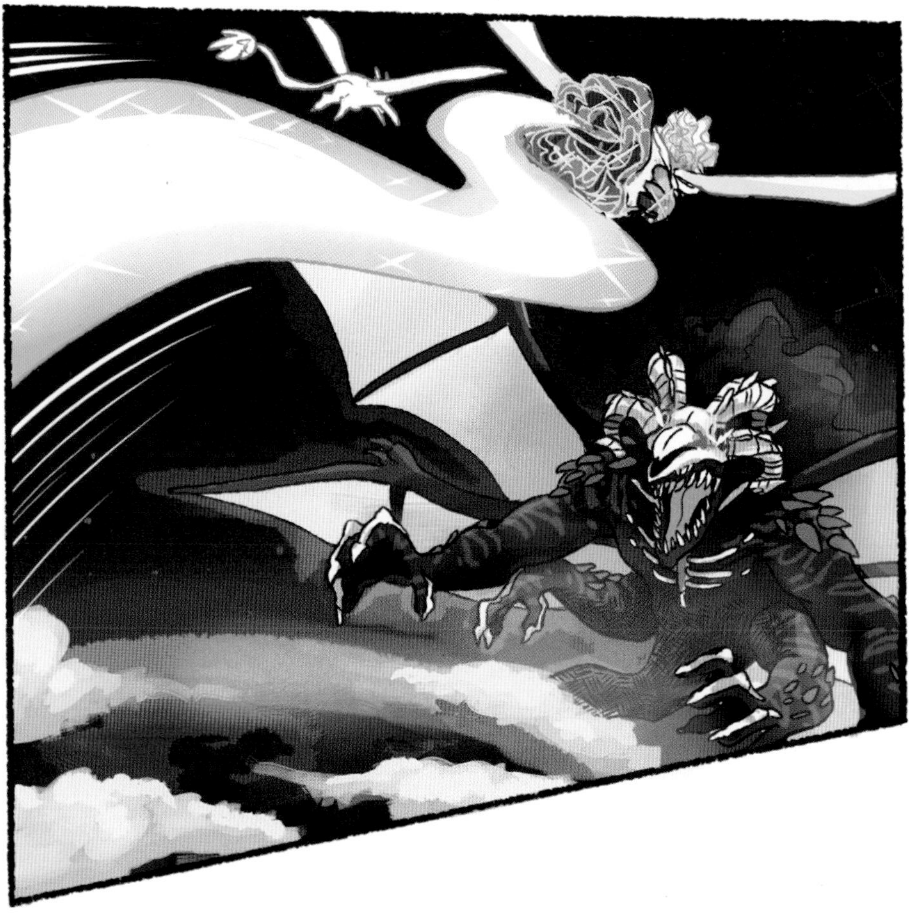

with bursting

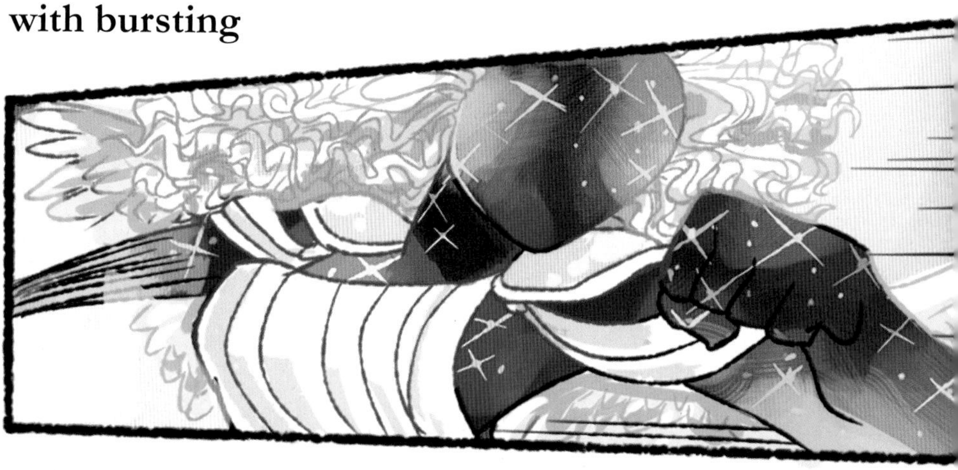

light!

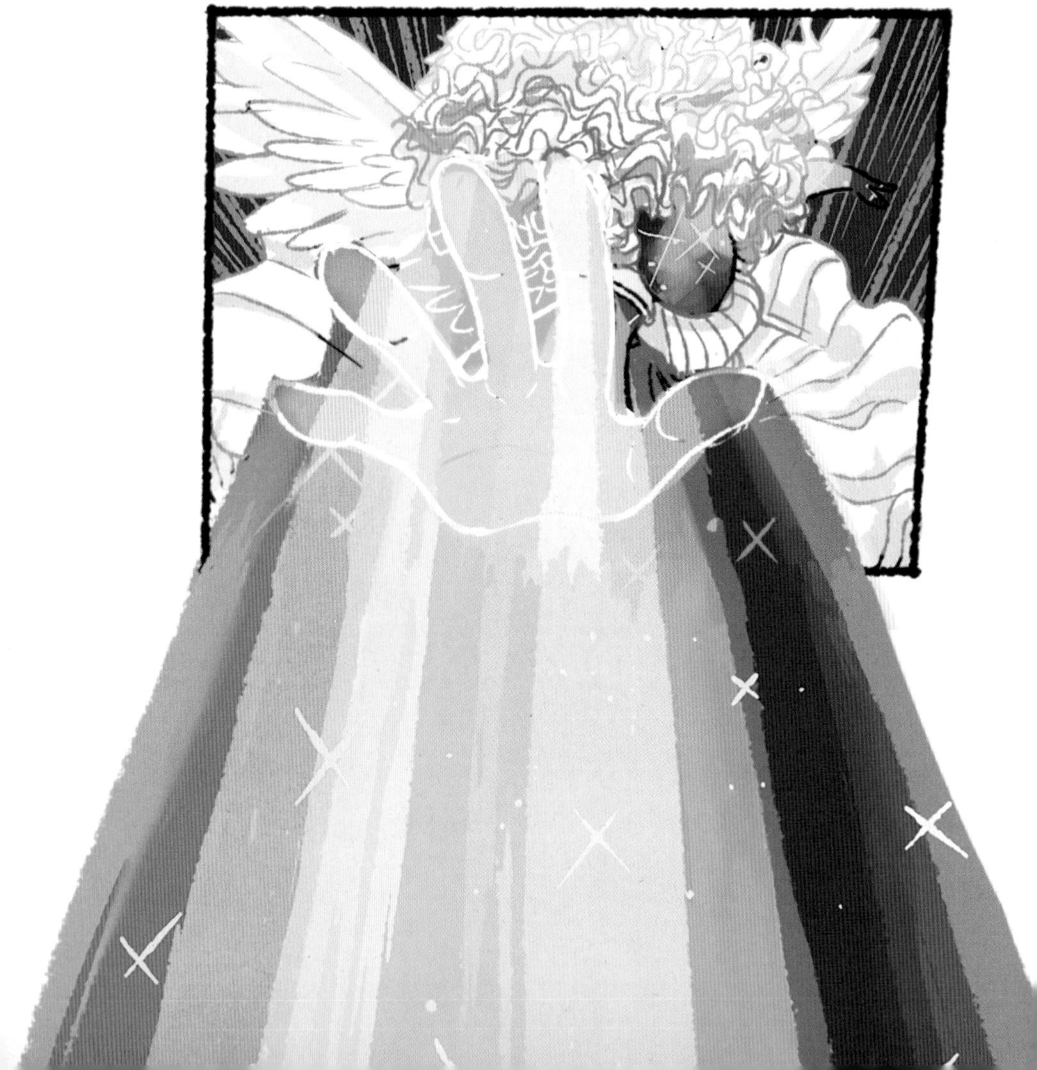

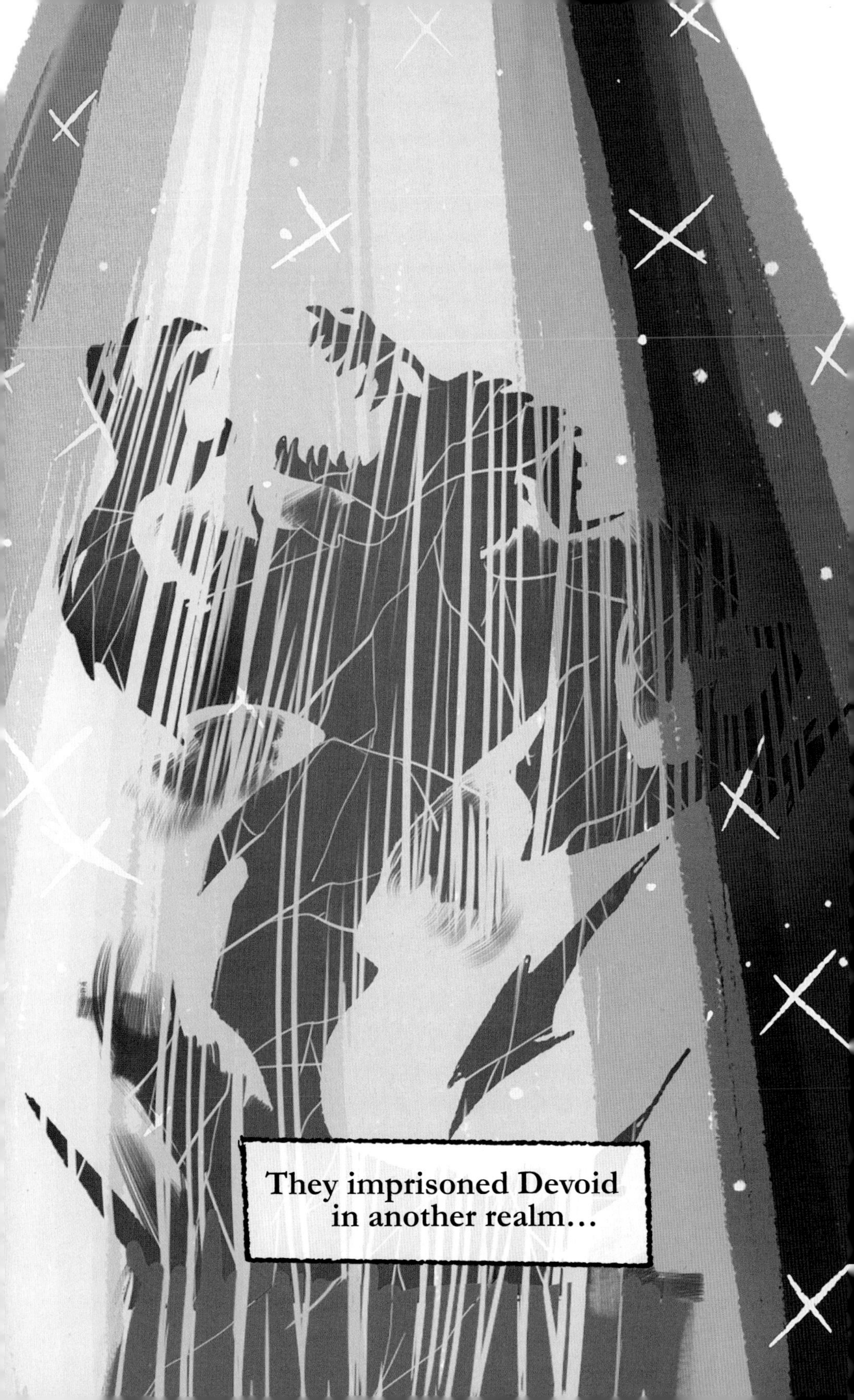
They imprisoned Devoid in another realm…

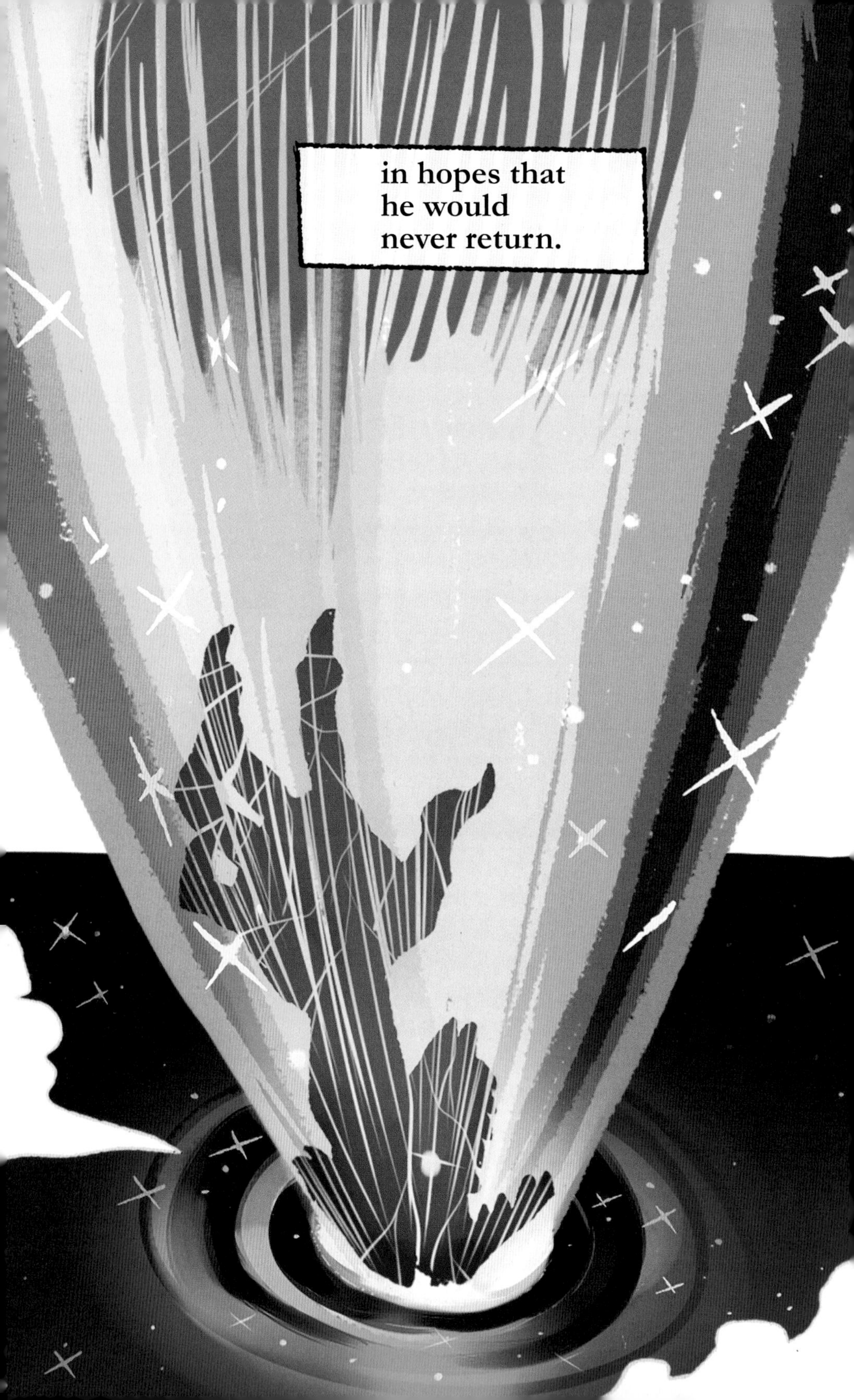
in hopes that he would never return.

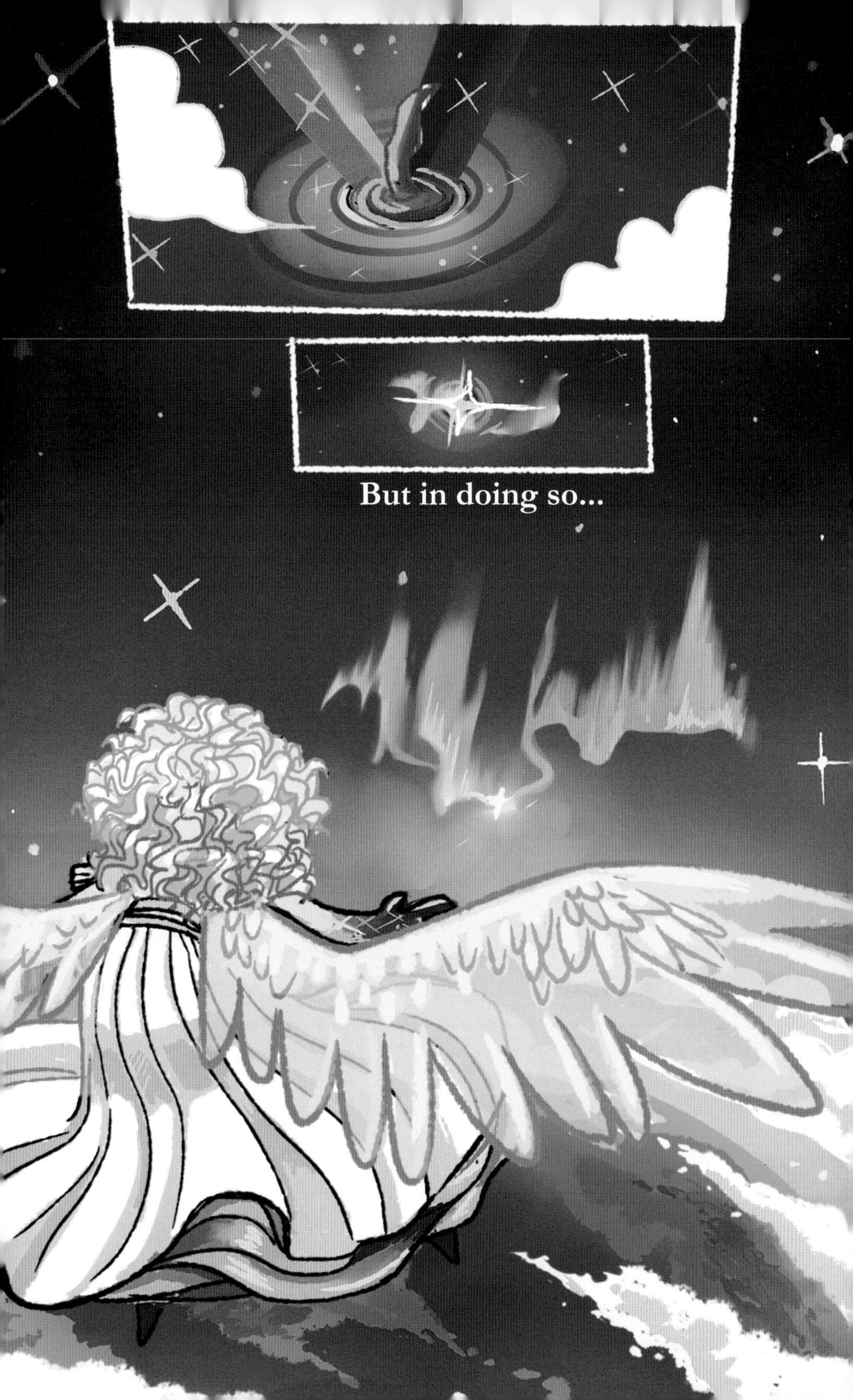
But in doing so...

**Aurora sacrificed
her very being . . .**

**to withhold
the seal…**

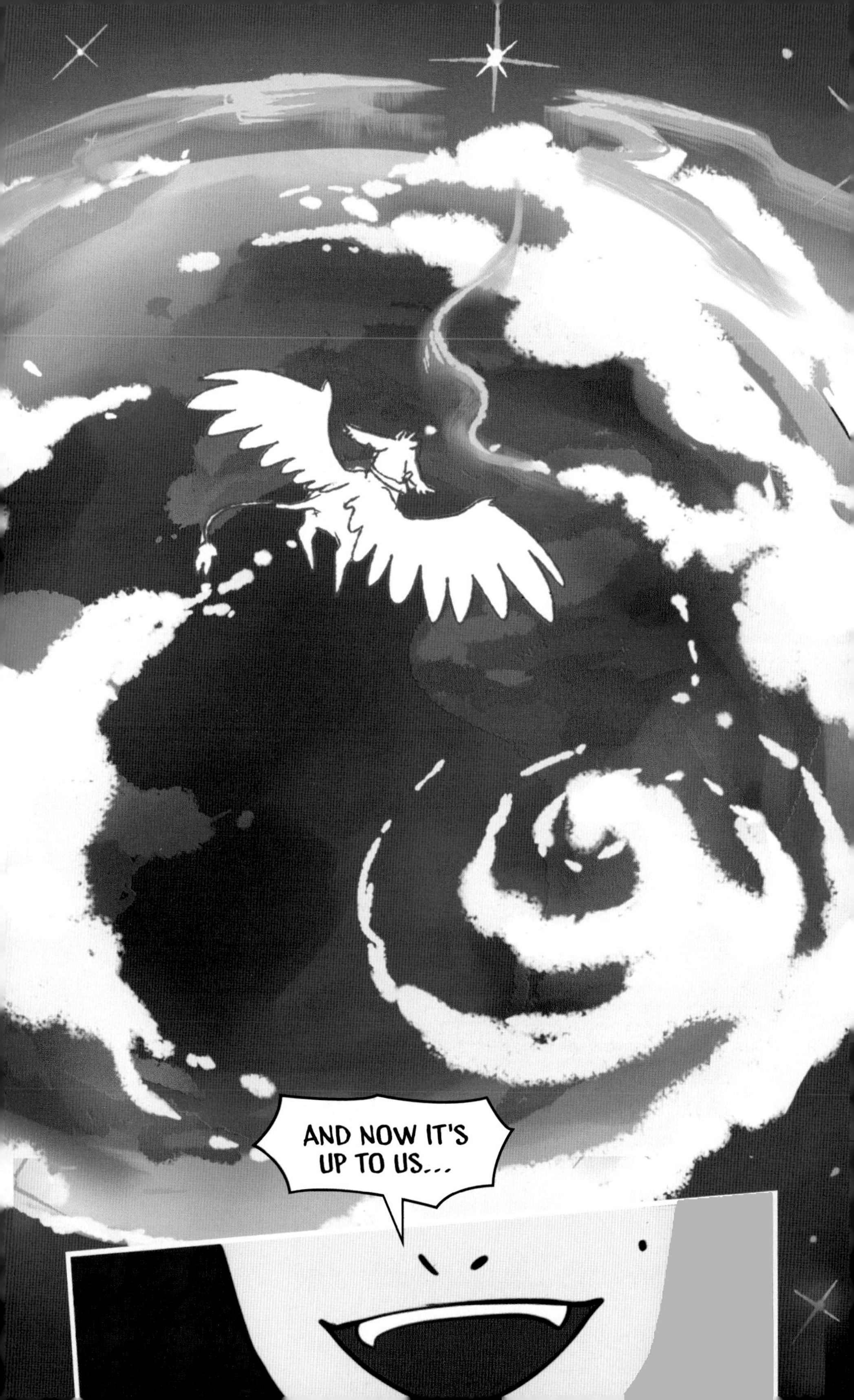
AND NOW IT'S UP TO US...

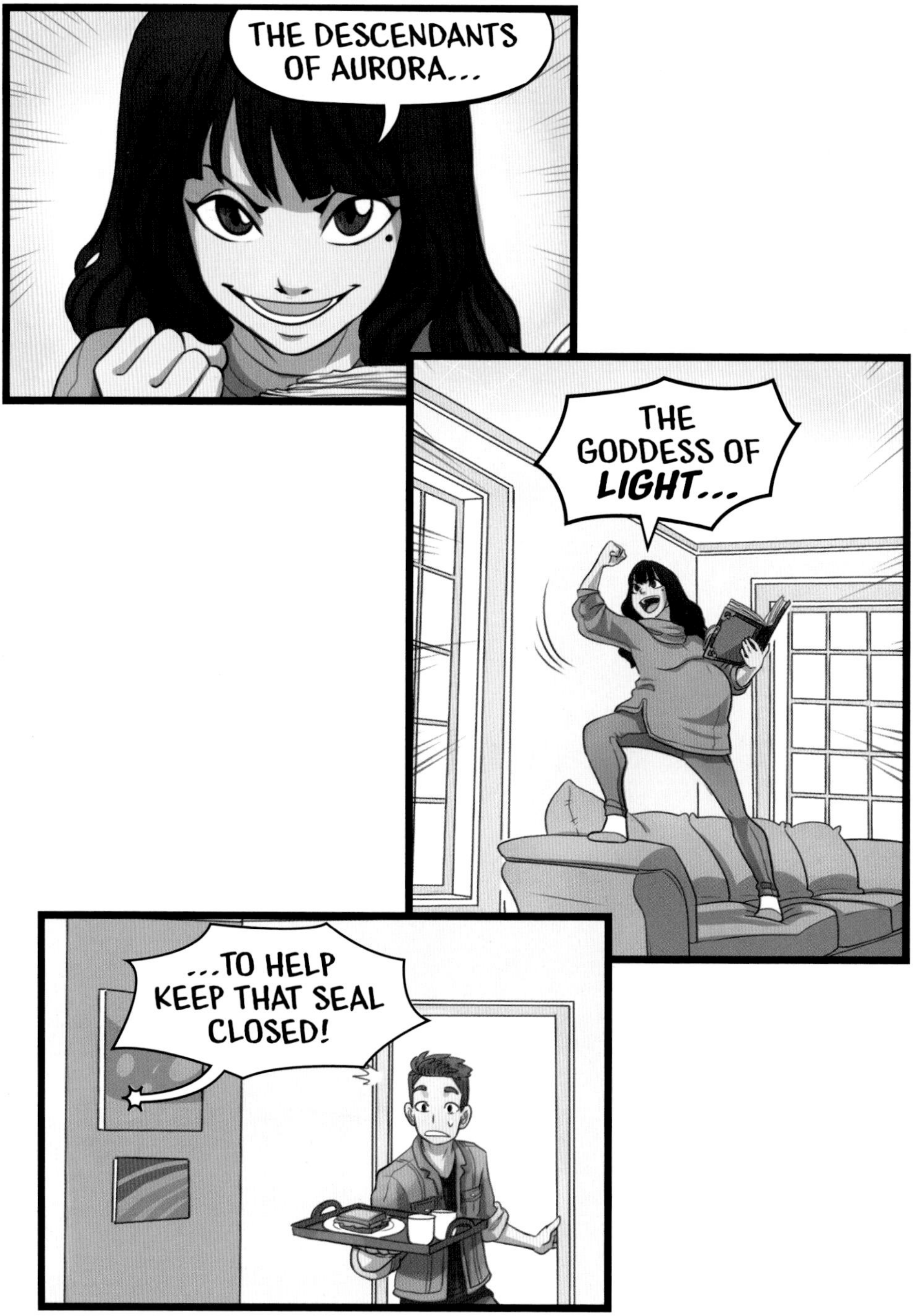
THE DESCENDANTS OF AURORA...
THE GODDESS OF LIGHT...
...TO HELP KEEP THAT SEAL CLOSED!

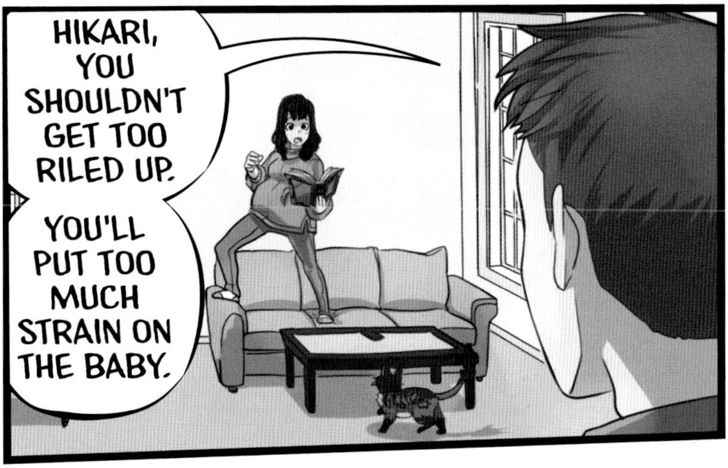
HIKARI, YOU SHOULDN'T GET TOO RILED UP.
YOU'LL PUT TOO MUCH STRAIN ON THE BABY.

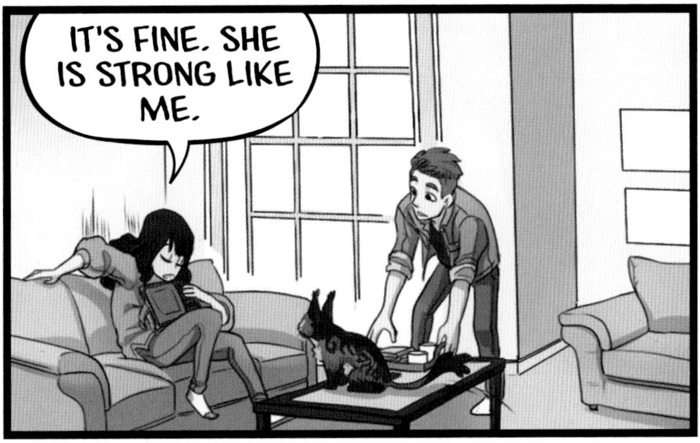
IT'S FINE. SHE IS STRONG LIKE ME.

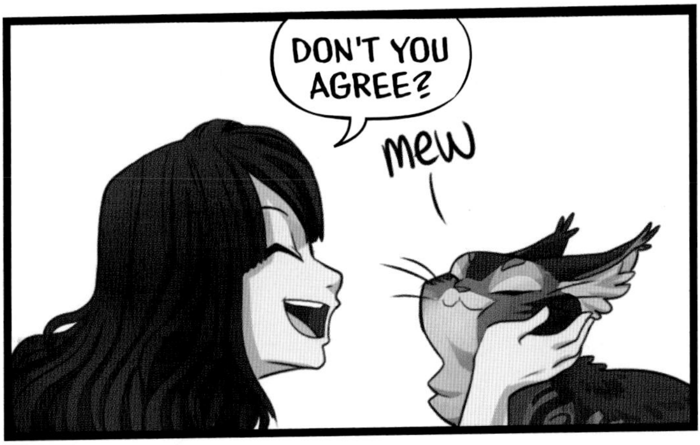
DON'T YOU AGREE?
mew

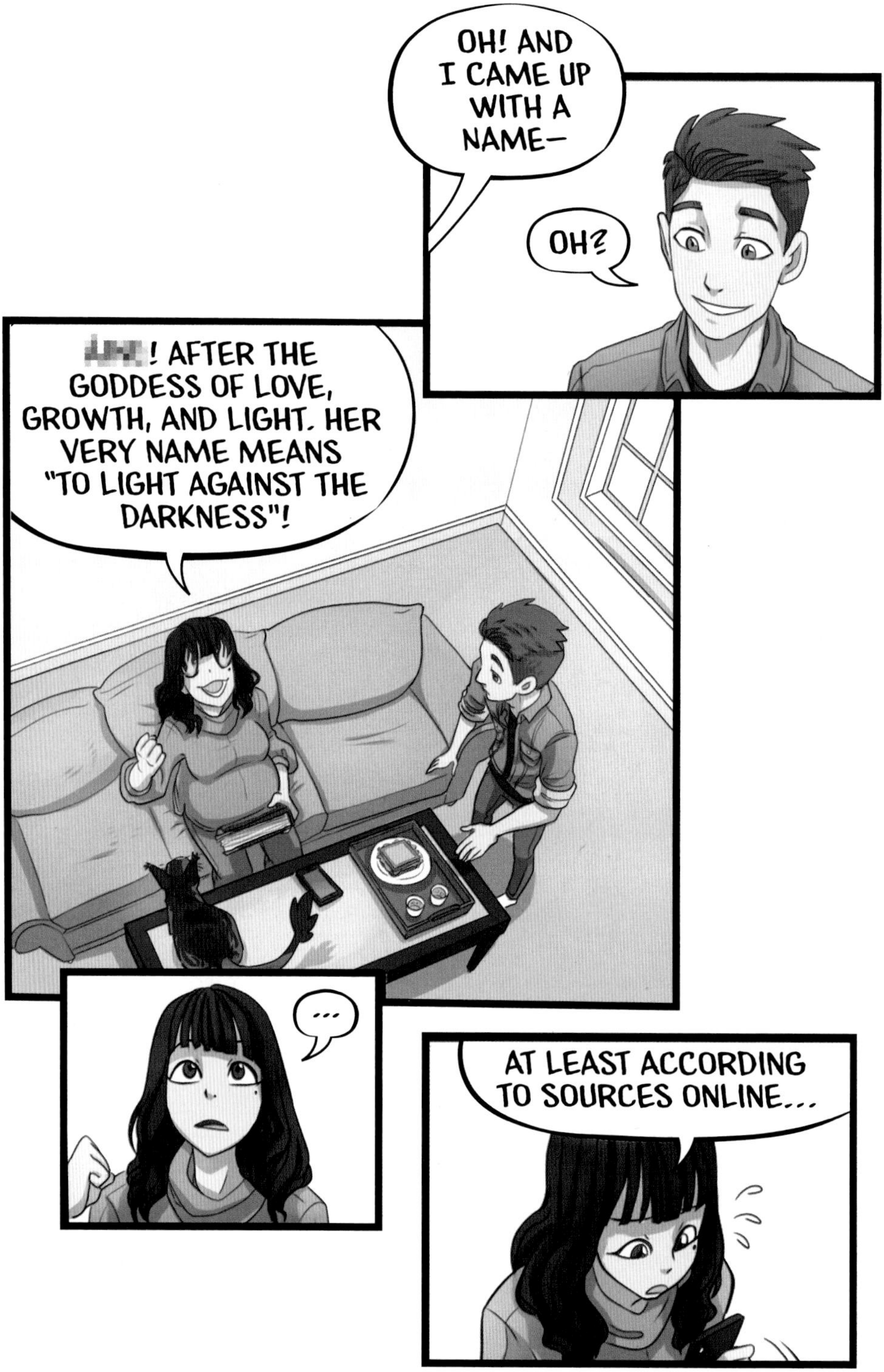
OH! AND I CAME UP WITH A NAME–
OH?
[redacted]! AFTER THE GODDESS OF LOVE, GROWTH, AND LIGHT. HER VERY NAME MEANS "TO LIGHT AGAINST THE DARKNESS"!
...
AT LEAST ACCORDING TO SOURCES ONLINE...

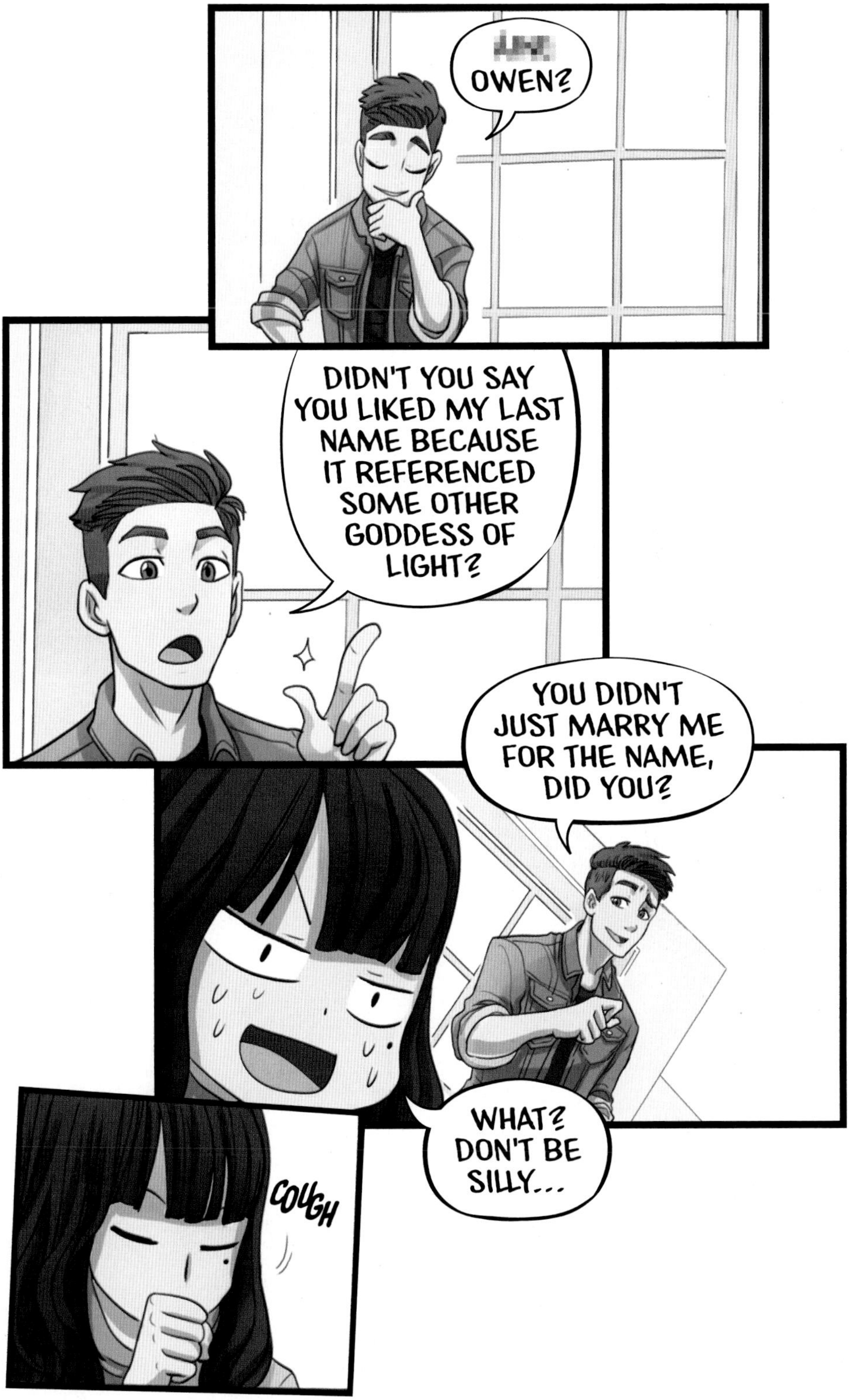
OWEN?
DIDN'T YOU SAY YOU LIKED MY LAST NAME BECAUSE IT REFERENCED SOME OTHER GODDESS OF LIGHT?
YOU DIDN'T JUST MARRY ME FOR THE NAME, DID YOU?
WHAT? DON'T BE SILLY...
COUGH

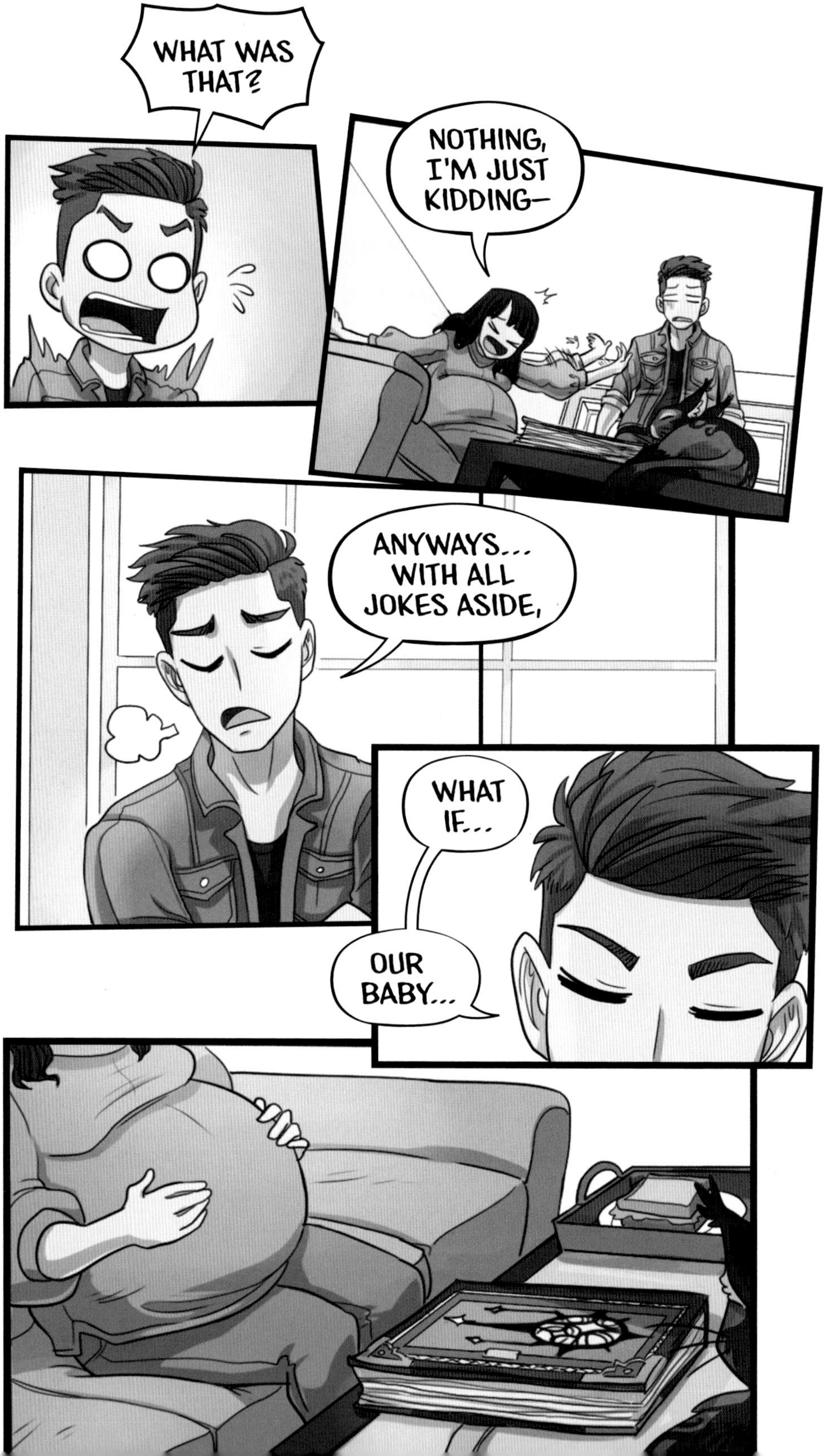
WHAT WAS THAT?
NOTHING, I'M JUST KIDDING—
ANYWAYS... WITH ALL JOKES ASIDE,
WHAT IF...
OUR BABY...

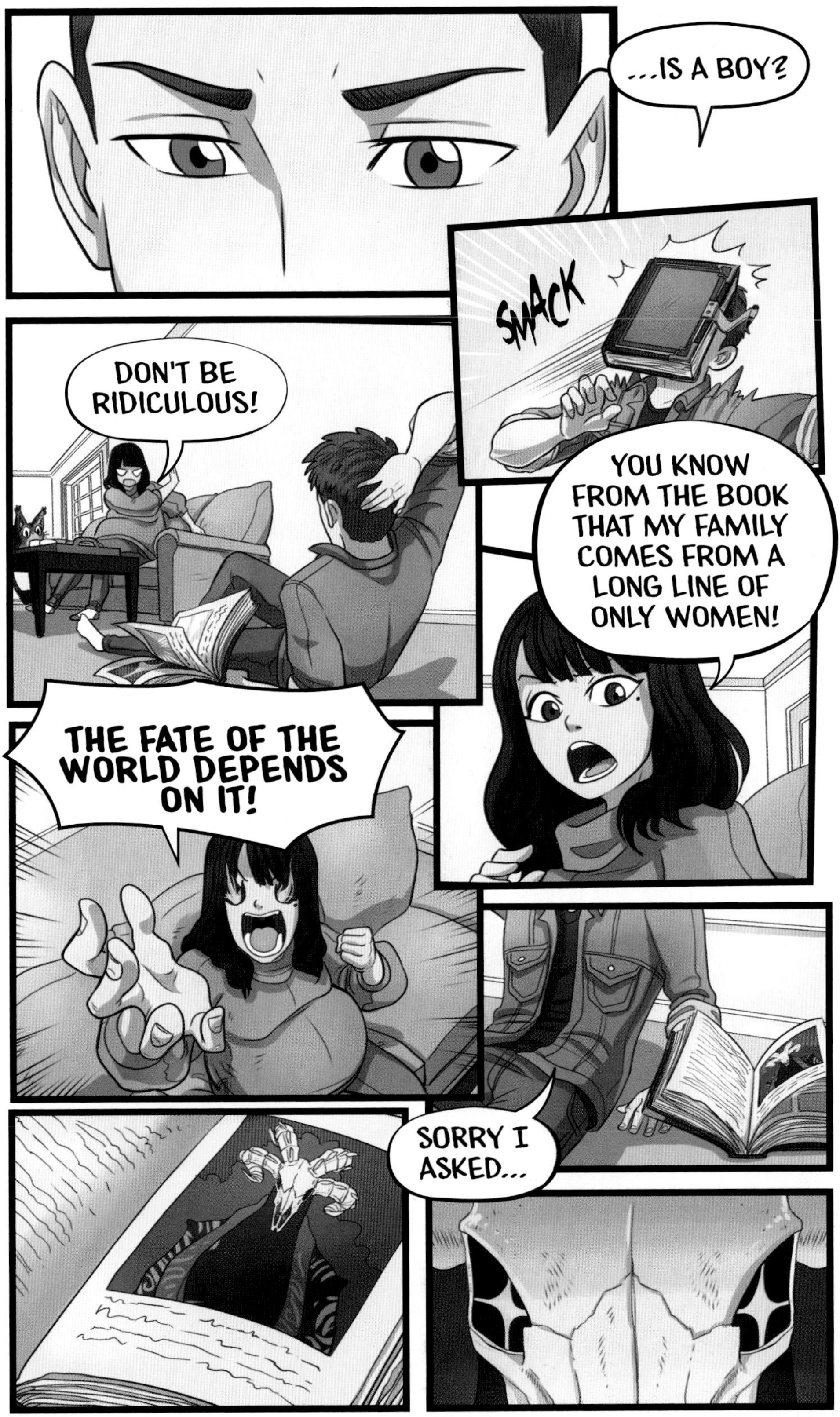
...IS A BOY?
SMACK
DON'T BE RIDICULOUS!
YOU KNOW FROM THE BOOK THAT MY FAMILY COMES FROM A LONG LINE OF ONLY WOMEN!
THE FATE OF THE WORLD DEPENDS ON IT!
SORRY I ASKED...

Episode 4:
MOMENT OF TRUTH

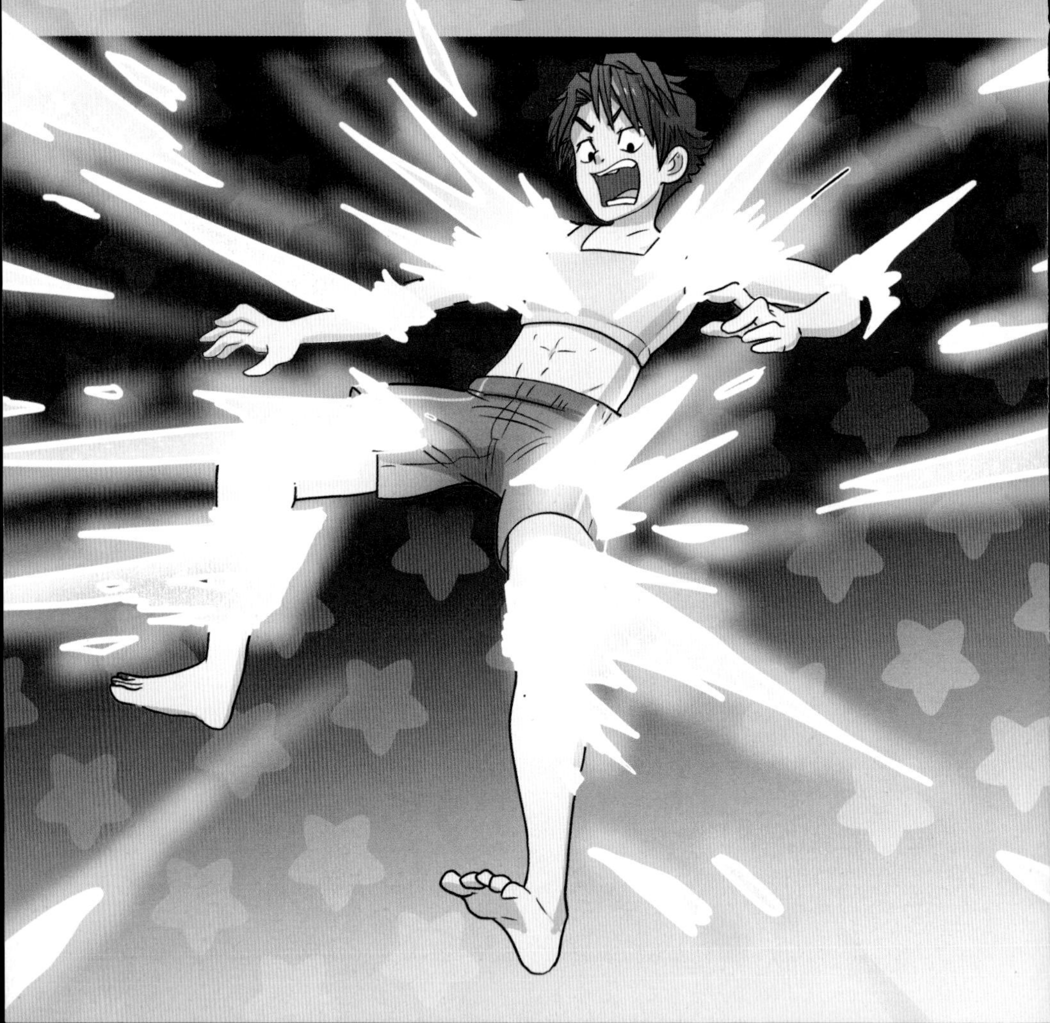

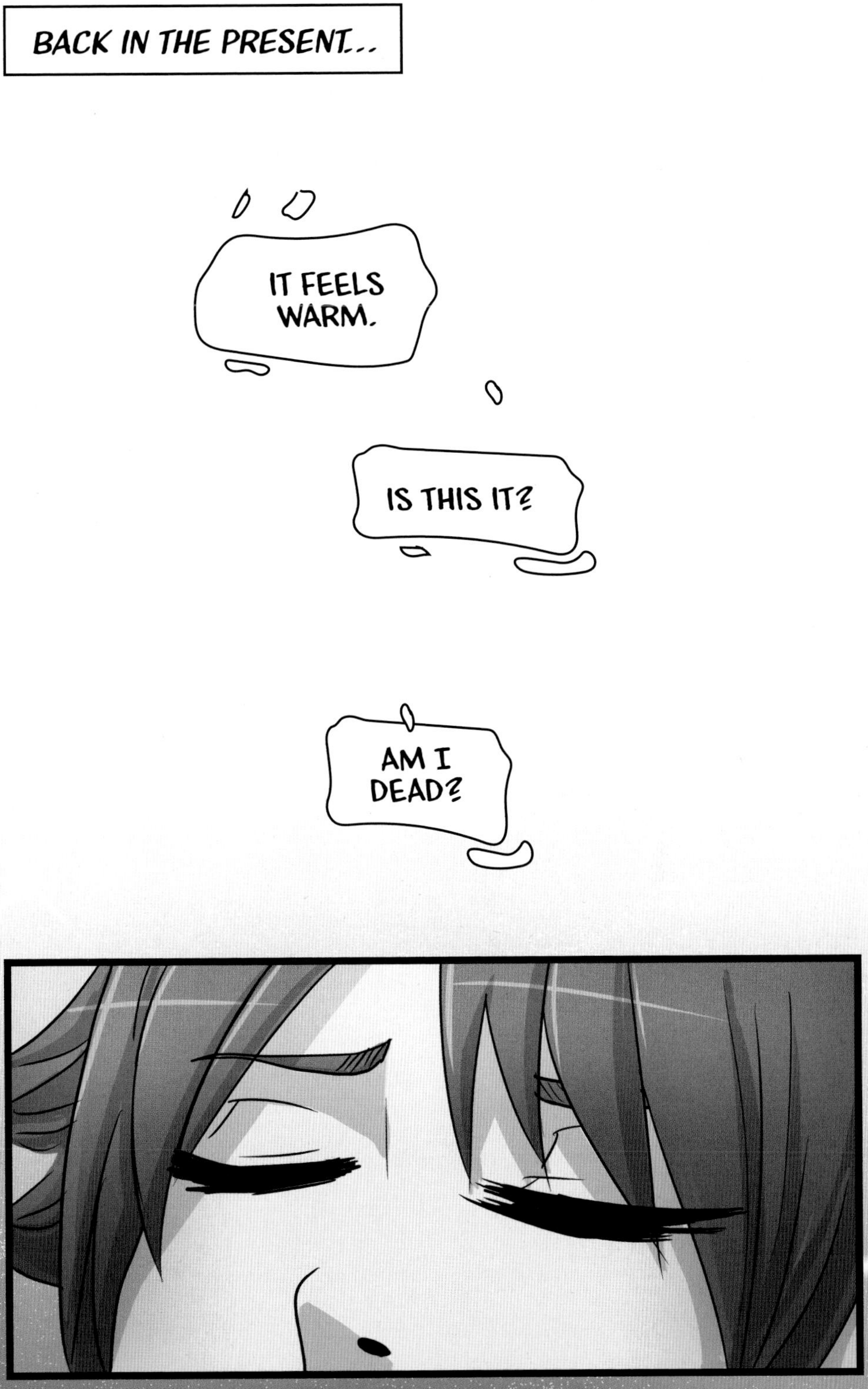
BACK IN THE PRESENT...
IT FEELS WARM.
IS THIS IT?
AM I DEAD?

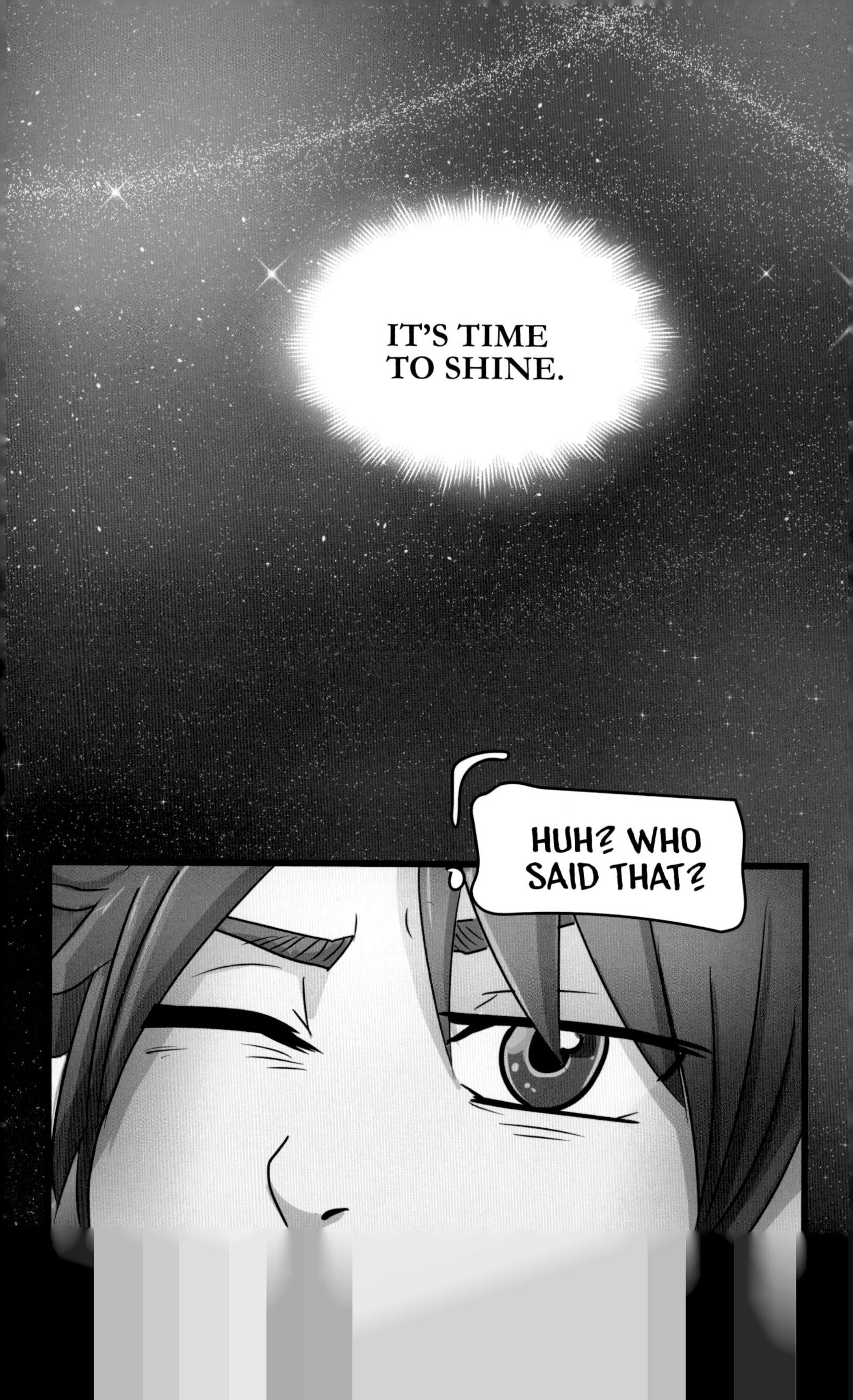
IT'S TIME
TO SHINE.
HUH? WHO
SAID THAT?

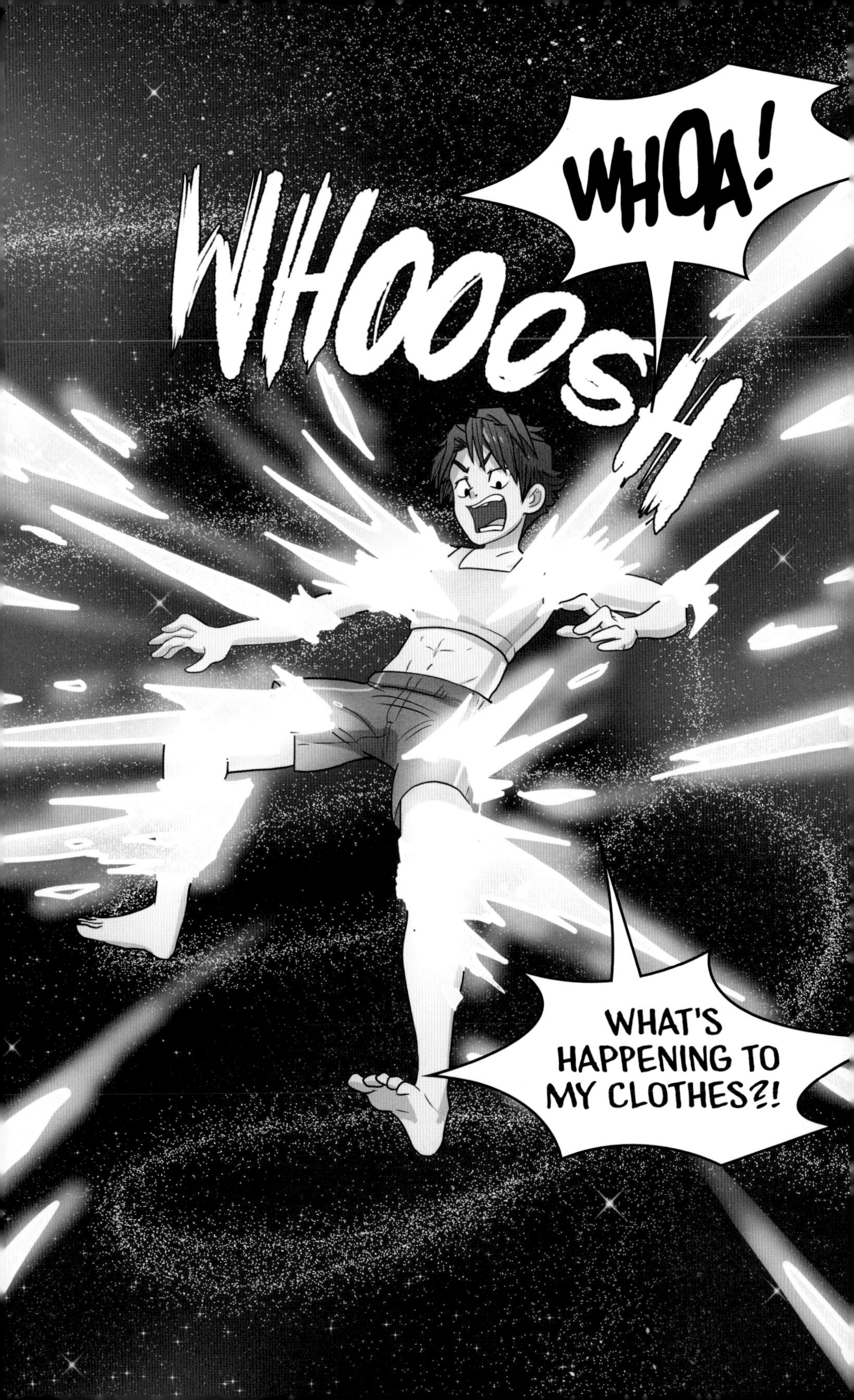
WHOOOSH
WHOA!
WHAT'S HAPPENING TO MY CLOTHES?!

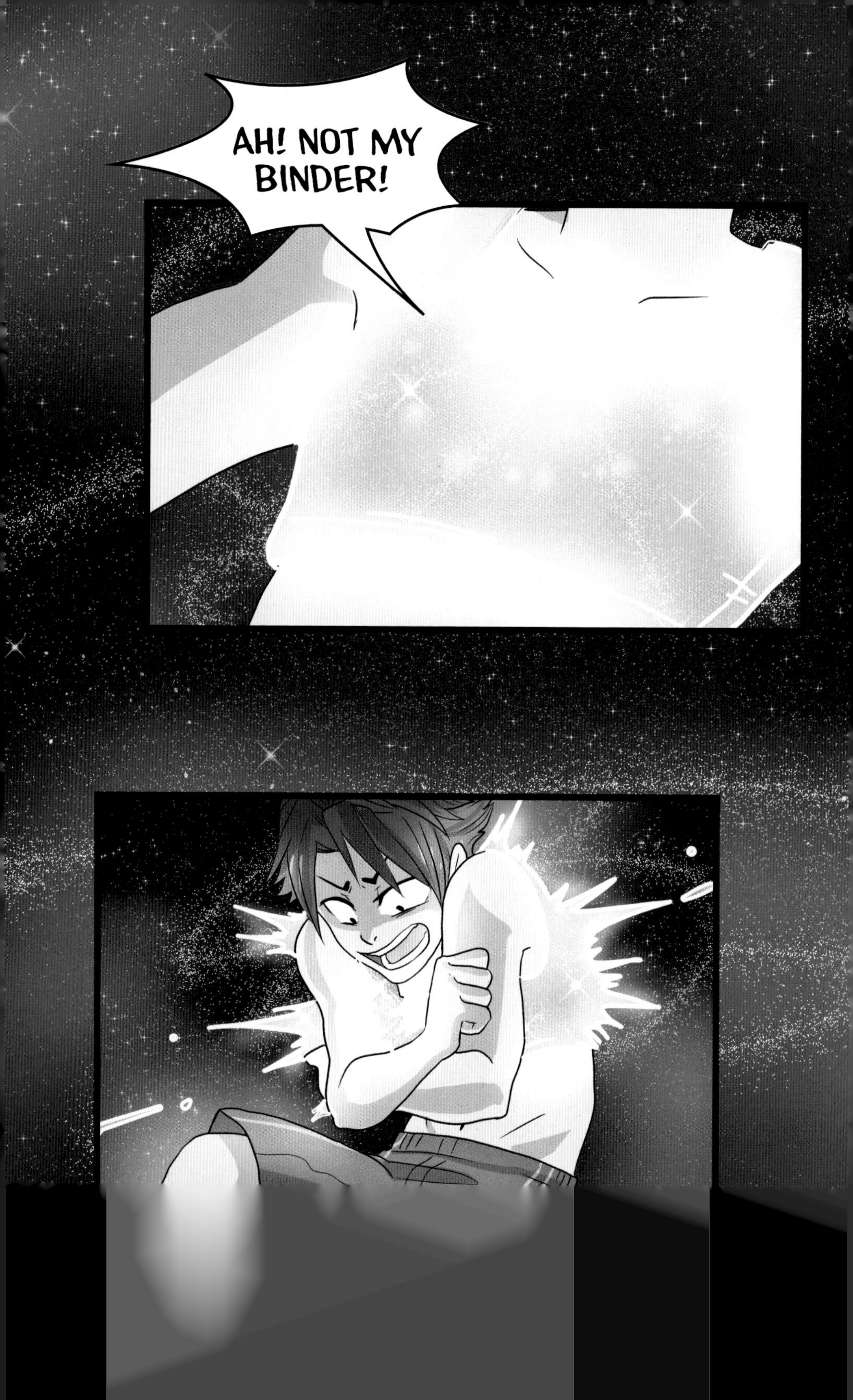
AH! NOT MY BINDER!

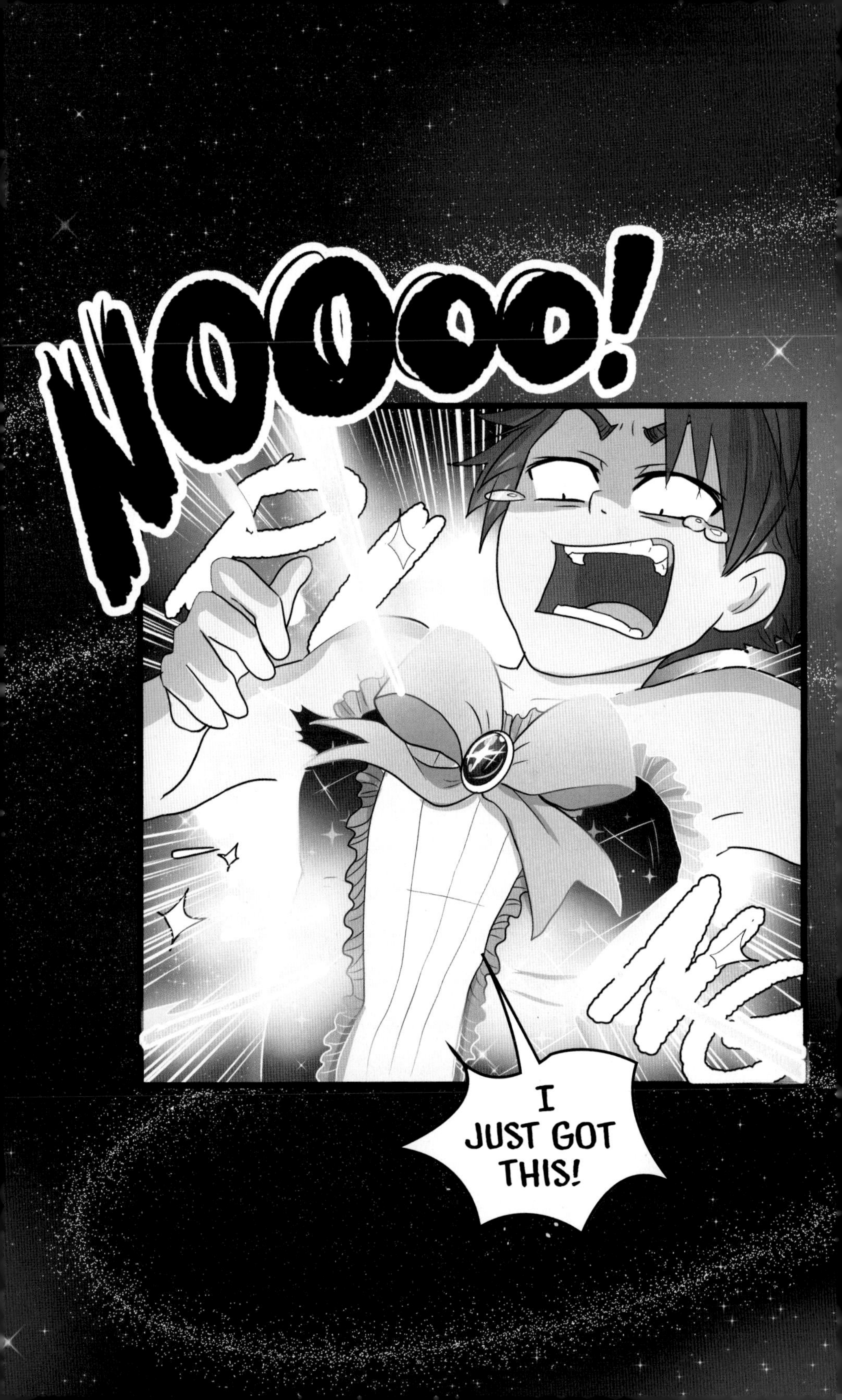
NOOOOO!
I JUST GOT THIS!

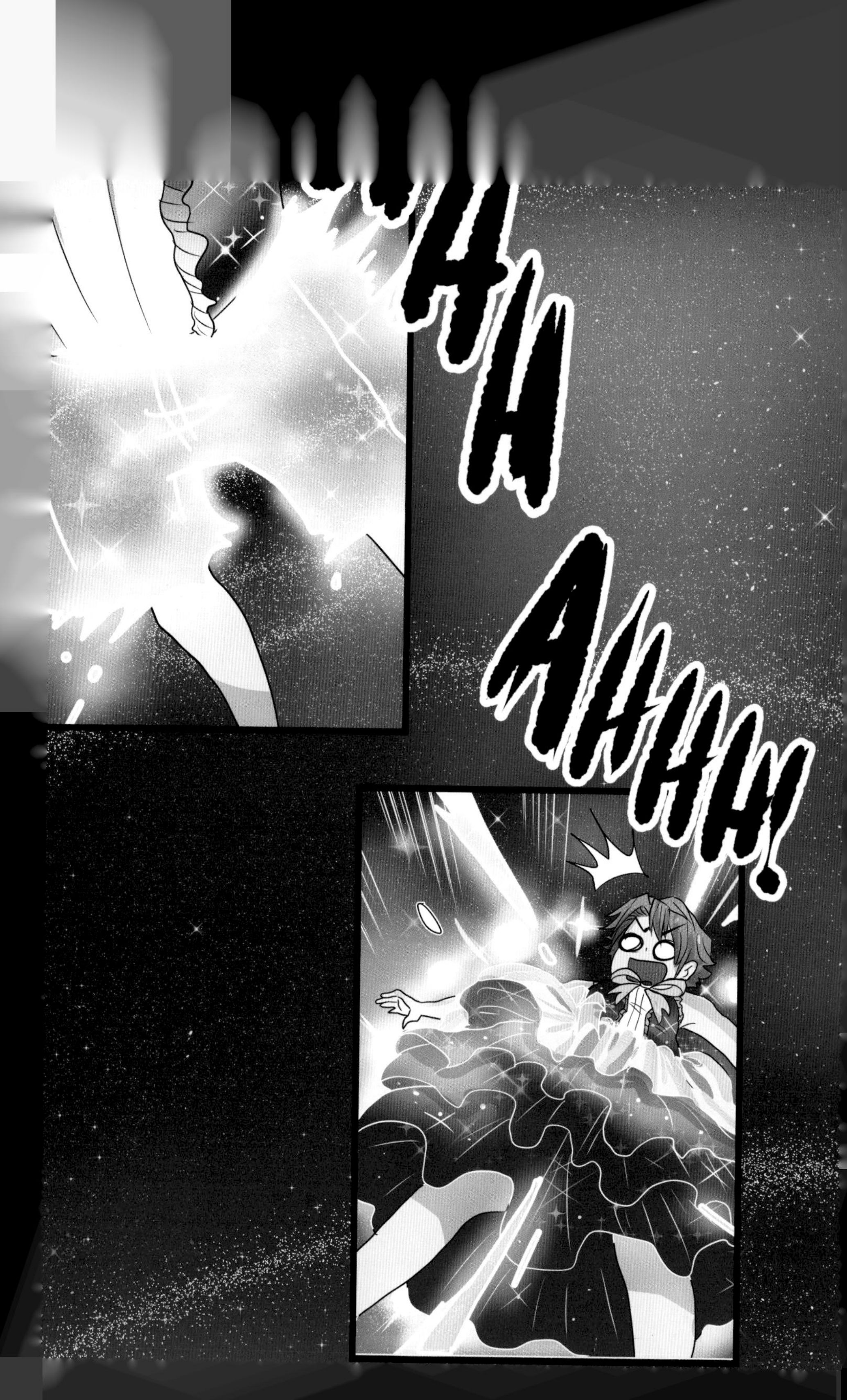
HHAHHHH!

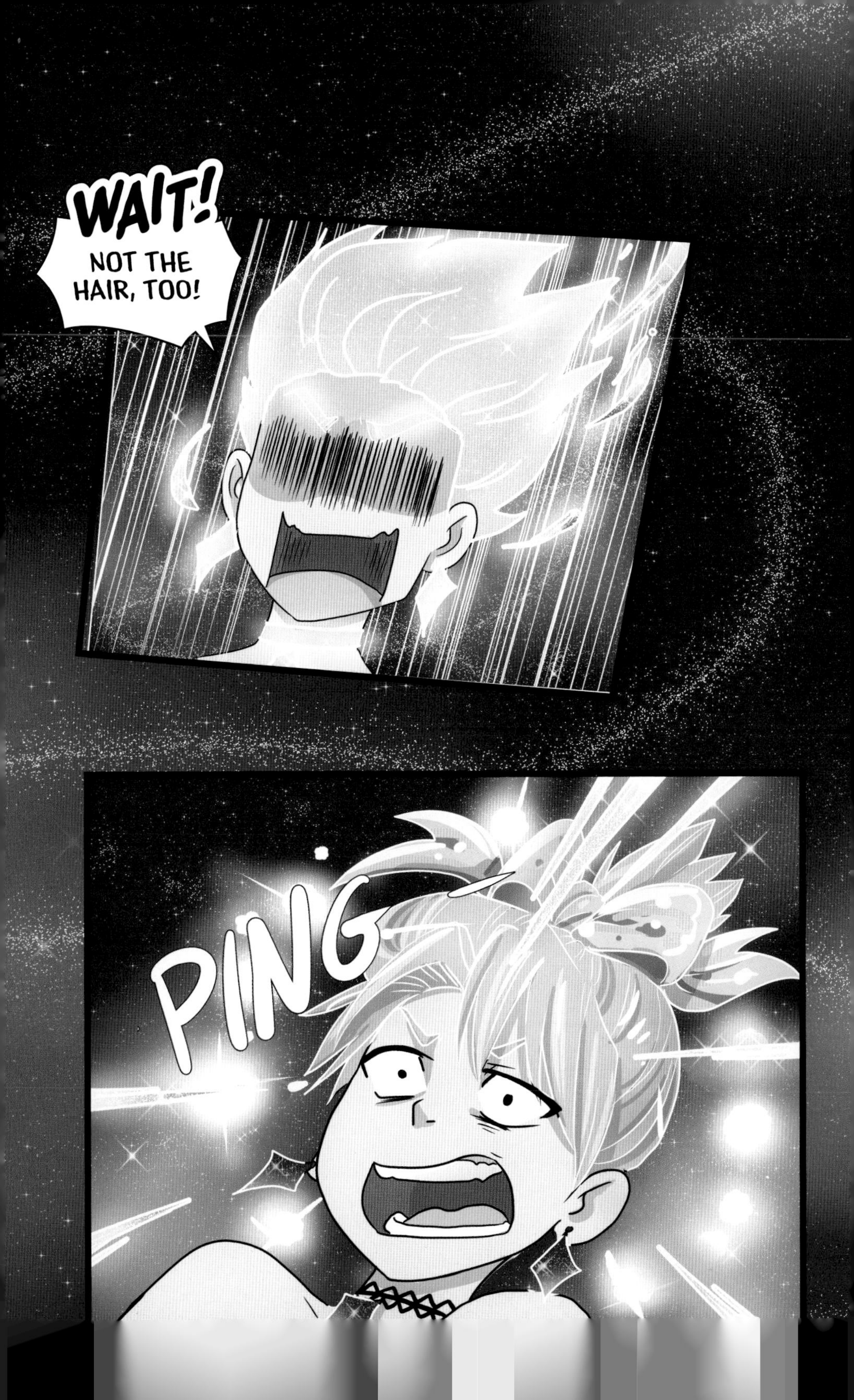
WAIT!
NOT THE HAIR, TOO!
PING

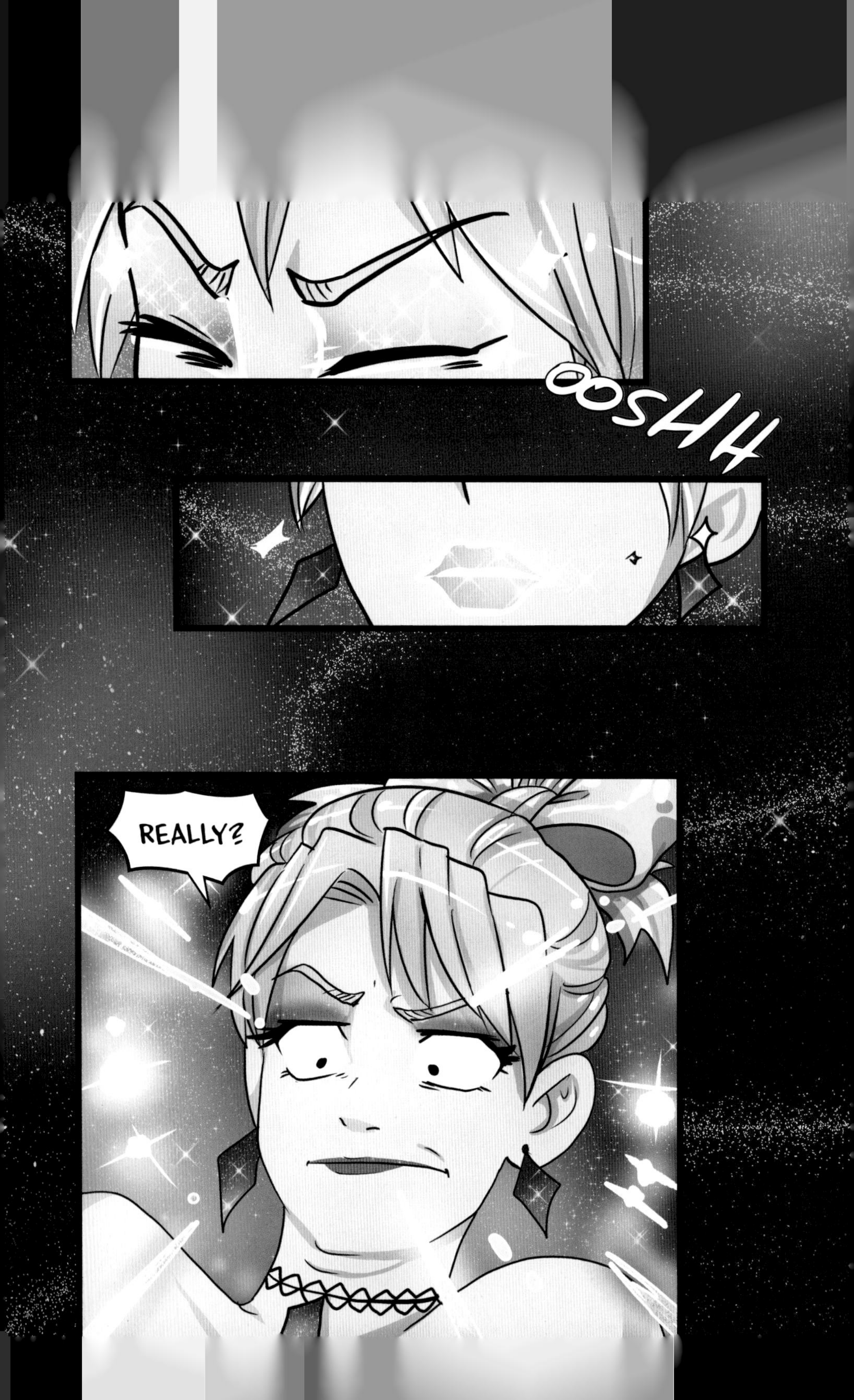

OOSHH
REALLY?

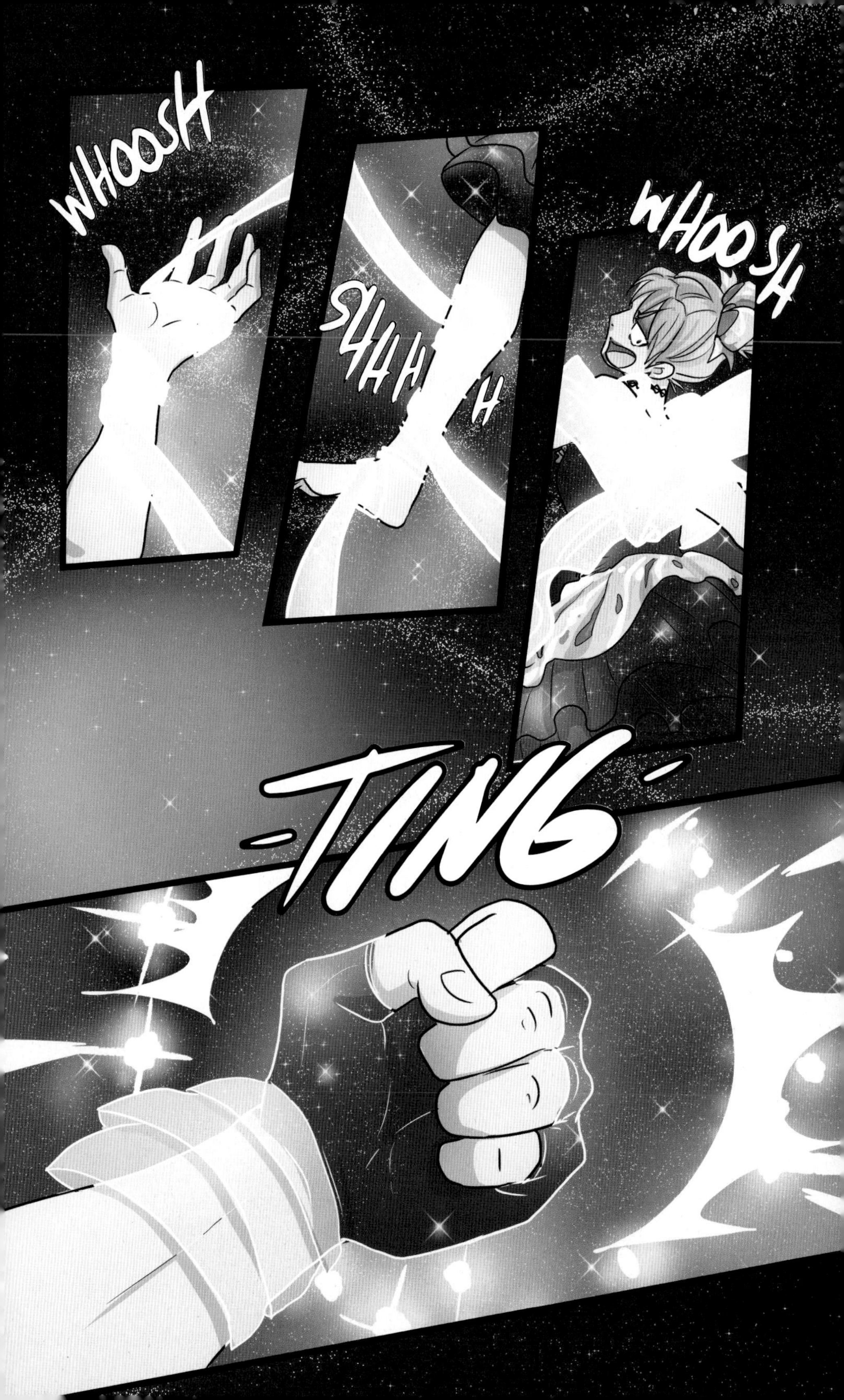
WHOOSH
SHHHH
WHOOSH
-TING-

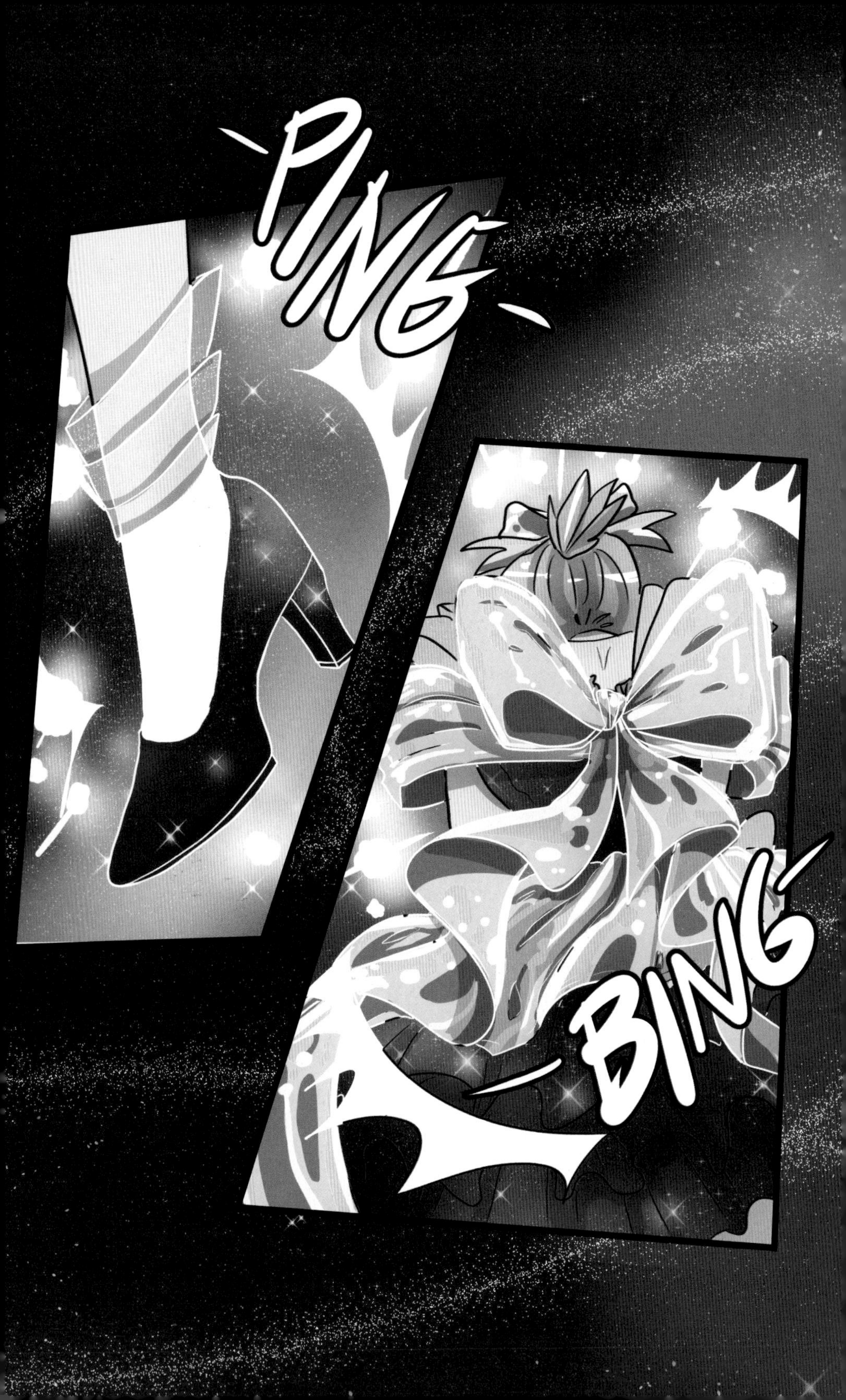
PING
BING

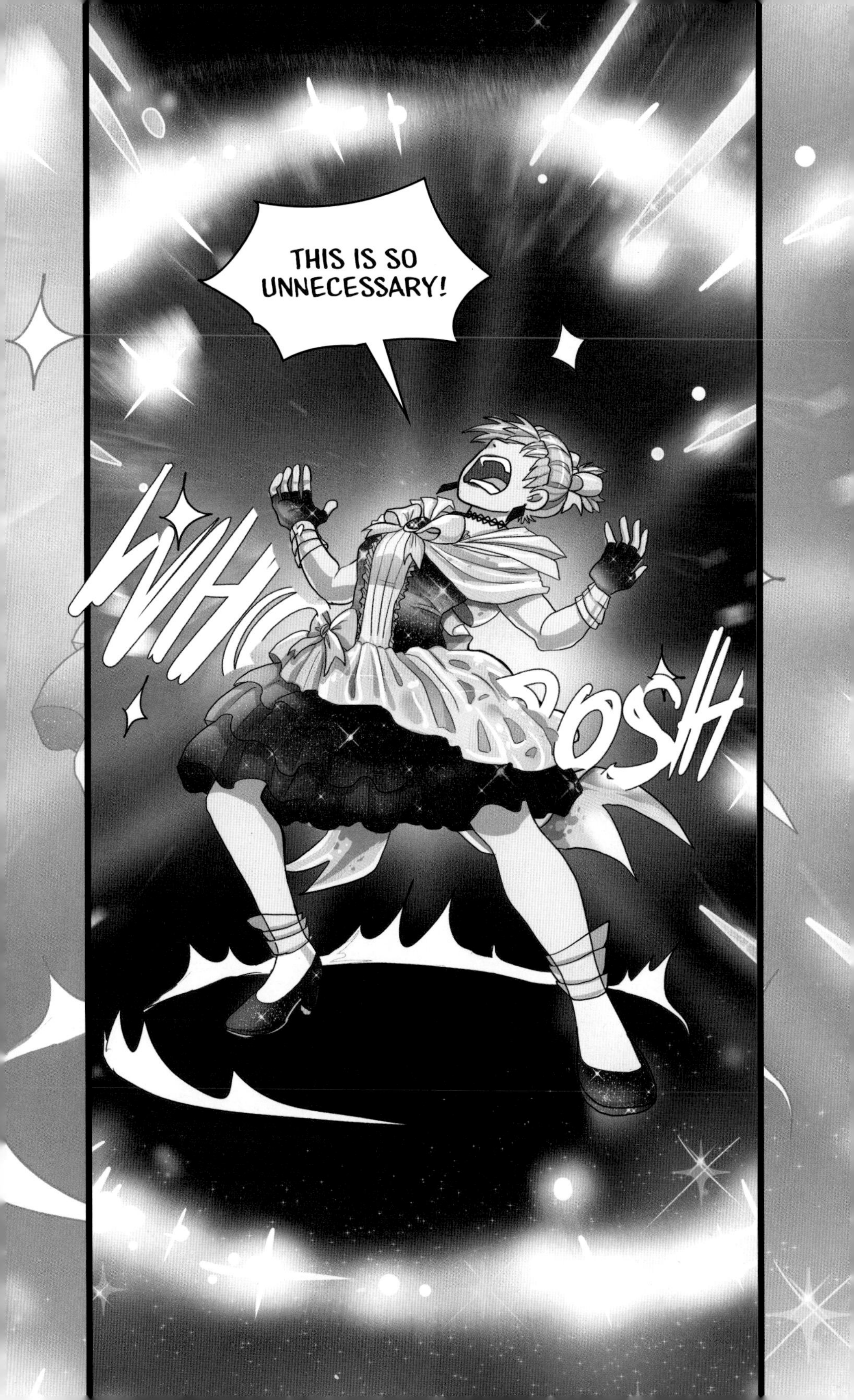
THIS IS SO UNNECESSARY!

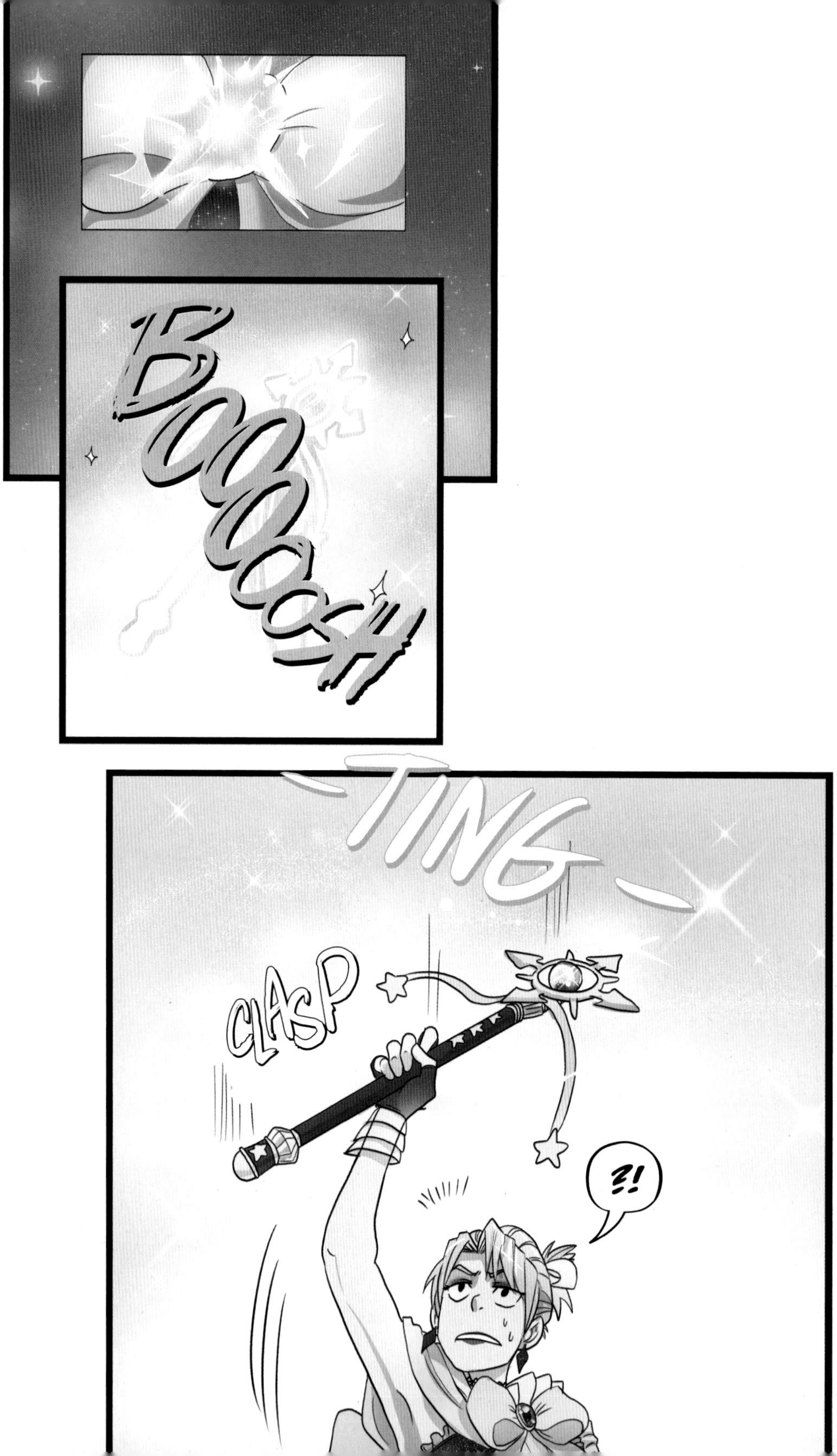
BOOOOOSH
TING
CLASP
?!

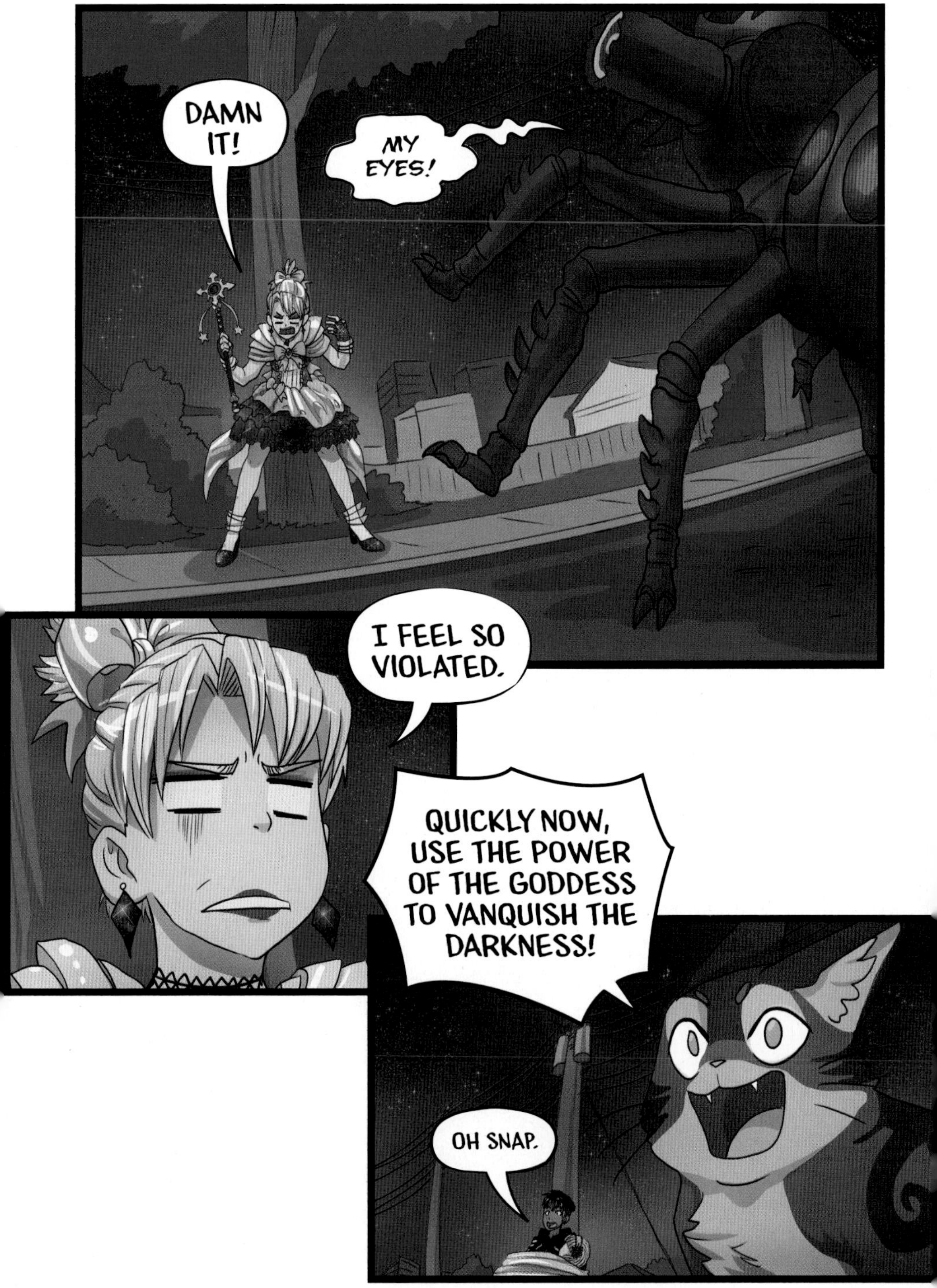

DAMN IT!
MY EYES!
I FEEL SO VIOLATED.
QUICKLY NOW, USE THE POWER OF THE GODDESS TO VANQUISH THE DARKNESS!
OH SNAP.

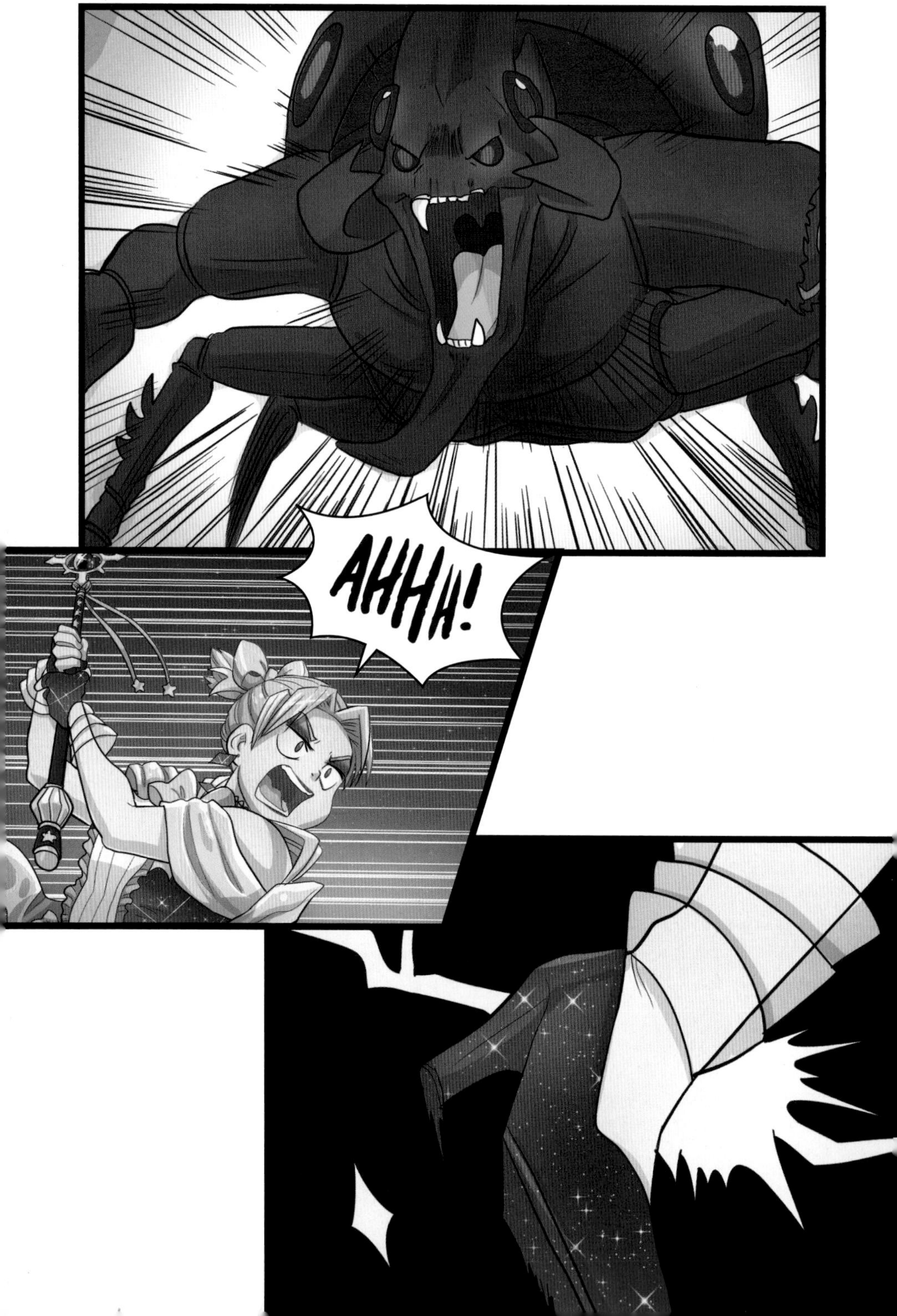
AHHH!

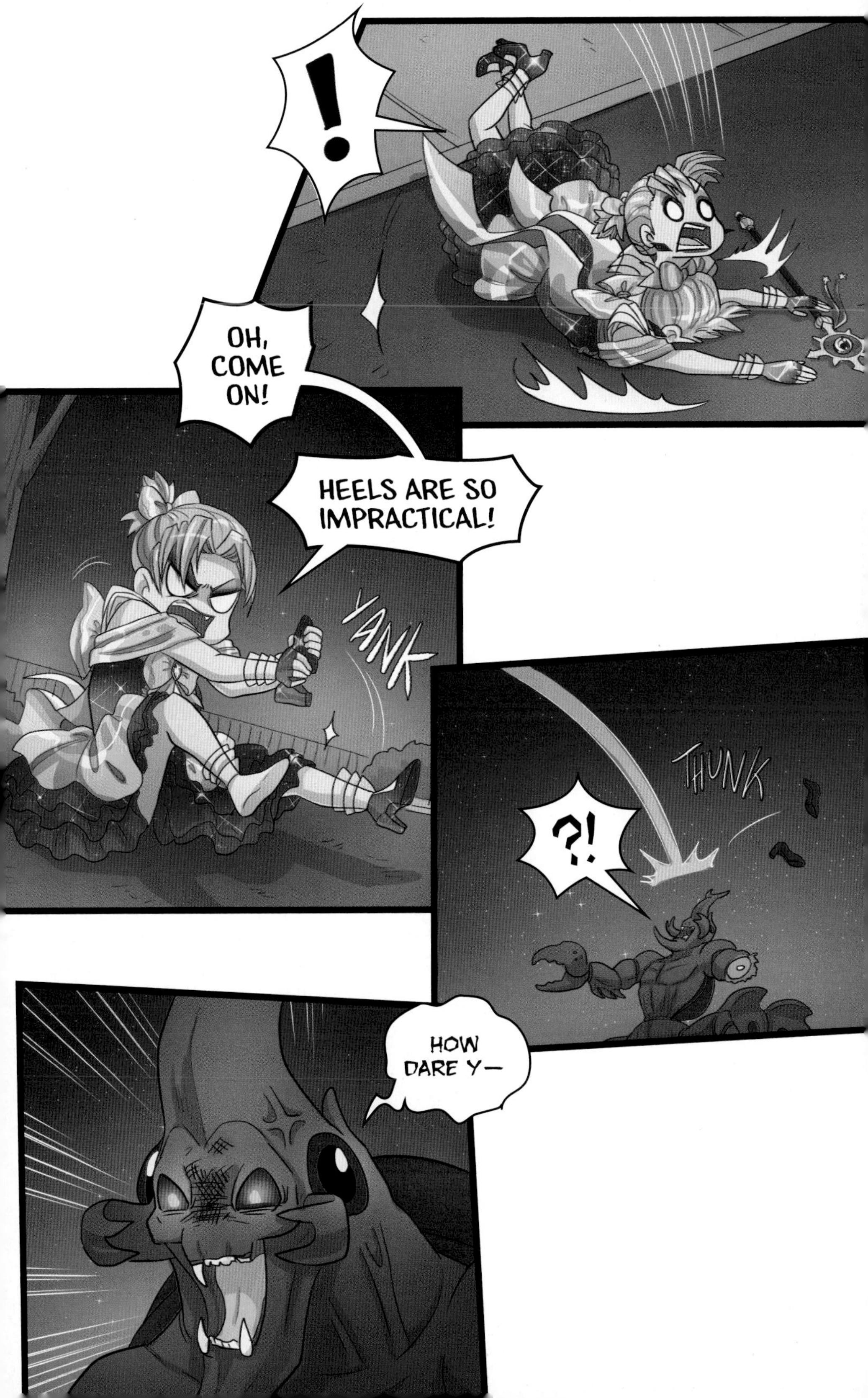
!
OH, COME ON!
HEELS ARE SO IMPRACTICAL!
YANK
THUNK
?!
HOW DARE Y—

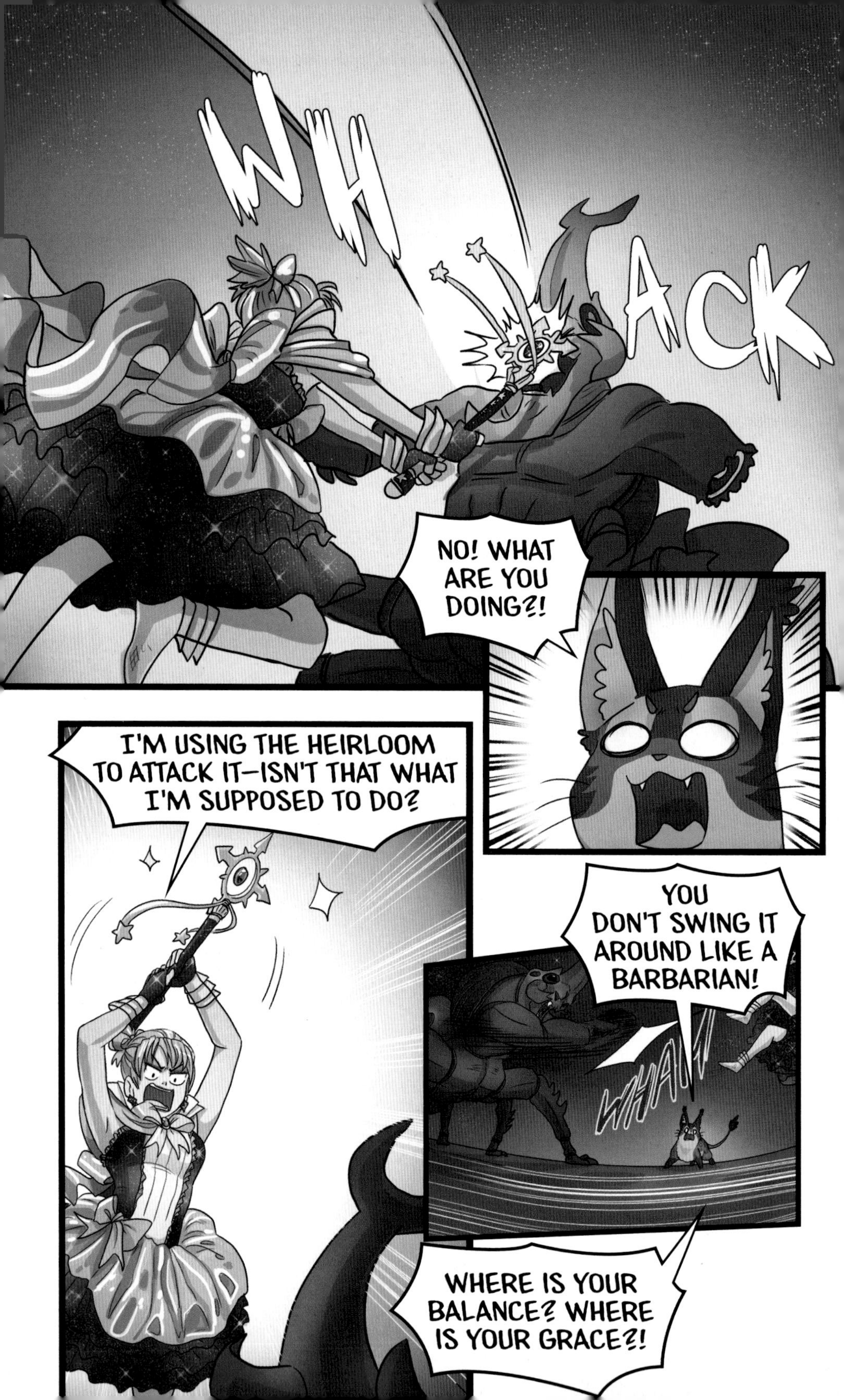
WHACK
NO! WHAT ARE YOU DOING?!
I'M USING THE HEIRLOOM TO ATTACK IT—ISN'T THAT WHAT I'M SUPPOSED TO DO?
YOU DON'T SWING IT AROUND LIKE A BARBARIAN!
WHAM
WHERE IS YOUR BALANCE? WHERE IS YOUR GRACE?!

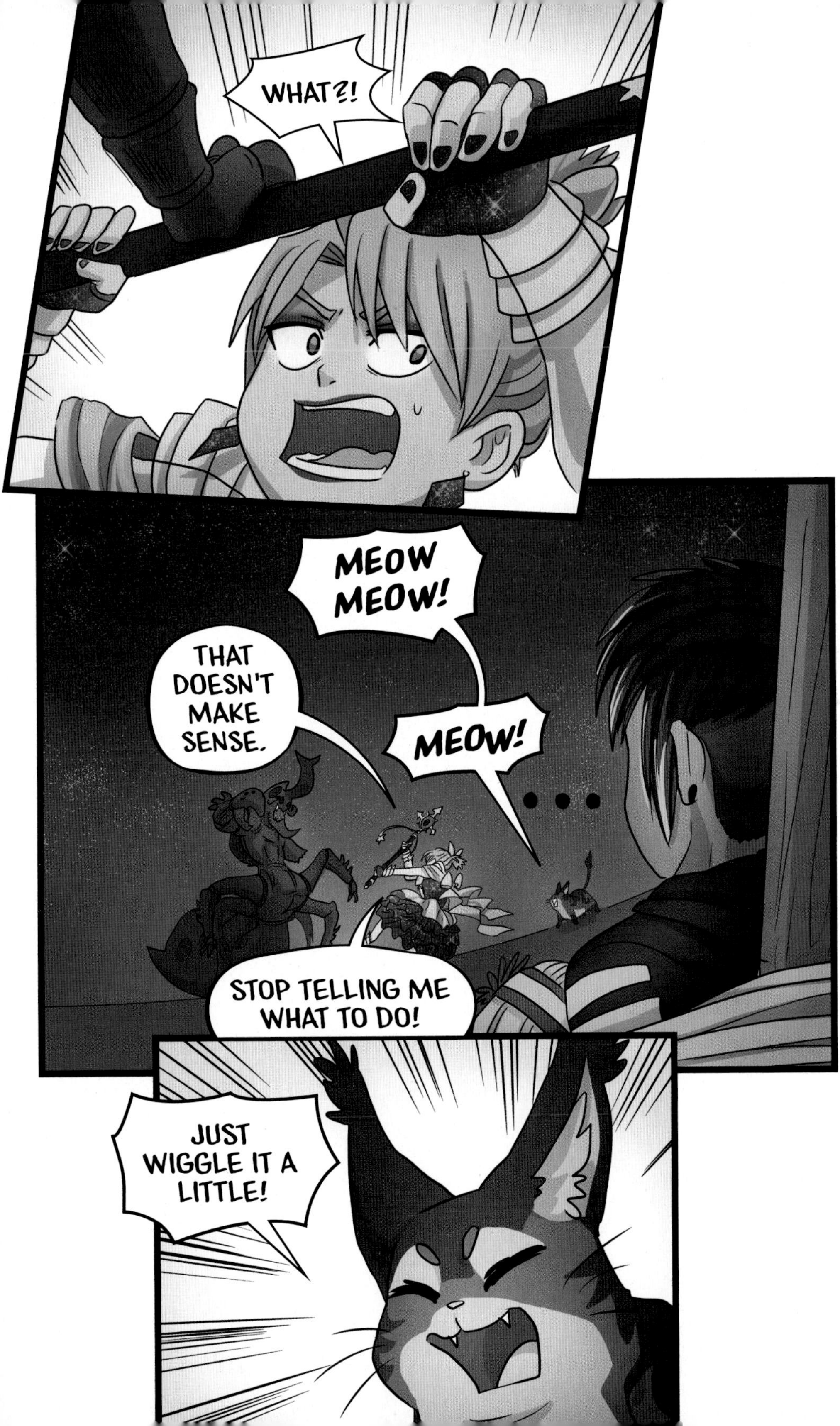
WHAT?!
MEOW MEOW!
THAT DOESN'T MAKE SENSE.
MEOW!
...
STOP TELLING ME WHAT TO DO!
JUST WIGGLE IT A LITTLE!

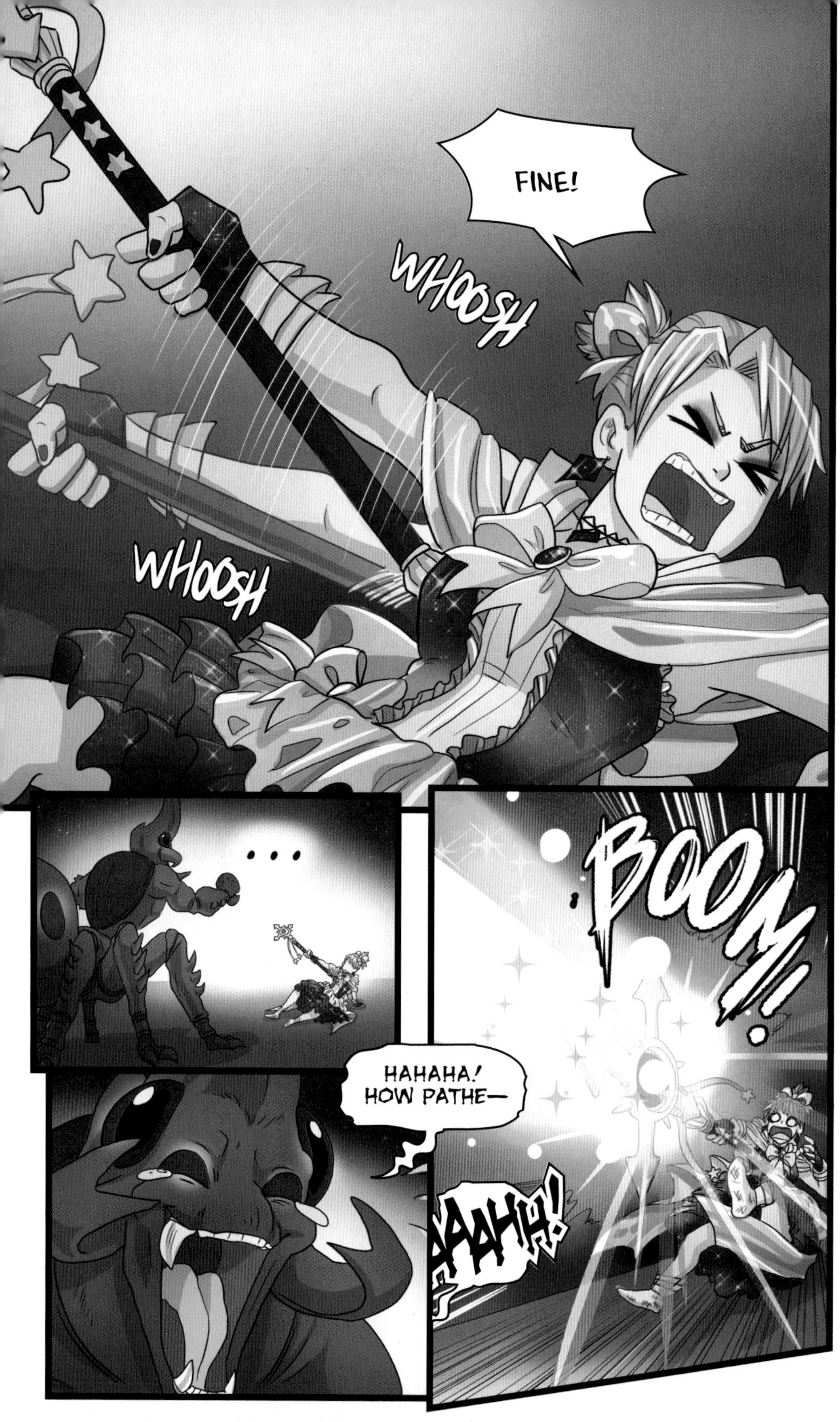
FINE!
WHOOSH
WHOOSH
...
BOOM!!
HAHAHA! HOW PATHE—
AAAHH!

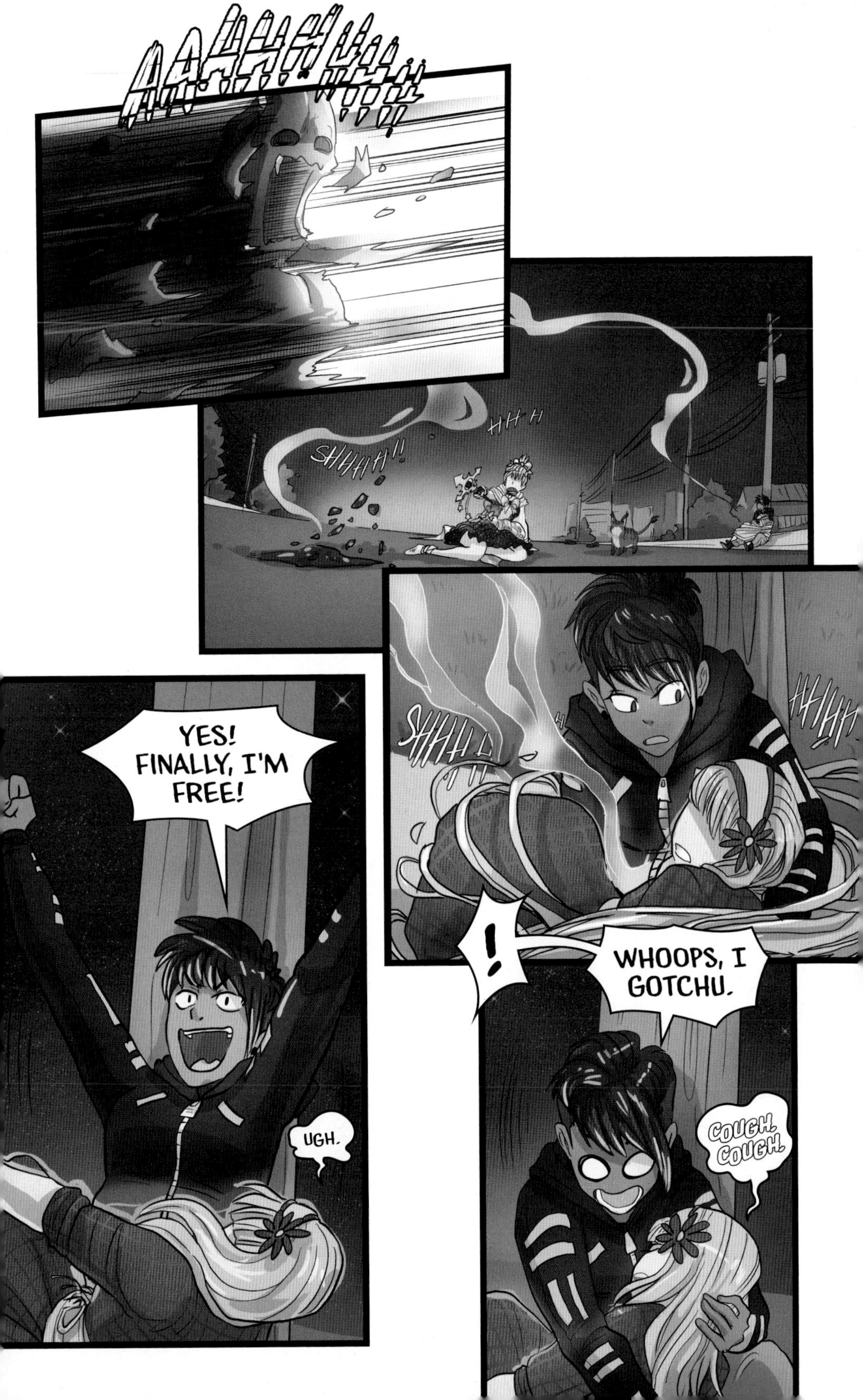
AAAAHHH!!
SHHHH!!
HHH H
SHHHH
HHHH
YES! FINALLY, I'M FREE!
UGH.
!
WHOOPS, I GOTCHU.
COUGH COUGH

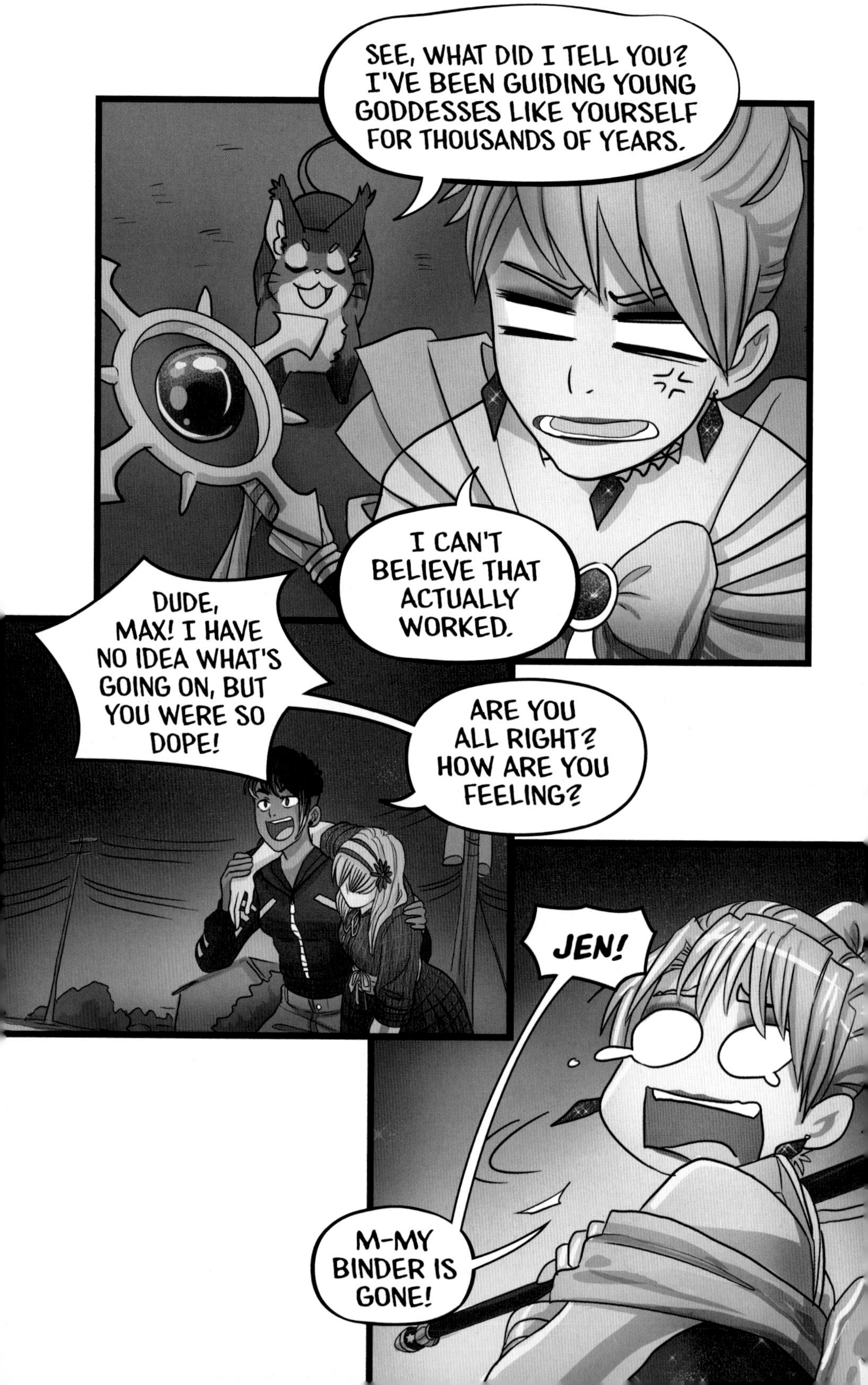
SEE, WHAT DID I TELL YOU? I'VE BEEN GUIDING YOUNG GODDESSES LIKE YOURSELF FOR THOUSANDS OF YEARS.
I CAN'T BELIEVE THAT ACTUALLY WORKED.
DUDE, MAX! I HAVE NO IDEA WHAT'S GOING ON, BUT YOU WERE SO DOPE!
ARE YOU ALL RIGHT? HOW ARE YOU FEELING?
JEN!
M-MY BINDER IS GONE!

Episode 5:
TROUBLES WITHIN

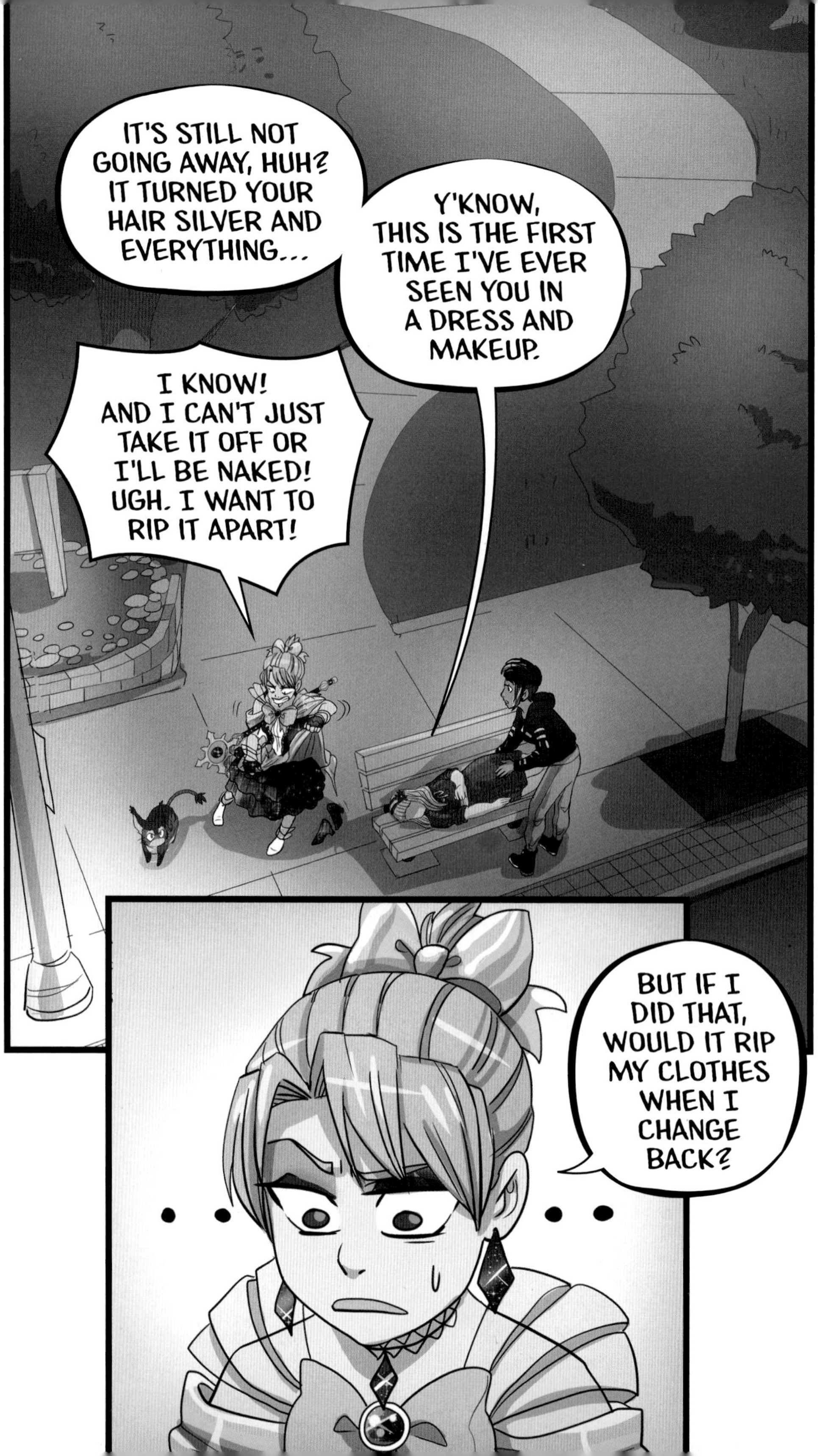
IT'S STILL NOT GOING AWAY, HUH? IT TURNED YOUR HAIR SILVER AND EVERYTHING...
Y'KNOW, THIS IS THE FIRST TIME I'VE EVER SEEN YOU IN A DRESS AND MAKEUP.
I KNOW! AND I CAN'T JUST TAKE IT OFF OR I'LL BE NAKED! UGH. I WANT TO RIP IT APART!
BUT IF I DID THAT, WOULD IT RIP MY CLOTHES WHEN I CHANGE BACK?
...
...

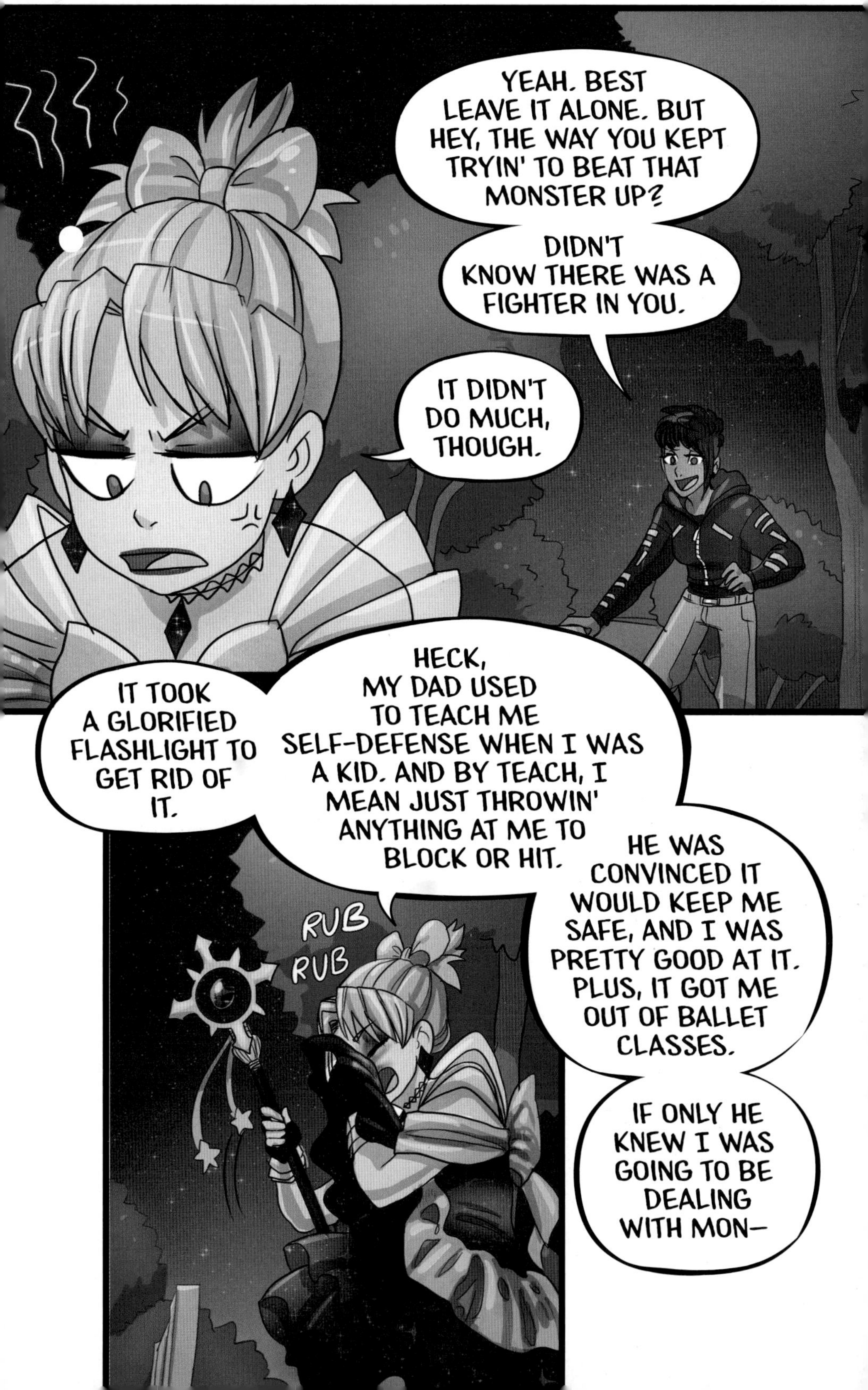
YEAH. BEST LEAVE IT ALONE. BUT HEY, THE WAY YOU KEPT TRYIN' TO BEAT THAT MONSTER UP?
DIDN'T KNOW THERE WAS A FIGHTER IN YOU.
IT DIDN'T DO MUCH, THOUGH.
IT TOOK A GLORIFIED FLASHLIGHT TO GET RID OF IT.
HECK, MY DAD USED TO TEACH ME SELF-DEFENSE WHEN I WAS A KID. AND BY TEACH, I MEAN JUST THROWIN' ANYTHING AT ME TO BLOCK OR HIT.
HE WAS CONVINCED IT WOULD KEEP ME SAFE, AND I WAS PRETTY GOOD AT IT. PLUS, IT GOT ME OUT OF BALLET CLASSES.
RUB
RUB
IF ONLY HE KNEW I WAS GOING TO BE DEALING WITH MON—

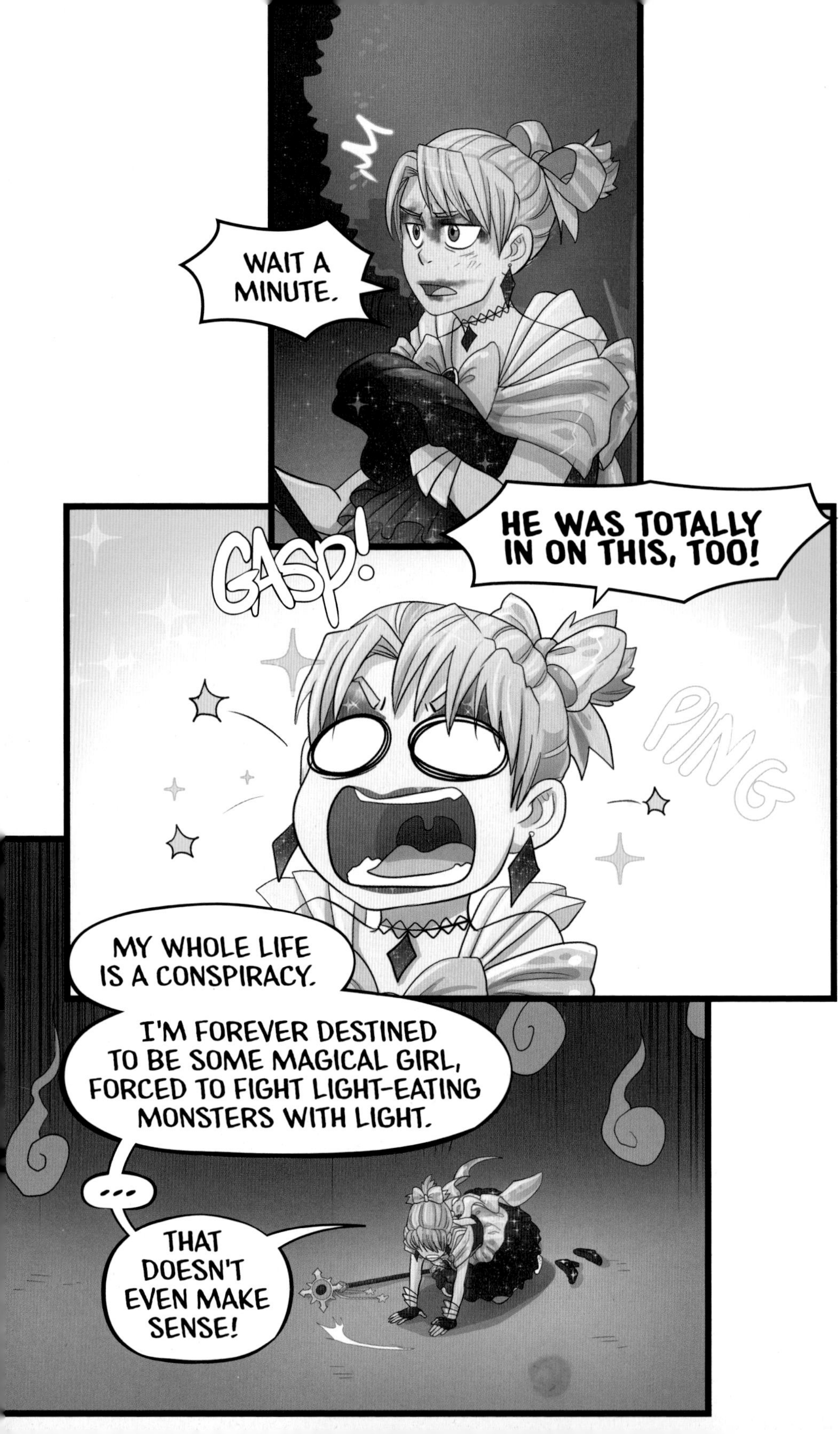

WAIT A MINUTE.
GASP!
HE WAS TOTALLY IN ON THIS, TOO!
PING
MY WHOLE LIFE IS A CONSPIRACY.
I'M FOREVER DESTINED TO BE SOME MAGICAL GIRL, FORCED TO FIGHT LIGHT-EATING MONSTERS WITH LIGHT.
...
THAT DOESN'T EVEN MAKE SENSE!

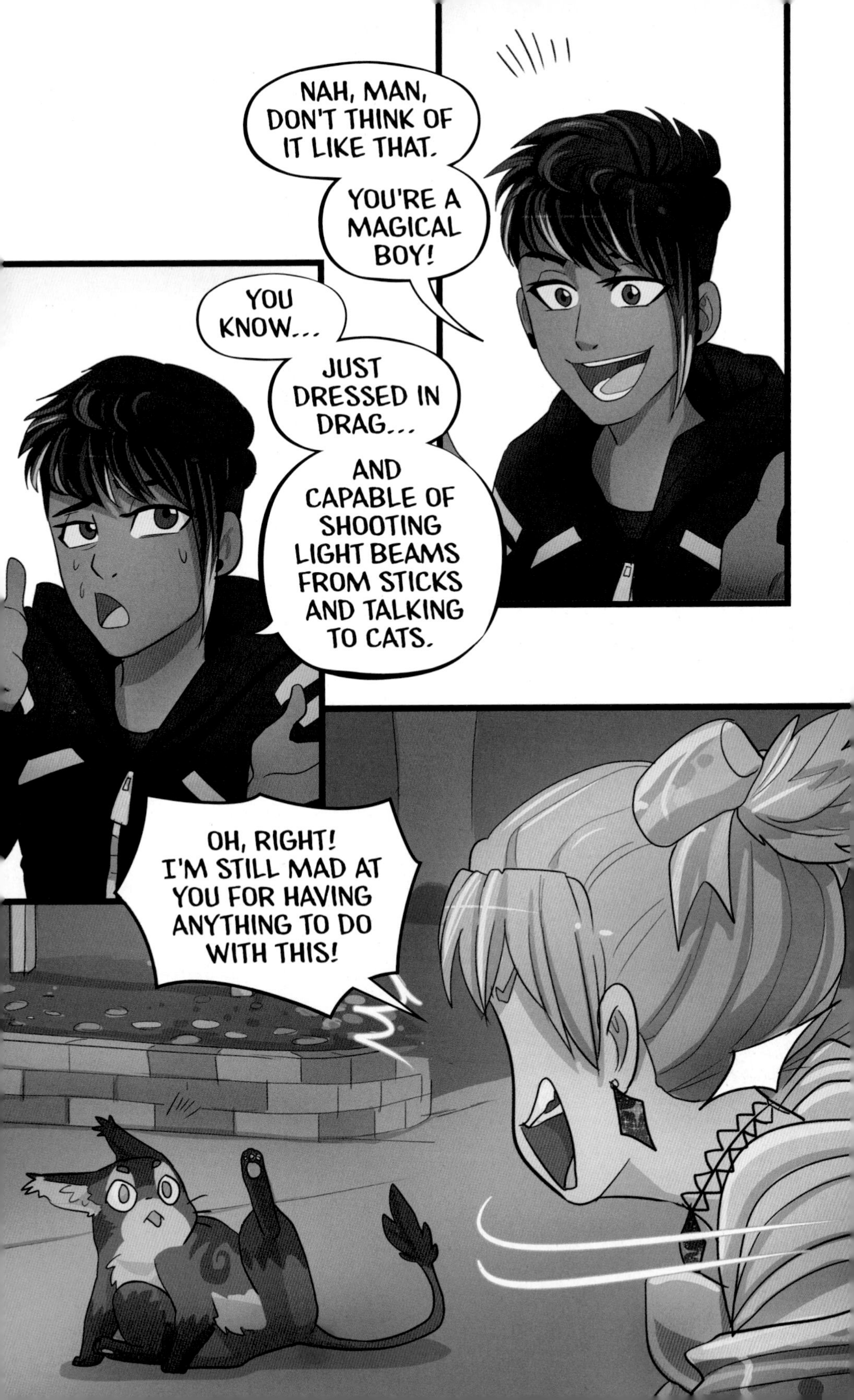
NAH, MAN, DON'T THINK OF IT LIKE THAT.
YOU'RE A MAGICAL BOY!
YOU KNOW...
JUST DRESSED IN DRAG...
AND CAPABLE OF SHOOTING LIGHT BEAMS FROM STICKS AND TALKING TO CATS.
OH, RIGHT! I'M STILL MAD AT YOU FOR HAVING ANYTHING TO DO WITH THIS!

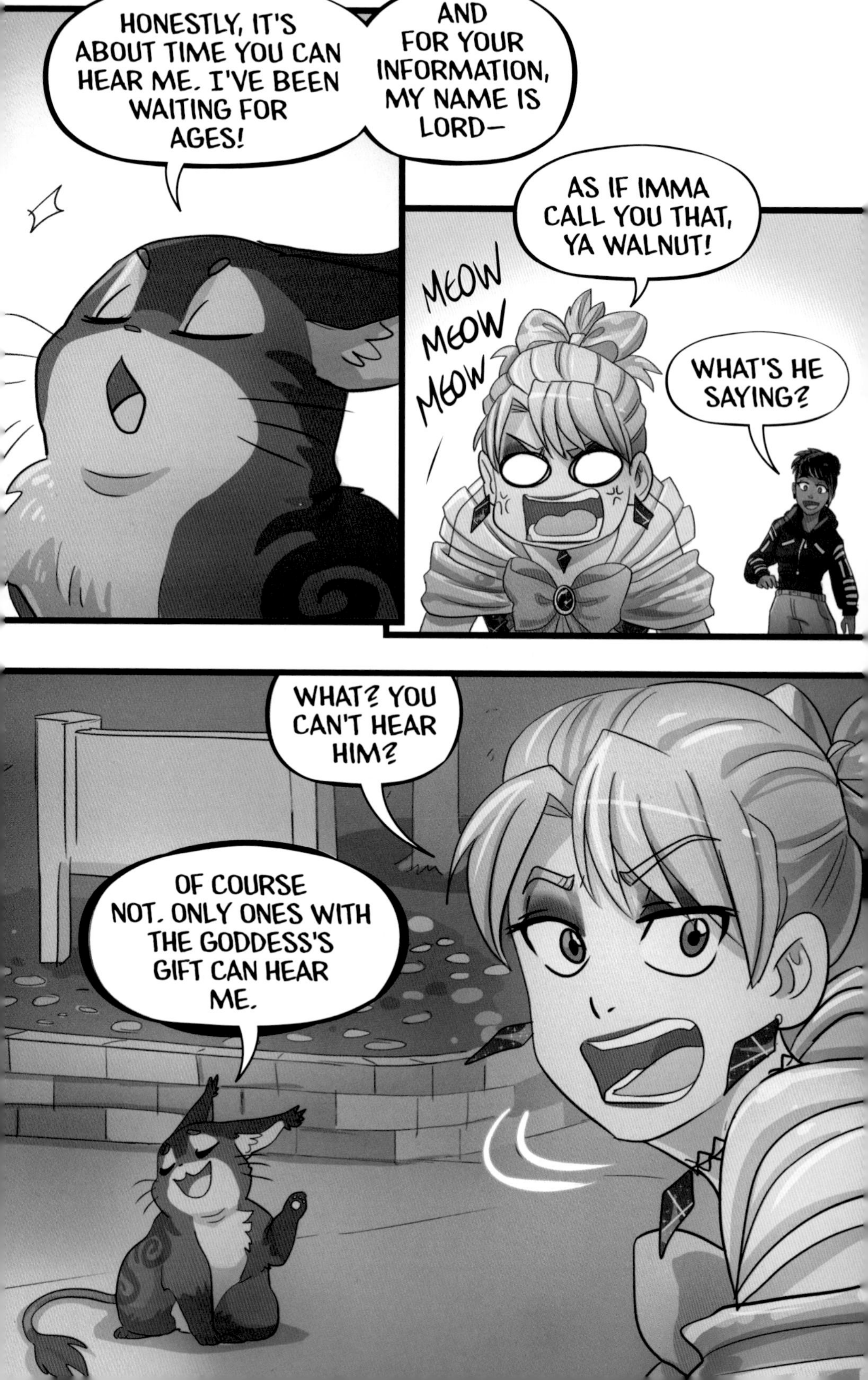
HONESTLY, IT'S ABOUT TIME YOU CAN HEAR ME. I'VE BEEN WAITING FOR AGES!
AND FOR YOUR INFORMATION, MY NAME IS LORD—
AS IF IMMA CALL YOU THAT, YA WALNUT!
MEOW MEOW MEOW
WHAT'S HE SAYING?
WHAT? YOU CAN'T HEAR HIM?
OF COURSE NOT. ONLY ONES WITH THE GODDESS'S GIFT CAN HEAR ME.

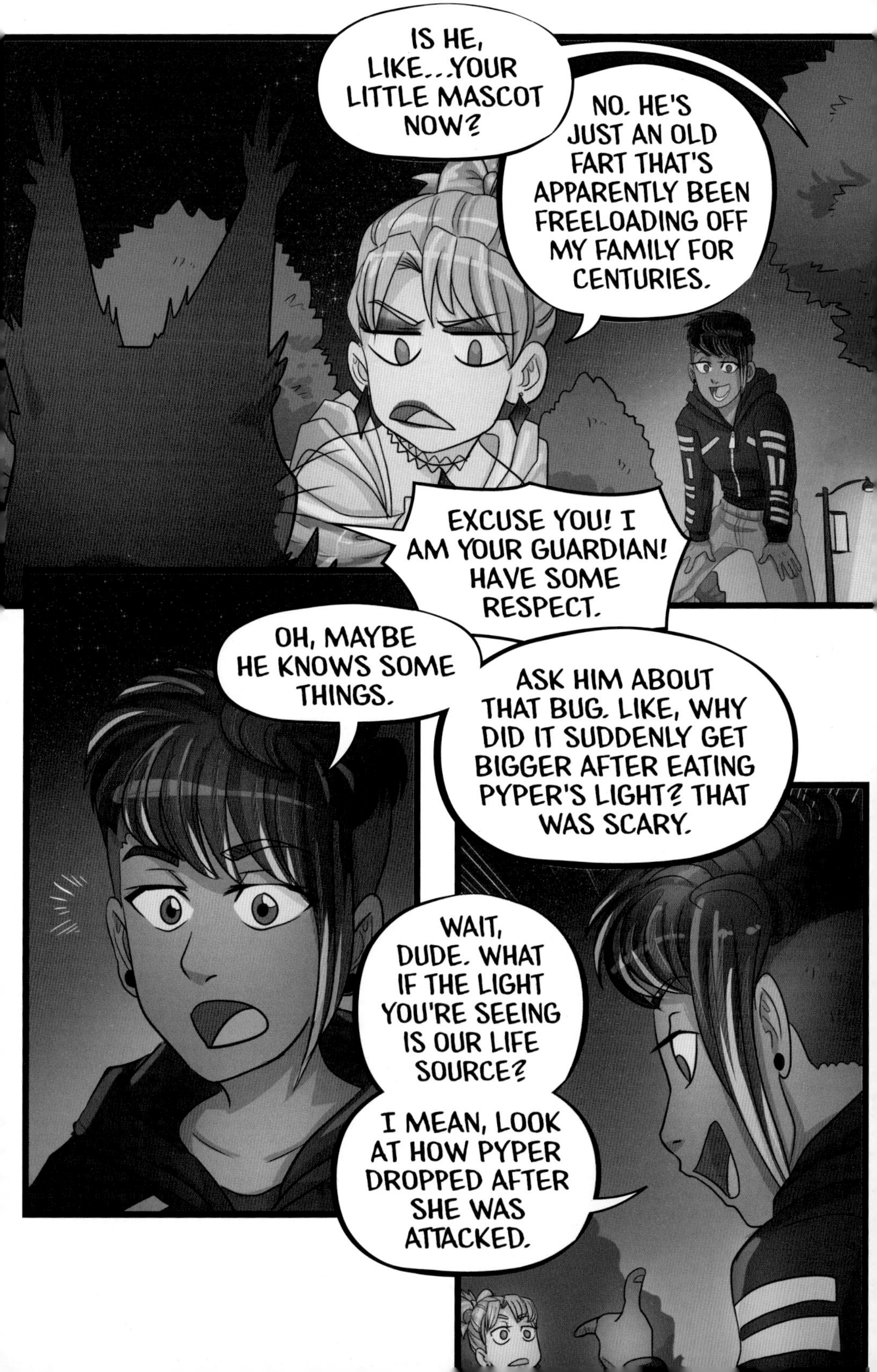
IS HE, LIKE...YOUR LITTLE MASCOT NOW?
NO. HE'S JUST AN OLD FART THAT'S APPARENTLY BEEN FREELOADING OFF MY FAMILY FOR CENTURIES.
EXCUSE YOU! I AM YOUR GUARDIAN! HAVE SOME RESPECT.
OH, MAYBE HE KNOWS SOME THINGS.
ASK HIM ABOUT THAT BUG. LIKE, WHY DID IT SUDDENLY GET BIGGER AFTER EATING PYPER'S LIGHT? THAT WAS SCARY.
WAIT, DUDE. WHAT IF THE LIGHT YOU'RE SEEING IS OUR LIFE SOURCE?
I MEAN, LOOK AT HOW PYPER DROPPED AFTER SHE WAS ATTACKED.

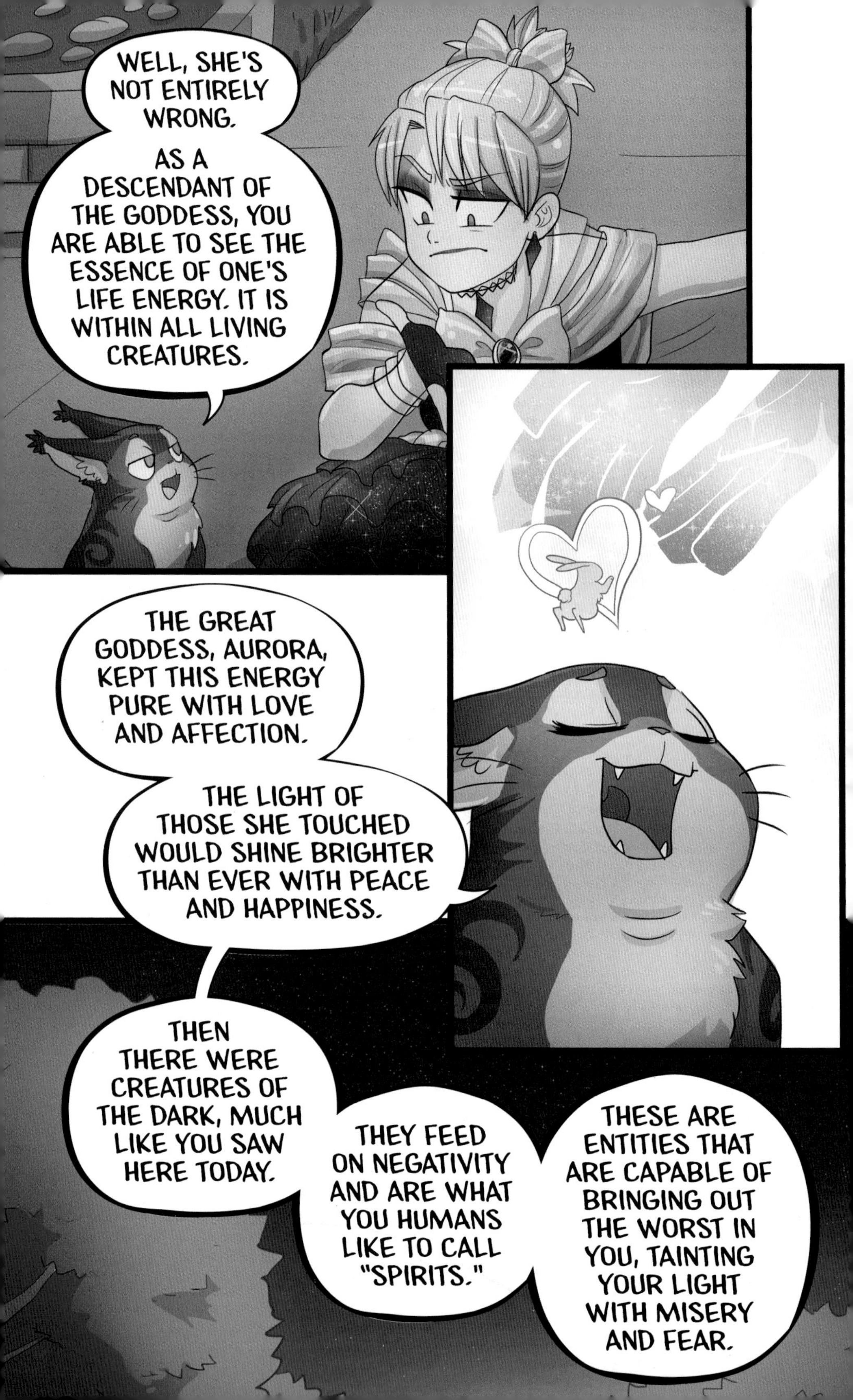
WELL, SHE'S NOT ENTIRELY WRONG.
AS A DESCENDANT OF THE GODDESS, YOU ARE ABLE TO SEE THE ESSENCE OF ONE'S LIFE ENERGY. IT IS WITHIN ALL LIVING CREATURES.
THE GREAT GODDESS, AURORA, KEPT THIS ENERGY PURE WITH LOVE AND AFFECTION.
THE LIGHT OF THOSE SHE TOUCHED WOULD SHINE BRIGHTER THAN EVER WITH PEACE AND HAPPINESS.
THEN THERE WERE CREATURES OF THE DARK, MUCH LIKE YOU SAW HERE TODAY.
THEY FEED ON NEGATIVITY AND ARE WHAT YOU HUMANS LIKE TO CALL "SPIRITS."
THESE ARE ENTITIES THAT ARE CAPABLE OF BRINGING OUT THE WORST IN YOU, TAINTING YOUR LIGHT WITH MISERY AND FEAR.

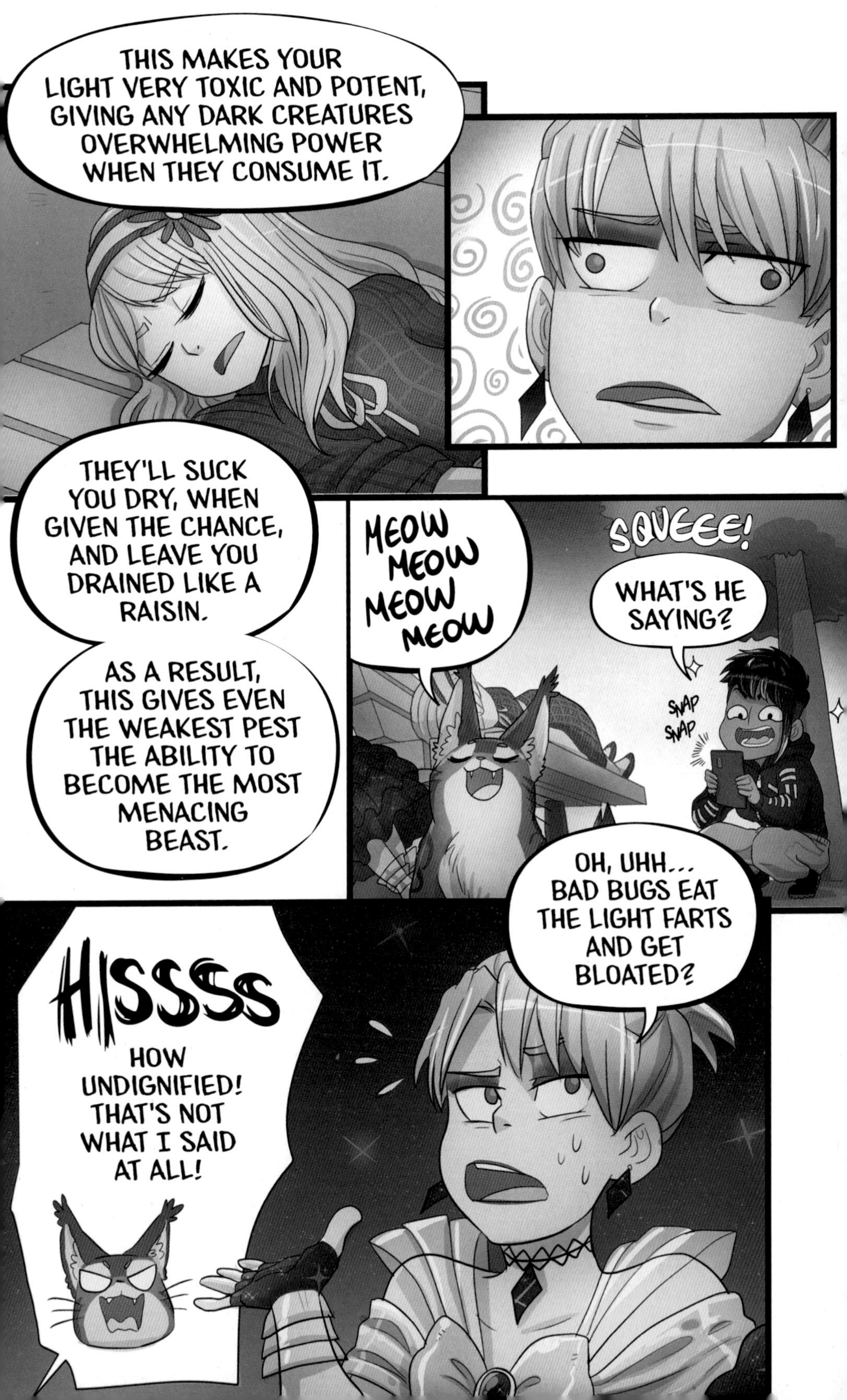
THIS MAKES YOUR LIGHT VERY TOXIC AND POTENT, GIVING ANY DARK CREATURES OVERWHELMING POWER WHEN THEY CONSUME IT.
THEY'LL SUCK YOU DRY, WHEN GIVEN THE CHANCE, AND LEAVE YOU DRAINED LIKE A RAISIN.
AS A RESULT, THIS GIVES EVEN THE WEAKEST PEST THE ABILITY TO BECOME THE MOST MENACING BEAST.
MEOW MEOW MEOW MEOW
SQUEEE!
WHAT'S HE SAYING?
SNAP SNAP
OH, UHH... BAD BUGS EAT THE LIGHT FARTS AND GET BLOATED?
HISSSS
HOW UNDIGNIFIED! THAT'S NOT WHAT I SAID AT ALL!

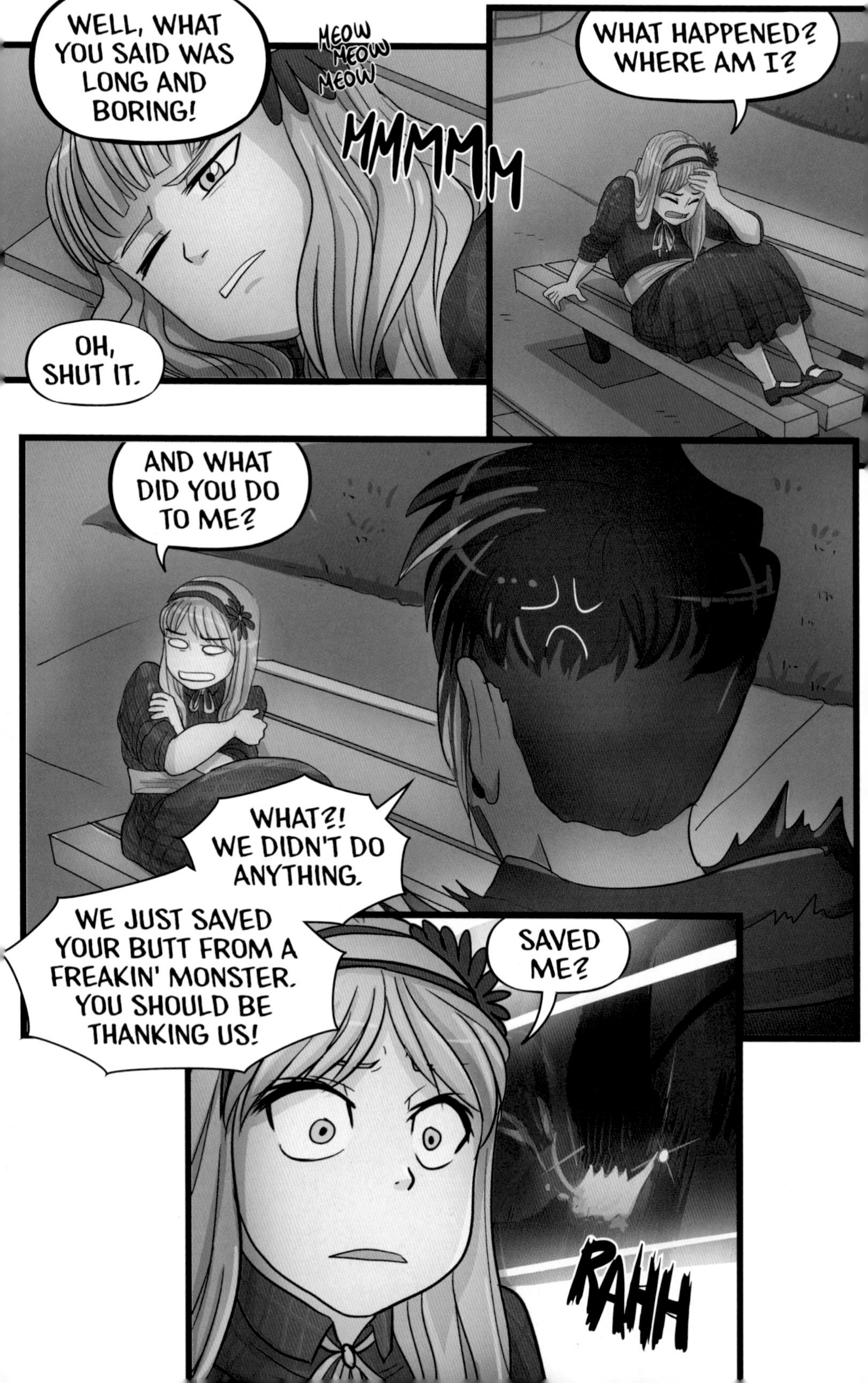
WELL, WHAT YOU SAID WAS LONG AND BORING!
MEOW MEOW MEOW
MMMMM
OH, SHUT IT.
WHAT HAPPENED? WHERE AM I?
AND WHAT DID YOU DO TO ME?
WHAT?! WE DIDN'T DO ANYTHING.
WE JUST SAVED YOUR BUTT FROM A FREAKIN' MONSTER. YOU SHOULD BE THANKING US!
SAVED ME?
RAHH

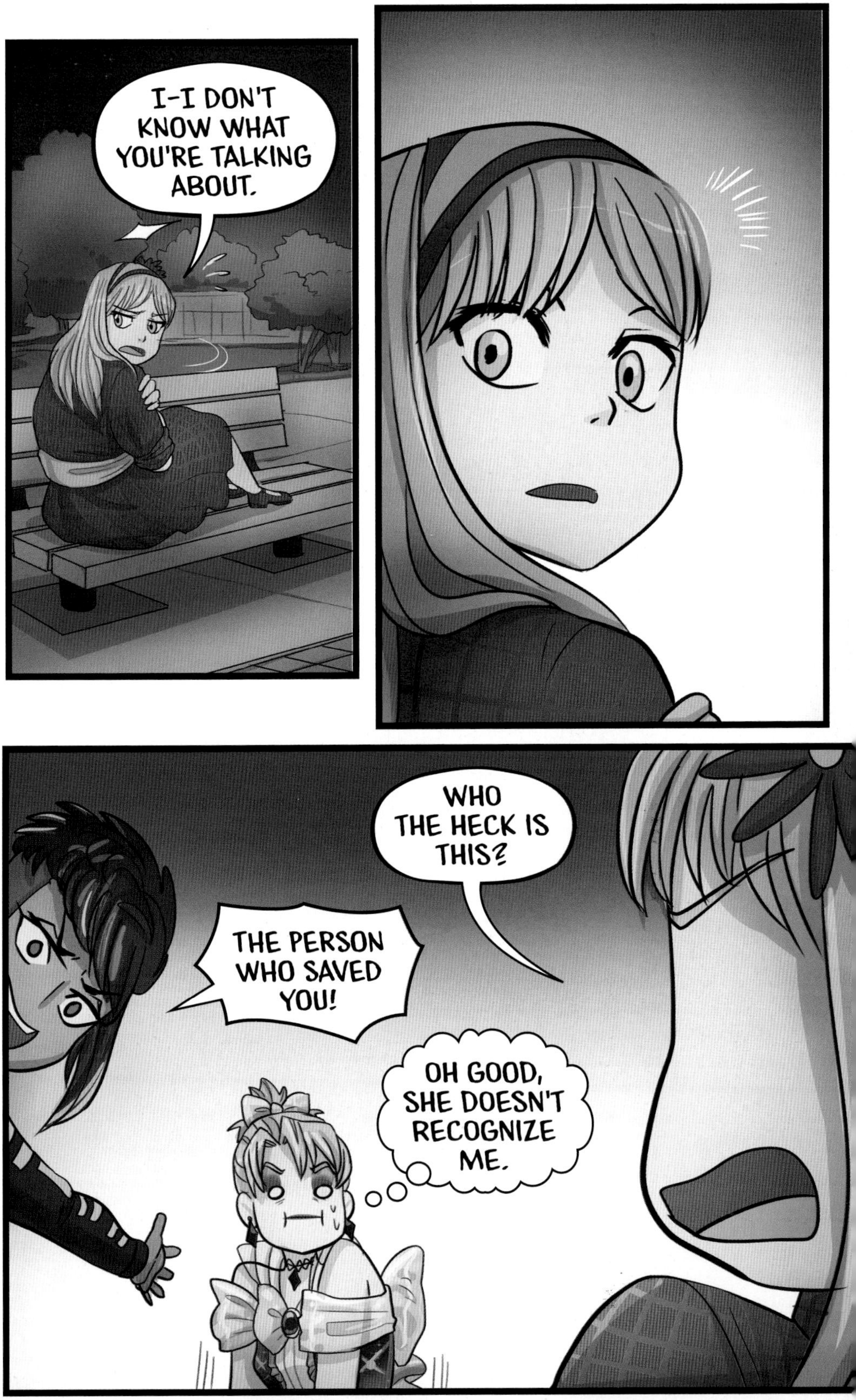
I-I DON'T KNOW WHAT YOU'RE TALKING ABOUT.
WHO THE HECK IS THIS?
THE PERSON WHO SAVED YOU!
OH GOOD, SHE DOESN'T RECOGNIZE ME.

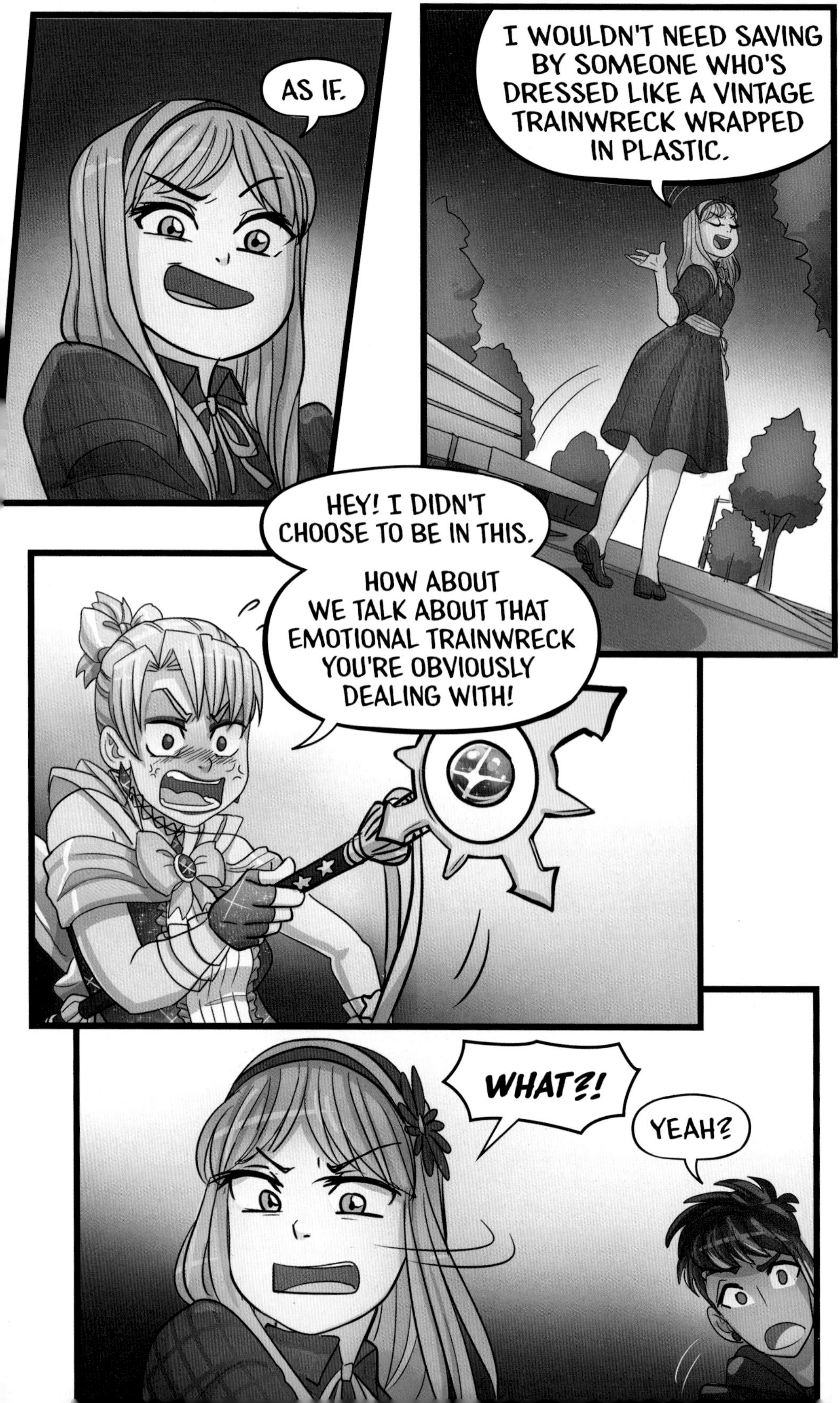
AS IF.
I WOULDN'T NEED SAVING BY SOMEONE WHO'S DRESSED LIKE A VINTAGE TRAINWRECK WRAPPED IN PLASTIC.
HEY! I DIDN'T CHOOSE TO BE IN THIS.
HOW ABOUT WE TALK ABOUT THAT EMOTIONAL TRAINWRECK YOU'RE OBVIOUSLY DEALING WITH!
WHAT?!
YEAH?

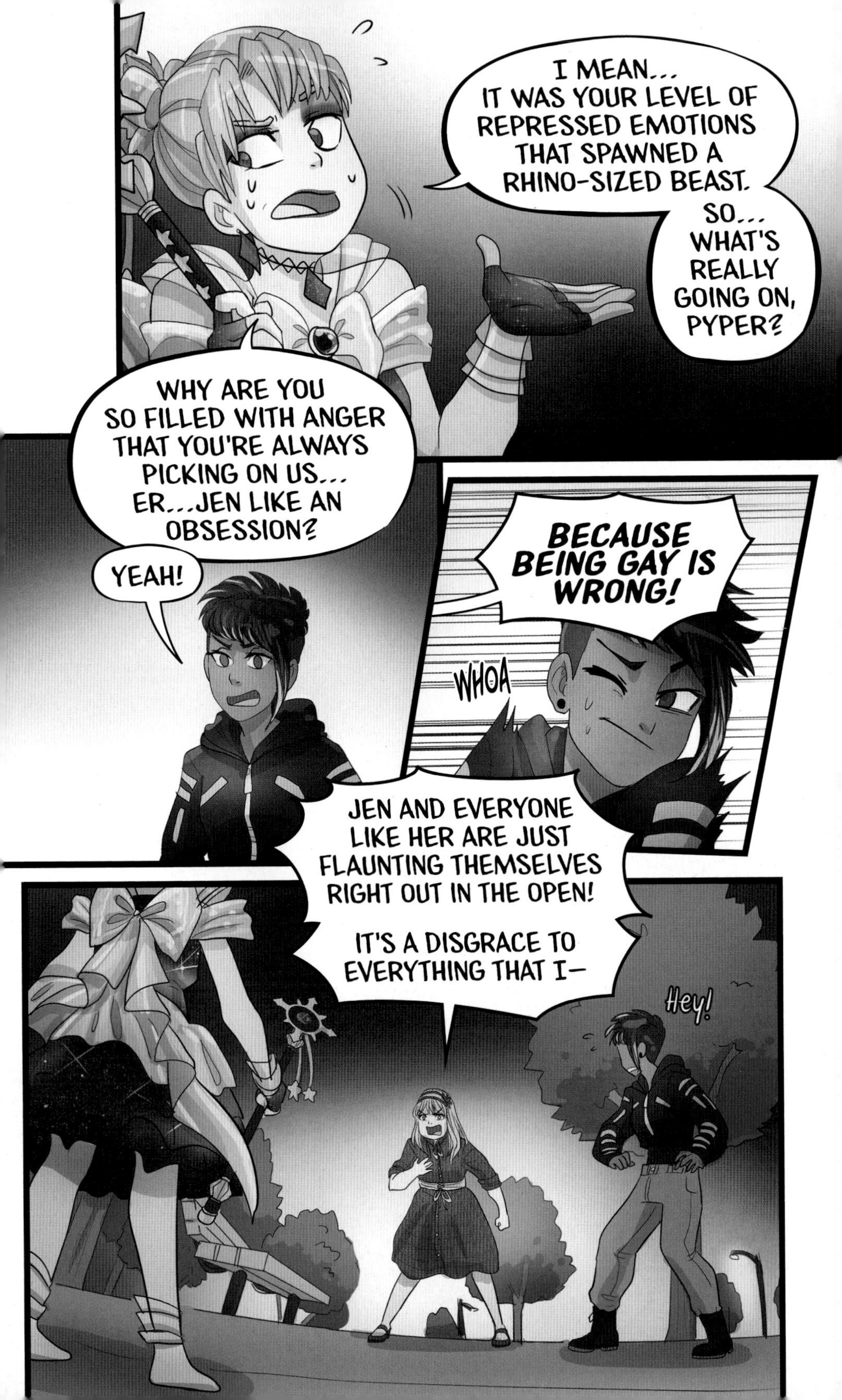
I MEAN... IT WAS YOUR LEVEL OF REPRESSED EMOTIONS THAT SPAWNED A RHINO-SIZED BEAST.
SO... WHAT'S REALLY GOING ON, PYPER?
WHY ARE YOU SO FILLED WITH ANGER THAT YOU'RE ALWAYS PICKING ON US... ER...JEN LIKE AN OBSESSION?
YEAH!
BECAUSE BEING GAY IS WRONG!
WHOA
JEN AND EVERYONE LIKE HER ARE JUST FLAUNTING THEMSELVES RIGHT OUT IN THE OPEN!
IT'S A DISGRACE TO EVERYTHING THAT I—
Hey!

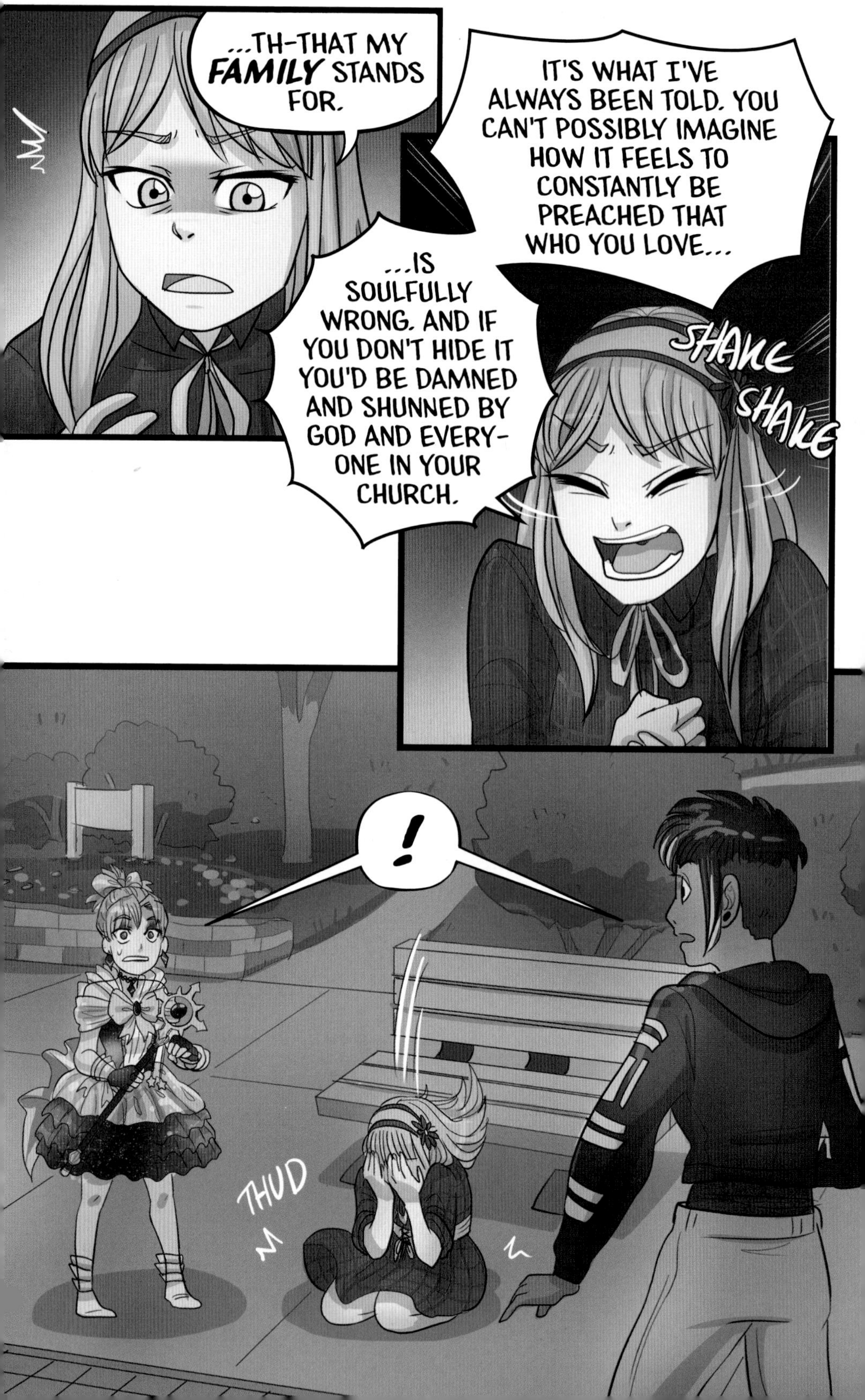
...TH-THAT MY FAMILY STANDS FOR.
IT'S WHAT I'VE ALWAYS BEEN TOLD. YOU CAN'T POSSIBLY IMAGINE HOW IT FEELS TO CONSTANTLY BE PREACHED THAT WHO YOU LOVE...
...IS SOULFULLY WRONG. AND IF YOU DON'T HIDE IT YOU'D BE DAMNED AND SHUNNED BY GOD AND EVERY-ONE IN YOUR CHURCH.
SHAKE
SHAKE
!
THUD

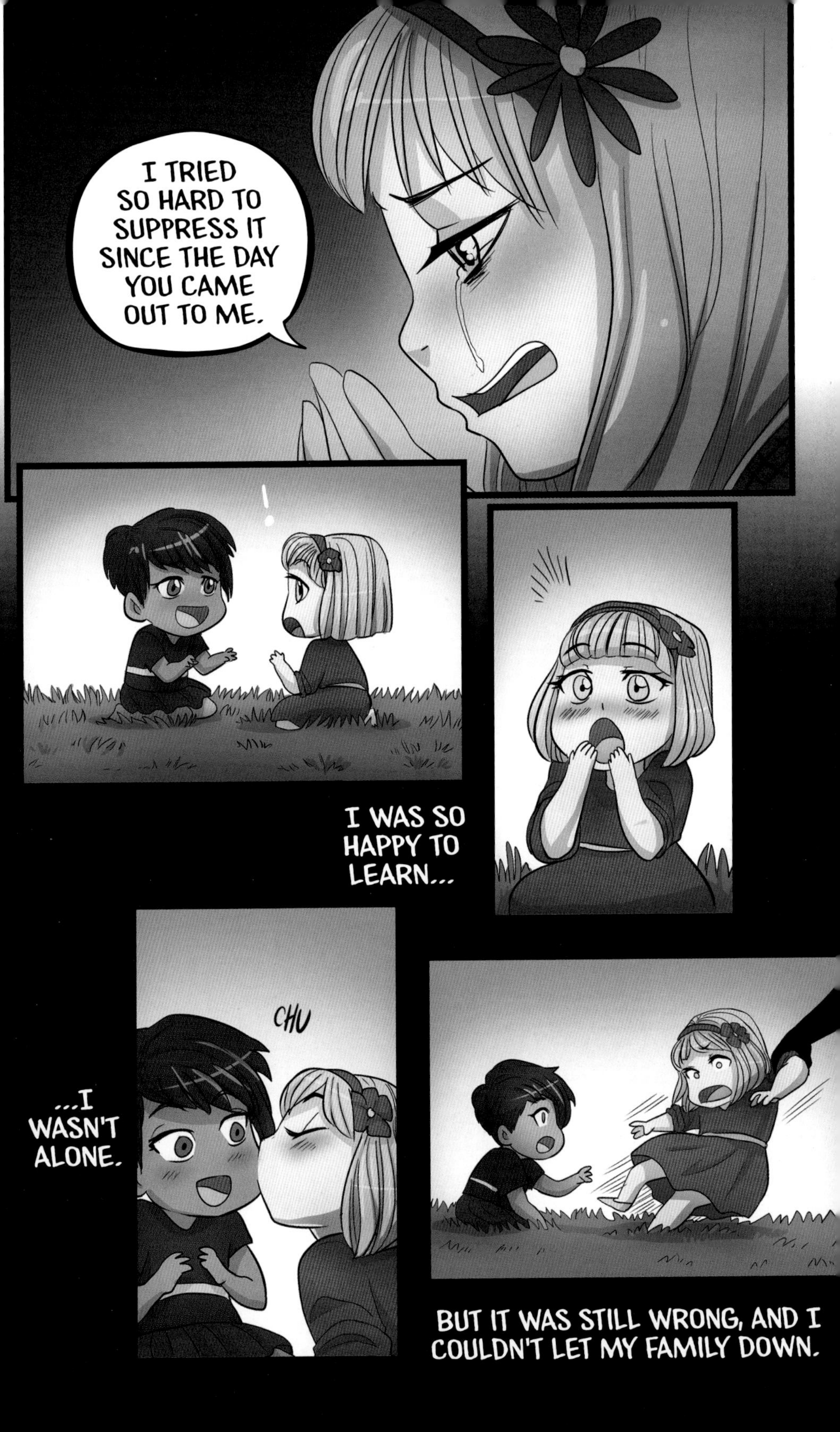
I TRIED SO HARD TO SUPPRESS IT SINCE THE DAY YOU CAME OUT TO ME.
!
I WAS SO HAPPY TO LEARN...
CHU
...I WASN'T ALONE.
BUT IT WAS STILL WRONG, AND I COULDN'T LET MY FAMILY DOWN.

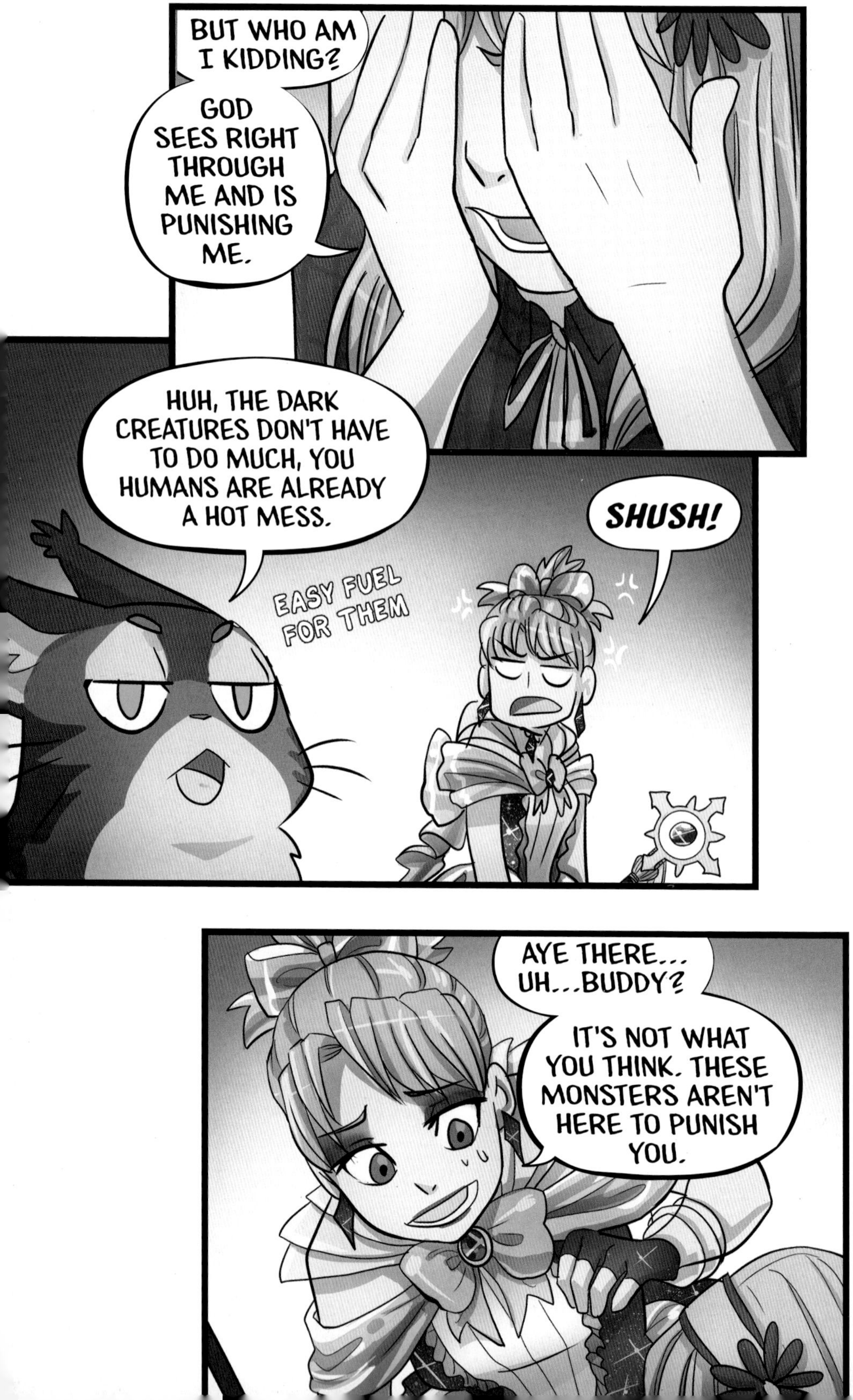
BUT WHO AM I KIDDING?
GOD SEES RIGHT THROUGH ME AND IS PUNISHING ME.
HUH, THE DARK CREATURES DON'T HAVE TO DO MUCH, YOU HUMANS ARE ALREADY A HOT MESS.
EASY FUEL FOR THEM
SHUSH!
AYE THERE... UH...BUDDY?
IT'S NOT WHAT YOU THINK. THESE MONSTERS AREN'T HERE TO PUNISH YOU.

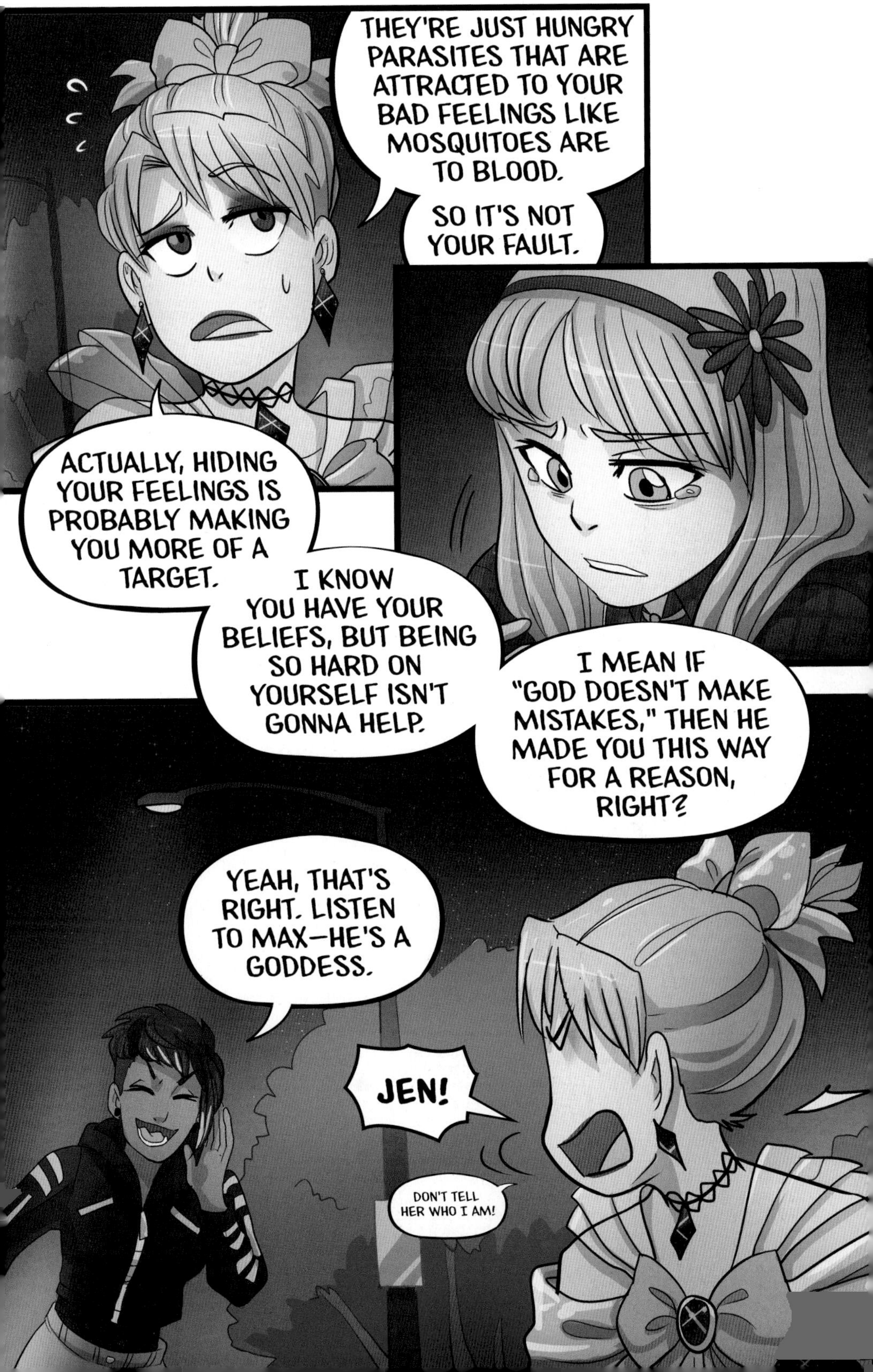
THEY'RE JUST HUNGRY PARASITES THAT ARE ATTRACTED TO YOUR BAD FEELINGS LIKE MOSQUITOES ARE TO BLOOD.
SO IT'S NOT YOUR FAULT.
ACTUALLY, HIDING YOUR FEELINGS IS PROBABLY MAKING YOU MORE OF A TARGET.
I KNOW YOU HAVE YOUR BELIEFS, BUT BEING SO HARD ON YOURSELF ISN'T GONNA HELP.
I MEAN IF "GOD DOESN'T MAKE MISTAKES," THEN HE MADE YOU THIS WAY FOR A REASON, RIGHT?
YEAH, THAT'S RIGHT. LISTEN TO MAX—HE'S A GODDESS.
JEN!
DON'T TELL HER WHO I AM!

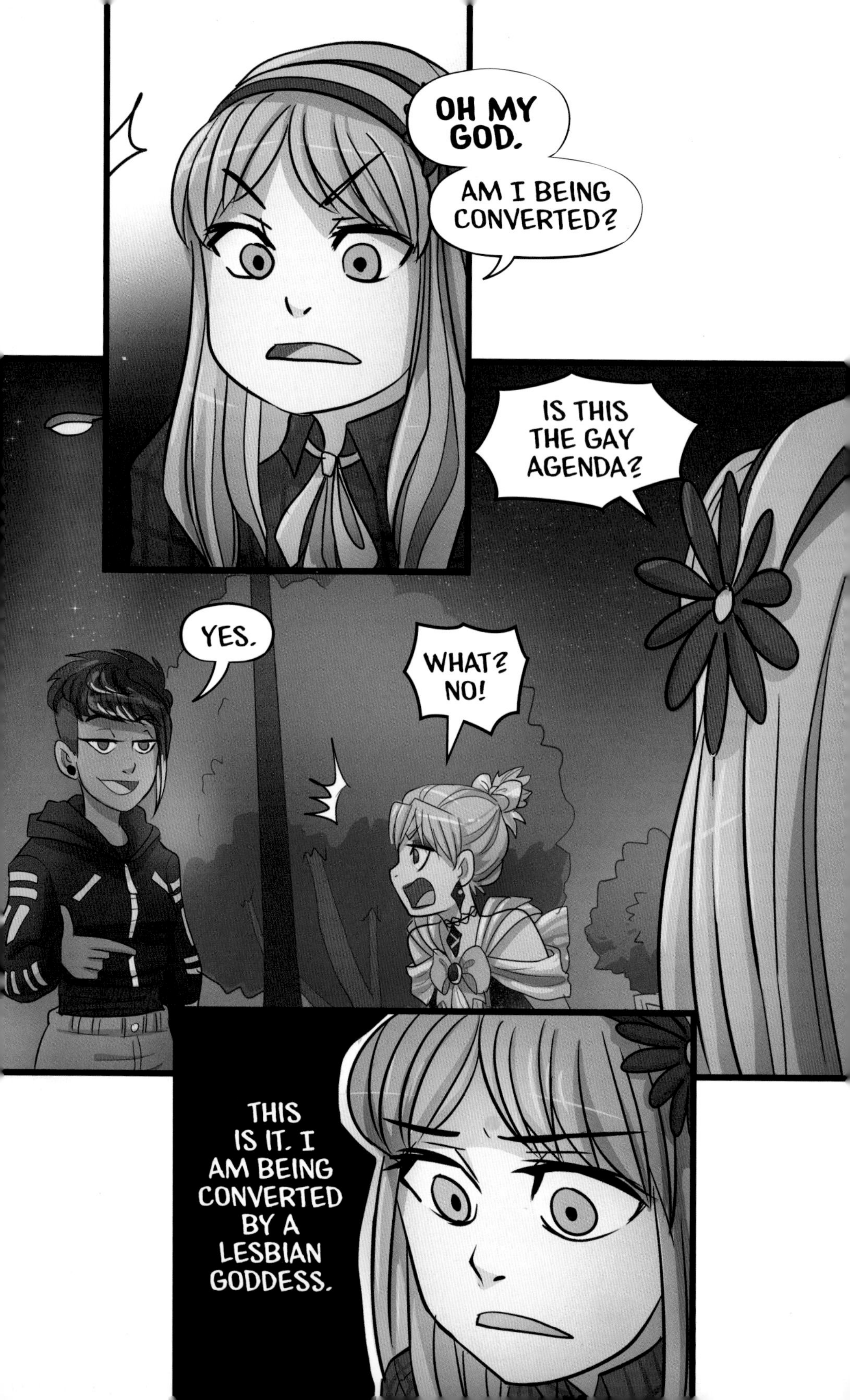
OH MY GOD.
AM I BEING CONVERTED?
IS THIS THE GAY AGENDA?
YES.
WHAT? NO!
THIS IS IT. I AM BEING CONVERTED BY A LESBIAN GODDESS.

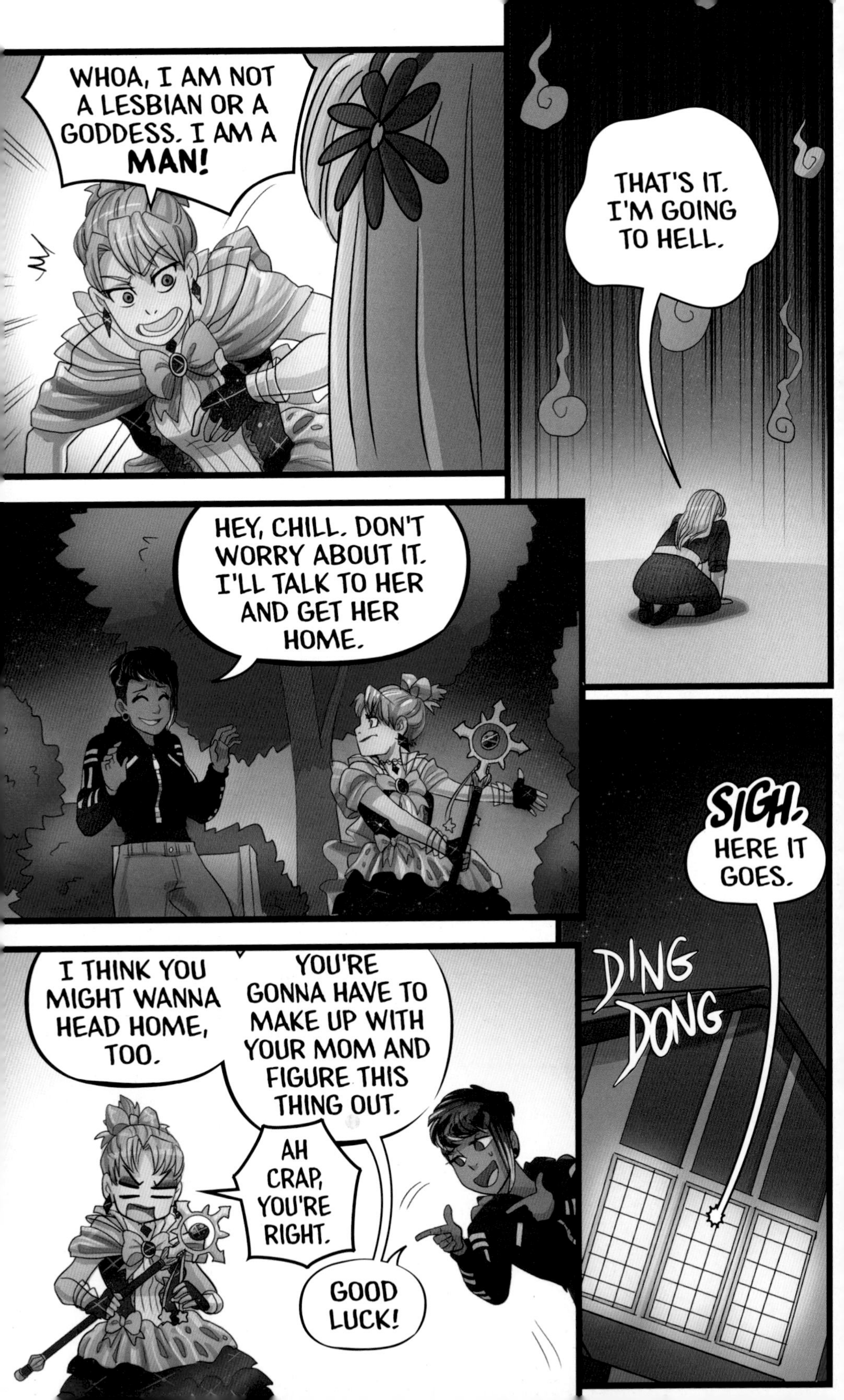

WHOA, I AM NOT A LESBIAN OR A GODDESS. I AM A **MAN!**
THAT'S IT. I'M GOING TO HELL.
HEY, CHILL. DON'T WORRY ABOUT IT. I'LL TALK TO HER AND GET HER HOME.
SIGH.
HERE IT GOES.
DING DONG
I THINK YOU MIGHT WANNA HEAD HOME, TOO.
YOU'RE GONNA HAVE TO MAKE UP WITH YOUR MOM AND FIGURE THIS THING OUT.
AH CRAP, YOU'RE RIGHT.
GOOD LUCK!

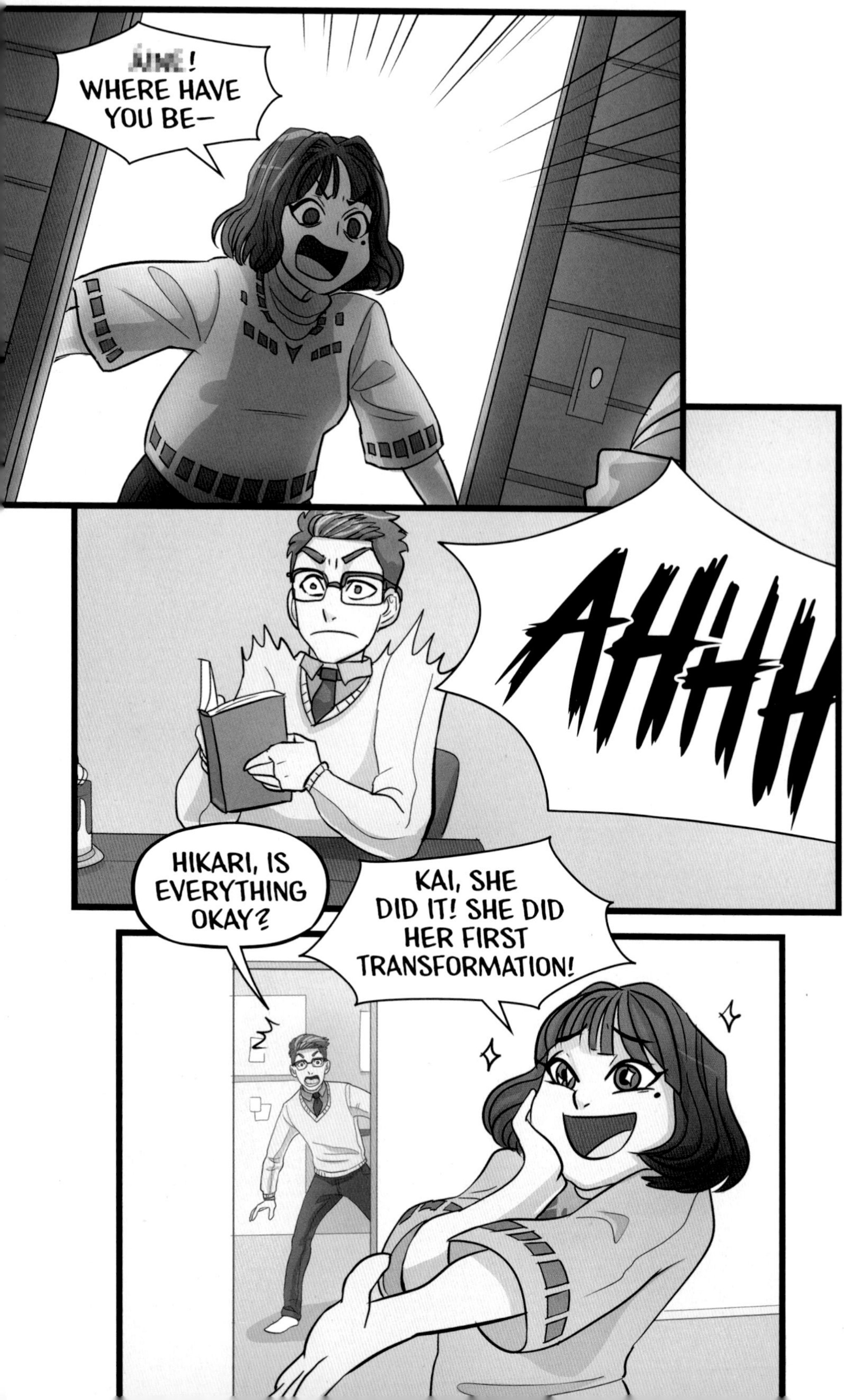
[redacted]! WHERE HAVE YOU BE–
AHHH
HIKARI, IS EVERYTHING OKAY?
KAI, SHE DID IT! SHE DID HER FIRST TRANSFORMATION!

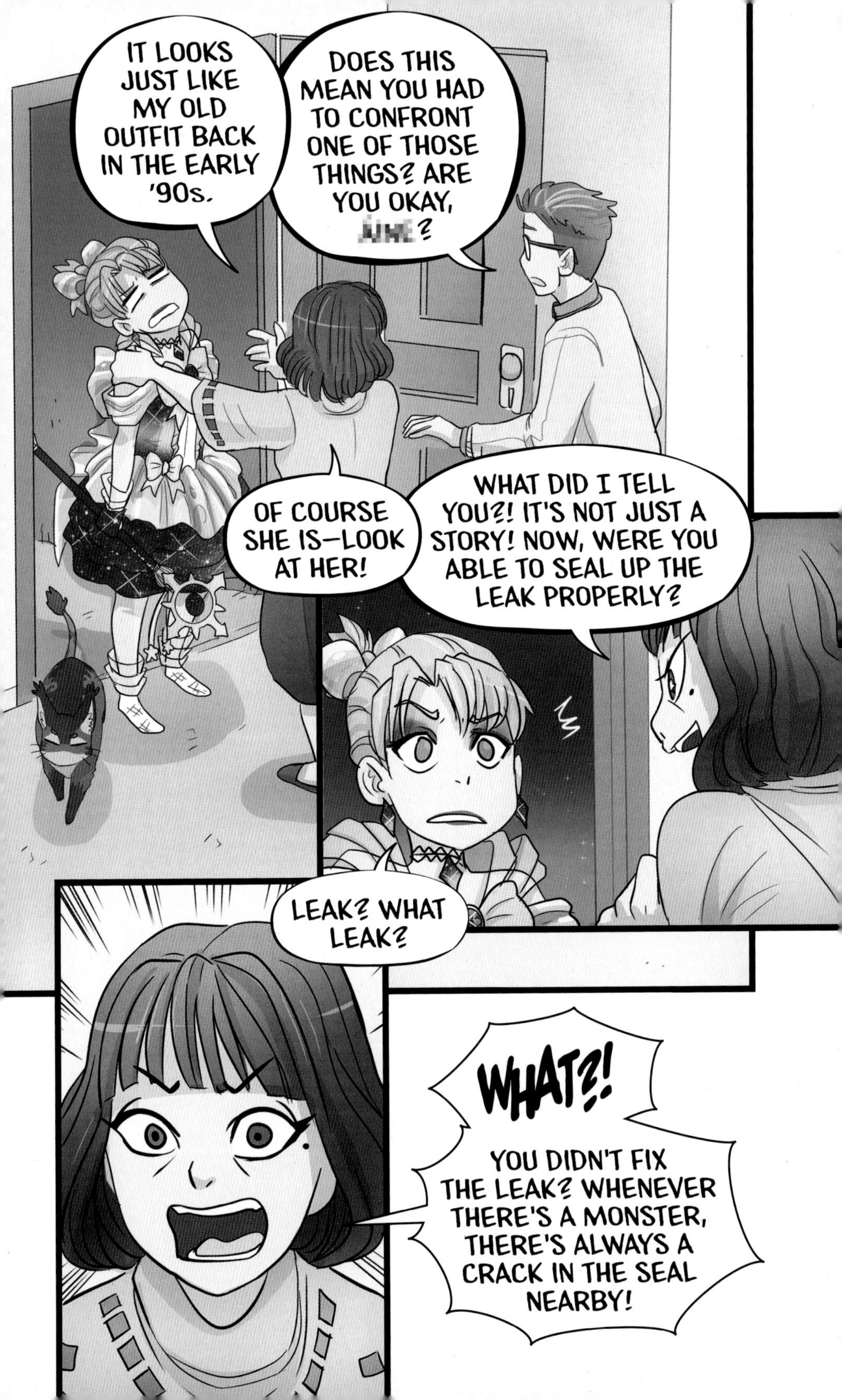
IT LOOKS JUST LIKE MY OLD OUTFIT BACK IN THE EARLY '90s.
DOES THIS MEAN YOU HAD TO CONFRONT ONE OF THOSE THINGS? ARE YOU OKAY, ?
OF COURSE SHE IS—LOOK AT HER!
WHAT DID I TELL YOU?! IT'S NOT JUST A STORY! NOW, WERE YOU ABLE TO SEAL UP THE LEAK PROPERLY?
LEAK? WHAT LEAK?
WHAT?!
YOU DIDN'T FIX THE LEAK? WHENEVER THERE'S A MONSTER, THERE'S ALWAYS A CRACK IN THE SEAL NEARBY!

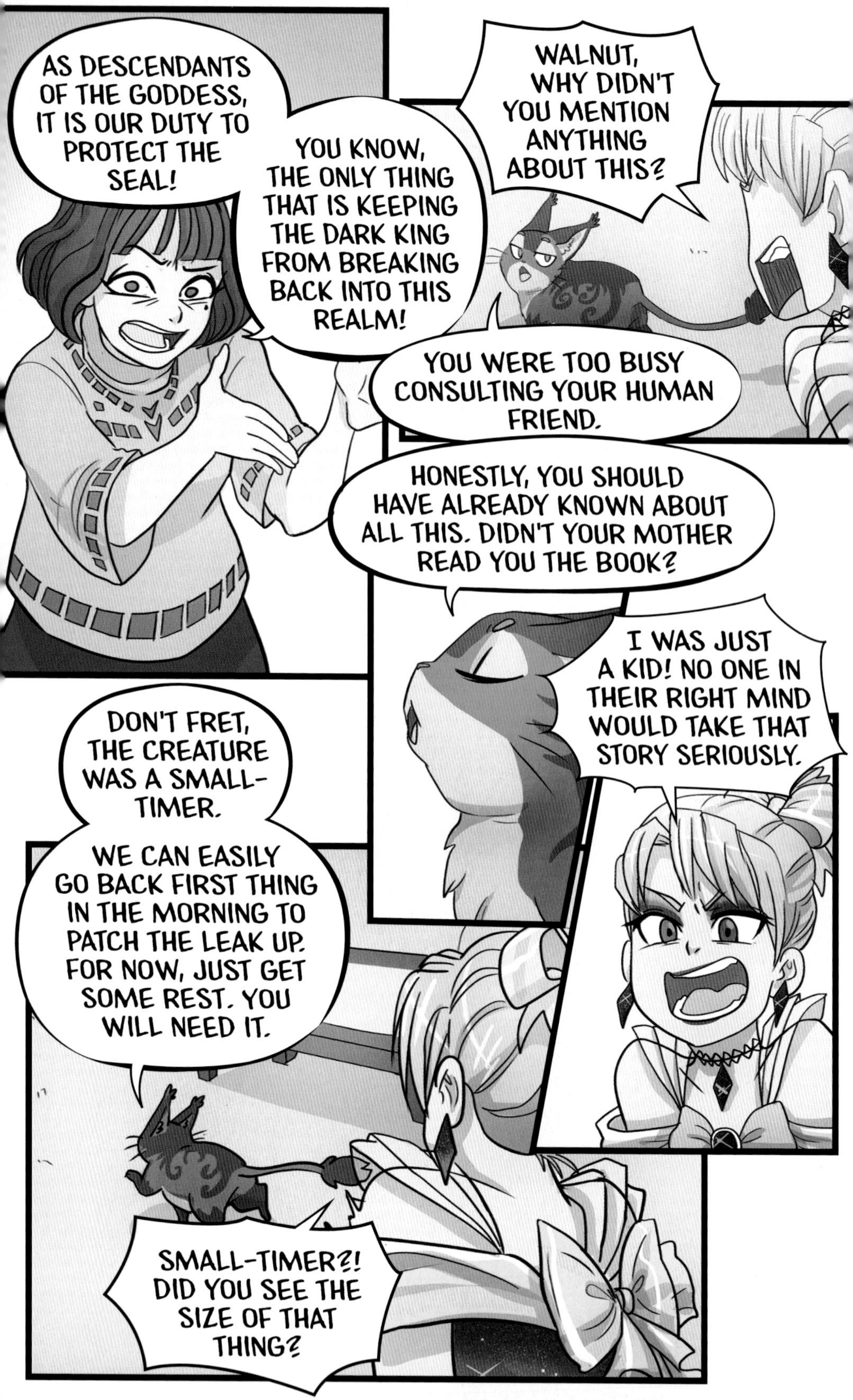
AS DESCENDANTS OF THE GODDESS, IT IS OUR DUTY TO PROTECT THE SEAL!
YOU KNOW, THE ONLY THING THAT IS KEEPING THE DARK KING FROM BREAKING BACK INTO THIS REALM!
WALNUT, WHY DIDN'T YOU MENTION ANYTHING ABOUT THIS?
YOU WERE TOO BUSY CONSULTING YOUR HUMAN FRIEND.
HONESTLY, YOU SHOULD HAVE ALREADY KNOWN ABOUT ALL THIS. DIDN'T YOUR MOTHER READ YOU THE BOOK?
I WAS JUST A KID! NO ONE IN THEIR RIGHT MIND WOULD TAKE THAT STORY SERIOUSLY.
DON'T FRET, THE CREATURE WAS A SMALL-TIMER.
WE CAN EASILY GO BACK FIRST THING IN THE MORNING TO PATCH THE LEAK UP. FOR NOW, JUST GET SOME REST. YOU WILL NEED IT.
SMALL-TIMER?! DID YOU SEE THE SIZE OF THAT THING?

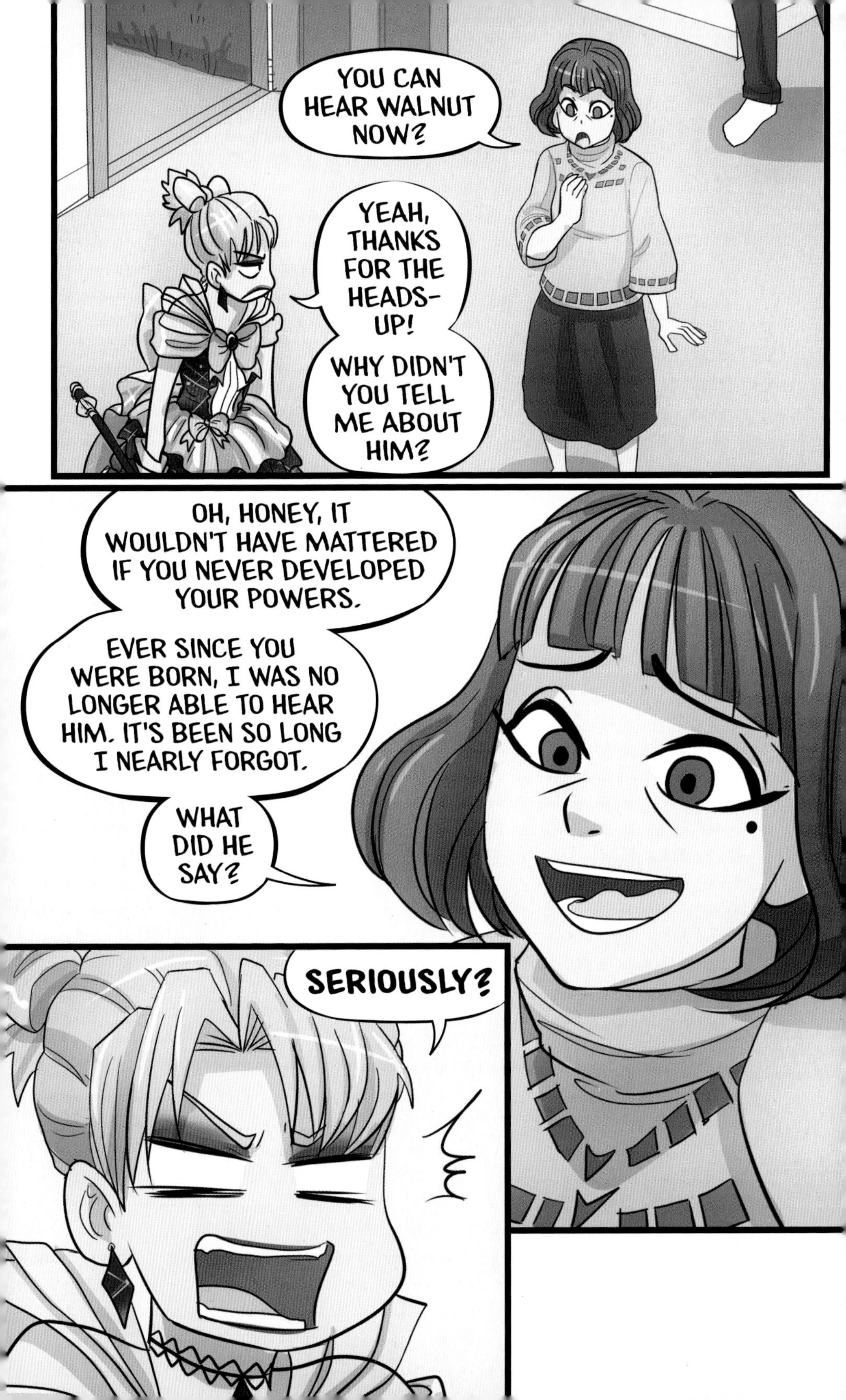
YOU CAN HEAR WALNUT NOW?
YEAH, THANKS FOR THE HEADS-UP!
WHY DIDN'T YOU TELL ME ABOUT HIM?
OH, HONEY, IT WOULDN'T HAVE MATTERED IF YOU NEVER DEVELOPED YOUR POWERS.
EVER SINCE YOU WERE BORN, I WAS NO LONGER ABLE TO HEAR HIM. IT'S BEEN SO LONG I NEARLY FORGOT.
WHAT DID HE SAY?
SERIOUSLY?

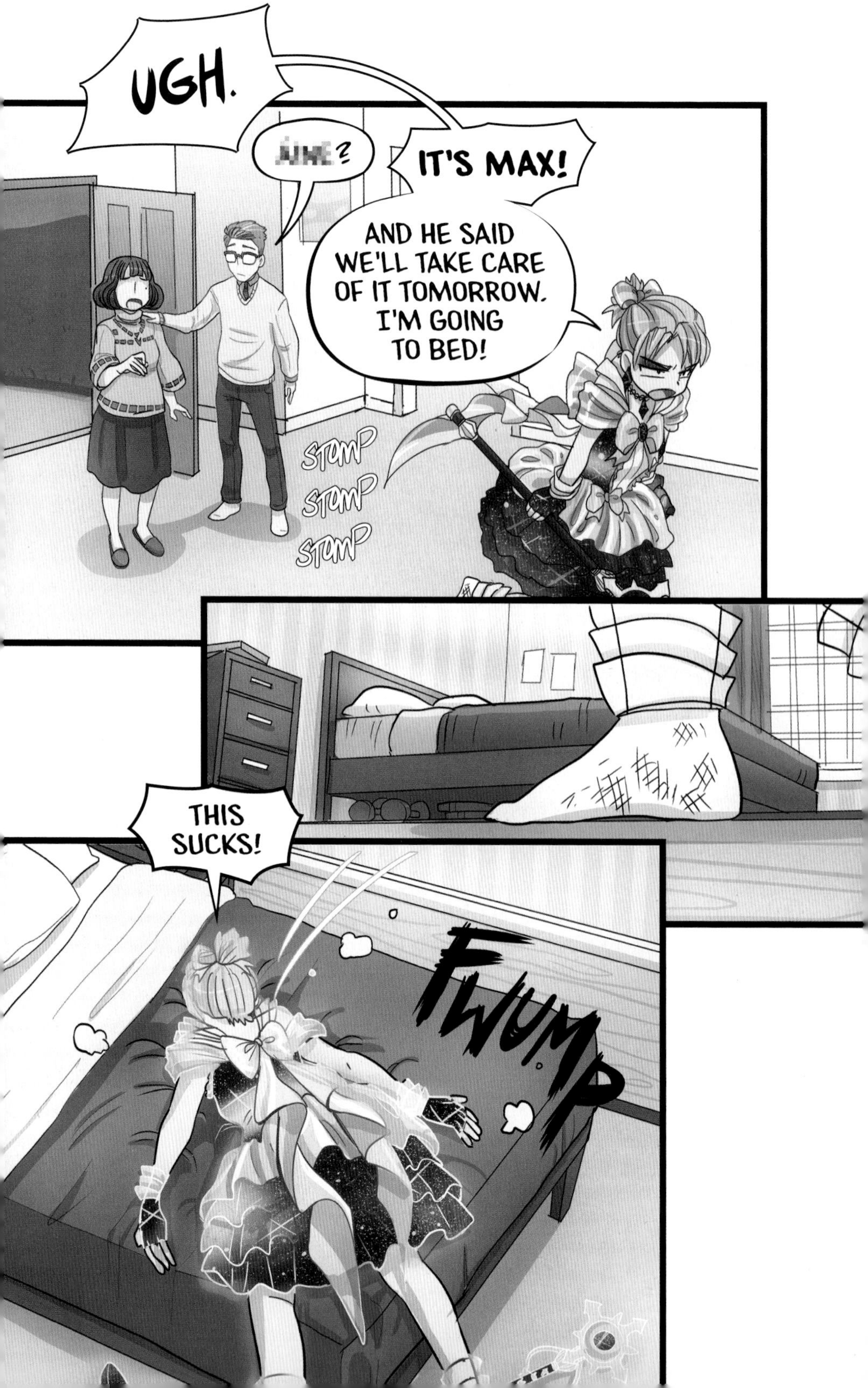

UGH.
?
IT'S MAX!
AND HE SAID WE'LL TAKE CARE OF IT TOMORROW. I'M GOING TO BED!
STOMP
STOMP
STOMP
THIS SUCKS!
FWUMP

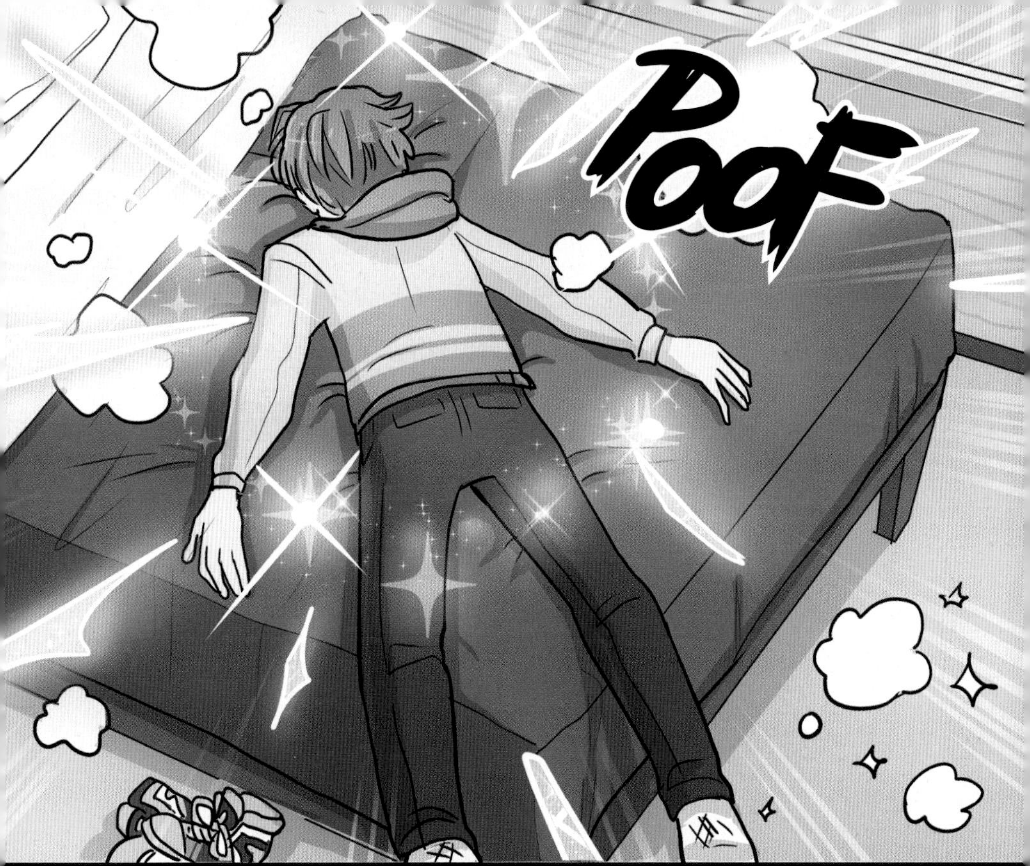
POOF

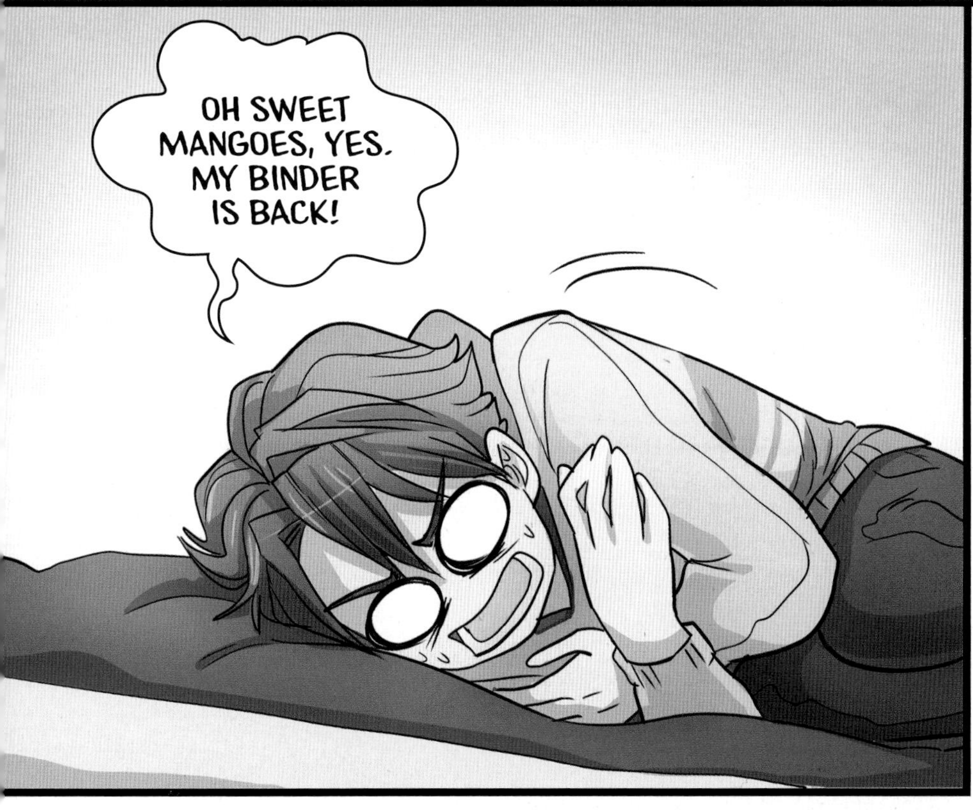
OH SWEET MANGOES, YES. MY BINDER IS BACK!

Episode 6:
TAKING INITIATIVE

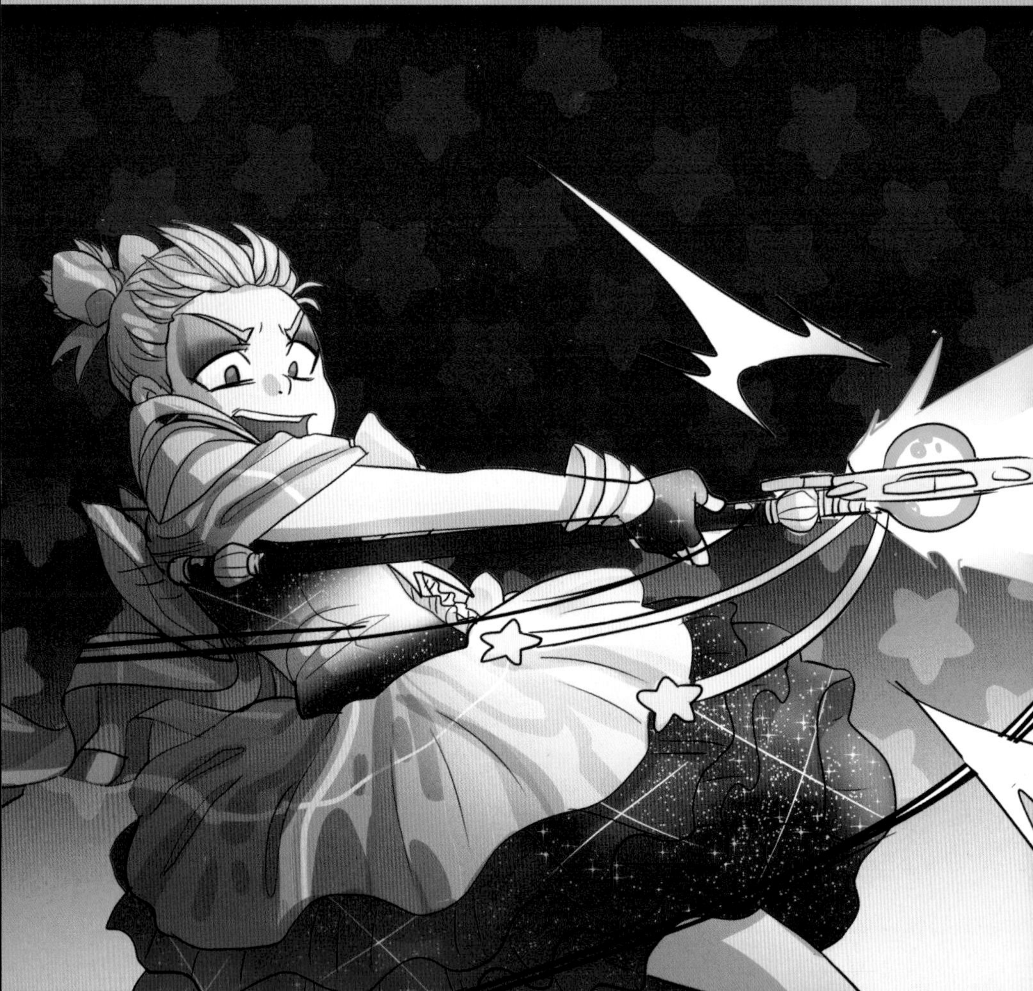

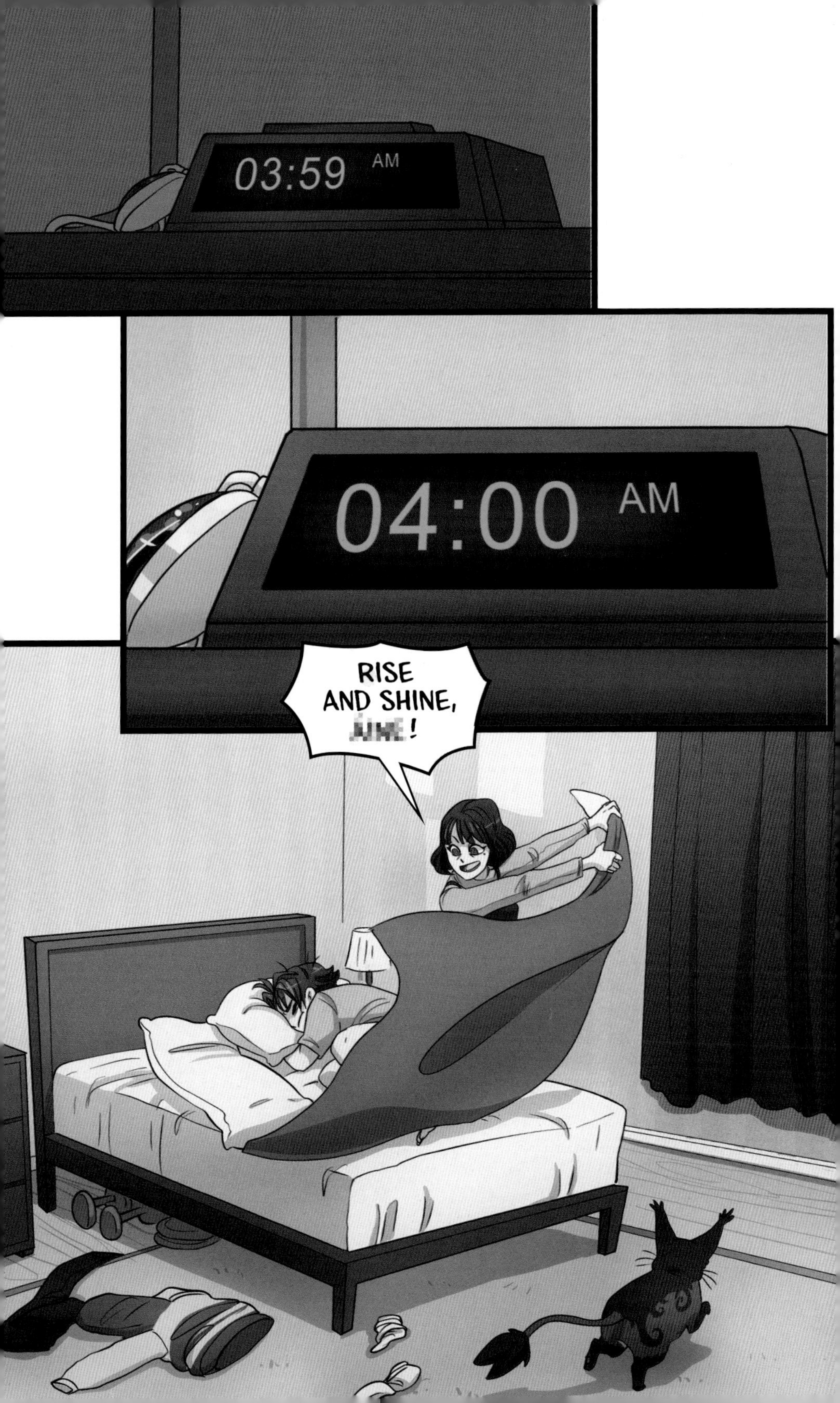
03:59 AM
04:00 AM
RISE AND SHINE, !

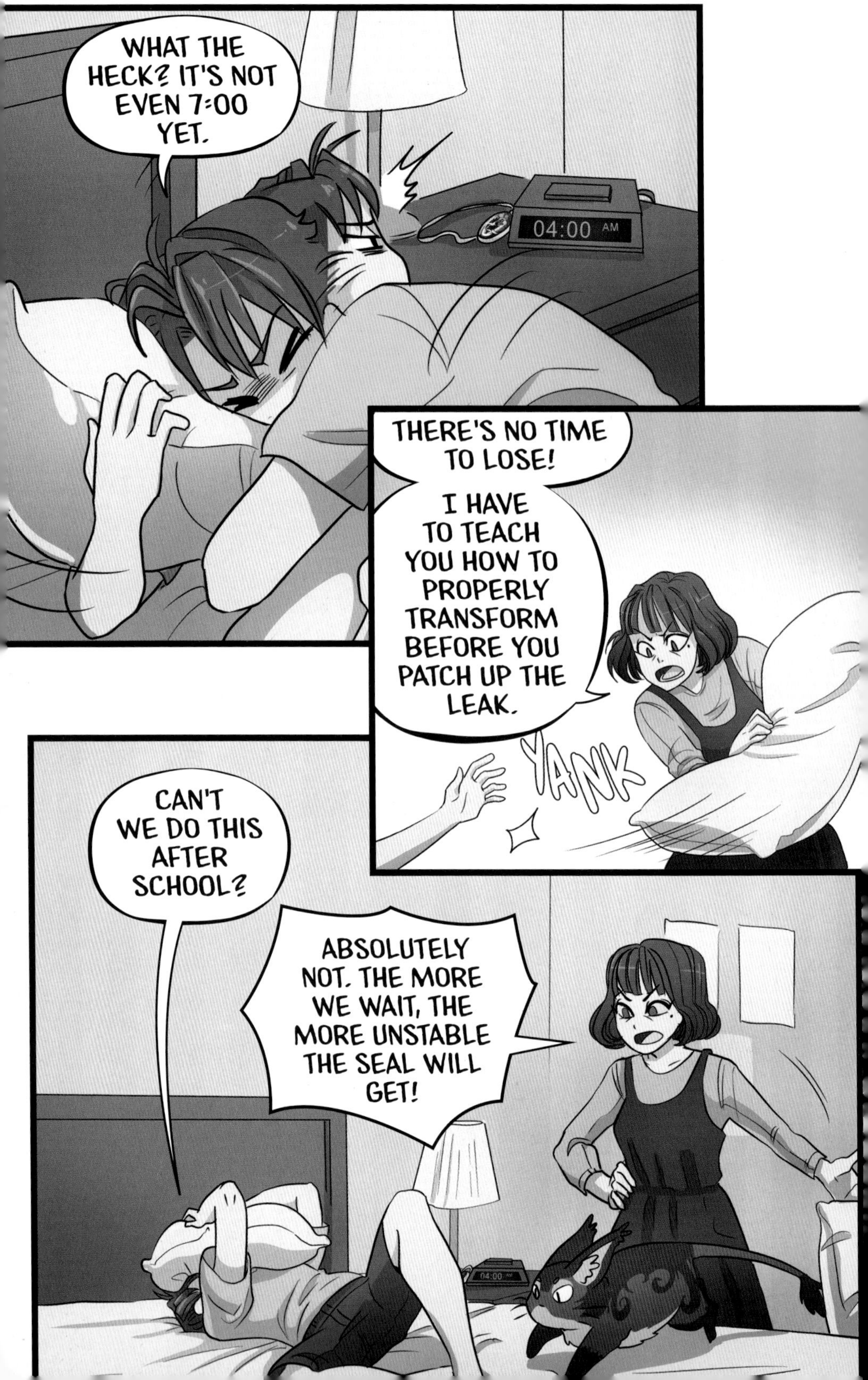
WHAT THE HECK? IT'S NOT EVEN 7:00 YET.
04:00 AM
THERE'S NO TIME TO LOSE!
I HAVE TO TEACH YOU HOW TO PROPERLY TRANSFORM BEFORE YOU PATCH UP THE LEAK.
YANK
CAN'T WE DO THIS AFTER SCHOOL?
ABSOLUTELY NOT. THE MORE WE WAIT, THE MORE UNSTABLE THE SEAL WILL GET!
04:00 AM

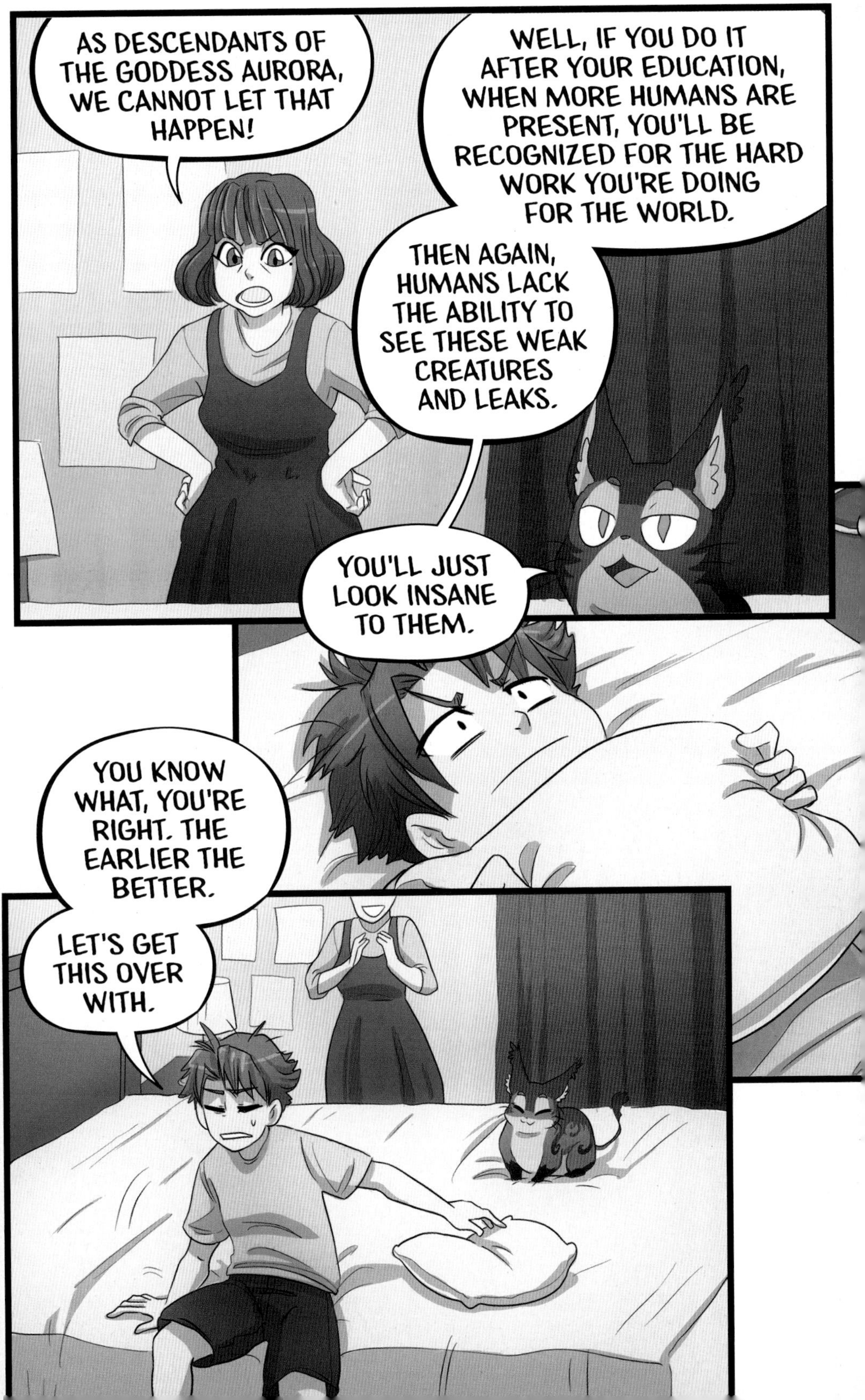
AS DESCENDANTS OF THE GODDESS AURORA, WE CANNOT LET THAT HAPPEN!
WELL, IF YOU DO IT AFTER YOUR EDUCATION, WHEN MORE HUMANS ARE PRESENT, YOU'LL BE RECOGNIZED FOR THE HARD WORK YOU'RE DOING FOR THE WORLD.
THEN AGAIN, HUMANS LACK THE ABILITY TO SEE THESE WEAK CREATURES AND LEAKS.
YOU'LL JUST LOOK INSANE TO THEM.
YOU KNOW WHAT, YOU'RE RIGHT. THE EARLIER THE BETTER.
LET'S GET THIS OVER WITH.

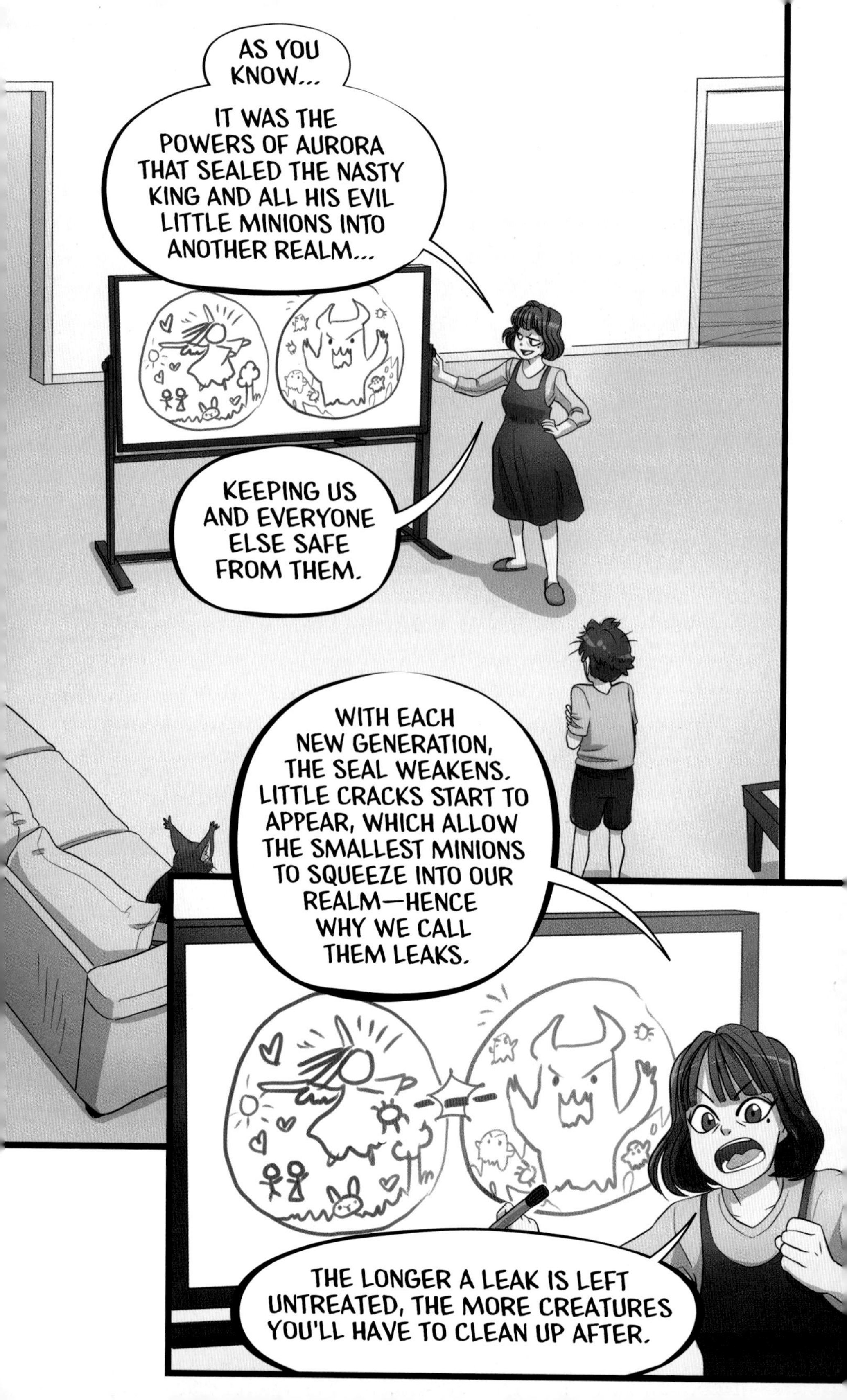
AS YOU KNOW...
IT WAS THE POWERS OF AURORA THAT SEALED THE NASTY KING AND ALL HIS EVIL LITTLE MINIONS INTO ANOTHER REALM...
KEEPING US AND EVERYONE ELSE SAFE FROM THEM.
WITH EACH NEW GENERATION, THE SEAL WEAKENS. LITTLE CRACKS START TO APPEAR, WHICH ALLOW THE SMALLEST MINIONS TO SQUEEZE INTO OUR REALM—HENCE WHY WE CALL THEM LEAKS.
THE LONGER A LEAK IS LEFT UNTREATED, THE MORE CREATURES YOU'LL HAVE TO CLEAN UP AFTER.

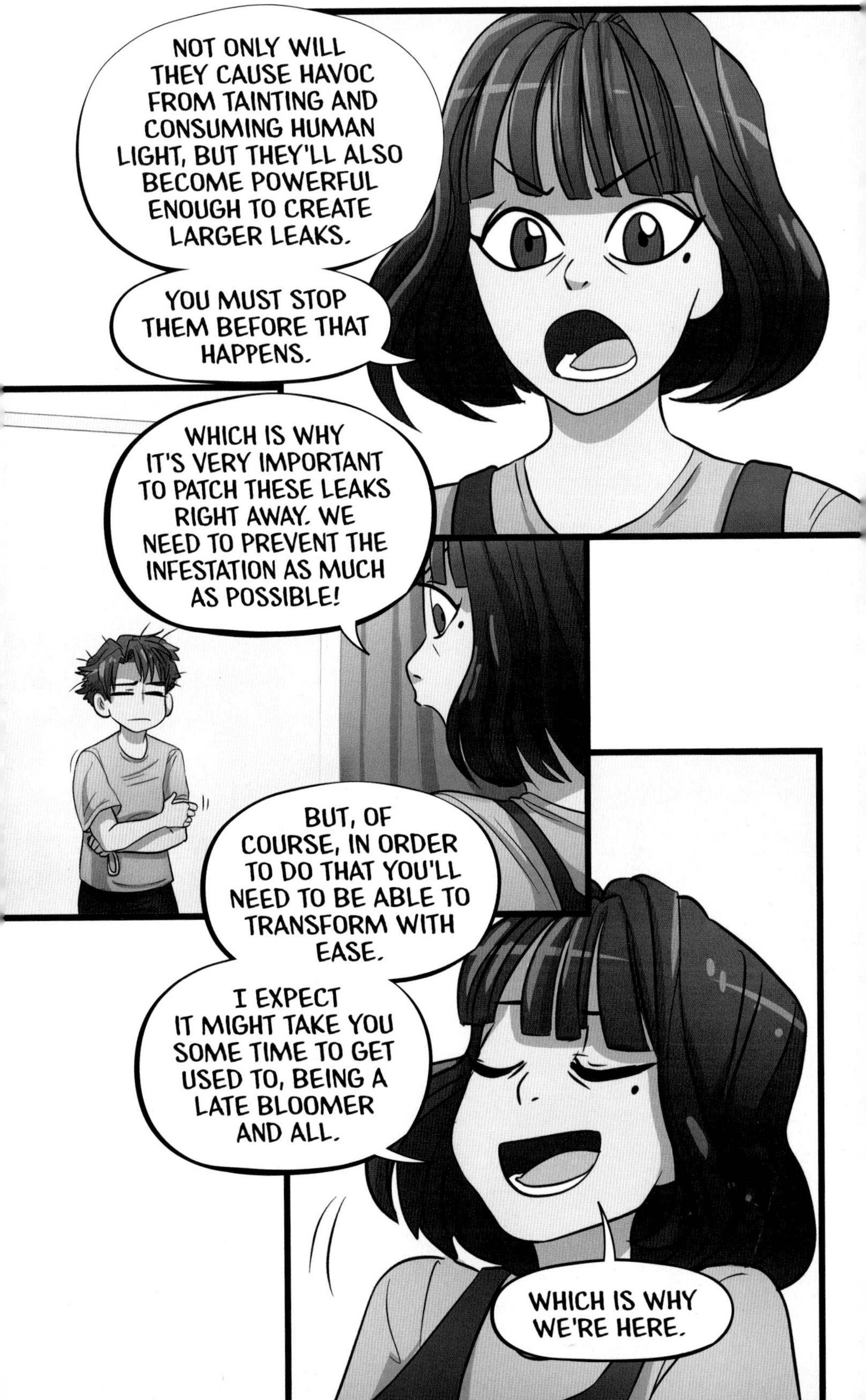
NOT ONLY WILL THEY CAUSE HAVOC FROM TAINTING AND CONSUMING HUMAN LIGHT, BUT THEY'LL ALSO BECOME POWERFUL ENOUGH TO CREATE LARGER LEAKS.
YOU MUST STOP THEM BEFORE THAT HAPPENS.
WHICH IS WHY IT'S VERY IMPORTANT TO PATCH THESE LEAKS RIGHT AWAY. WE NEED TO PREVENT THE INFESTATION AS MUCH AS POSSIBLE!
BUT, OF COURSE, IN ORDER TO DO THAT YOU'LL NEED TO BE ABLE TO TRANSFORM WITH EASE.
I EXPECT IT MIGHT TAKE YOU SOME TIME TO GET USED TO, BEING A LATE BLOOMER AND ALL.
WHICH IS WHY WE'RE HERE.

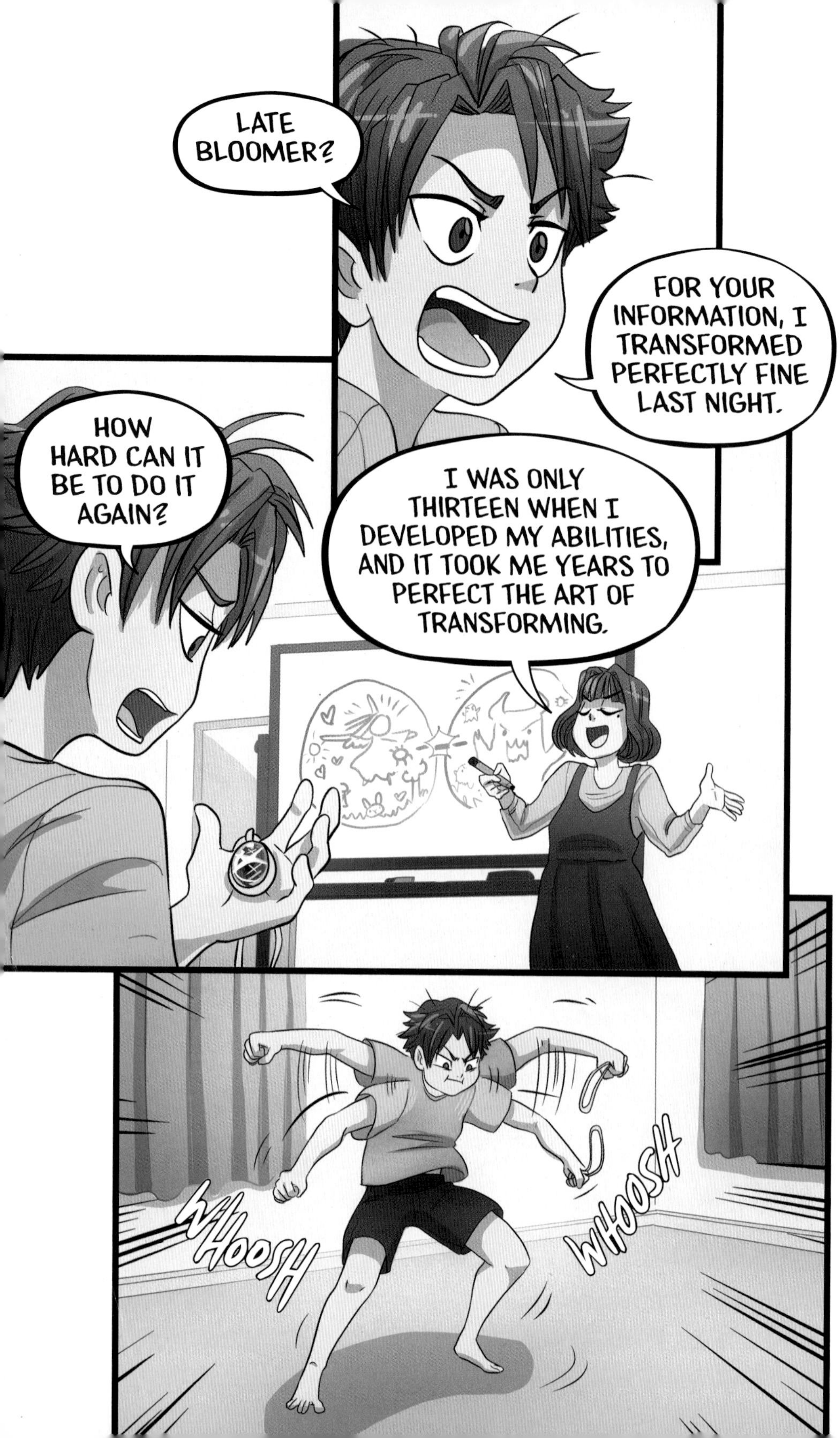
LATE BLOOMER?
FOR YOUR INFORMATION, I TRANSFORMED PERFECTLY FINE LAST NIGHT.
HOW HARD CAN IT BE TO DO IT AGAIN?
I WAS ONLY THIRTEEN WHEN I DEVELOPED MY ABILITIES, AND IT TOOK ME YEARS TO PERFECT THE ART OF TRANSFORMING.
WHOOSH
WHOOSH

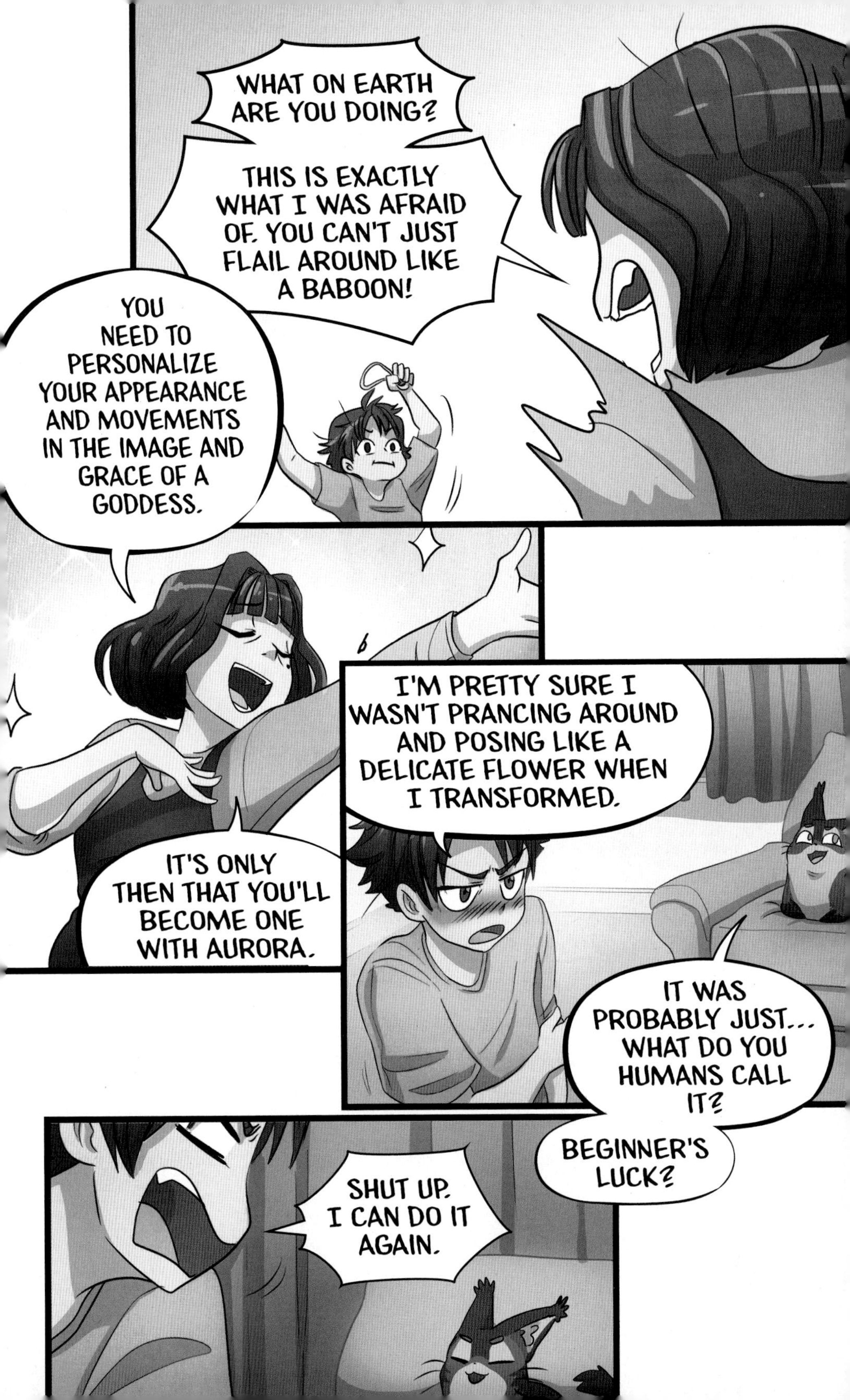

WHAT ON EARTH ARE YOU DOING?
THIS IS EXACTLY WHAT I WAS AFRAID OF. YOU CAN'T JUST FLAIL AROUND LIKE A BABOON!
YOU NEED TO PERSONALIZE YOUR APPEARANCE AND MOVEMENTS IN THE IMAGE AND GRACE OF A GODDESS.
IT'S ONLY THEN THAT YOU'LL BECOME ONE WITH AURORA.
I'M PRETTY SURE I WASN'T PRANCING AROUND AND POSING LIKE A DELICATE FLOWER WHEN I TRANSFORMED.
IT WAS PROBABLY JUST... WHAT DO YOU HUMANS CALL IT?
BEGINNER'S LUCK?
SHUT UP. I CAN DO IT AGAIN.

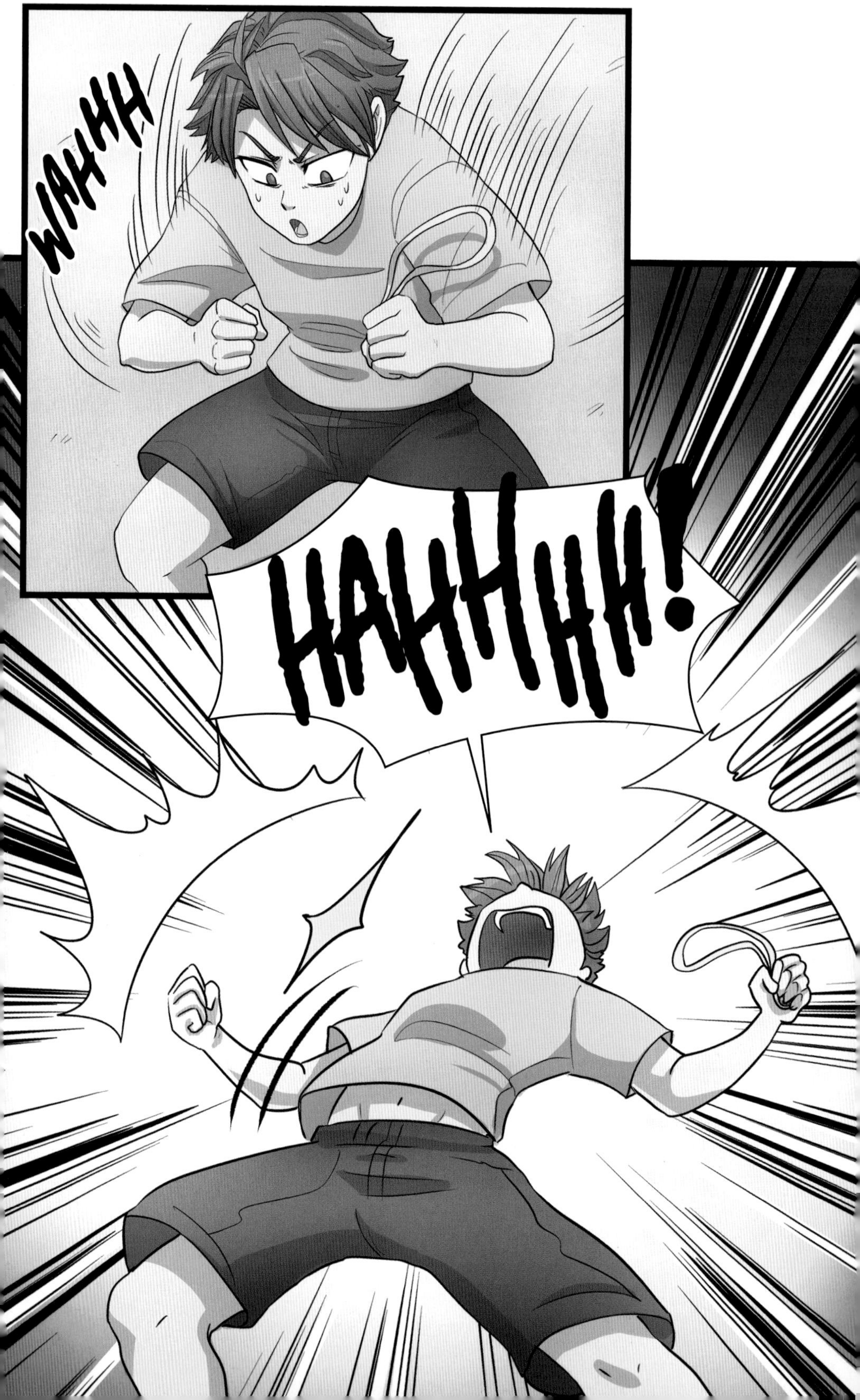
WAHHH
HAHHHHH!

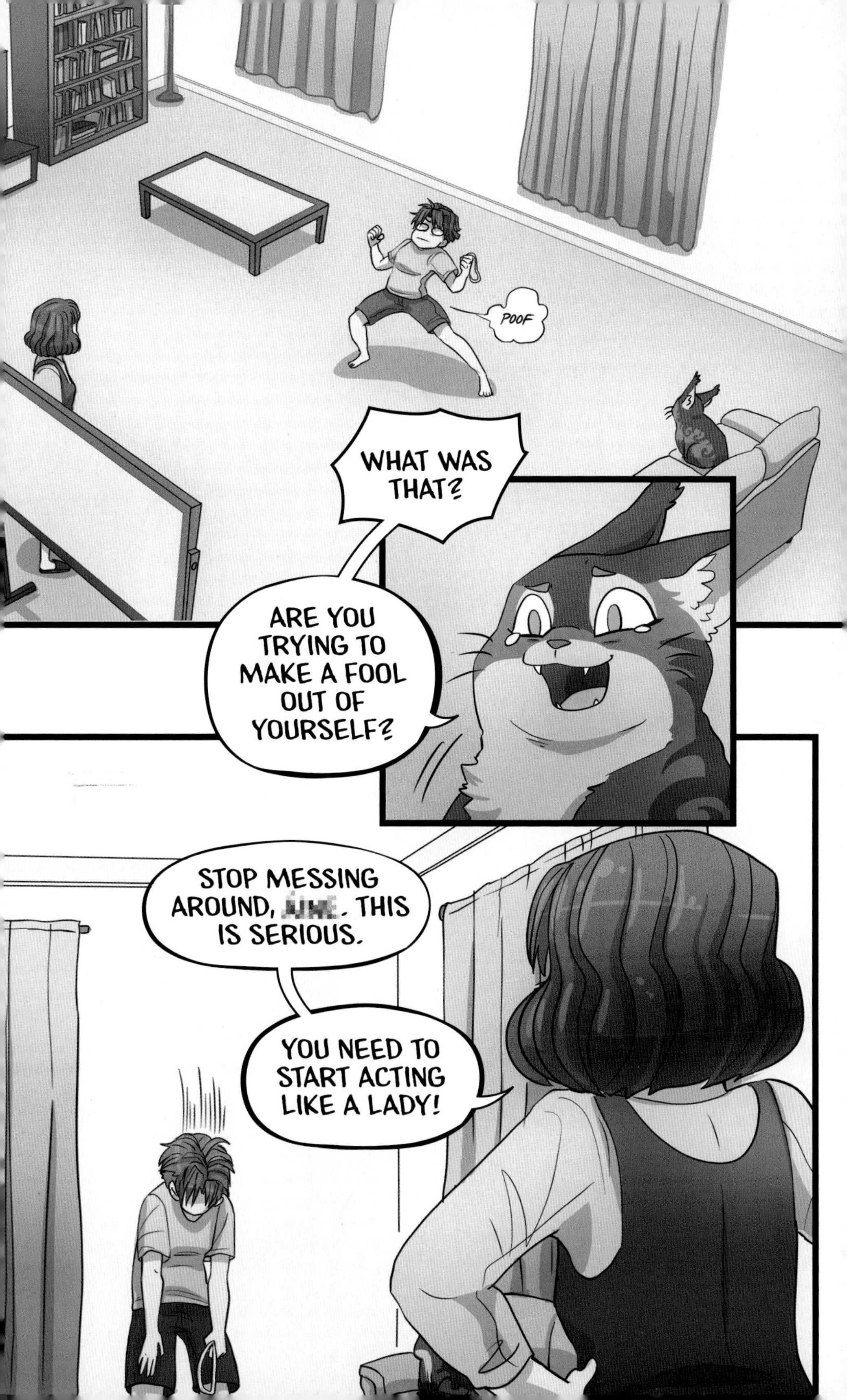
POOF
WHAT WAS THAT?
ARE YOU TRYING TO MAKE A FOOL OUT OF YOURSELF?
STOP MESSING AROUND, . THIS IS SERIOUS.
YOU NEED TO START ACTING LIKE A LADY!

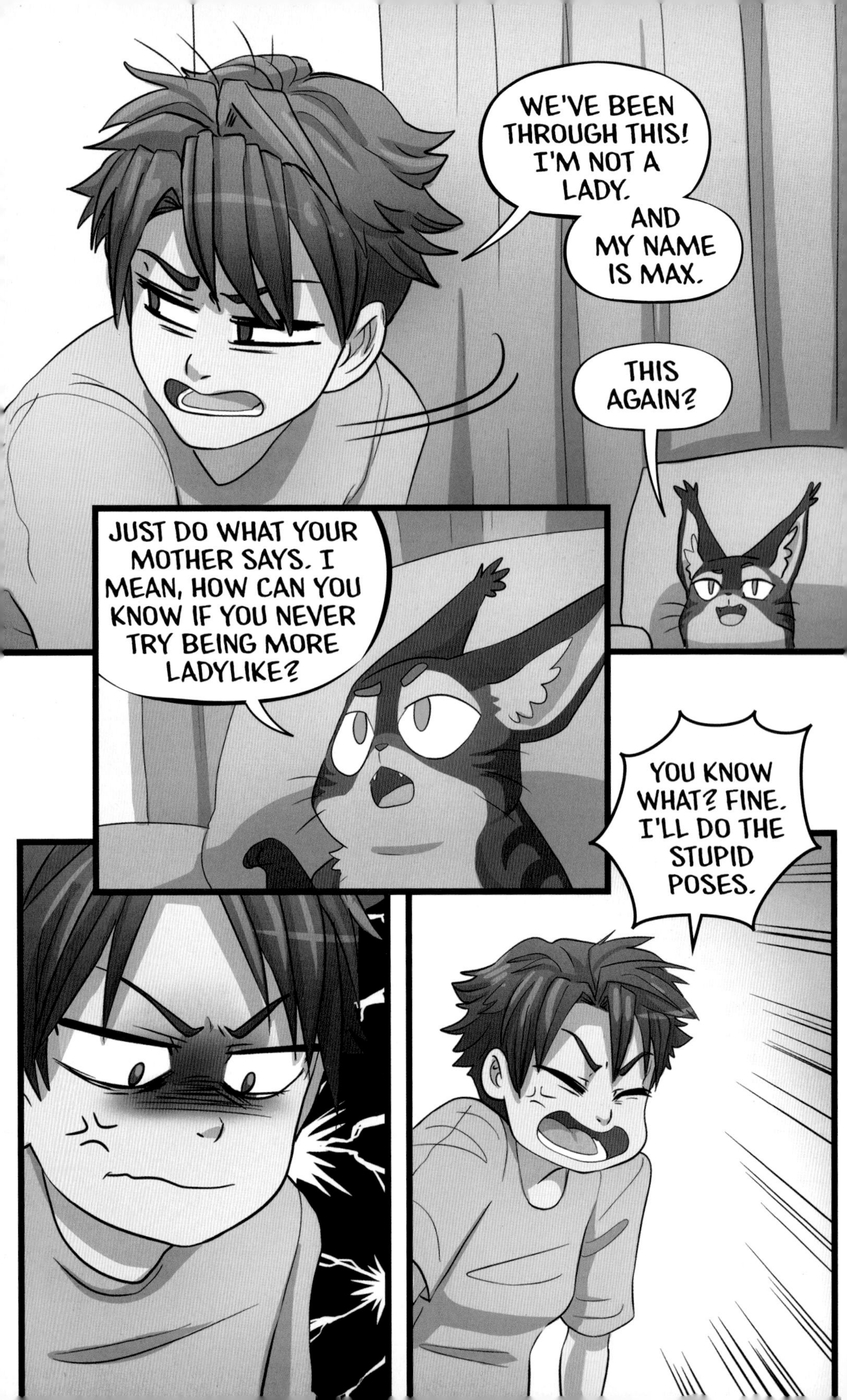
WE'VE BEEN THROUGH THIS! I'M NOT A LADY.
AND MY NAME IS MAX.
THIS AGAIN?
JUST DO WHAT YOUR MOTHER SAYS. I MEAN, HOW CAN YOU KNOW IF YOU NEVER TRY BEING MORE LADYLIKE?
YOU KNOW WHAT? FINE. I'LL DO THE STUPID POSES.

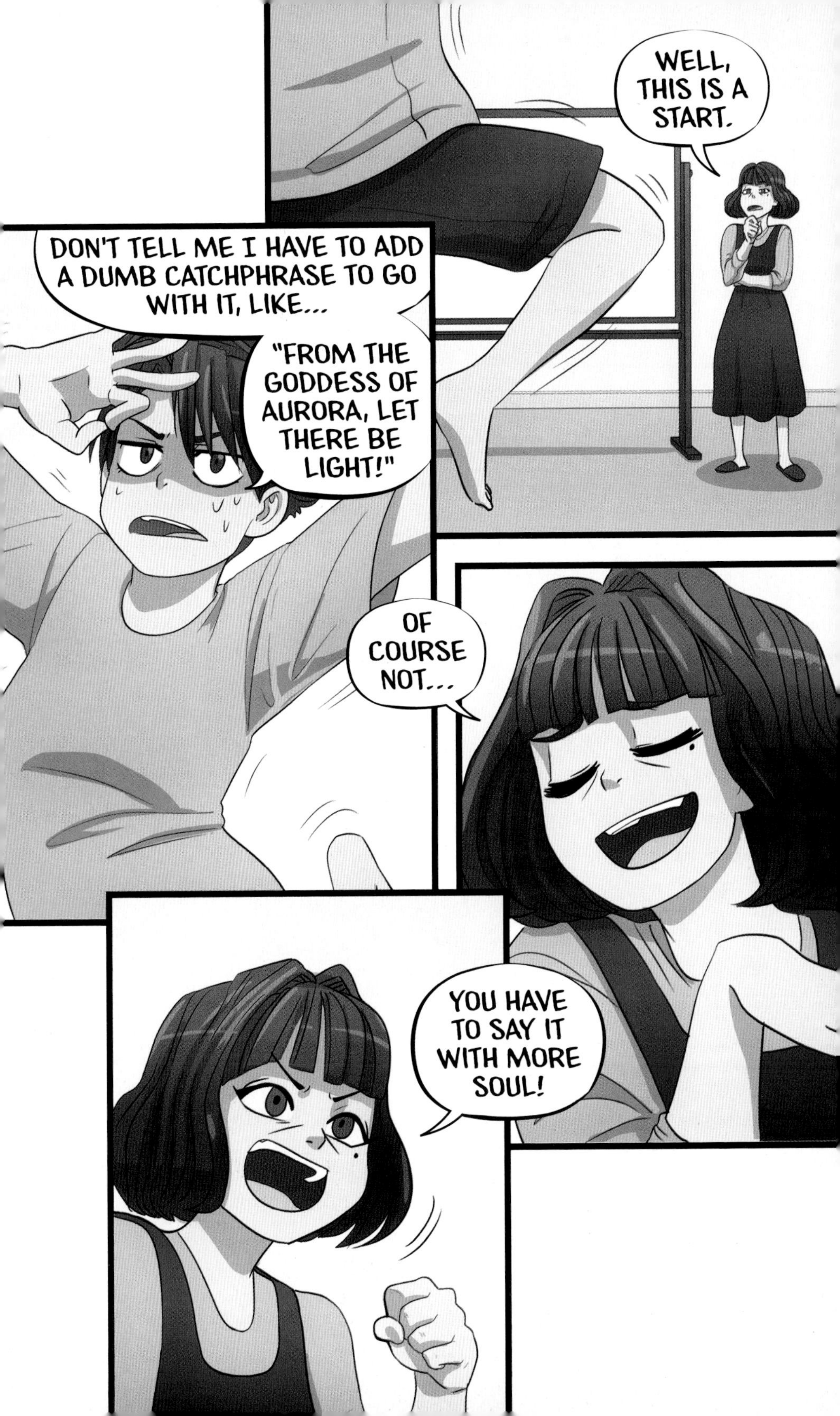
WELL, THIS IS A START.
DON'T TELL ME I HAVE TO ADD A DUMB CATCHPHRASE TO GO WITH IT, LIKE...
"FROM THE GODDESS OF AURORA, LET THERE BE LIGHT!"
OF COURSE NOT...
YOU HAVE TO SAY IT WITH MORE SOUL!

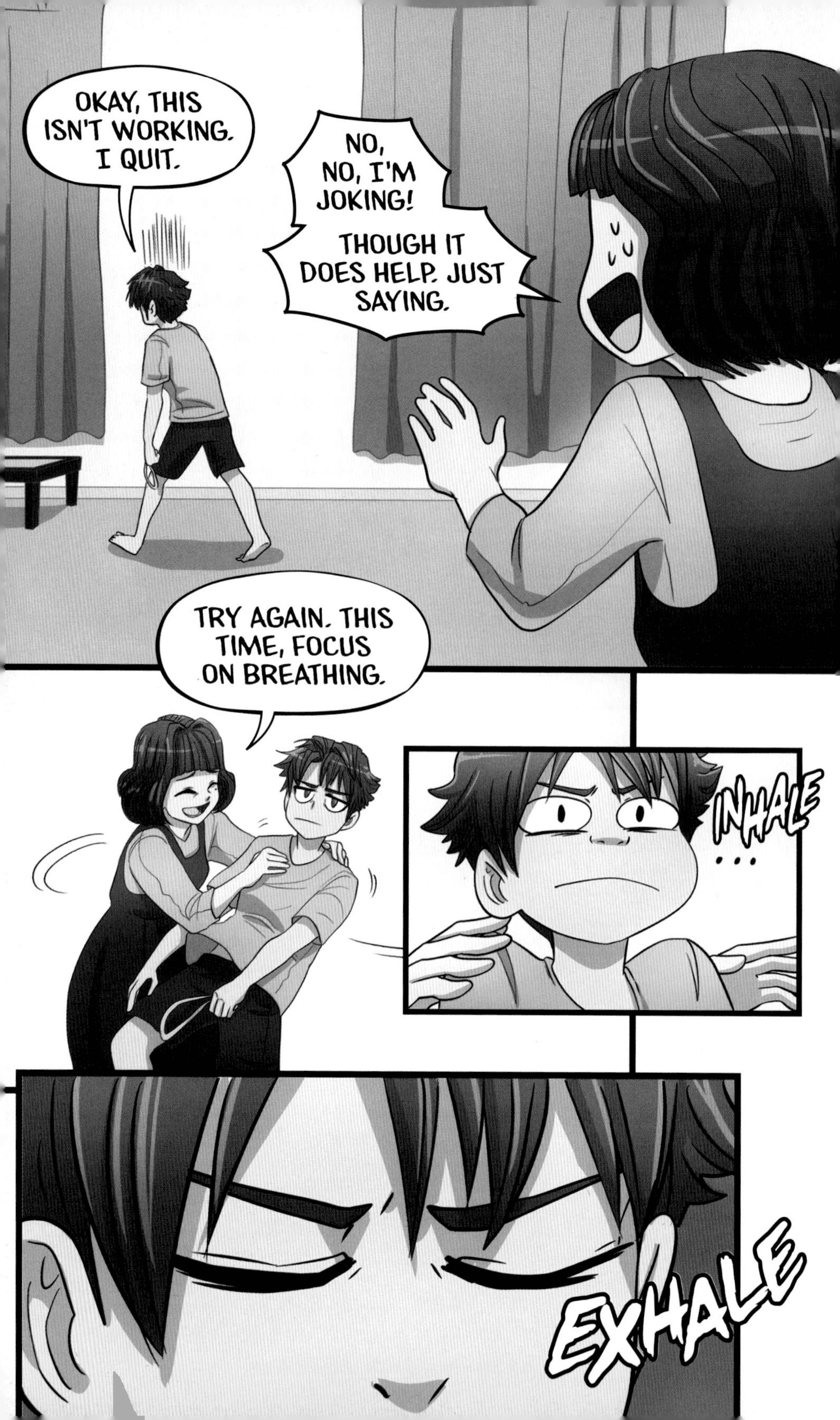
OKAY, THIS ISN'T WORKING. I QUIT.
NO, NO, I'M JOKING!
THOUGH IT DOES HELP. JUST SAYING.
TRY AGAIN. THIS TIME, FOCUS ON BREATHING.
INHALE
...
EXHALE

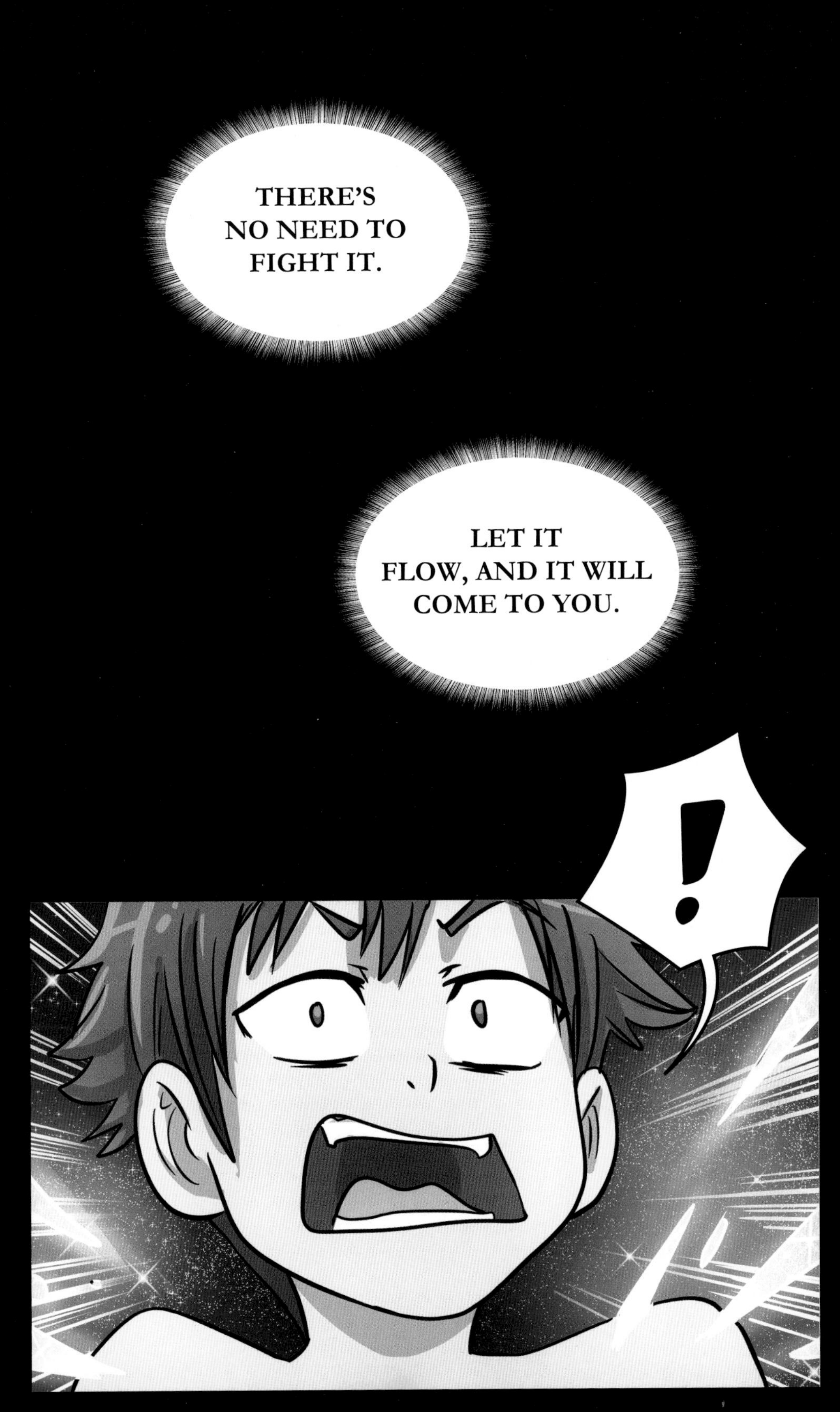

THERE'S NO NEED TO FIGHT IT.
LET IT FLOW, AND IT WILL COME TO YOU.
!

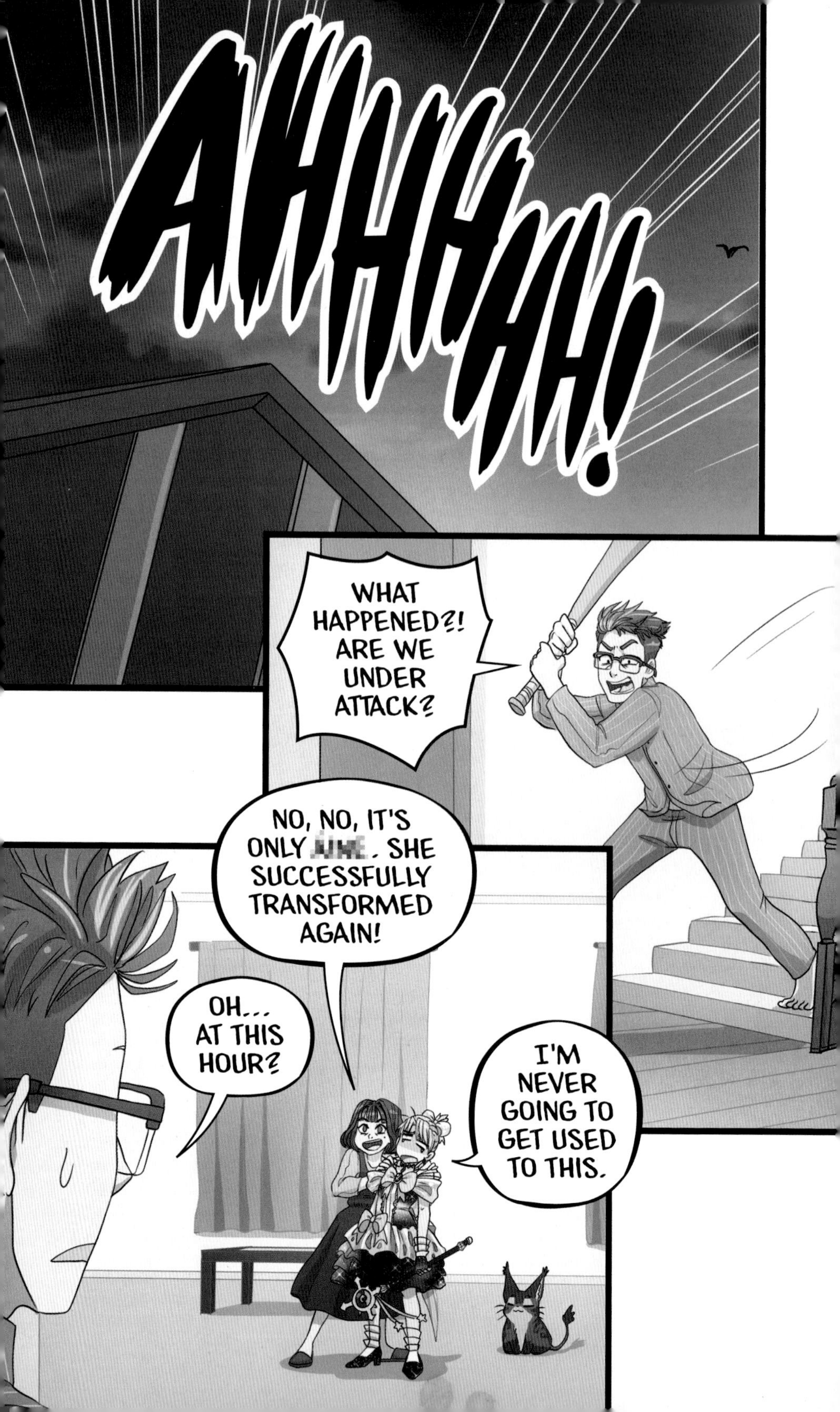
AHHHHHH!
WHAT HAPPENED?! ARE WE UNDER ATTACK?
NO, NO, IT'S ONLY . SHE SUCCESSFULLY TRANSFORMED AGAIN!
OH... AT THIS HOUR?
I'M NEVER GOING TO GET USED TO THIS.

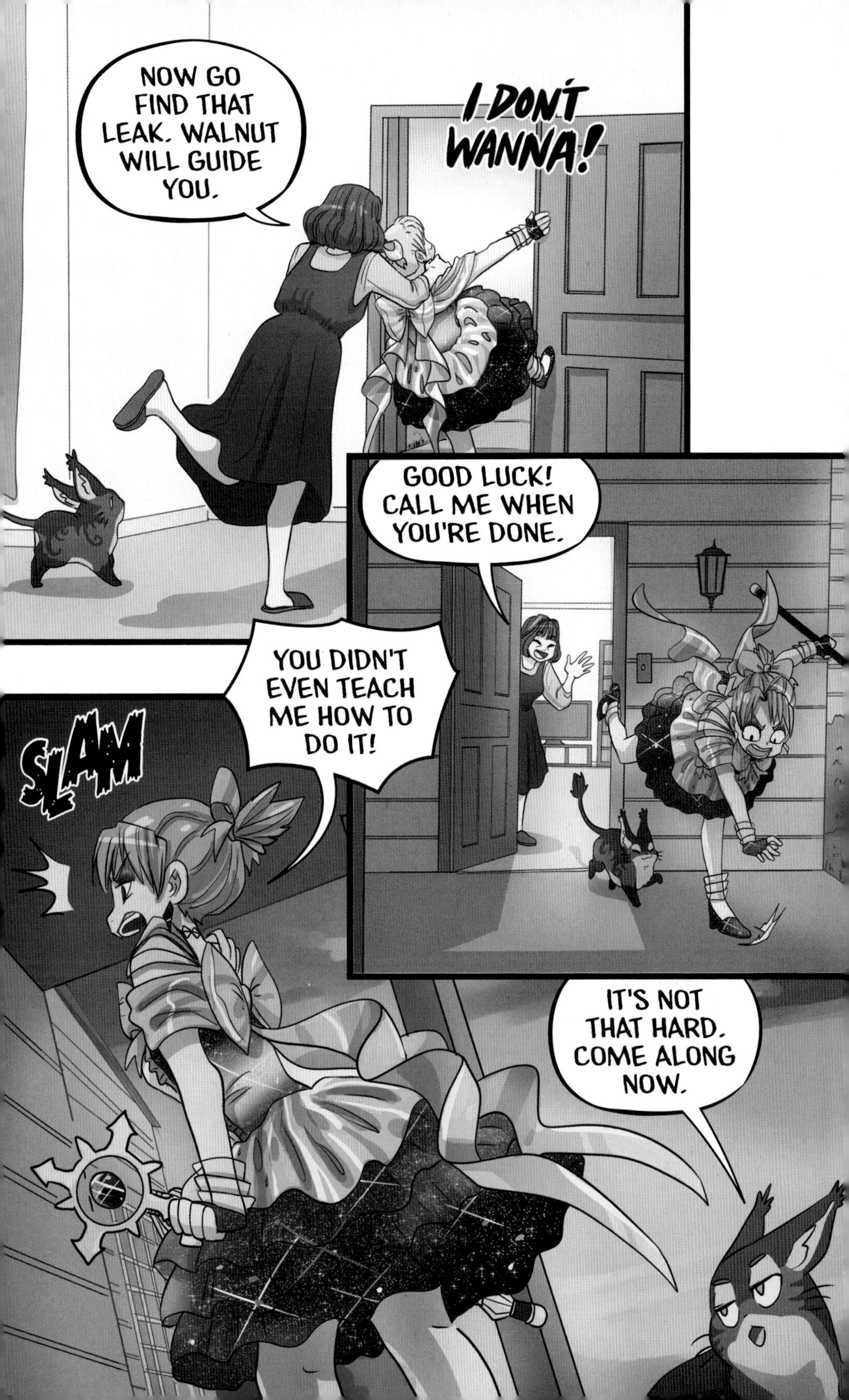
NOW GO FIND THAT LEAK. WALNUT WILL GUIDE YOU.
I DON'T WANNA!
GOOD LUCK! CALL ME WHEN YOU'RE DONE.
YOU DIDN'T EVEN TEACH ME HOW TO DO IT!
SLAM
IT'S NOT THAT HARD. COME ALONG NOW.

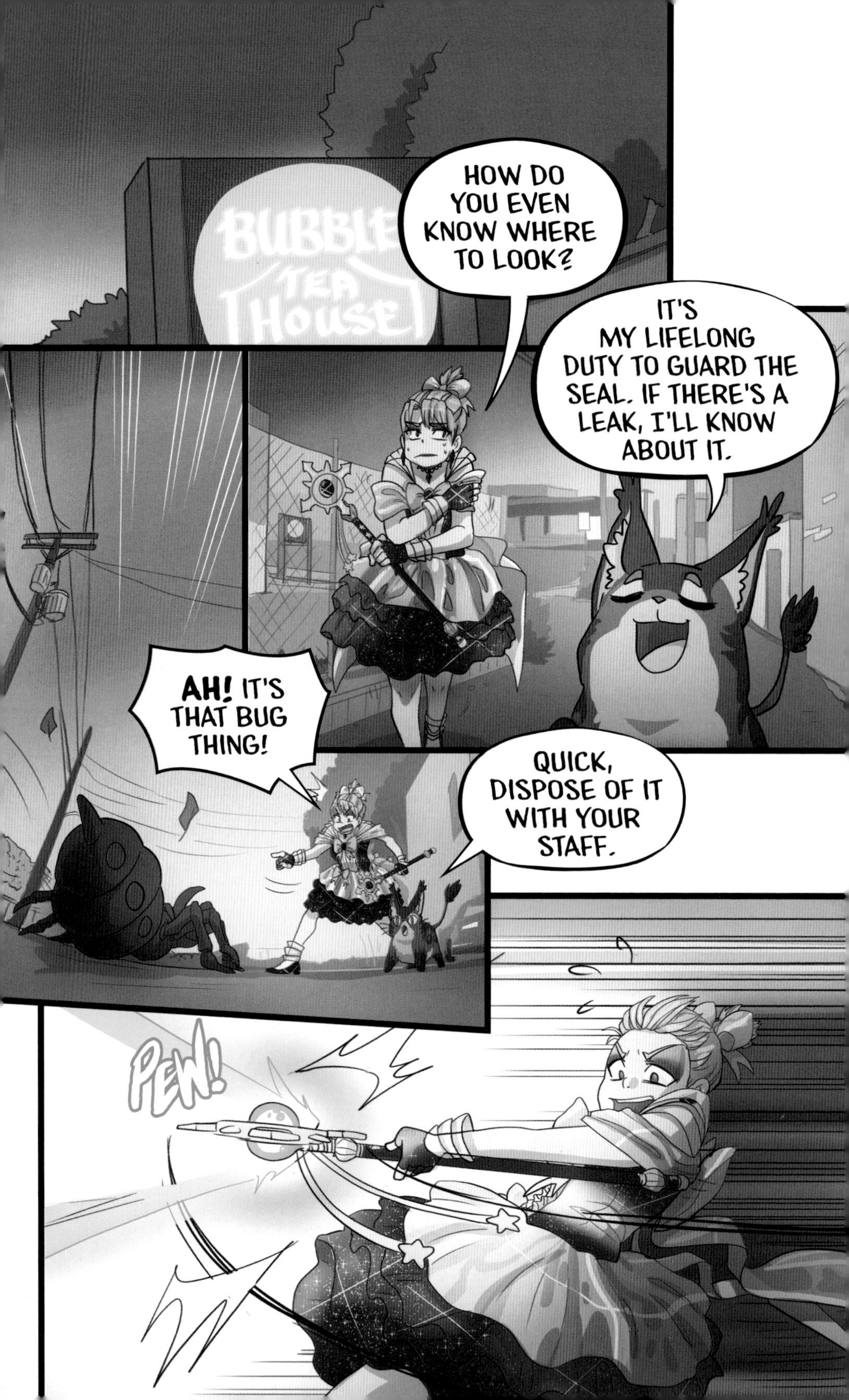
BUBBLE TEA HOUSE
HOW DO YOU EVEN KNOW WHERE TO LOOK?
IT'S MY LIFELONG DUTY TO GUARD THE SEAL. IF THERE'S A LEAK, I'LL KNOW ABOUT IT.
AH! IT'S THAT BUG THING!
QUICK, DISPOSE OF IT WITH YOUR STAFF.
PEW!

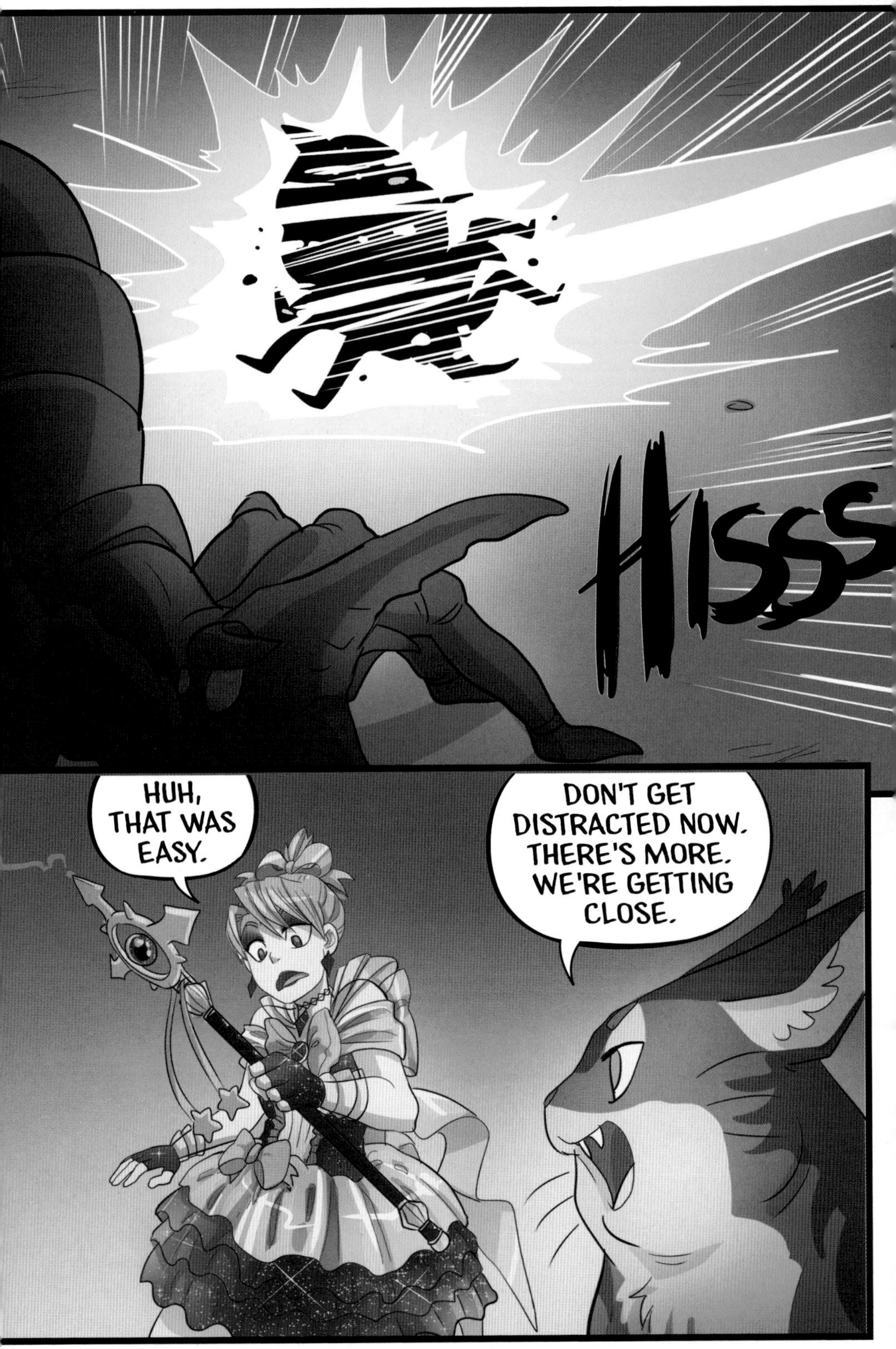
HISSS
HUH, THAT WAS EASY.
DON'T GET DISTRACTED NOW. THERE'S MORE. WE'RE GETTING CLOSE.

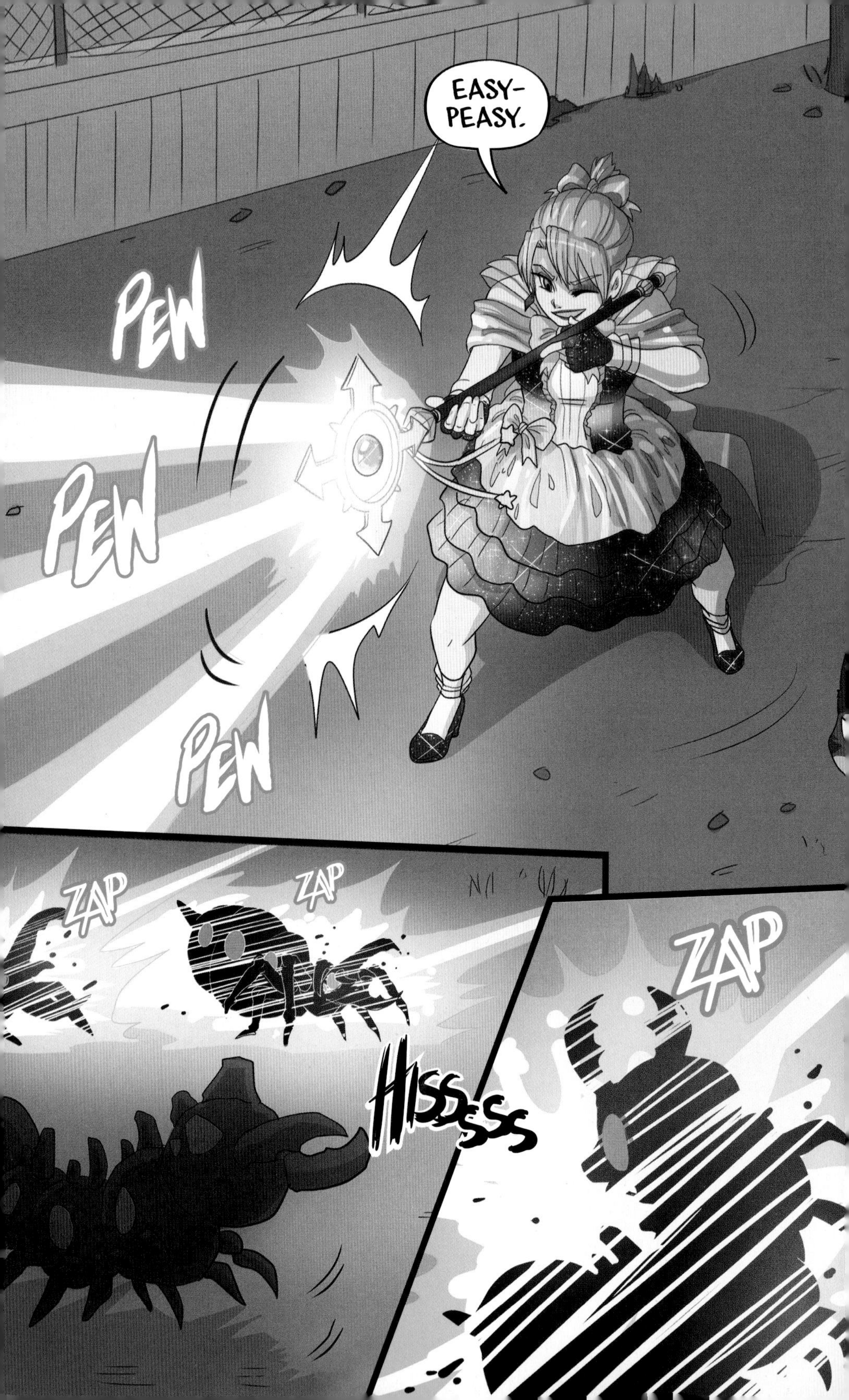
EASY-PEASY.
PEW
PEW
PEW
ZAP
ZAP
ZAP
HISSSSS

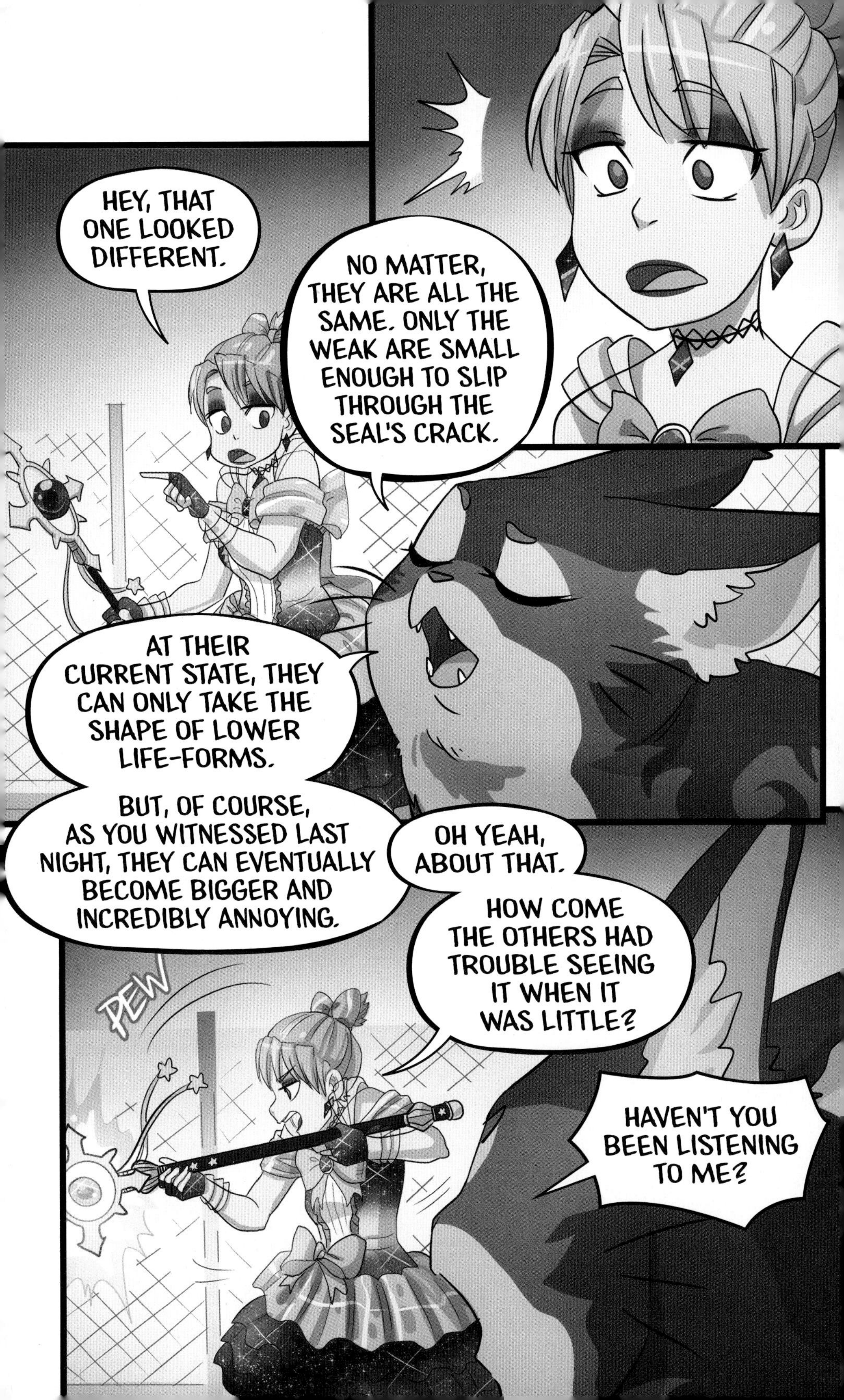
HEY, THAT ONE LOOKED DIFFERENT.
NO MATTER, THEY ARE ALL THE SAME. ONLY THE WEAK ARE SMALL ENOUGH TO SLIP THROUGH THE SEAL'S CRACK.
AT THEIR CURRENT STATE, THEY CAN ONLY TAKE THE SHAPE OF LOWER LIFE-FORMS.
BUT, OF COURSE, AS YOU WITNESSED LAST NIGHT, THEY CAN EVENTUALLY BECOME BIGGER AND INCREDIBLY ANNOYING.
OH YEAH, ABOUT THAT.
HOW COME THE OTHERS HAD TROUBLE SEEING IT WHEN IT WAS LITTLE?
PEW
HAVEN'T YOU BEEN LISTENING TO ME?

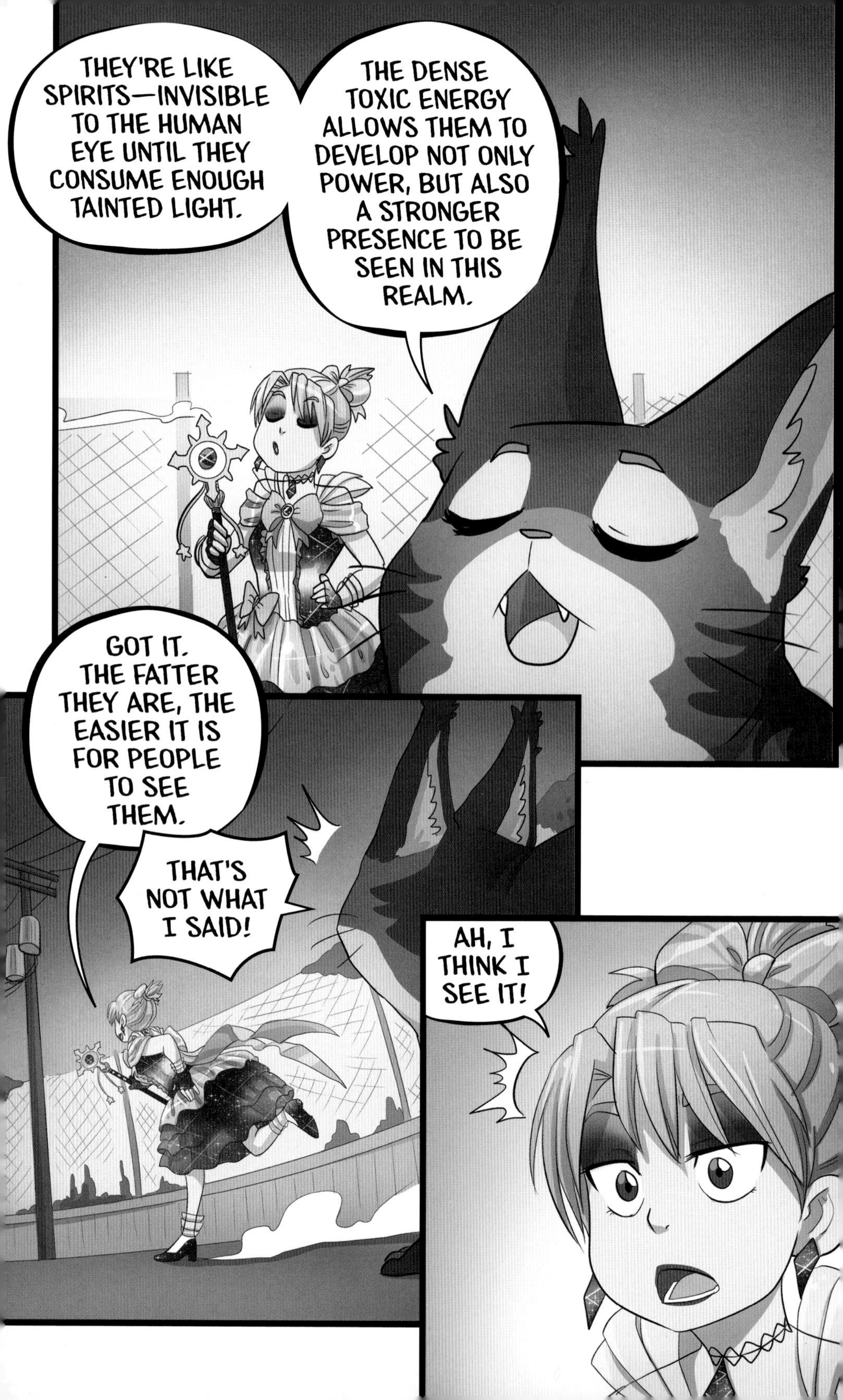
THEY'RE LIKE SPIRITS—INVISIBLE TO THE HUMAN EYE UNTIL THEY CONSUME ENOUGH TAINTED LIGHT.
THE DENSE TOXIC ENERGY ALLOWS THEM TO DEVELOP NOT ONLY POWER, BUT ALSO A STRONGER PRESENCE TO BE SEEN IN THIS REALM.
GOT IT. THE FATTER THEY ARE, THE EASIER IT IS FOR PEOPLE TO SEE THEM.
THAT'S NOT WHAT I SAID!
AH, I THINK I SEE IT!

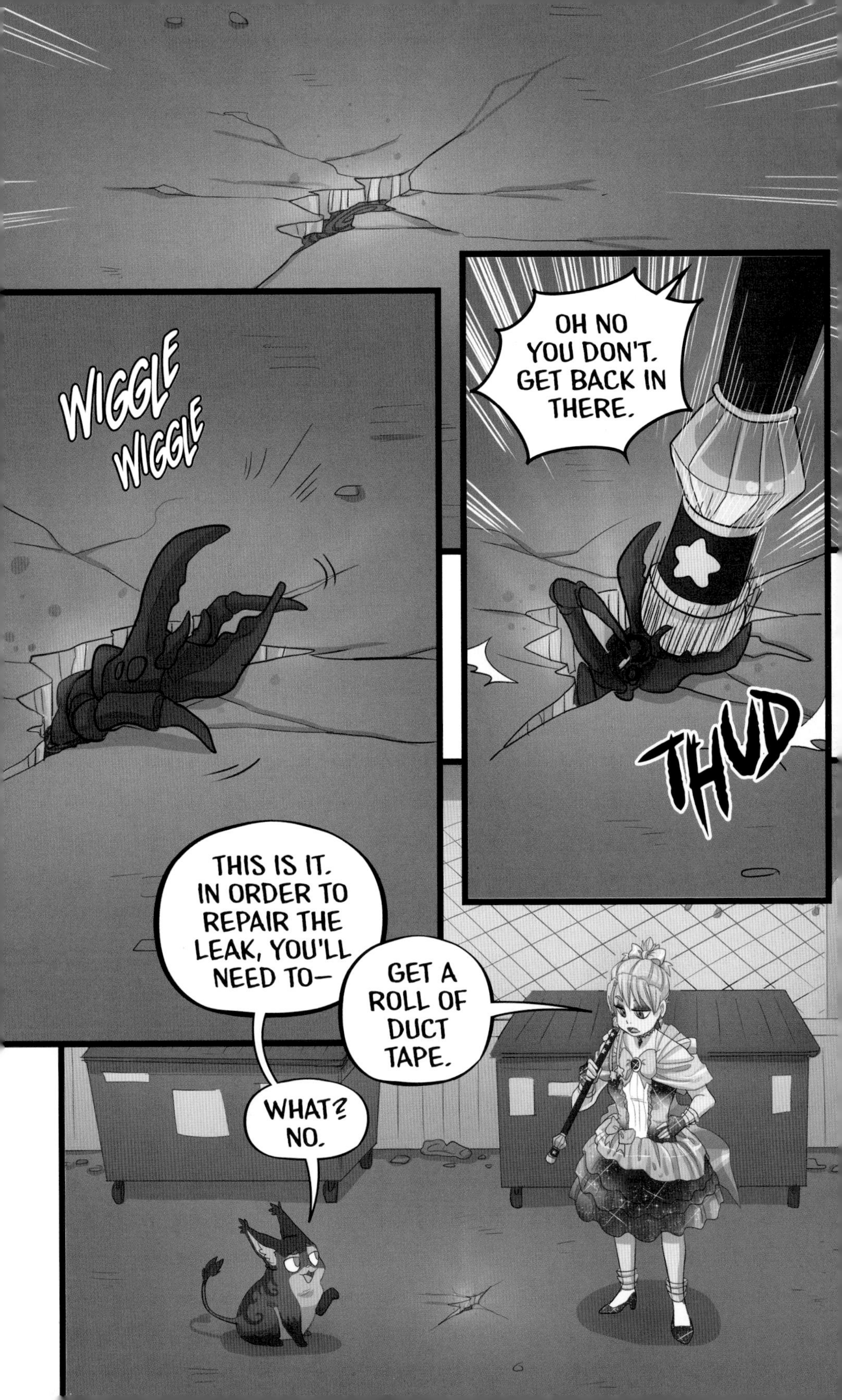
WIGGLE
WIGGLE
OH NO YOU DON'T. GET BACK IN THERE.
THUD
THIS IS IT. IN ORDER TO REPAIR THE LEAK, YOU'LL NEED TO—
GET A ROLL OF DUCT TAPE.
WHAT? NO.

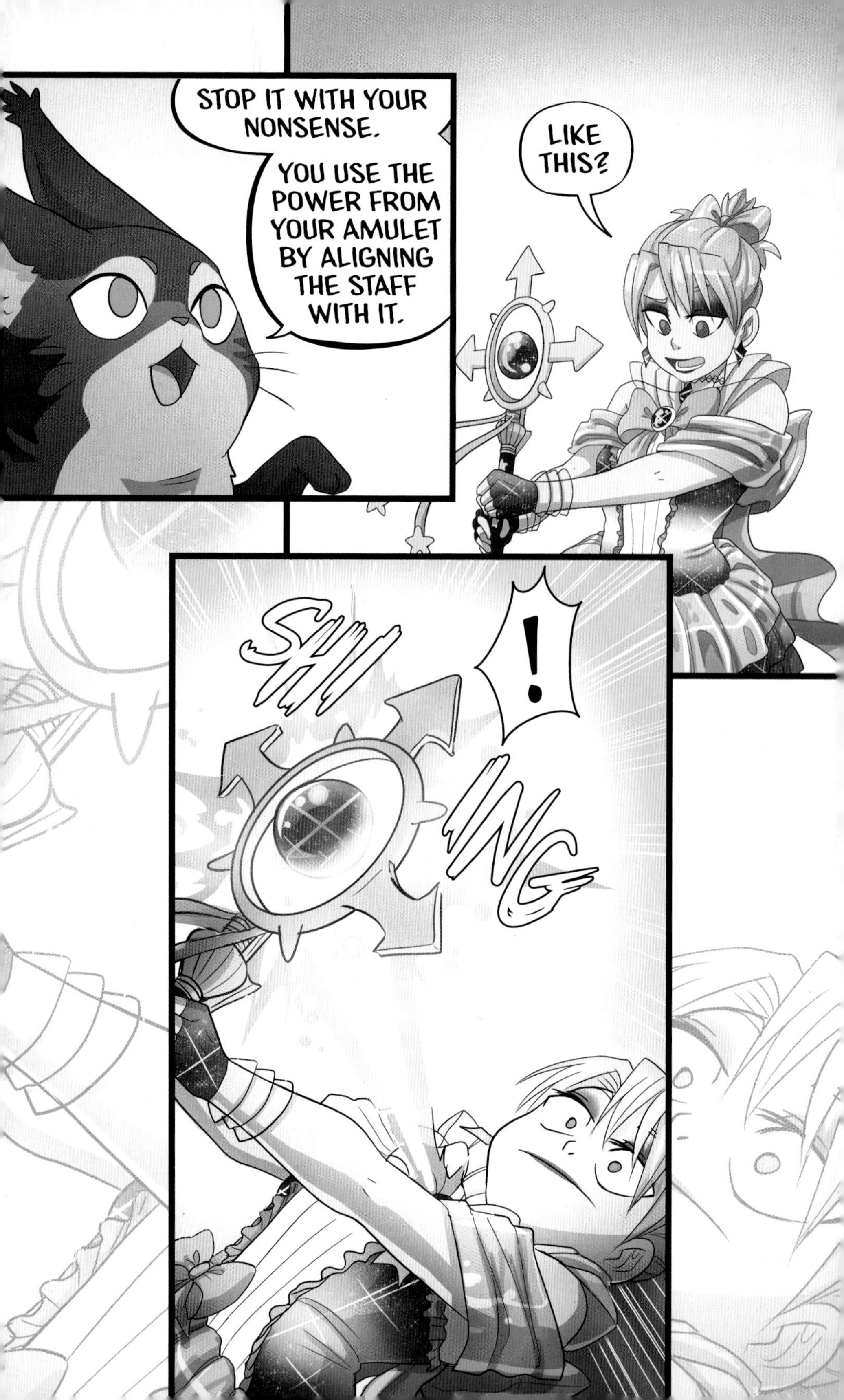

STOP IT WITH YOUR NONSENSE.
YOU USE THE POWER FROM YOUR AMULET BY ALIGNING THE STAFF WITH IT.
LIKE THIS?
SHIING
!

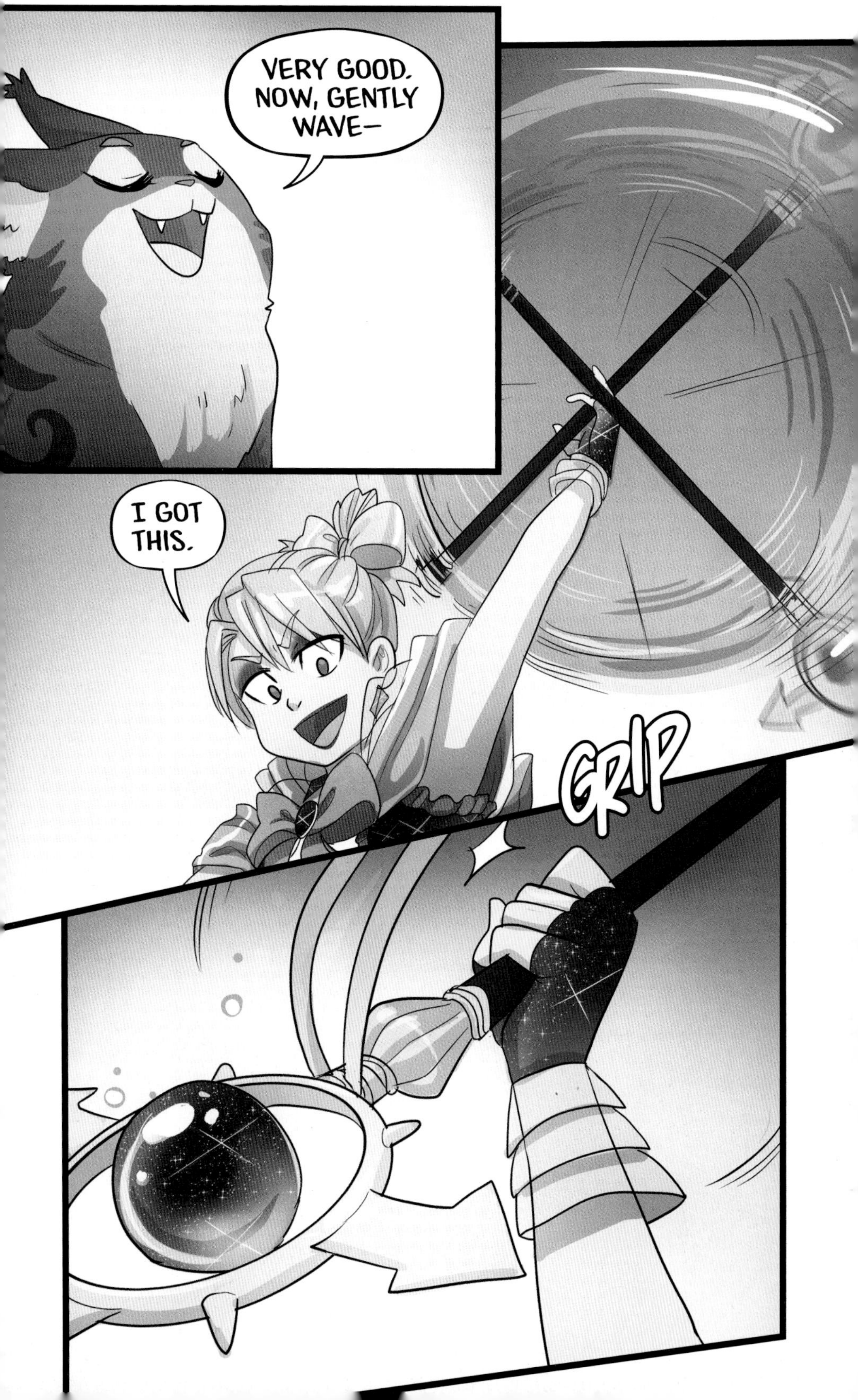
VERY GOOD. NOW, GENTLY WAVE—
I GOT THIS.
GRIP

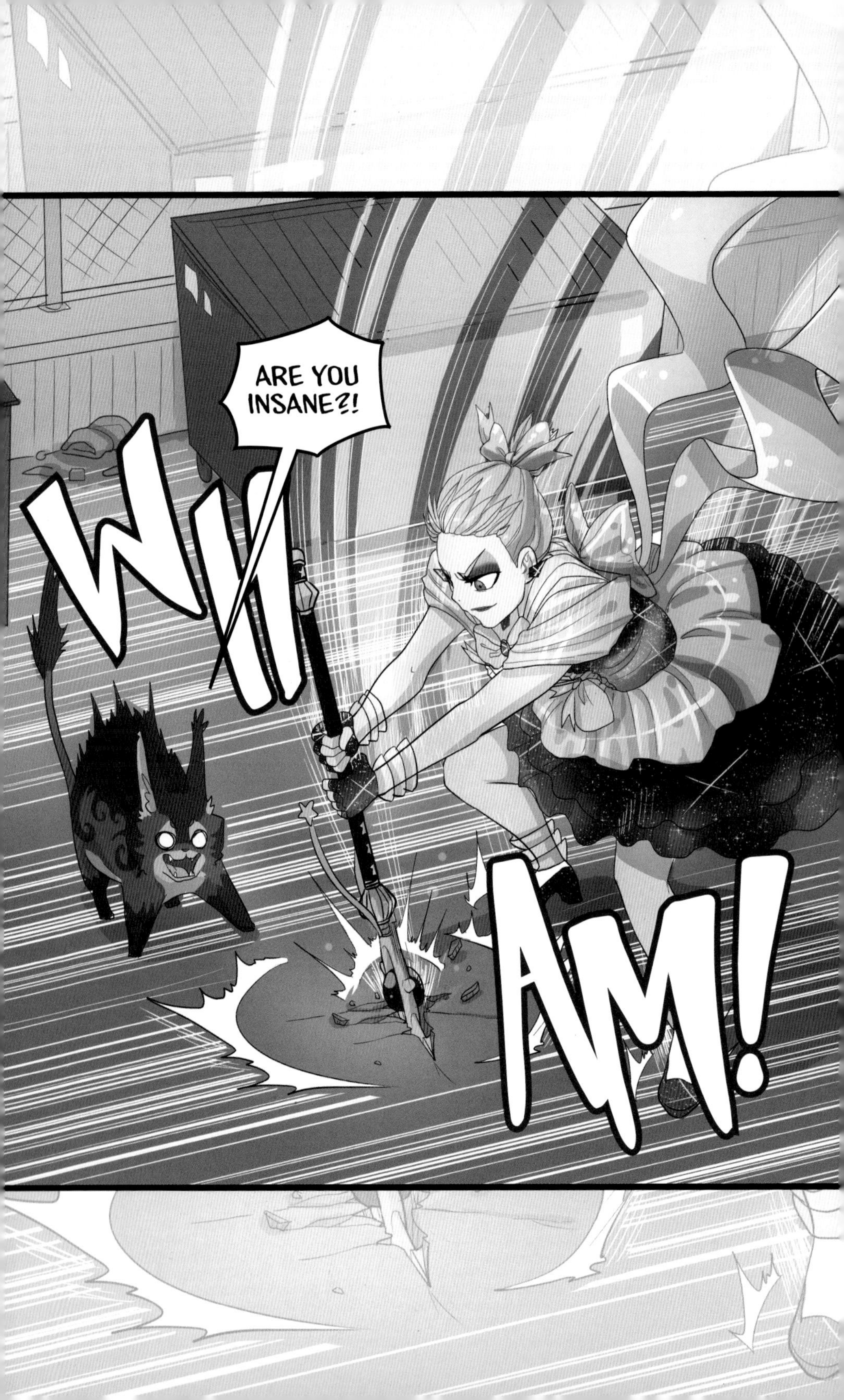
ARE YOU INSANE?!
WHAM!

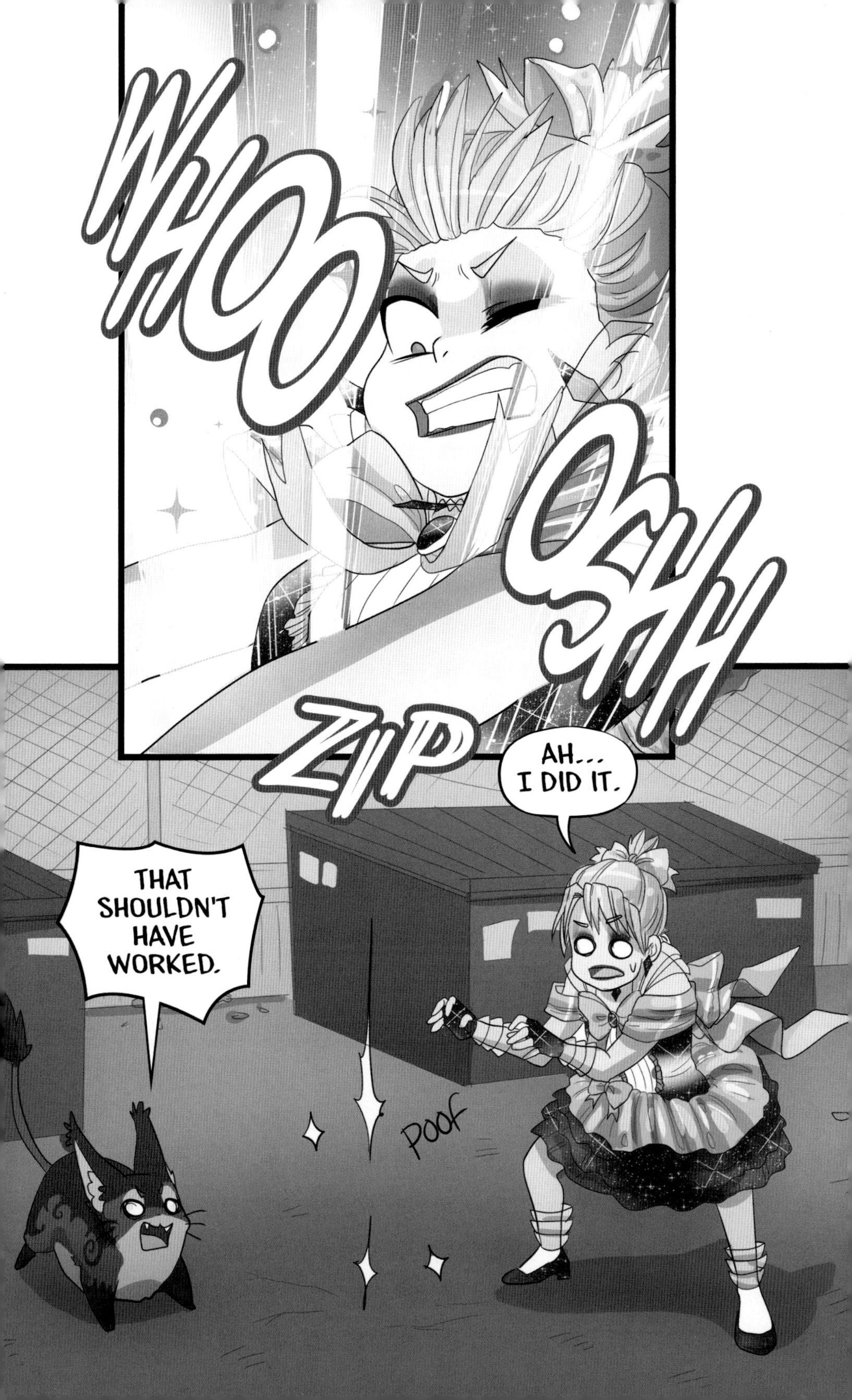
WHOOOSH
ZIP
AH... I DID IT.
THAT SHOULDN'T HAVE WORKED.
POOF

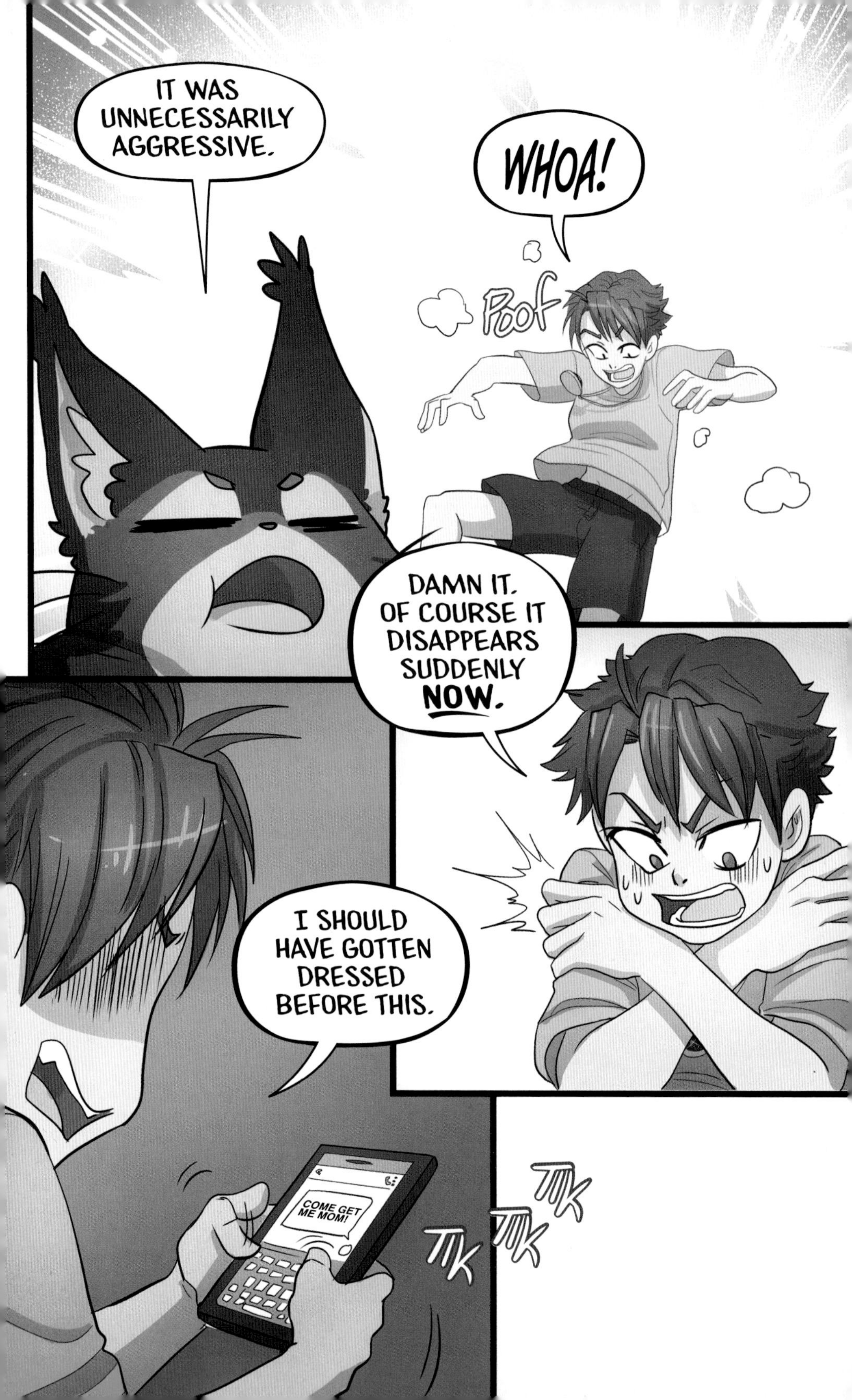
IT WAS UNNECESSARILY AGGRESSIVE.
WHOA!
Poof
DAMN IT. OF COURSE IT DISAPPEARS SUDDENLY NOW.
I SHOULD HAVE GOTTEN DRESSED BEFORE THIS.
COME GET ME MOM!
TIK
TIK
TIK

Episode 7:
TAKE ME FOR A MAN

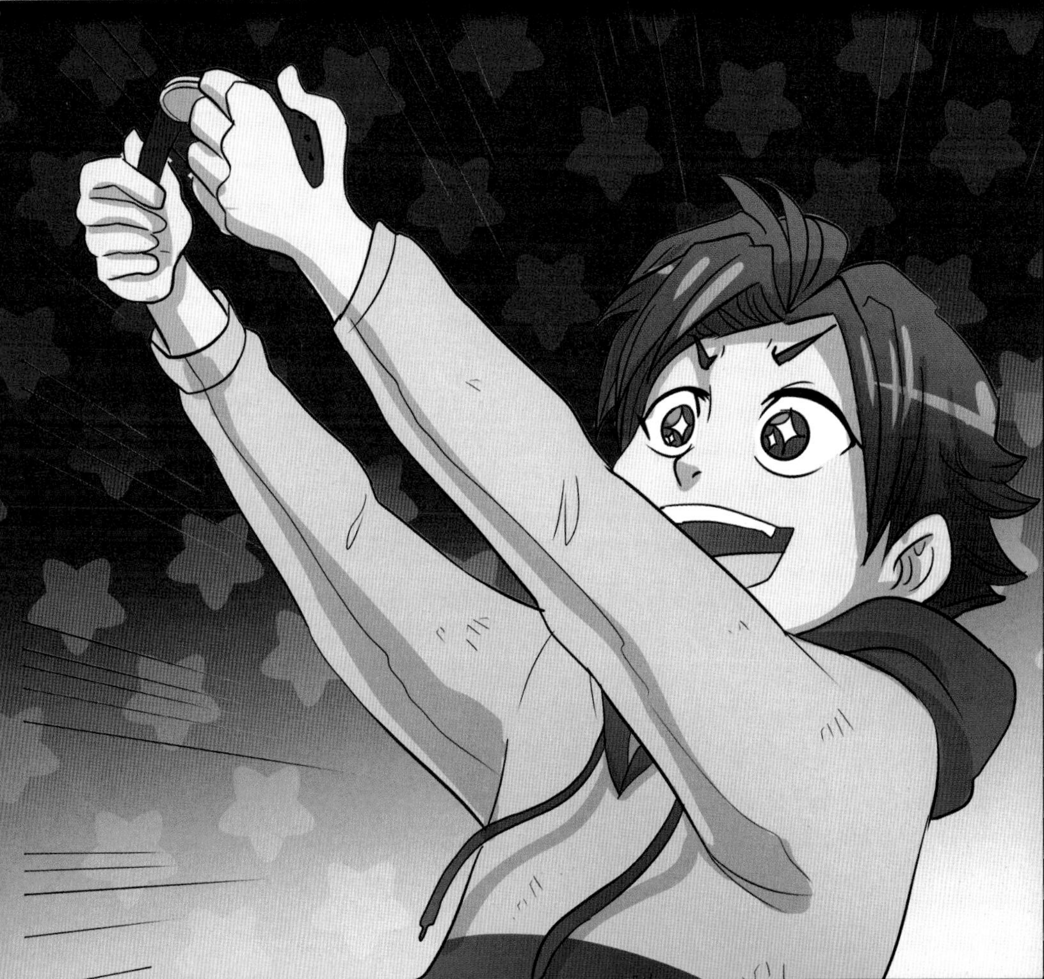

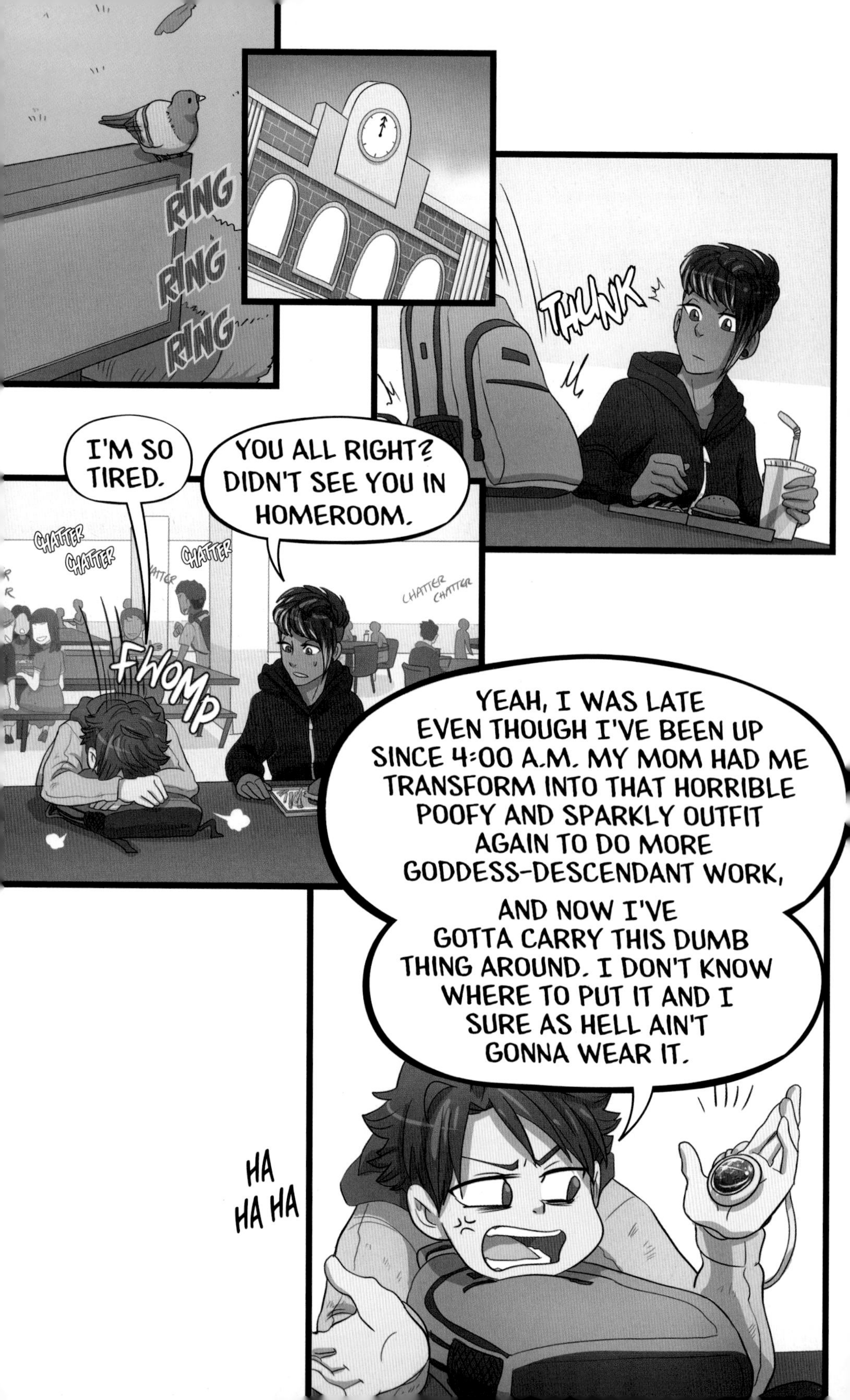
RING
RING
RING
THUNK
CHATTER
CHATTER
CHATTER
CHATTER CHATTER
FWOMP
I'M SO TIRED.
YOU ALL RIGHT? DIDN'T SEE YOU IN HOMEROOM.
YEAH, I WAS LATE EVEN THOUGH I'VE BEEN UP SINCE 4:00 A.M. MY MOM HAD ME TRANSFORM INTO THAT HORRIBLE POOFY AND SPARKLY OUTFIT AGAIN TO DO MORE GODDESS-DESCENDANT WORK,
AND NOW I'VE GOTTA CARRY THIS DUMB THING AROUND. I DON'T KNOW WHERE TO PUT IT AND I SURE AS HELL AIN'T GONNA WEAR IT.
HA HA HA

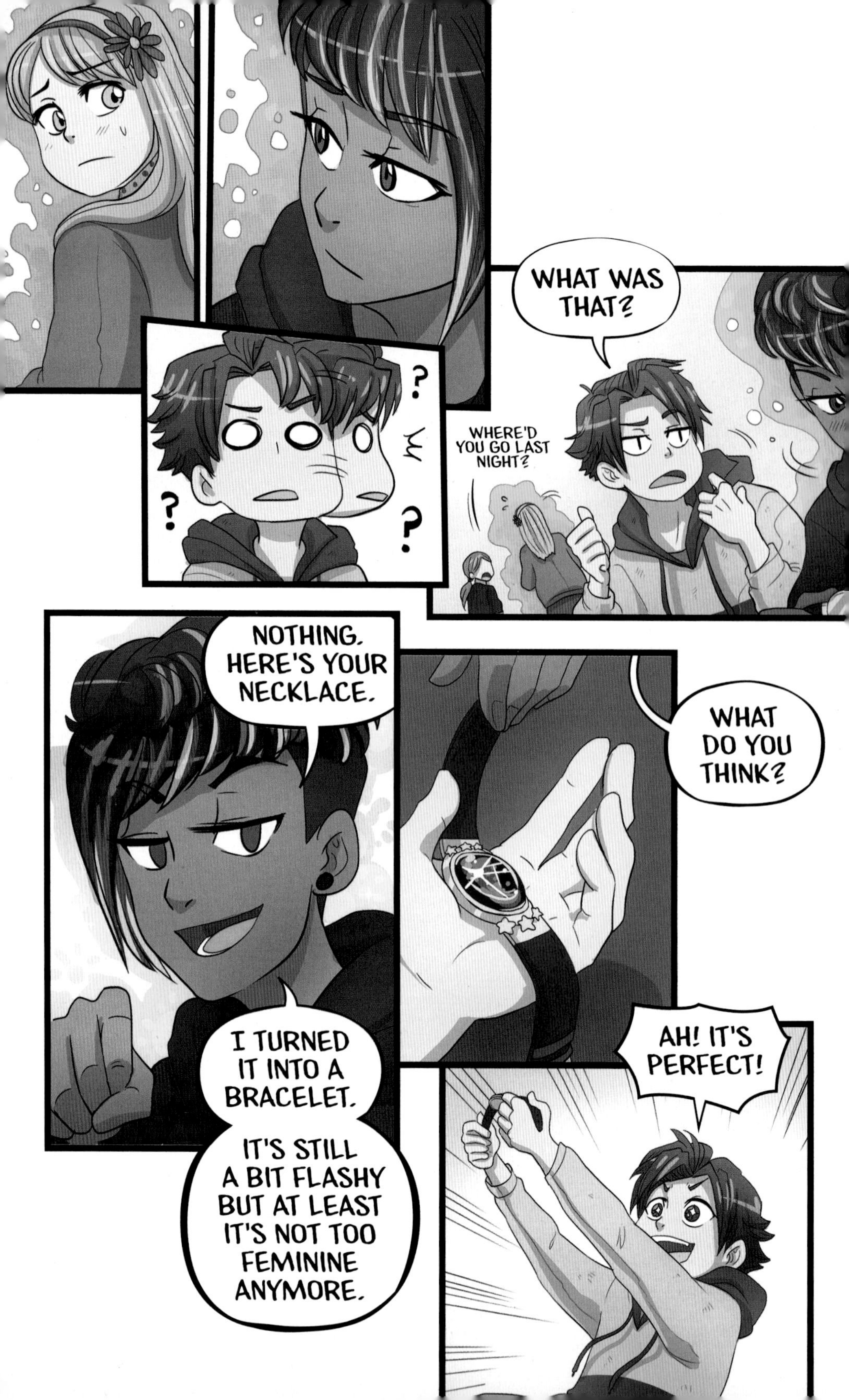
WHAT WAS THAT?
WHERE'D YOU GO LAST NIGHT?
NOTHING. HERE'S YOUR NECKLACE.
I TURNED IT INTO A BRACELET.
IT'S STILL A BIT FLASHY BUT AT LEAST IT'S NOT TOO FEMININE ANYMORE.
WHAT DO YOU THINK?
AH! IT'S PERFECT!

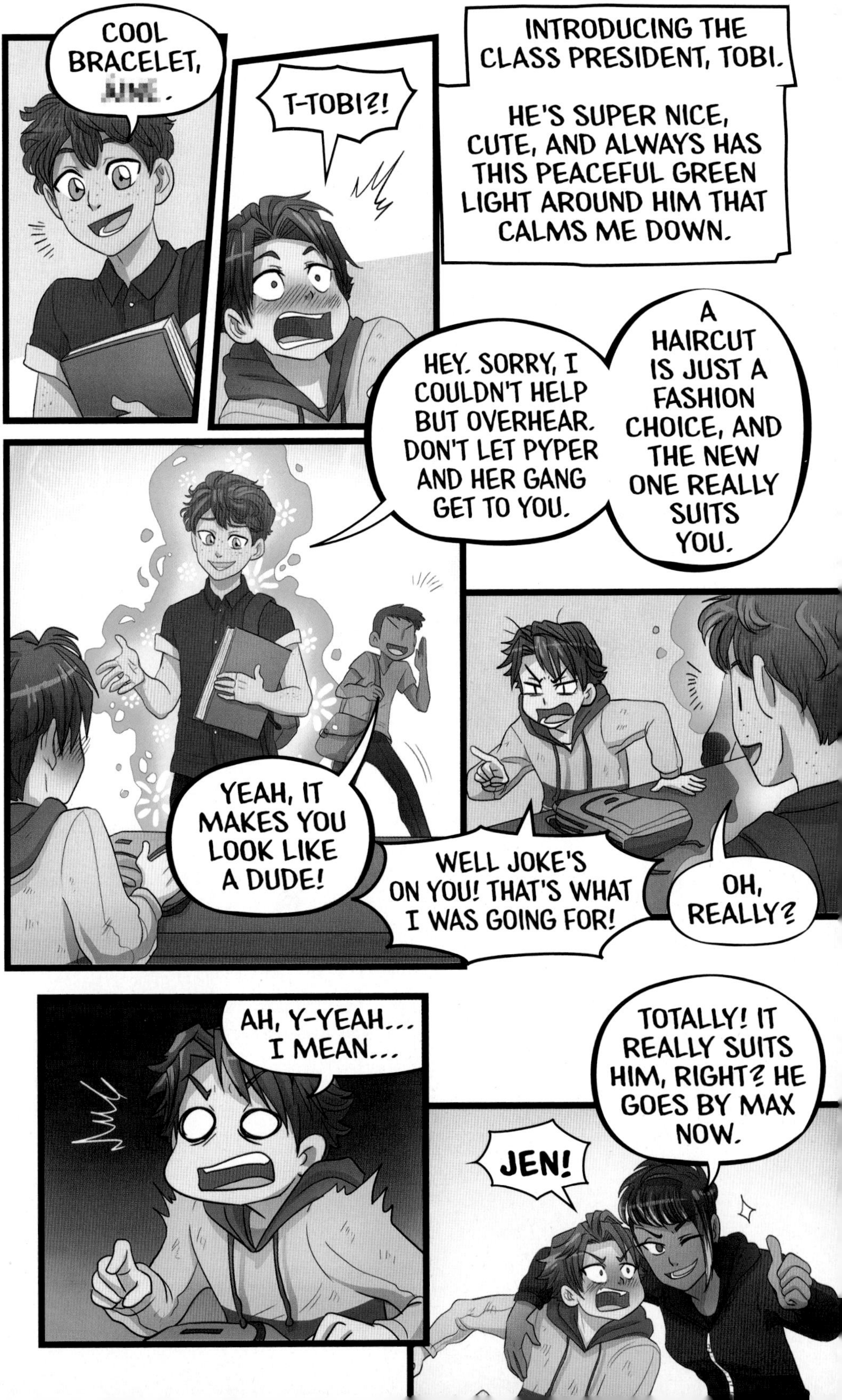
COOL BRACELET,
T-TOBI?!
INTRODUCING THE CLASS PRESIDENT, TOBI.
HE'S SUPER NICE, CUTE, AND ALWAYS HAS THIS PEACEFUL GREEN LIGHT AROUND HIM THAT CALMS ME DOWN.
HEY. SORRY, I COULDN'T HELP BUT OVERHEAR. DON'T LET PYPER AND HER GANG GET TO YOU.
A HAIRCUT IS JUST A FASHION CHOICE, AND THE NEW ONE REALLY SUITS YOU.
YEAH, IT MAKES YOU LOOK LIKE A DUDE!
WELL JOKE'S ON YOU! THAT'S WHAT I WAS GOING FOR!
OH, REALLY?
AH, Y-YEAH... I MEAN...
TOTALLY! IT REALLY SUITS HIM, RIGHT? HE GOES BY MAX NOW.
JEN!

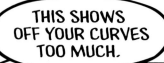

THIS SHOWS OFF YOUR CURVES TOO MUCH.

HELLO, SIR, DID YOU FIND EVERYTHING YOU NEED ALL RIGHT?

WHAT? ARE YOU TALKING TO ME?

OH, I'M SORRY, MA'AM. YES, DO YOU NEED ANY HELP WITH ANYTHING?

NO, I'M GOOD.

HOW ABOUT YOU, MA'AM?

OH, COME ON!

HAHA, SORRY. WE'RE GOOD.

HERE, MAX. TRY THIS ONE.

SINCE YOU LIKE HOODIES, HERE'S SOME DIFFERENT OPTIONS.

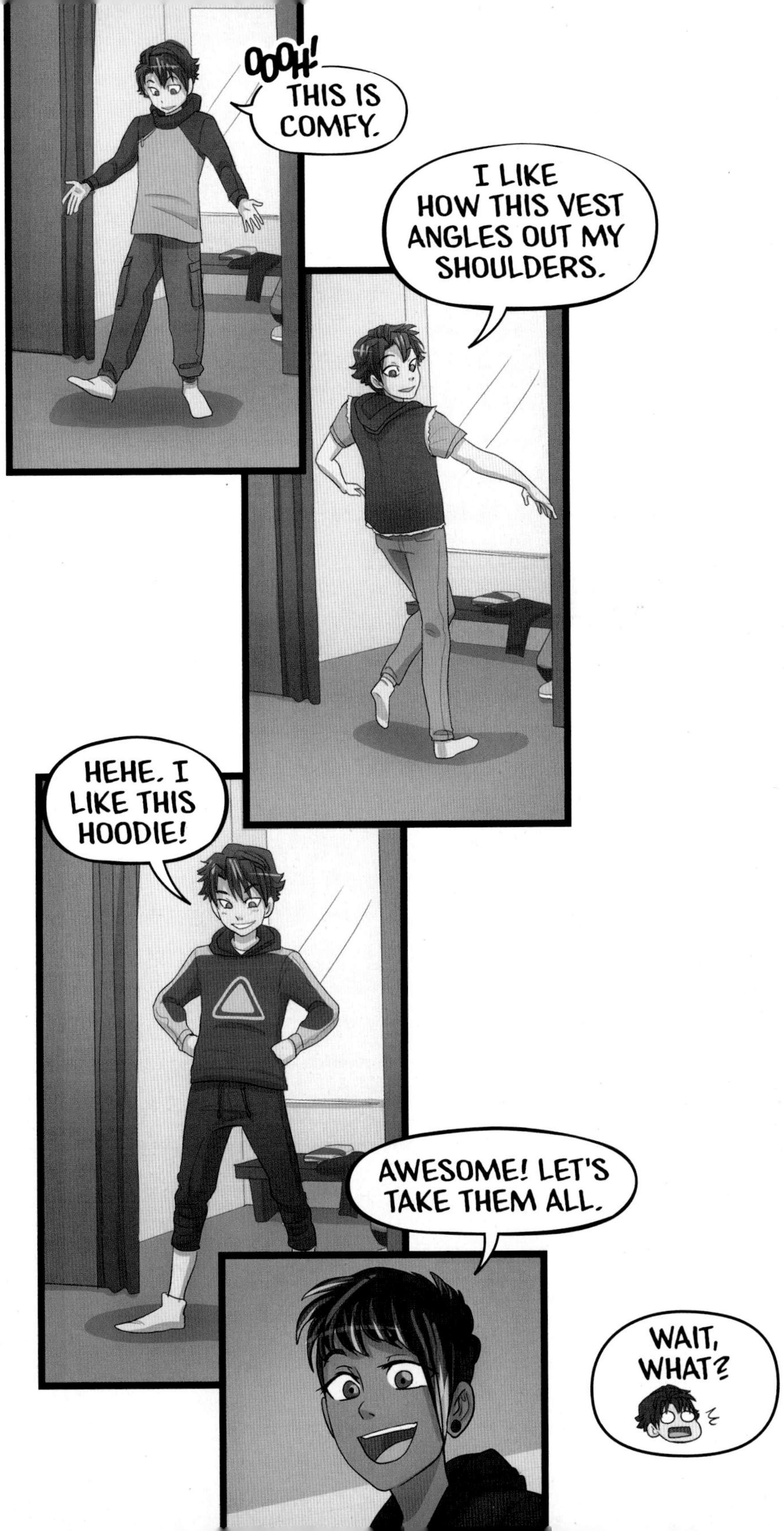
OOOH! THIS IS COMFY.
I LIKE HOW THIS VEST ANGLES OUT MY SHOULDERS.
HEHE. I LIKE THIS HOODIE!
AWESOME! LET'S TAKE THEM ALL.
WAIT, WHAT?

203

Episode 8:
HOW'S IT GOING TO BE?

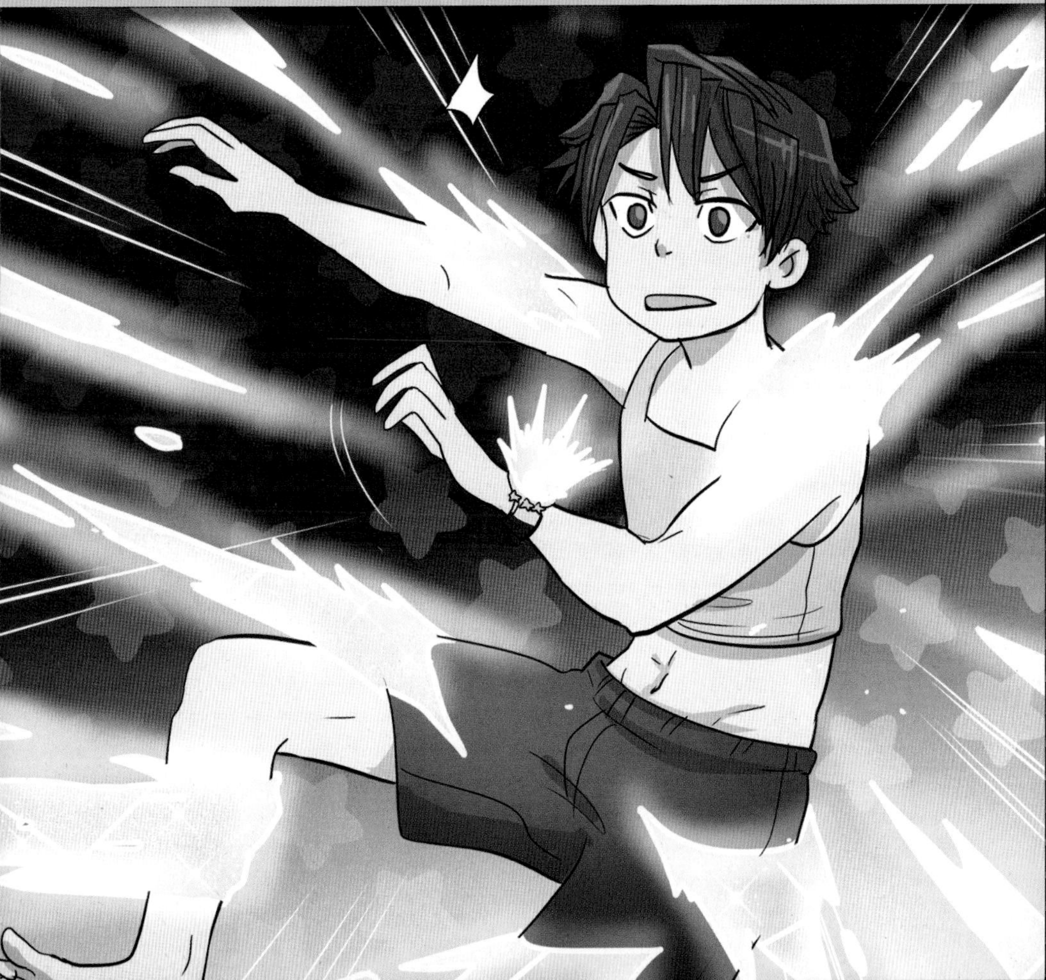

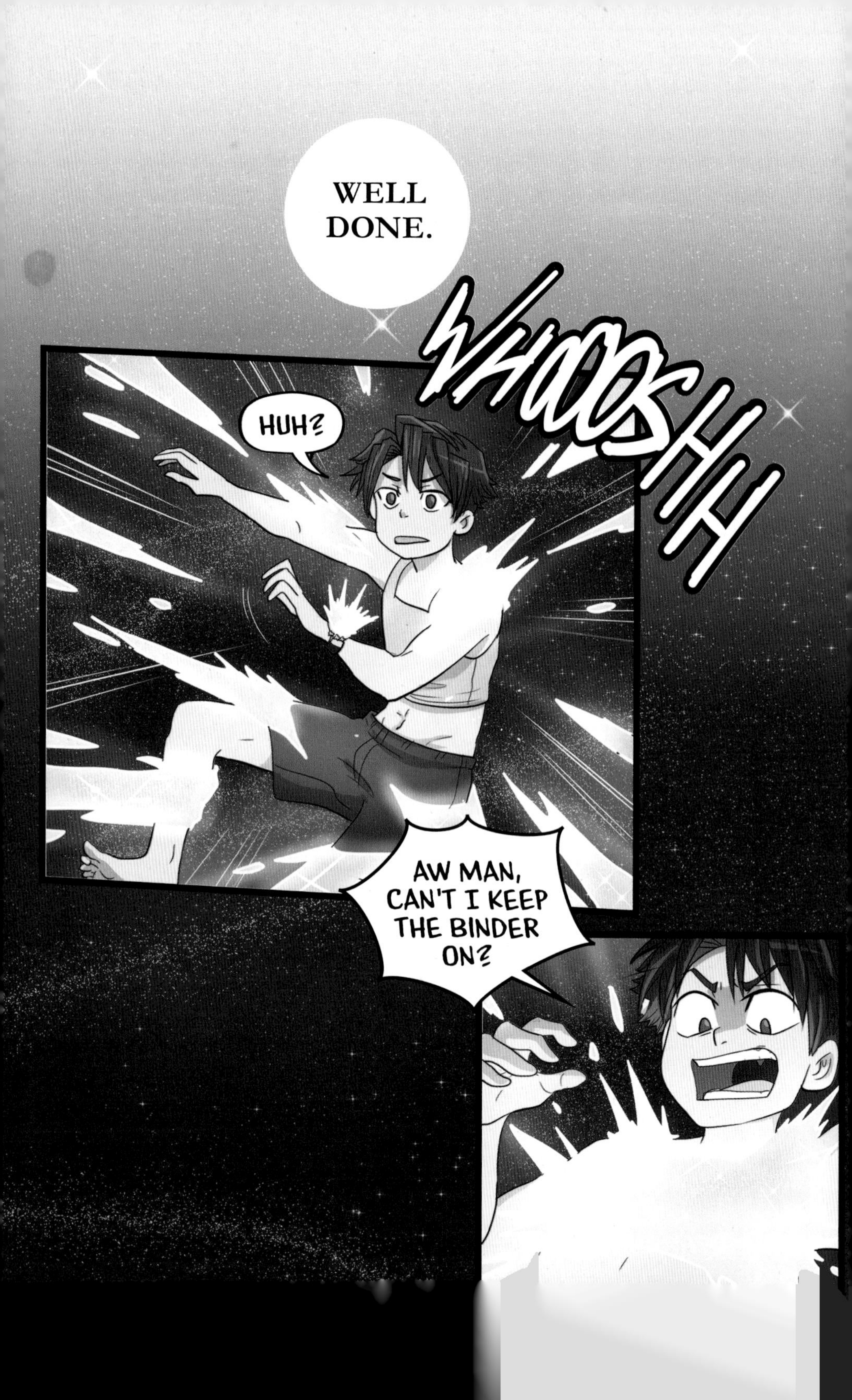
WELL DONE.
WHOOSHHH
HUH?
AW MAN, CAN'T I KEEP THE BINDER ON?

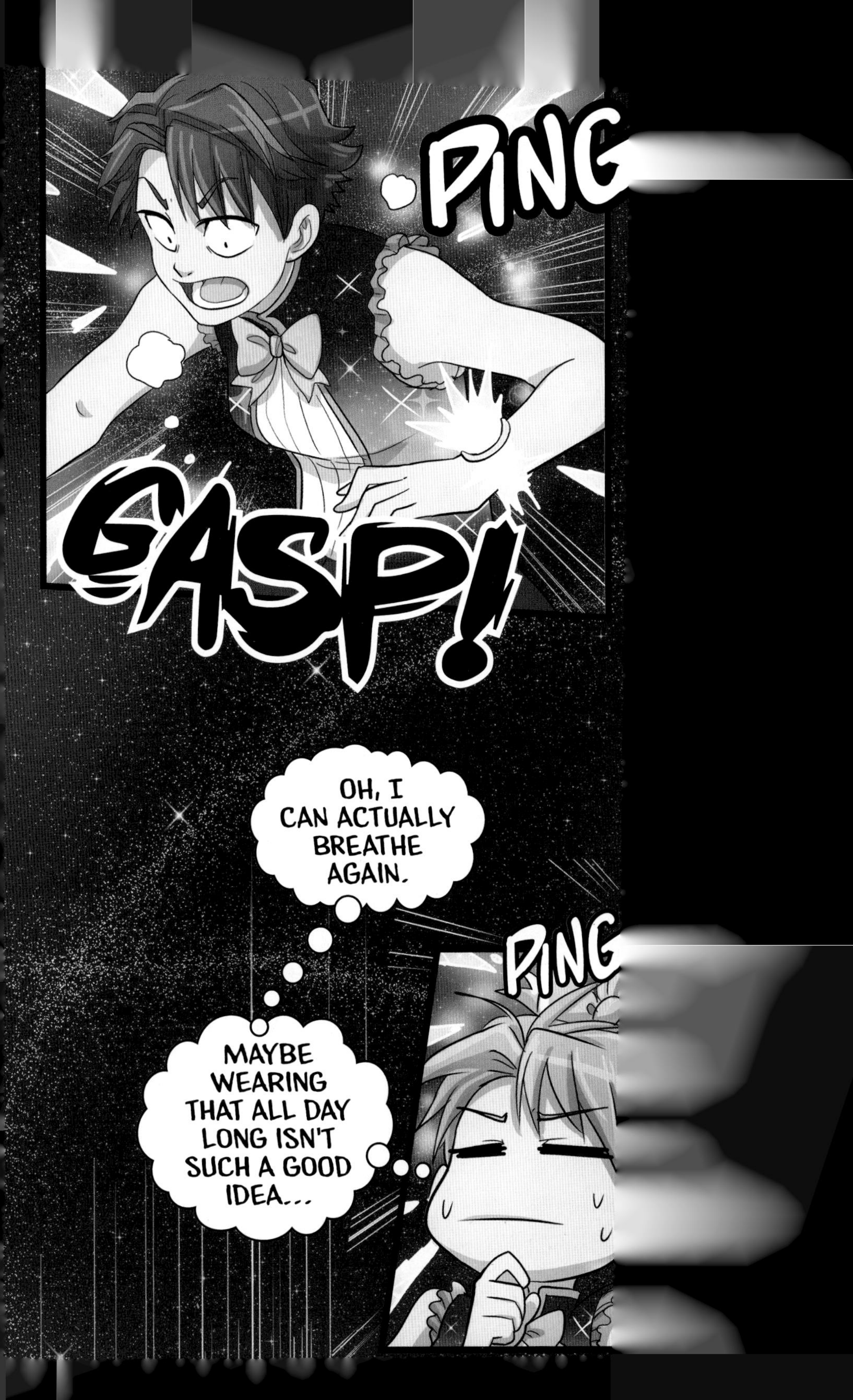

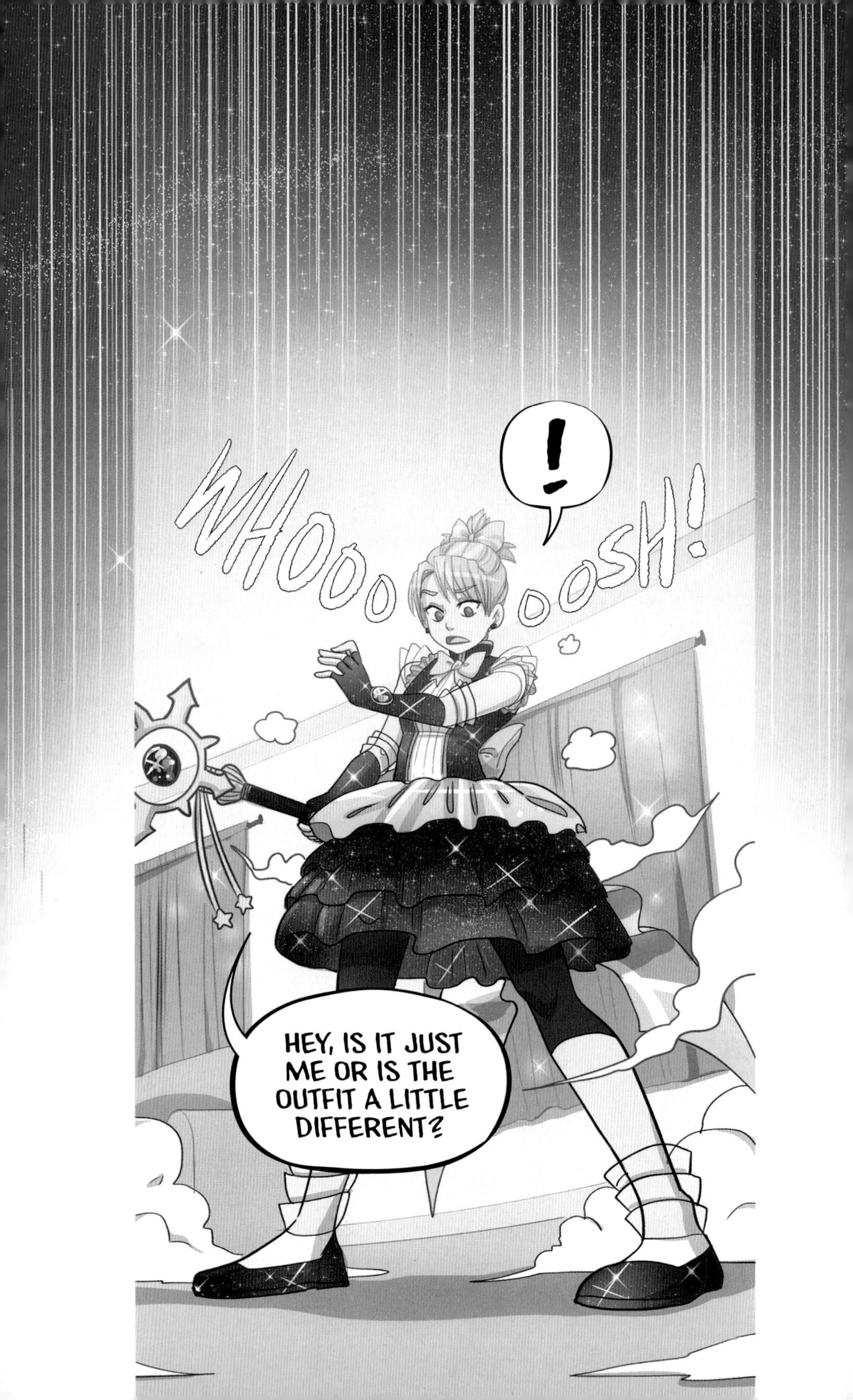

WHOOOO OOSH!
!
HEY, IS IT JUST ME OR IS THE OUTFIT A LITTLE DIFFERENT?

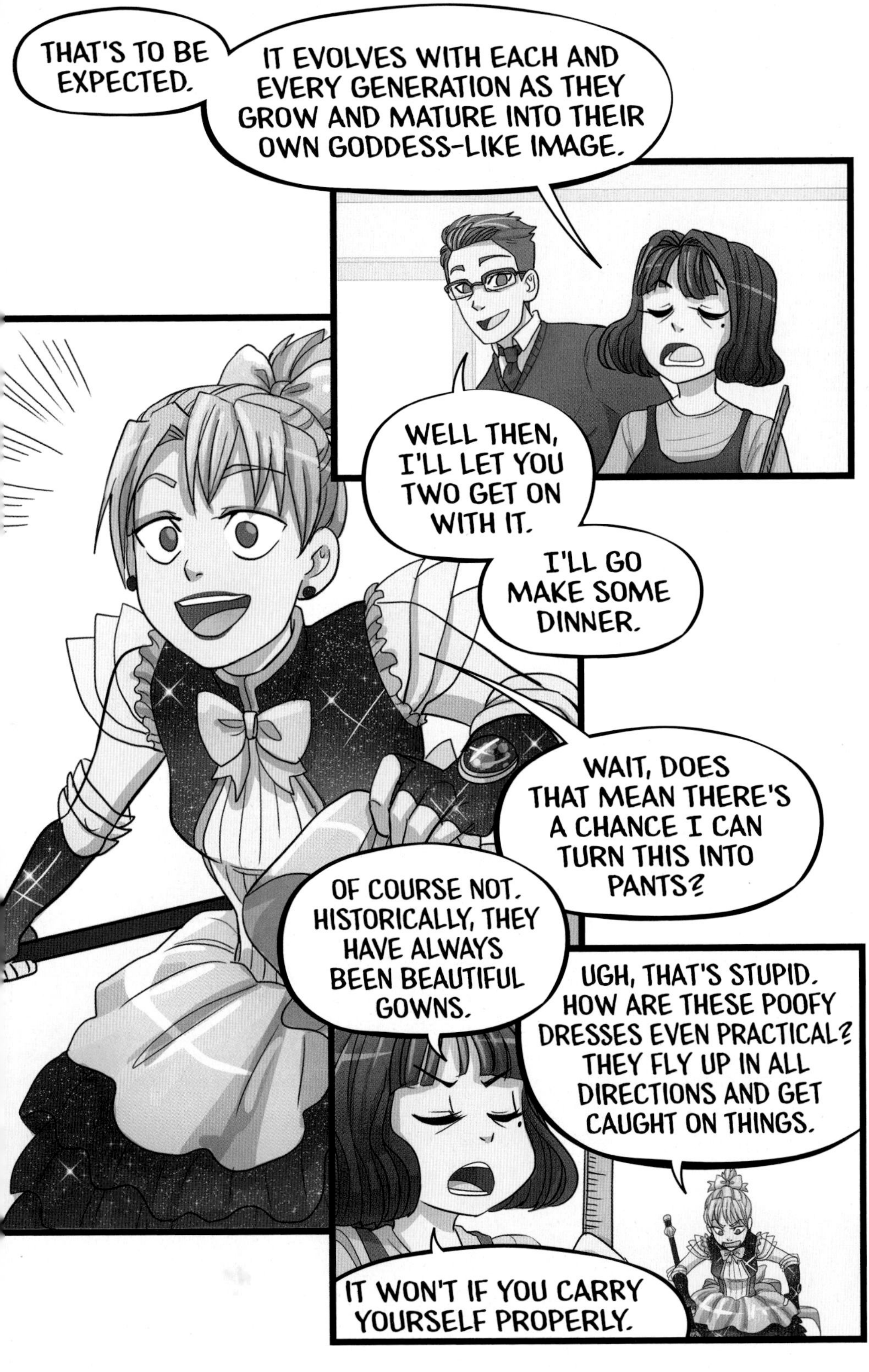
THAT'S TO BE EXPECTED.
IT EVOLVES WITH EACH AND EVERY GENERATION AS THEY GROW AND MATURE INTO THEIR OWN GODDESS-LIKE IMAGE.
WELL THEN, I'LL LET YOU TWO GET ON WITH IT.
I'LL GO MAKE SOME DINNER.
WAIT, DOES THAT MEAN THERE'S A CHANCE I CAN TURN THIS INTO PANTS?
OF COURSE NOT. HISTORICALLY, THEY HAVE ALWAYS BEEN BEAUTIFUL GOWNS.
UGH, THAT'S STUPID. HOW ARE THESE POOFY DRESSES EVEN PRACTICAL? THEY FLY UP IN ALL DIRECTIONS AND GET CAUGHT ON THINGS.
IT WON'T IF YOU CARRY YOURSELF PROPERLY.

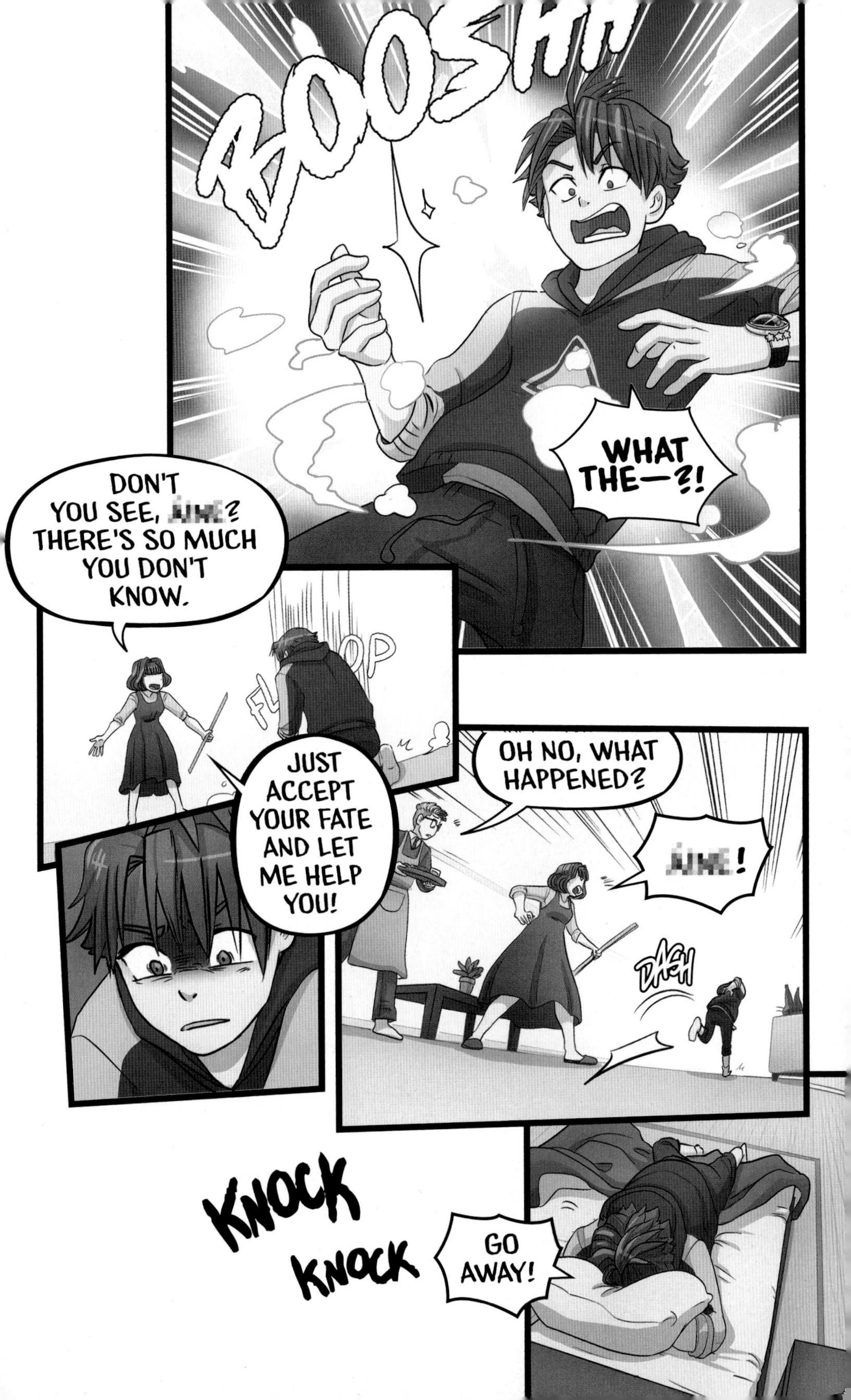
BOOSH
WHAT THE—?!
DON'T YOU SEE, [redacted]? THERE'S SO MUCH YOU DON'T KNOW.
JUST ACCEPT YOUR FATE AND LET ME HELP YOU!
OH NO, WHAT HAPPENED?
[redacted]!
DASH
KNOCK
KNOCK
GO AWAY!

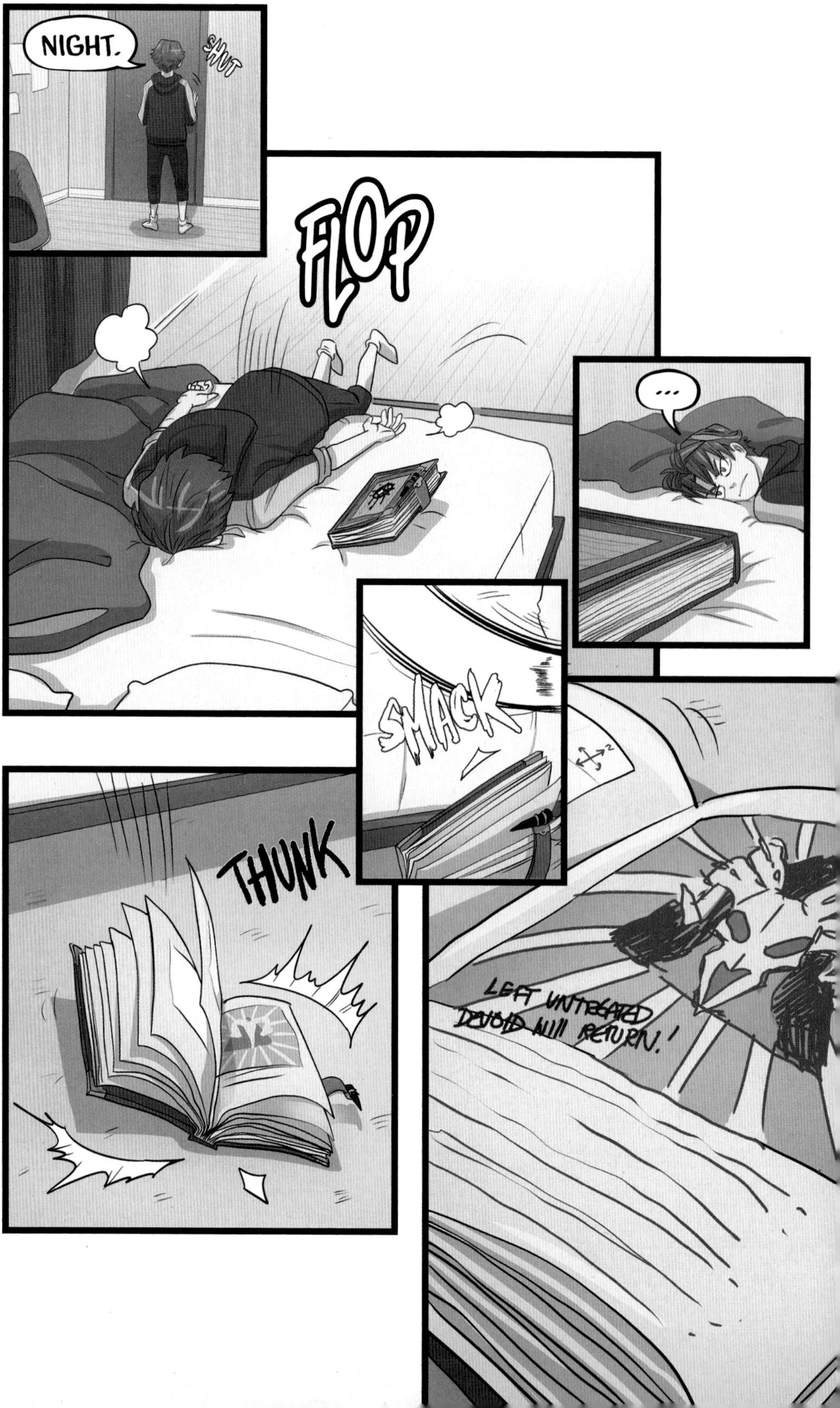
NIGHT.
SHUT
FLOP
...
SMACK
THUNK
LEFT UNTREATED
DEVOID WILL RETURN!

EPISODE 9: UNAVOIDABLE

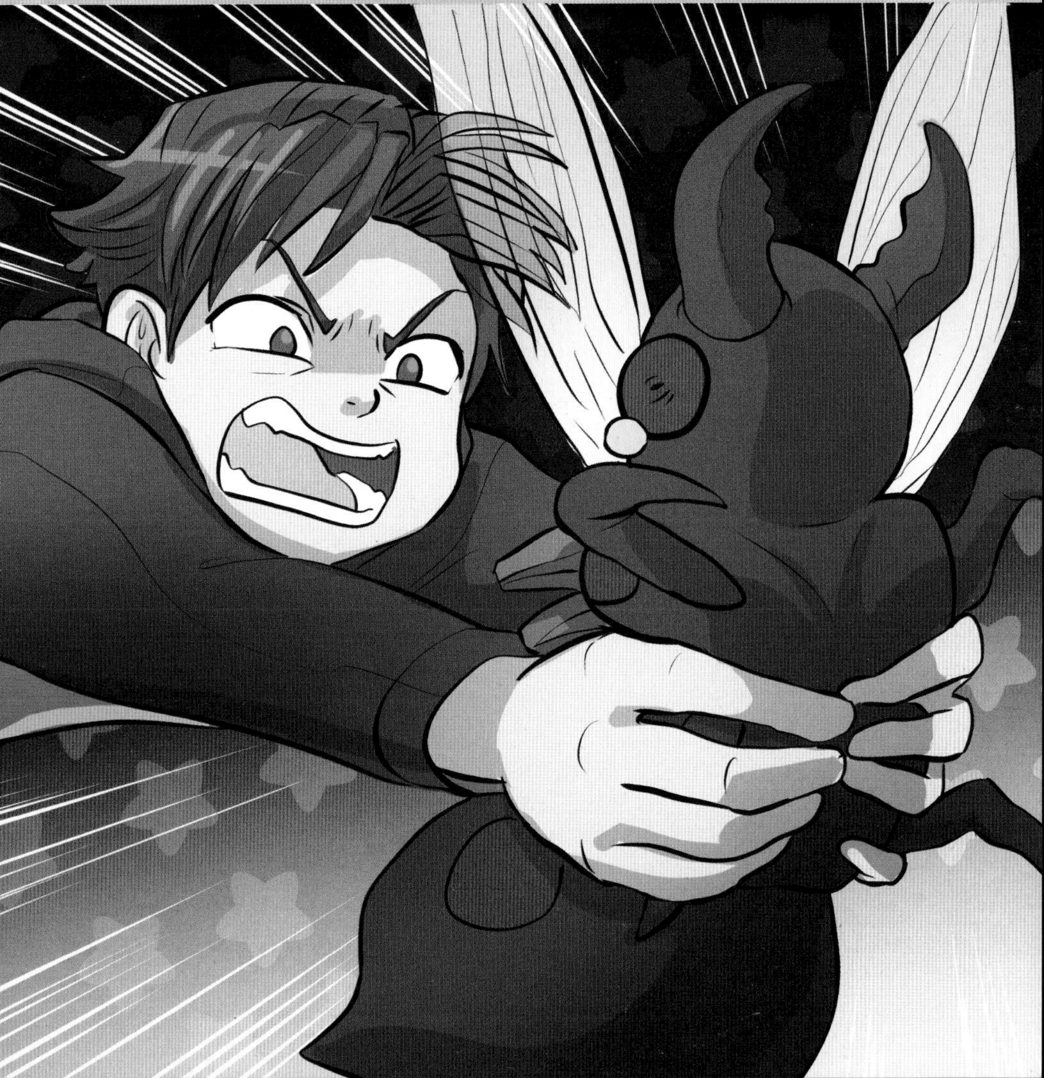

226

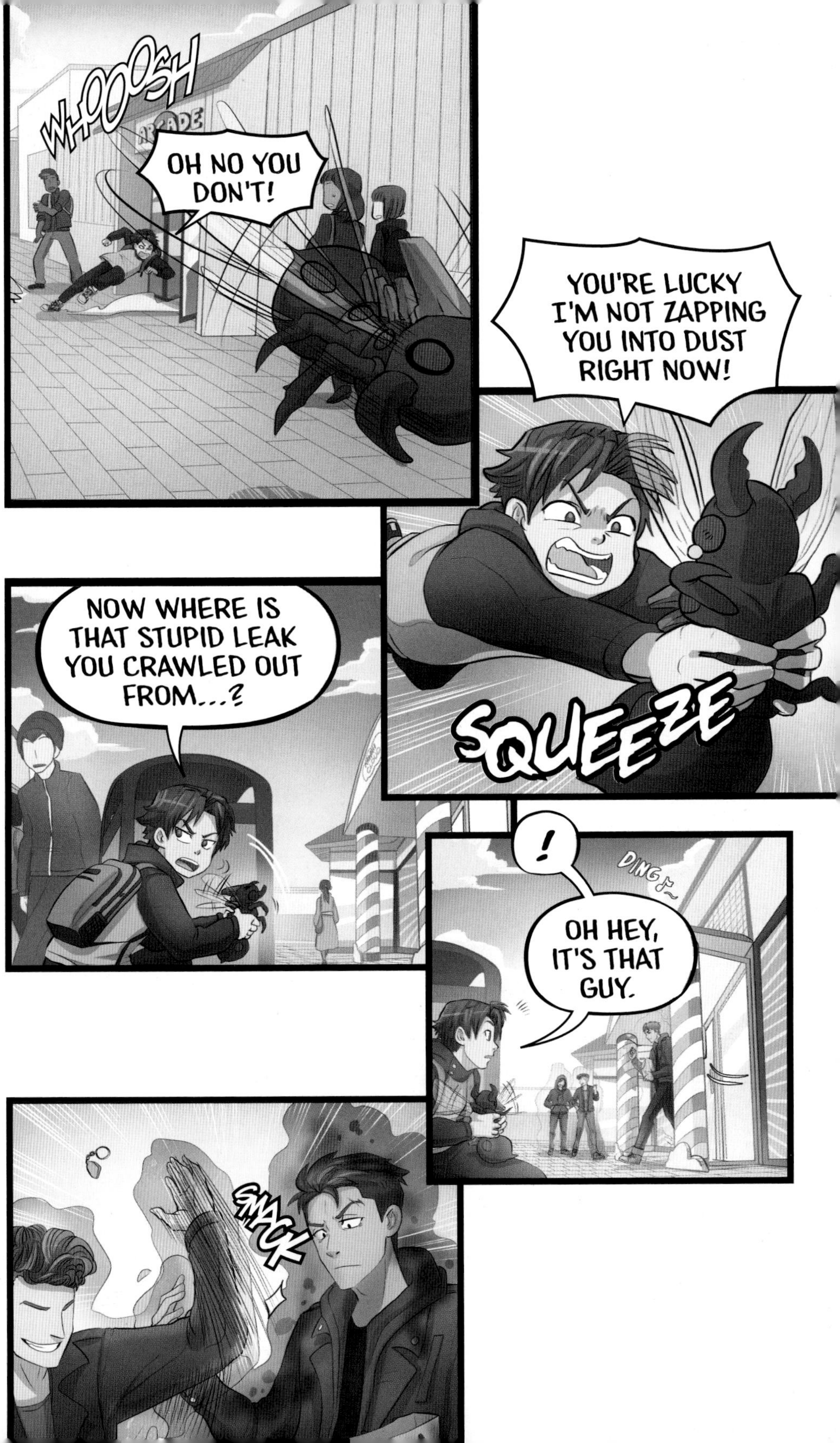
WHOOOSH
OH NO YOU DON'T!
YOU'RE LUCKY I'M NOT ZAPPING YOU INTO DUST RIGHT NOW!
SQUEEZE
NOW WHERE IS THAT STUPID LEAK YOU CRAWLED OUT FROM...?
!
DING
OH HEY, IT'S THAT GUY.
SMACK

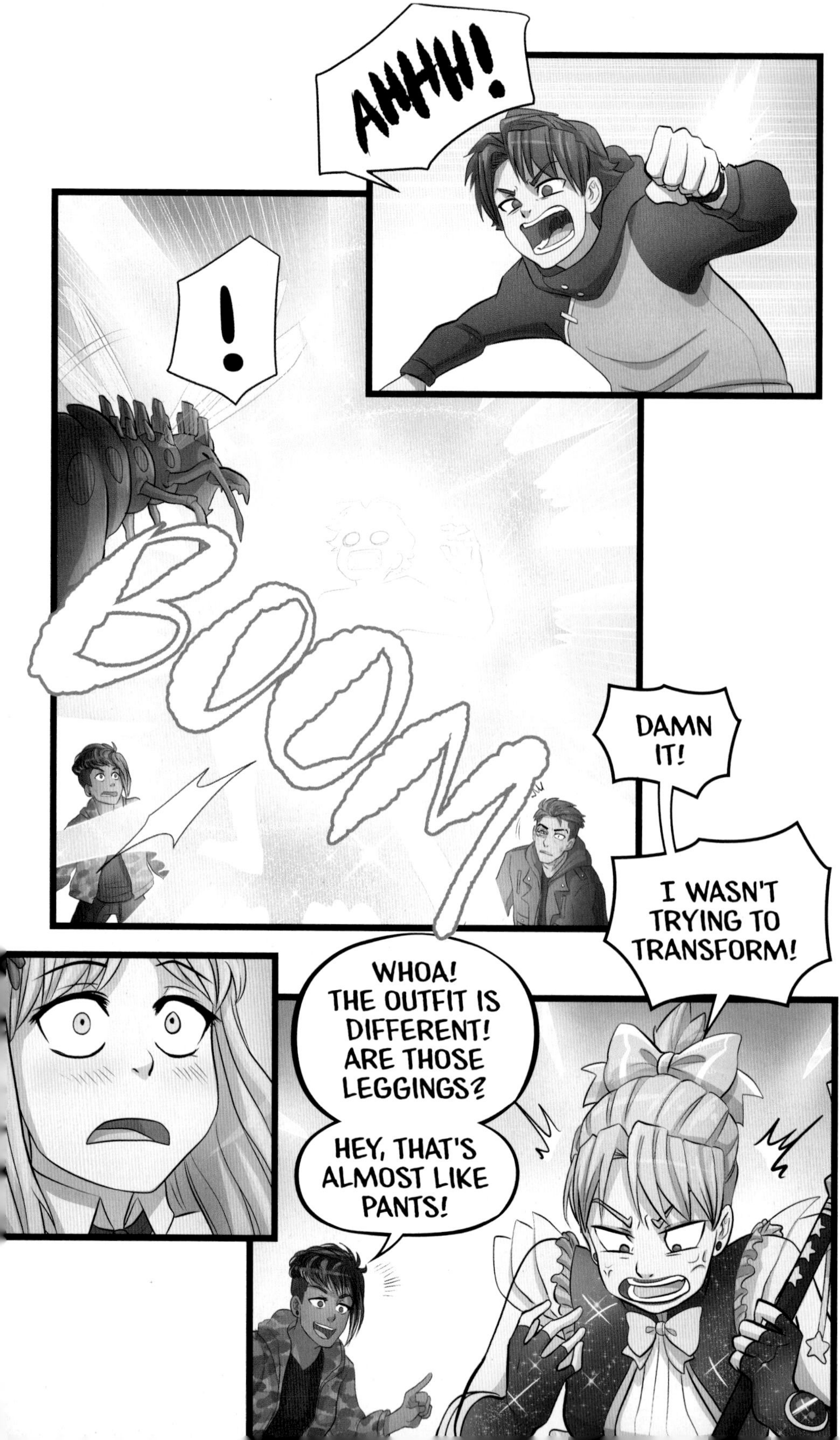
AHHH!
!
BOOM
DAMN IT!
I WASN'T TRYING TO TRANSFORM!
WHOA! THE OUTFIT IS DIFFERENT! ARE THOSE LEGGINGS?
HEY, THAT'S ALMOST LIKE PANTS!

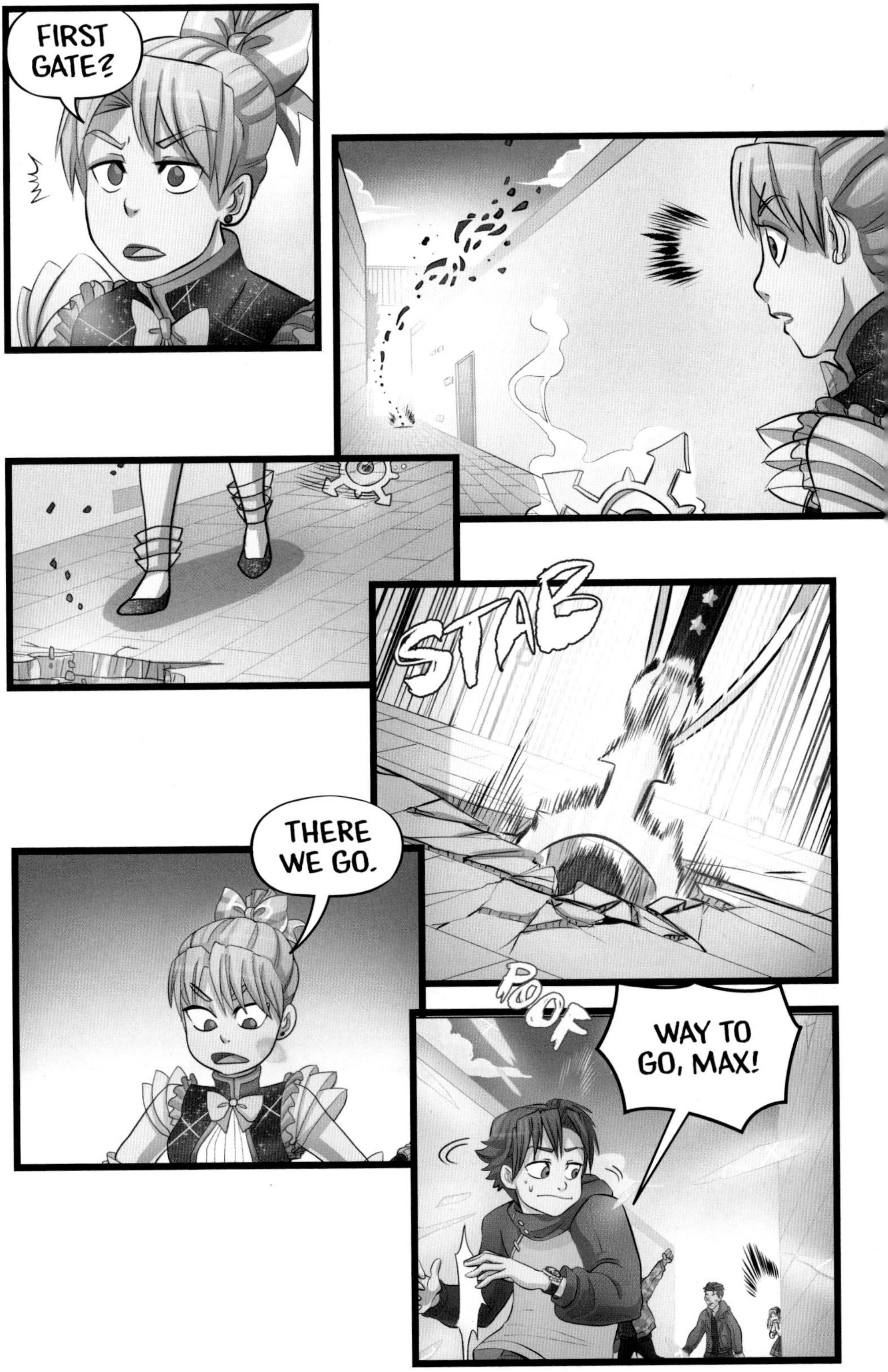
FIRST GATE?
STAB
THERE WE GO.
POOF
WAY TO GO, MAX!

EPISODE 10:
BE A MAN

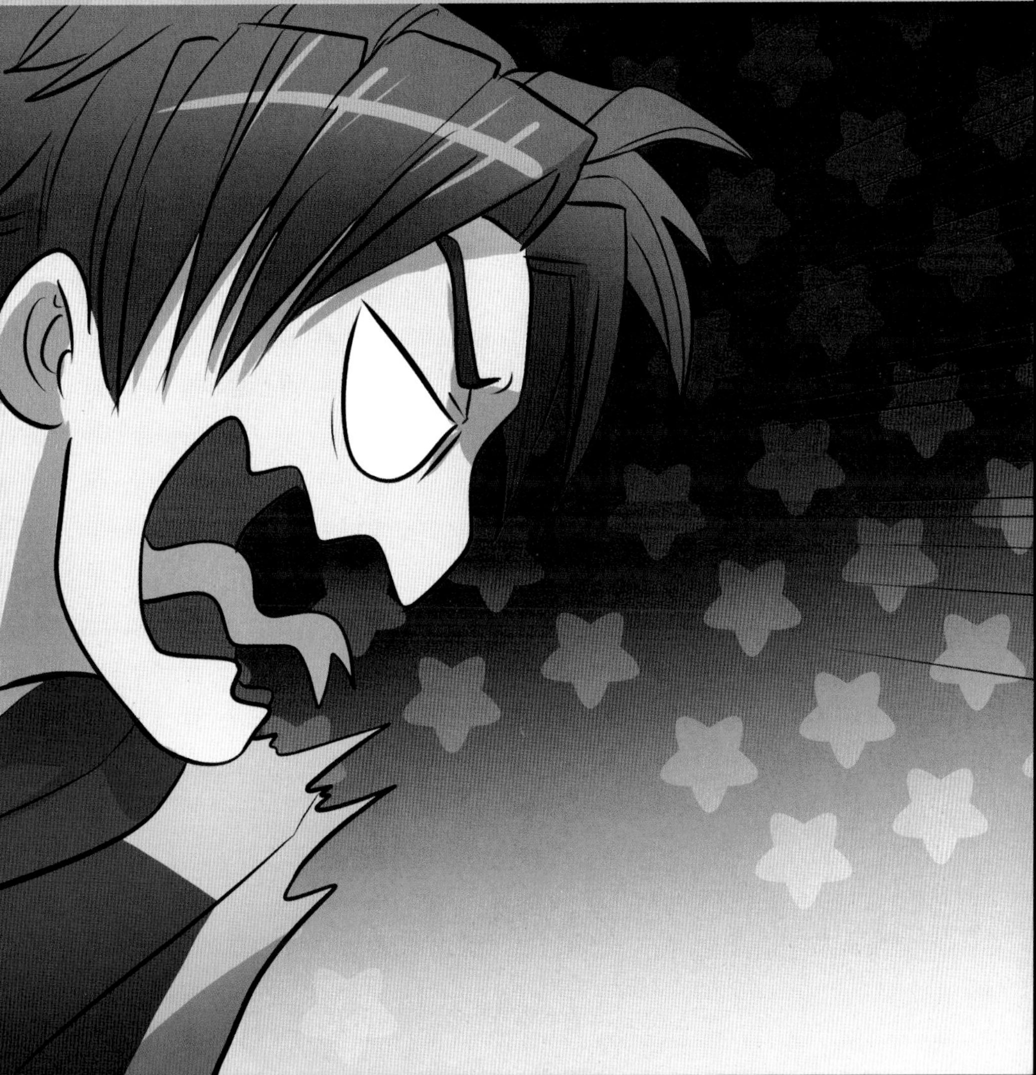

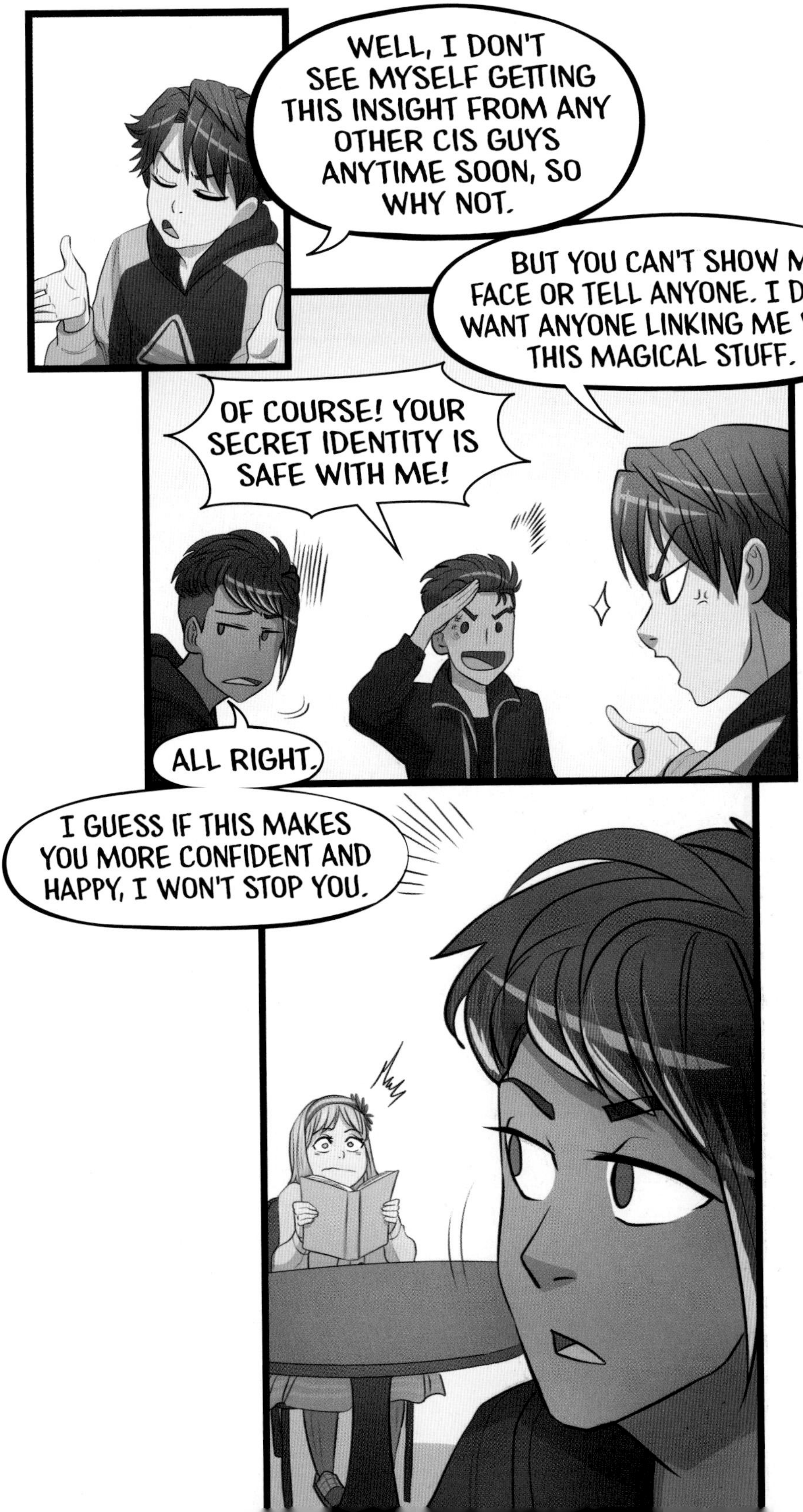
WELL, I DON'T SEE MYSELF GETTING THIS INSIGHT FROM ANY OTHER CIS GUYS ANYTIME SOON, SO WHY NOT.
BUT YOU CAN'T SHOW MY FACE OR TELL ANYONE. I DON'T WANT ANYONE LINKING ME WITH THIS MAGICAL STUFF.
OF COURSE! YOUR SECRET IDENTITY IS SAFE WITH ME!
ALL RIGHT.
I GUESS IF THIS MAKES YOU MORE CONFIDENT AND HAPPY, I WON'T STOP YOU.

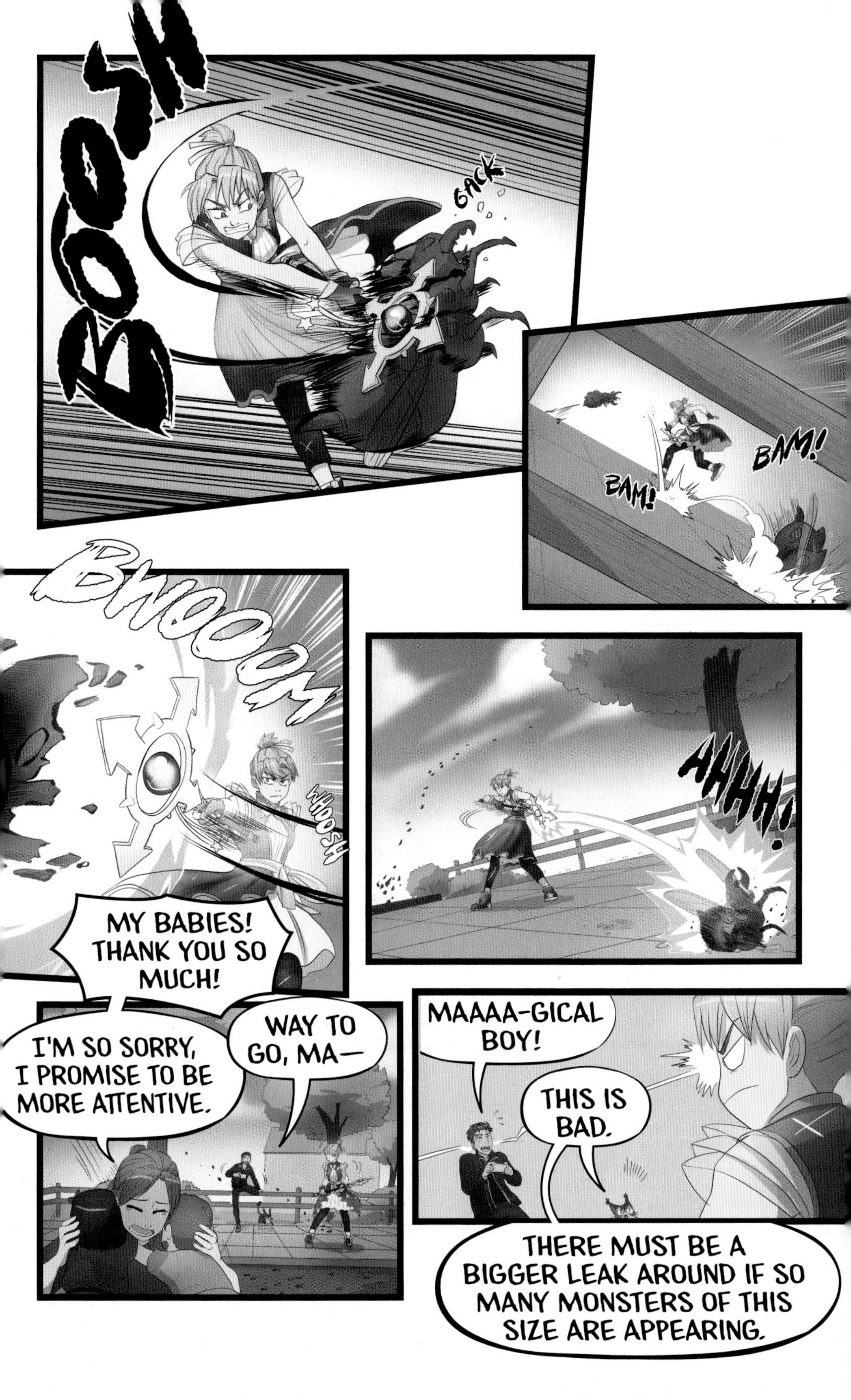
BOOSH
GACK
BAM!
BAM!
BWOOOOM
WHOOSH
AHHH!
MY BABIES! THANK YOU SO MUCH!
I'M SO SORRY, I PROMISE TO BE MORE ATTENTIVE.
WAY TO GO, MA—
MAAAA-GICAL BOY!
THIS IS BAD.
THERE MUST BE A BIGGER LEAK AROUND IF SO MANY MONSTERS OF THIS SIZE ARE APPEARING.

ONE OF THESE PESTS MENTIONED A "GATE" IS OPEN YESTERDAY. DOES THAT MEAN ANYTHING?

EXCUSE YOU, TH MONSTER GAVE ME TH INFORMATION AS I WA ANNIHILATING IT!

IMPOSSIBLE. IT'S TOO SOON FOR THAT...UNLESS YOU HAVEN'T BEEN DOING YOUR JOB.

NOW, WHAT'S THIS GATE BUSINESS?

YOU WOULD HAVE ALREADY KNOWN IF YOU'D READ THE BOOK.

WHY WOULD I READ IF YOU COULD JUST TELL ME? YOU'RE SUPPOSED TO BE HELPING ME.

MEOW!

WHAT'S YOUR SIDEKICK SAYING?

HE'S NOT MY SIDEKICK!

HEY! WHERE'RE YOU GOING?!

I NEED TO FOCUS ON FINDING THIS GATE.

FOR NOW, FIND THE LEAK THESE CREATURES ESCAPED FROM JUST NOW.

U-UM.

!

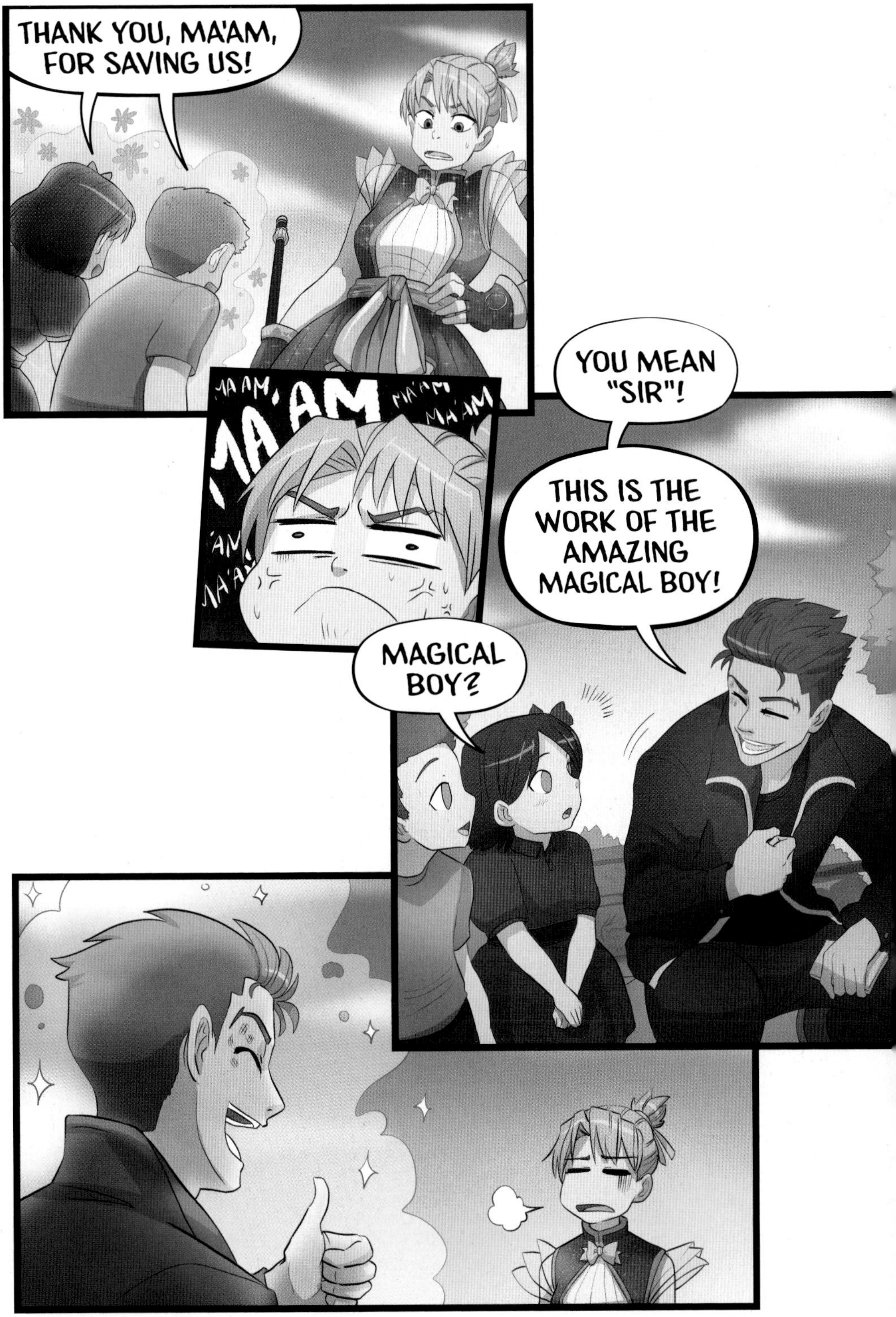
THANK YOU, MA'AM, FOR SAVING US!
MA'AM
MA'AM
MA'AM
MA'AM
MA'AM
MA'AM
YOU MEAN "SIR"!
THIS IS THE WORK OF THE AMAZING MAGICAL BOY!
MAGICAL BOY?

Episode 11:
CRUSH IT

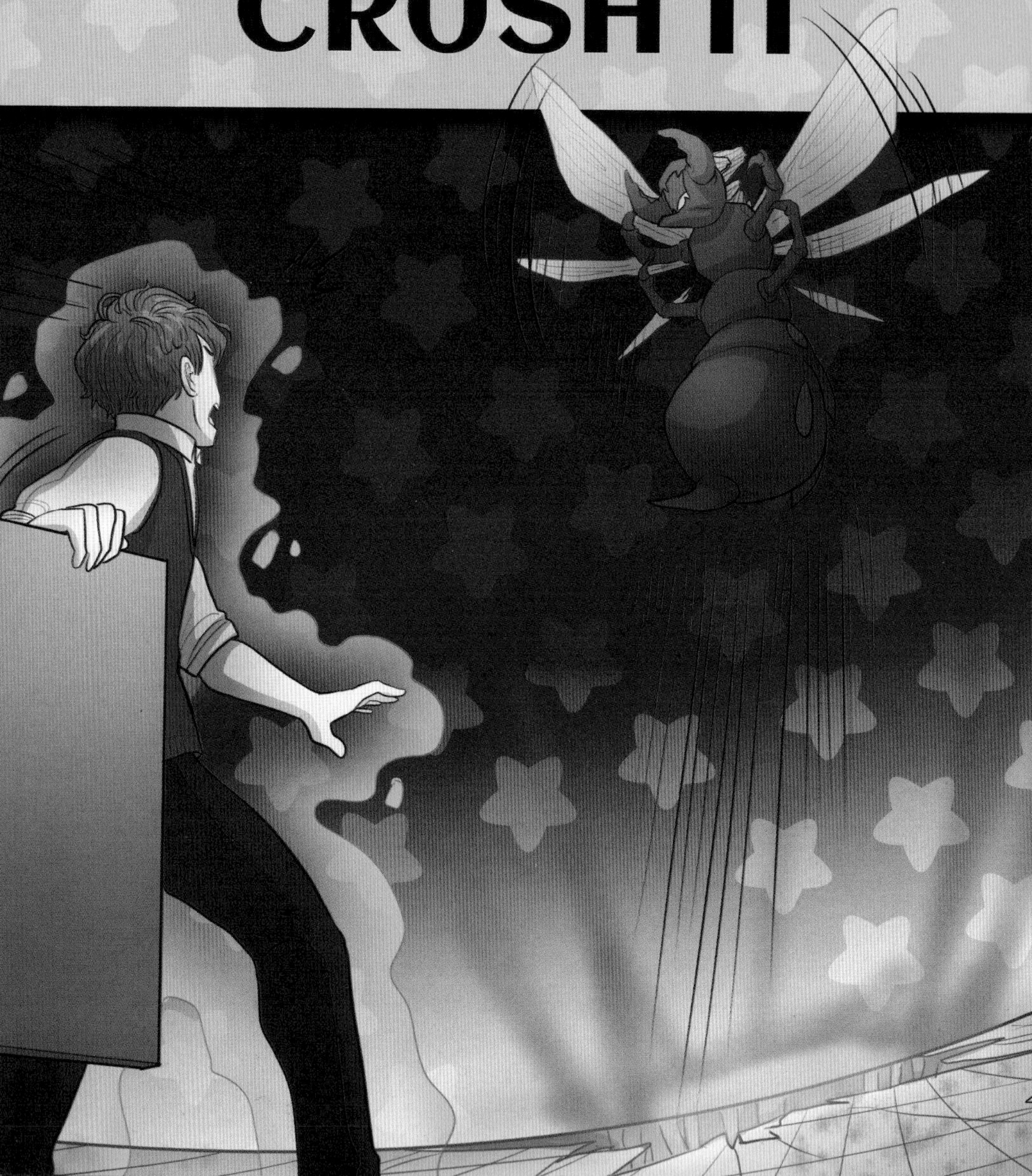

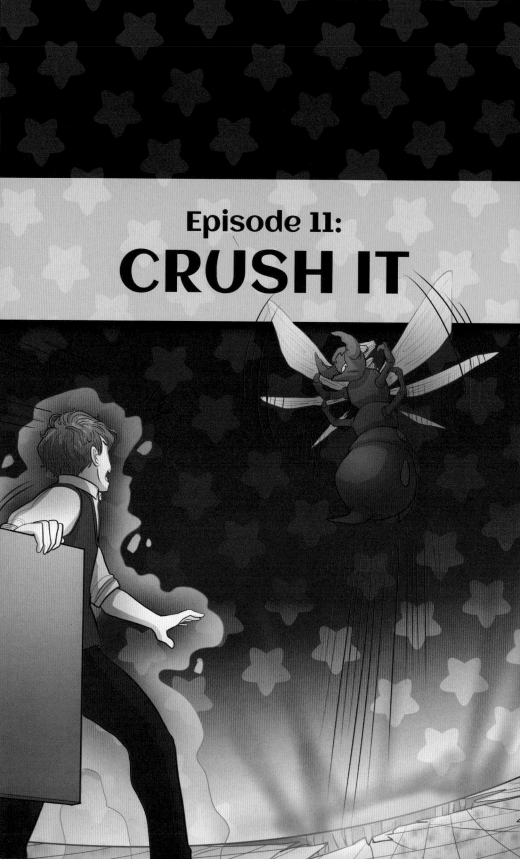

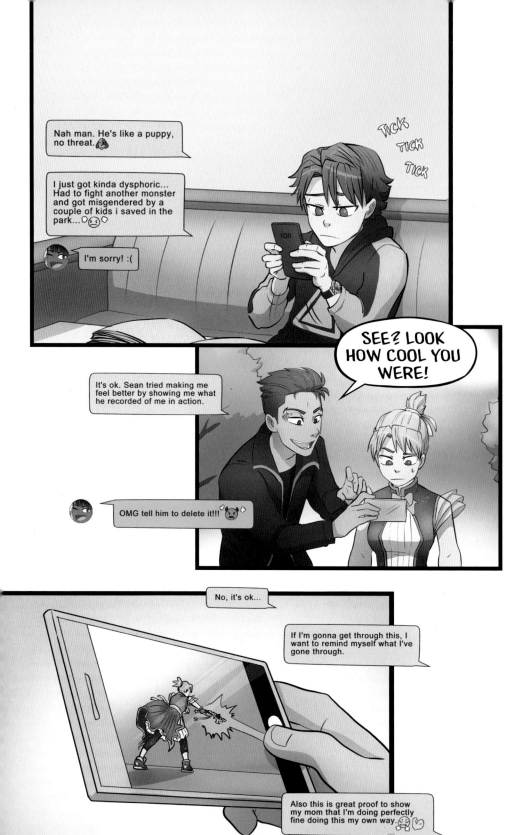

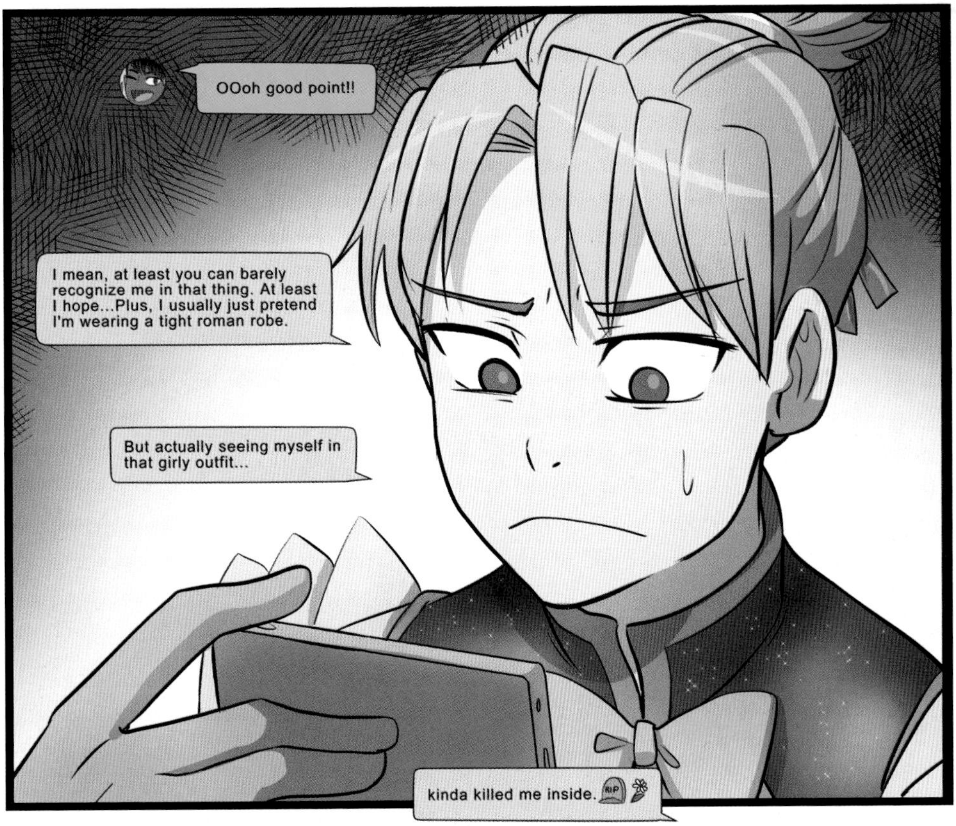
OOoh good point!!
I mean, at least you can barely recognize me in that thing. At least I hope...Plus, I usually just pretend I'm wearing a tight roman robe.
But actually seeing myself in that girly outfit...
kinda killed me inside.

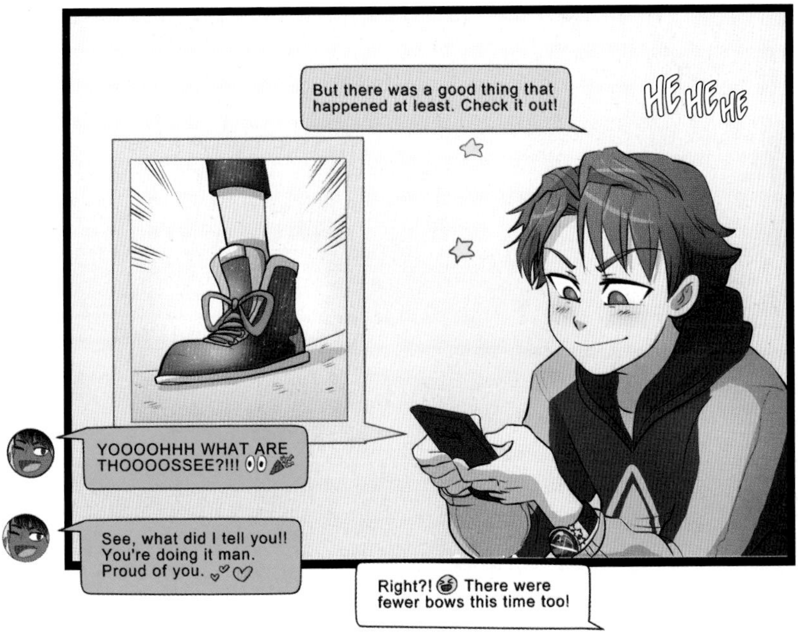
But there was a good thing that happened at least. Check it out!
HE HE HE
YOOOOHHH WHAT ARE THOOOOSSEE?!!!
See, what did I tell you!! You're doing it man. Proud of you.
Right?! There were fewer bows this time too!

267

271

Episode 12:
CONFRONTATION

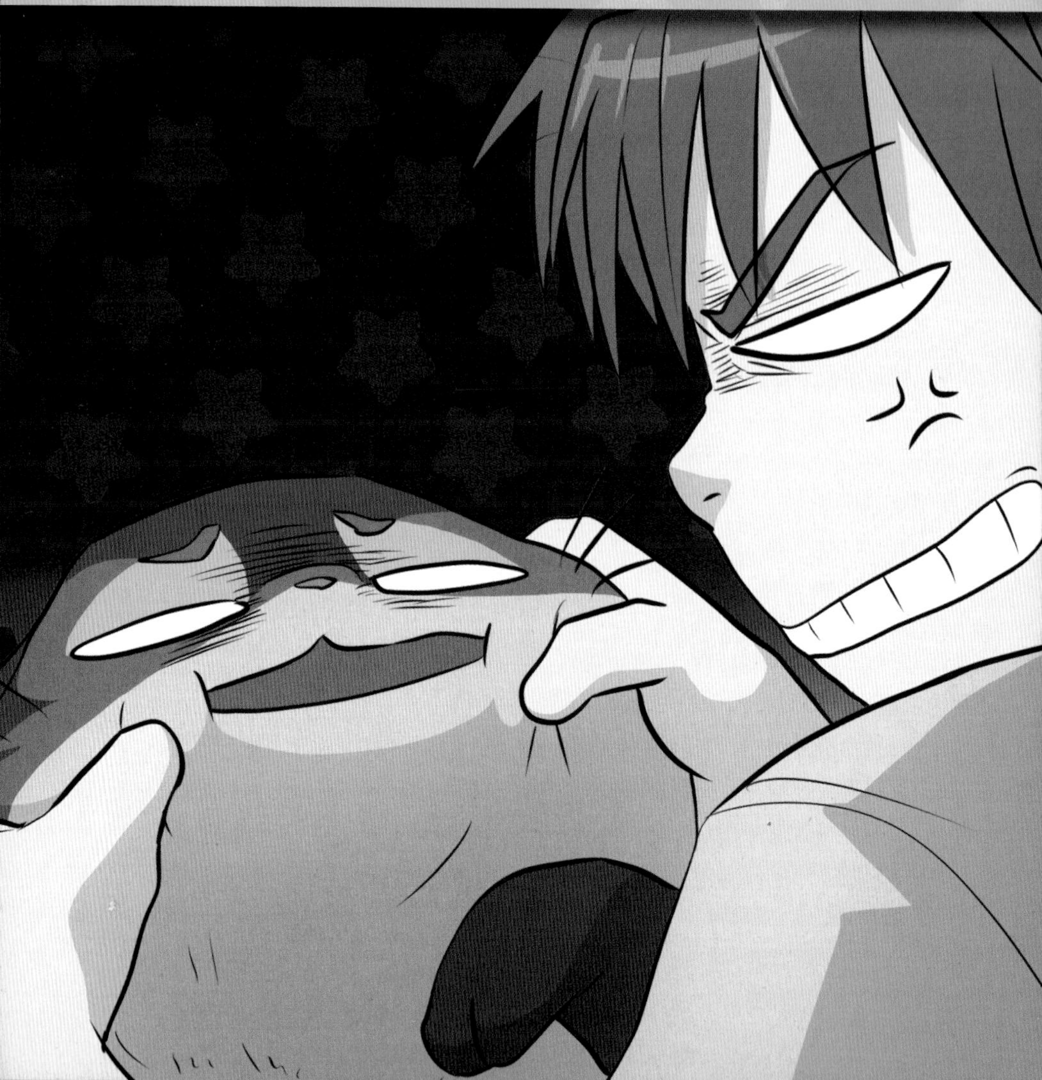

YOU WERE SO BEAUTIFUL. IT'D BE SUCH A WASTE TO HIDE IT.

I THINK YOU SHOULD WEAR A DRESS MORE OFTEN.

WHAT ARE YOU SAYING, TOBI?

THIS CAN'T BE HAPPENING.

THUNK

NOW HE REALLY DOESN'T SEE ME AS A MAN.

AM I EVEN MAN ENOUGH? WHO AM I TRYING TO FOOL?

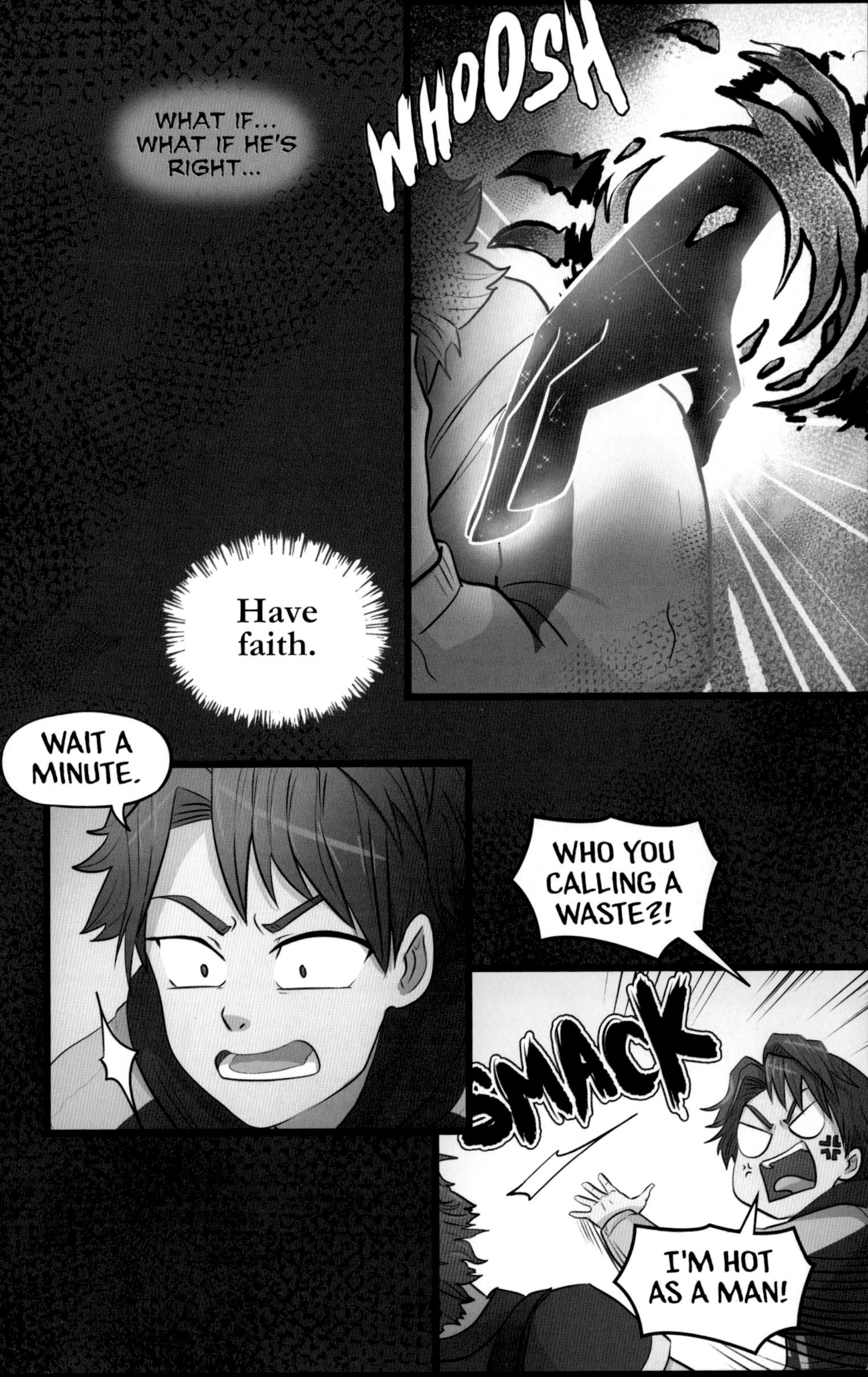
WHAT IF...
WHAT IF HE'S
RIGHT...
WHOOSH
Have
faith.
WAIT A
MINUTE.
WHO YOU
CALLING A
WASTE?!
SMACK
I'M HOT
AS A MAN!

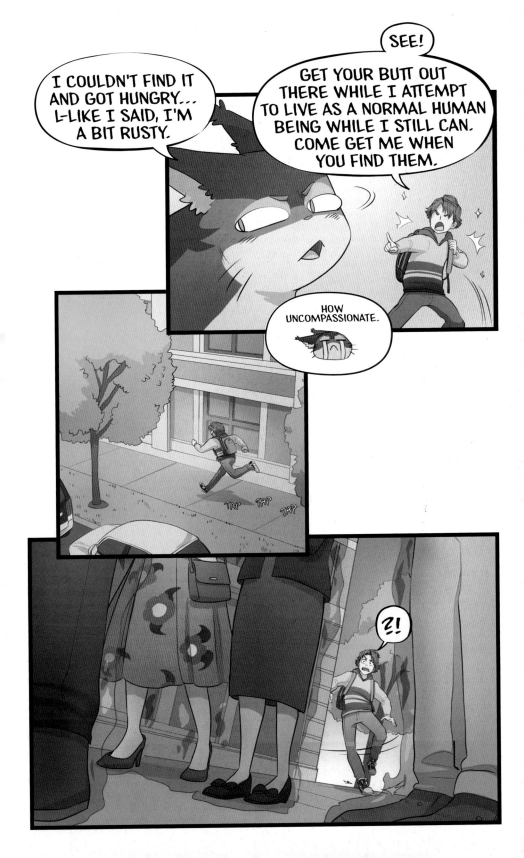

Episode 13:
TEAM
MAGICAL BOY

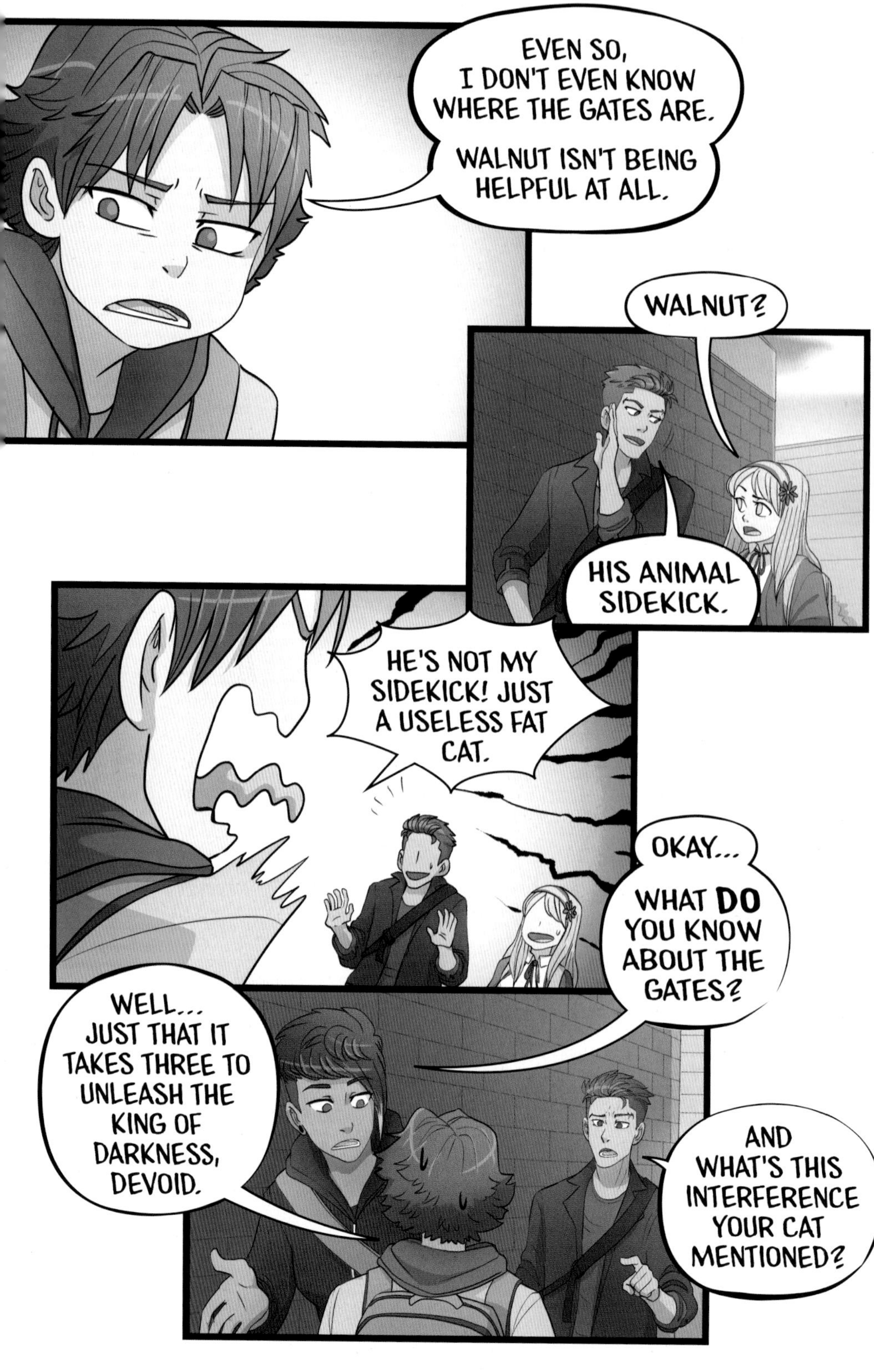
EVEN SO, I DON'T EVEN KNOW WHERE THE GATES ARE.
WALNUT ISN'T BEING HELPFUL AT ALL.
WALNUT?
HIS ANIMAL SIDEKICK.
HE'S NOT MY SIDEKICK! JUST A USELESS FAT CAT.
OKAY...
WHAT **DO** YOU KNOW ABOUT THE GATES?
WELL... JUST THAT IT TAKES THREE TO UNLEASH THE KING OF DARKNESS, DEVOID.
AND WHAT'S THIS INTERFERENCE YOUR CAT MENTIONED?

Episode 14:
WALK IN THE PARK

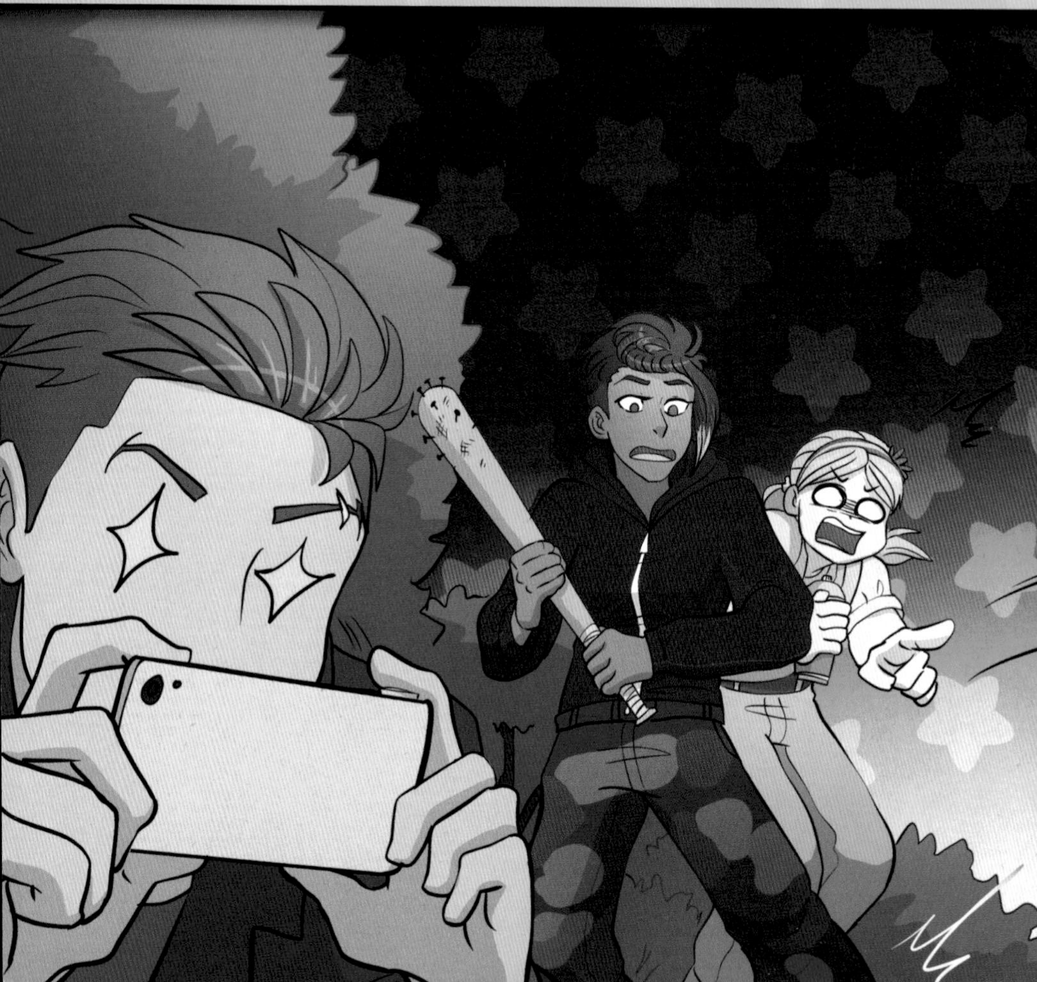

Episode 15:
WITHIN THE FOREST

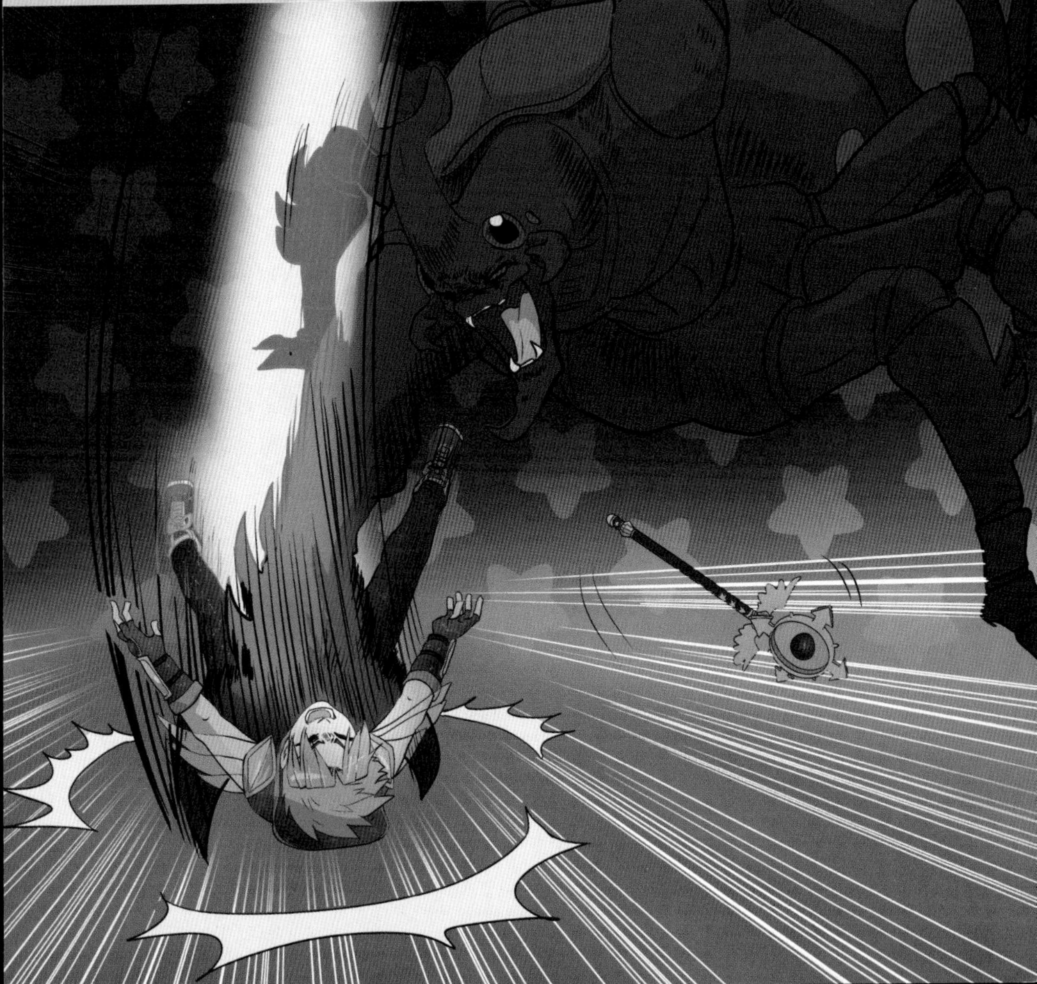

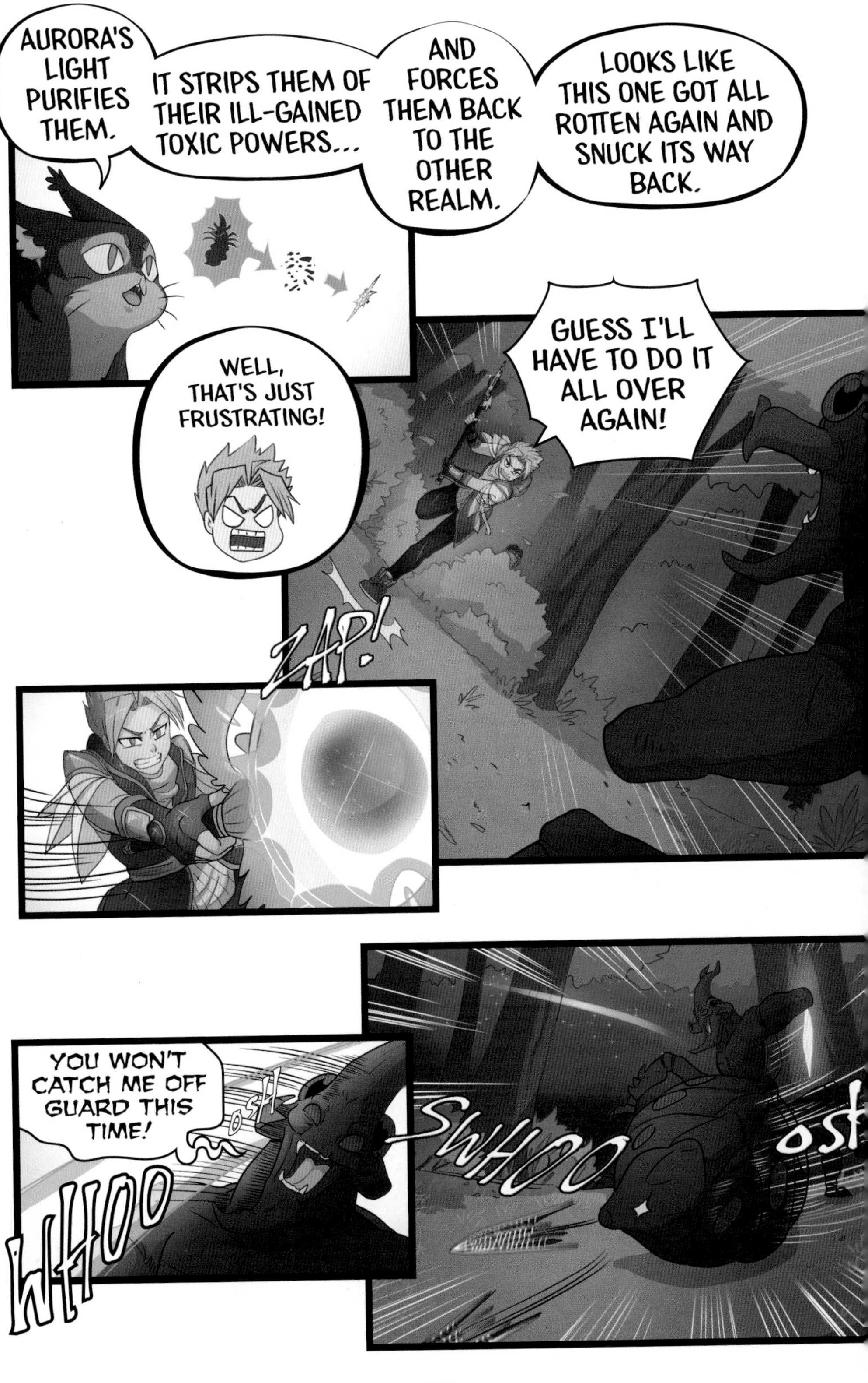
AURORA'S LIGHT PURIFIES THEM.
IT STRIPS THEM OF THEIR ILL-GAINED TOXIC POWERS...
AND FORCES THEM BACK TO THE OTHER REALM.
LOOKS LIKE THIS ONE GOT ALL ROTTEN AGAIN AND SNUCK ITS WAY BACK.
WELL, THAT'S JUST FRUSTRATING!
GUESS I'LL HAVE TO DO IT ALL OVER AGAIN!
ZAP!
YOU WON'T CATCH ME OFF GUARD THIS TIME!
WHOOSH
-SWHOOOSH

PUNT

YOU LITTLE...!

OH NO YOU DON'T!

BAM!

!

HOW DOES IT FEEL TO HAVE FAILED SO BADLY COMPARED TO THE OTHER GODDESSES?

STOMP

YOU WERE A FOOL TO BRING THEM WITH YOU.

MAX!

I'M OUT OF BUG SPRAY!

I'M GONNA NEED A BIGGER PAN.

I'LL CRUSH ALL THE HOPE THEY HAVE FOR YOU AND USE THEIR TAINTED LIGHT TO POWER UP MY GATE. HAHAHA!

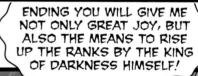

ENDING YOU WILL GIVE ME NOT ONLY GREAT JOY, BUT ALSO THE MEANS TO RISE UP THE RANKS BY THE KING OF DARKNESS HIMSELF!

PRESS

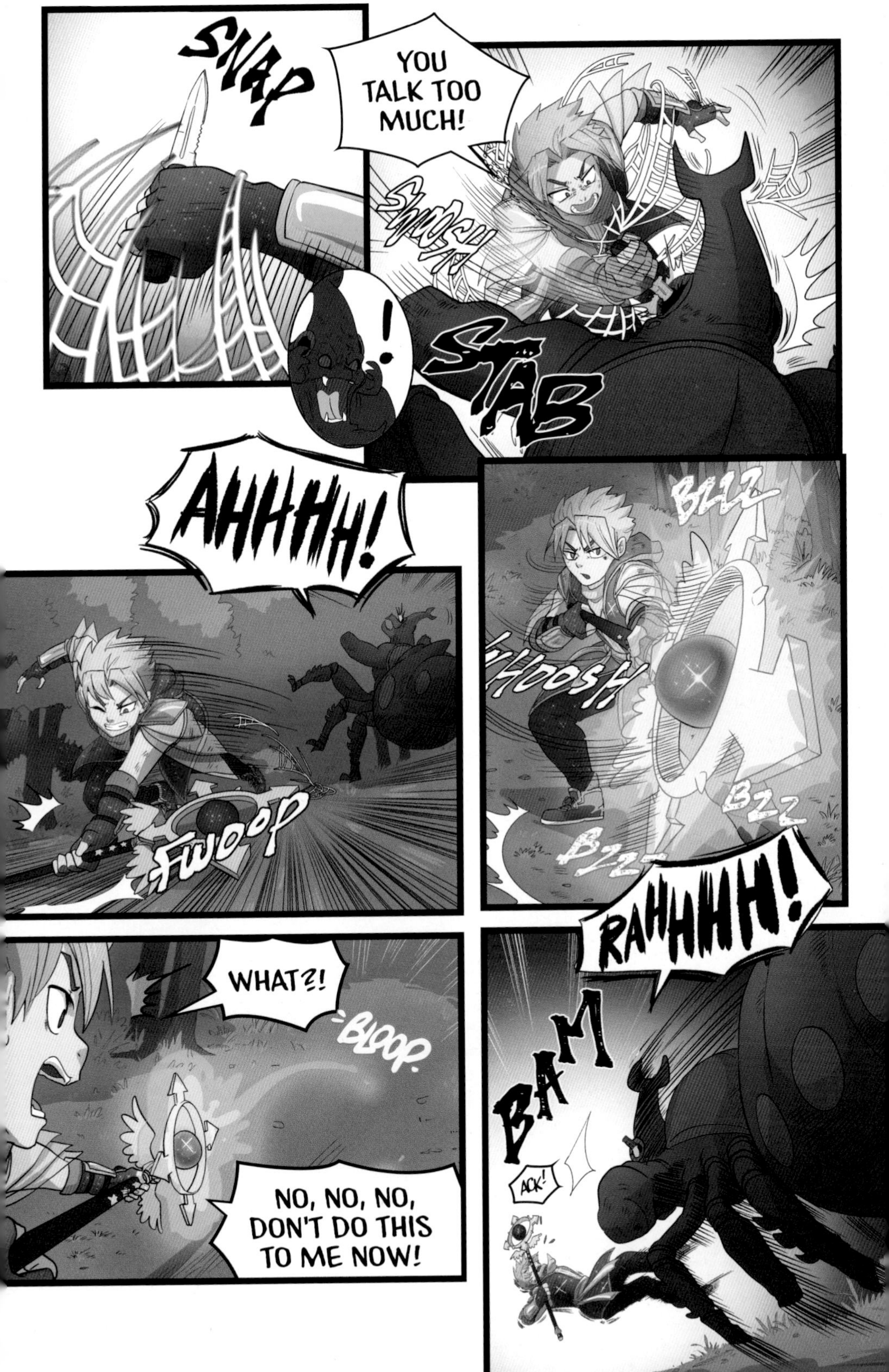
SNAP
YOU TALK TOO MUCH!
SHOOSH
!
STAB
AHHHH!
FWOOP
BZZZ
WHOOSH
BZZ
BZZZ
WHAT?!
BLOOP
NO, NO, NO, DON'T DO THIS TO ME NOW!
RAHHHH!
BAM
ACK!

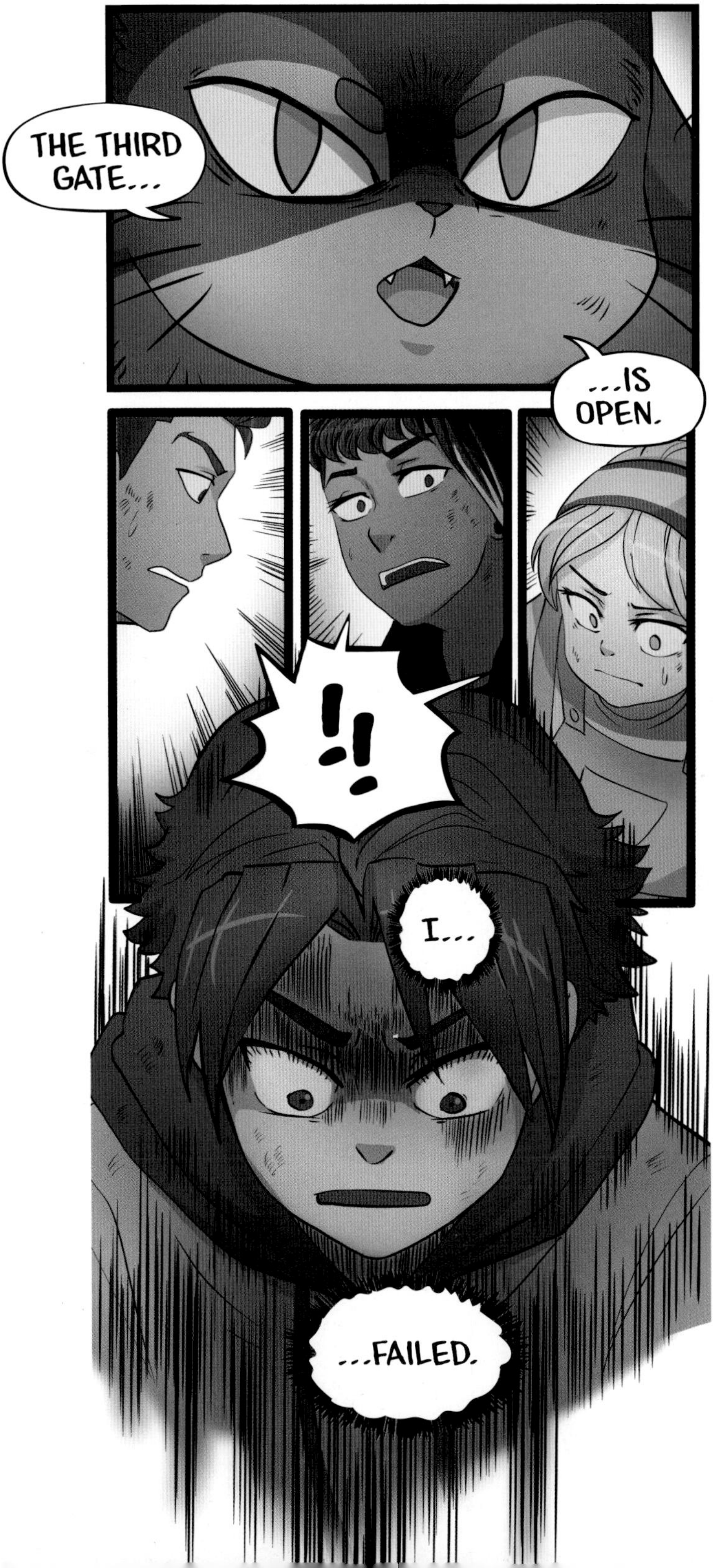
THE THIRD GATE...
...IS OPEN.
!!
I...
...FAILED.